Mary E. Pearce, a Londoner by birth, now lives in the relative peace of Gloucestershire. She tackled various jobs – shop assistant, filing clerk, waitress, usherette – before settling down to write seriously in the 1960s. Her career began with the appearance of short stories in magazines and has led to the publication of nine highly successful novels which have been translated into Dutch, French, German, Italian, Japanese, Norwegian and Portuguese, as well as being bestsellers in America.

'An author with a rare feel for country life and speech' *Sunday Telegraph*

'Warm and vivid' *Publishers Weekly*

'About the human nature of people which is Mary Pearce's secret . . . The dialogue both convinces and entertains' *Manchester Evening News*

'All the characters are drawn with warm understanding and humour' *Eastern Daily Press*

D1334754

MARY E. PEARCE OMNIBUS

The Land Endures
and
Seedtime and Harvest

WARNER BOOKS

A *Warner* Book

This omnibus edition published by Warner Books in 2000

Omnibus edition © Mary E. Pearce 2000

The Land Endures first published in Great Britain in 1978
by Macdonald and Jane's Publishers.
First published in paperback by Warner Books in 1994.
Seedtime and Harvest first published in Great Britain in 1980
by Macdonald & Co (Publishers).
First published in paperback by Warner Books in 1992.

The Land Endures copyright © Mary E. Pearce 1978
Seedtime and Harvest copyright © Mary E. Pearce 1975

A CIP catalogue record for this book
is available from the British Library.

ISBN 0 7515 3132 4

Printed and bound in Great Britain by
Mackays of Chatham plc, Chatham, Kent

Warner Books
A Division of
Little, Brown and Company (UK)
Brettenham House
Lancaster Place
London WC2E 7EN

For
Kathleen and Eric

THE LAND ENDURES

Chapter 1

The farmhouse welcomed them from the beginning. They felt they belonged there, all of them, as though the place cast a spell on them. Stephen had had his doubts, of course, and sometimes Gwen had shared in them, for the purchase had not been an easy one, and the outgoing farmer, Mr Gould, had driven a hard bargain over the valuation of the standing crops. But that was behind them; a thing of the past. Holland Farm was now theirs, even if it did have a mortgage on it, and when they clip-clopped into the yard and saw the old, quiet house waiting for them, they knew they had made the right decision.

The house was not quiet for long. As Stephen and Gwen stood in the hall, waiting the arrival of the furniture van, the children ran from room to room, making their own discoveries. After the tiny house at Springs, the space of the farmhouse delighted them. Their voices rang out, echoing, and their feet pounded the bare boards.

"Is it possible," Stephen said, "that four children can make so much noise?"

"Does it distress you?" Gwen asked. She followed him into the big kitchen. She still worried about him, ceaselessly, for the war had left its mark on him, and even now, more than a year after his discharge, his nerves were still badly frayed. "Shall I tell them to be quiet?"

"God, no! Let them yell. They never had the chance in Prior's Walk."

And yell the children certainly did. It seemed they meant to make up for the past.

"Chris! Come and look! This bedroom is vast!"

"Never mind the bedroom. You come up here. There's a secret cupboard in this wall."

"I can see the cattle from up here. *Our* cattle. And some

1

sheep. Yoo-hoo, Joanna, why don't you come?"

"Where's Jamesy calling from?"

"He's up in the attic. So's little Emma."

"The furniture's coming!" Jamesy shrieked. "I've seen the van coming up the track."

"It's miles away yet," Joanna said, glancing out of the nearest window. "It'll take all day, the rate it's going."

But downstairs they ran, in search of their parents, and found them in the kitchen-cum-living room, where three casement windows looked out on the yard and where, in the big blackleaded iron range, the wood ashes were still warm, although the Goulds had been gone two days. There was a bundle of sticks in the hearth, together with a heap of logs: a gesture of Mr Gould's goodwill. Stephen threw the sticks into the stove and blew on the ashes until they caught. Soon he had the split logs alight, and the children's faces were lit by the flames.

"The furniture's coming," Chris said.

"Is it?" said Stephen. He looked at his watch. "Two o'clock. Bang on the nail."

"As soon as they've unpacked the kettle," said Gwen, "make sure they bring it to me."

It was cold for early October. They would all be glad of a cup of tea.

Gradually, as the carpets were laid and the furniture was carried in, the house became more and more their own, beginning with the kitchen-cum-living-room, the most important room in the house. Wing-chair; book case; old sagging couch; the Monet print and the oval mirror: all these soon had a place and looked as though they had been there for years; but some disagreement arose as to where the dining-table and chairs should stand, and the carved mahogany sideboard, and the desk that had come from Stephen's office. The removal men had their own ideas and the foreman especially argued with passion.

"Oh, well!" Gwen said. "I can always alter things afterwards."

But when, on leaving, the men came into the kitchen again, to receive Stephen's tip, the foreman looked round at their handiwork and touched Gwen's arm.

2

"You won't better that!" he said to her. "Not if you try for a hundred years!"

And he was right, as Gwen afterwards had to admit, for even when spring-cleaning time came round and the furniture had to be shifted about, she found herself putting it back again, item by item, as before. Holland Farm was like that. It was not a place that invited change.

The weather was wet the day they moved in and remained wet throughout the weekend, but the four children were perfectly happy, poking into cupboards, attics, cellars, till the house had yielded all its secrets. Under a floorboard in the attic they found a broken china mug, a spinning-top, and a small wooden doll.

"The Goulds had no children," Stephen said, "and they lived in this house nearly fifty years."

"Visitors' children, perhaps," said Gwen.

But there were other discoveries: drawings of animals on the walls, revealed when the wallpaper was removed; a girl's name, Rosina Lane, entwined in a pattern of vine-leaves; and, under another loose floorboard, a bunch of herbs in a sealed jar that bore a label and these faded words: "Gathered by me on Midsummer's Eve: Cicely Lane, aged eleven; year of grace, 1860."

The two sisters, if sisters they were, would now be old ladies of seventy or more, but to the Wayman children, coming to the house in 1919, Cicely and Rosina Lane were still two children like themselves, held up as models to one another or used to excuse some fall from grace. "Cicely would never have bitten her nails," Joanna said to little Emma, and Jamesy, having borrowed something without permission, said scornfully: "Rosina would never have made such a fuss about a rotten box of paints!"

* * * * *

After the house, there were the farm buildings to be explored: stables, cowsheds, cartsheds, barns; and all around lay the meadows and fields, almost two hundred and fifty acres, spreading their slopes to the south-west, and running down to the Derrent brook. The freedom of it went to their heads; released from school at the weekends, they ran wild from dawn to dusk; clattered into the house for meals, and bundled out again in a rush, the instant they were given leave.

"Look after Emma!" Gwen would call, but they would be gone like mad things, helter-skelter across the yard, with Emma trotting along behind.

"No doubt what *they* think of Holland Farm," Stephen said. "How did we manage to keep all that energy pent up close in the house at Springs?" And sometimes he would say to his wife: "What do *you* feel, now we're here?"

"Ask me in a few years' time!"

It was only a joke, and they both knew it. Leaving Springs and buying the farm was the best thing they had ever done. There were no regrets on either side. They wondered why they had waited so long.

It was the war that had made up their minds, by showing them where their values lay. Stephen had been gassed in 1918, and the doctor's advice had been very blunt.

"Get out of doors as much as you can. It's the only thing for lungs like yours. If you go back to your damned office, you'll be asking for trouble, no doubt of that!"

So Stephen sold his partnership in the legal firm of Hallam and Dobbs and worked for a year on a farm near Springs, helping an ex-Army man like himself, and learning something about the land. He had always had a hankering to farm, and Gwen was a Worcestershire farmer's daughter. They had no one to consider but themselves and their children, for Gwen's parents were both dead and so were Stephen's, and the only relations they had left in the world were his two cousins, who lived in India. Land prices were high just then, but he had the money from his partnership and a small gratuity from the Army, and, after raising a mortgage, he was able to buy Holland Farm. His own house and his own land! What better investment could there be for the future of his family? But he worried sometimes, nevertheless.

"I *must* make a go of it," he said. "I can't afford to make mistakes."

"Of course we shall make a go of it! Why shouldn't we?"

4

Gwen said.

Why not indeed? Farm prices were pretty good, having risen throughout the war, and there were government guarantees. But Stephen knew that the good times would probably not last forever. He therefore went cautiously and was always ready to take advice, either from the neighbouring farmers or from the men who worked for him. These men were there when he took the farm. He made no changes but hoped for the best.

"They're not a bad bunch," Gould had said. "There's only one you've got to watch and you'll soon find out which one that is. He belongs to the union. You'll soon hear from *him*!"

Stephen thought this was prejudice. He was inclined to be amused.

"Is there only one union man among them?"

"One's enough!" Gould had said.

The man in question was Morton George. He had a watchful, suspicious manner, but never looked you in the eye. Stephen decided to reserve judgment. Of the eight men there, he found he liked Bob Tupper best. The others, when they gave advice, made a mystery of the reasons behind it, but Bob Tupper gave it straight.

"I shouldn't plough the Home Field yet, 'cos that'll still be workable later on, even when it's wet. I'd start with the Freelands and the Goose Ground – they're dry enough now but they won't be for long."

It was the same when buying stock. Bob would go with him to the sales and, with a few quiet words in his ear, tell him what to guard against.

"Not only in the cow," as Stephen, laughing, said to Gwen, "but in the farmer who's selling her!"

Bob knew the district inside out; he was an expert in everything; and Stephen was thankful to have such a man. Bob was in his early forties. Except for two years away in the war, he had been at Holland Farm since the age of eleven, thirty-two years in all, longer than any other man there.

"You should be foreman by rights," Stephen said.

"Mr Gould didn't hold with that, setting one man above the rest. He didn't hold with paying the extra wages neither."

"I'm not Mr Gould," Stephen said.

Most of the other men were pleased when Bob's new status became known. Their jibes were friendly, good-humoured, broad.

"Twopence to speak to you now, is it, Bob?"

"Shouldn't you wear a bowler hat?"

"Will the news be printed in *The Gazette*?"

Billy Rye said the promotion made little difference that he could see.

"Bob's been telling us what to do for donkey's years. It's just been made official, that's all."

Only Morton George seemed less than pleased. He lounged in the office doorway, nibbling a straw.

"I suppose it's on account of the war."

"What do you mean?" Stephen asked.

"Well, you're both old soldiers, you and him."

"That's got nothing to do with it. Bob is the senior man here. It's only right to recognize that."

"We should've voted among ourselves. That's the proper way to get a foreman."

"Now look here –" Stephen began, but was interrupted by Billy Rye.

"If we *had've* voted," Billy said, "Bob would be foreman just the same cos he's the best man for the job and we all know it." And then, to make light of it all, Billy gave Bob Tupper a nudge. "If I don't get a drink outa you after that, I shall want to know the reason why!"

Bob Tupper was not the only war veteran at Holland Farm. Nate Hopson was another. On November the eleventh, Armistice Day, these two men arrived for work wearing sprigs of evergreen in their caps, and later on that same morning, carting muck from the muck-bury, they stopped work at eleven o'clock and, removing their caps, stood bare-headed in the rain, remembering their fallen comrades.

It was not true that Stephen favoured these veterans, but it was inevitable that he should feel some kinship with them. The war had left its stamp on him and them, as on all those men who had gone to the edge of the pit and looked in, and that stamp could be recognized at a glance. Tupper and

6

Hopson saw at once that Stephen had been out at the Front. They heard the huskiness in his voice and knew he had suffered poisoning by gas. They noticed the three crooked fingers of his right hand and the deep scar running up his arm, and they recognized it as a shrapnel wound. And they, although they bore no visible scars, were just as easily known to him. They had a certain look in their eyes, as though they marvelled at everything they saw and yet were weary in their souls.

They gave themselves away, too, in their habits of speech and the jokes they made, as when Bob referred to his sandwiches as "wads" or gave the time as "thirteen-fifteen." Once, when the cattle were being driven up an unfenced track between two fields and kept straying out over the ploughland on one side, Tupper, walking behind the plough, shouted to Hopson, in charge of the herd: "Watch your dressing by the right there!"

Stephen would smile on hearing these things, even while he shrank inside. Neither he nor they ever talked of the war. They tried to put it out of their minds, though they couldn't of course, and would never be able to, all their lives. Still, something was salvaged from the waste: the kinship was there, and it made him smile.

As for Morton George, who sneered behind Stephen's back, it was partly because he felt left out.

"What do you talk about, you and him? All about how you beat the Hun?"

"The trouble with Mort is, he's jealous," said Nate.

"He should've said so before," said Bob. "He could've had my place out there if only he'd asked me in 1916."

"He was too busy running the union."

"Oh, you can laugh!" George exclaimed. "Who got your wages up to forty-eight-and-six a week?"

"I shall have to do something about that union of yours."

"Join it, d'you mean?"

"I shall have to remember it in my prayers!"

* * * * *

Stephen was determined from the beginning that Gwen

should have help in the house, and it happened that there were two women already there, who had worked for Mr and Mrs Gould and were now willing to work for the Waymans. Gwen had been ill with 'flu the previous winter, and the illness had pulled her down badly. She herself would never admit it; she liked to think she was as strong as a horse; but Stephen was concerned for her, and tried to save her all he could.

The duties of a farmer's wife overflowed the house itself. The dairy claimed a lot of her time, and there were the chickens, the turkeys, the geese. There were sickly lambs to hand-rear and often a calf that had to be weaned, and later on, at harvest times, she would be needed in the fields. It was useless for Stephen to say that Gwen must not do all these things: she wanted to do everything; it was therefore a comfort to him when Mrs Bessemer agreed to stay on, for she was a cheerful Amazon, with mighty arms and enormous hands, who would surely make nothing of the household chores.

But Gwen and he soon perceived that although Mrs Bessemer would polish fanatically at the tops of tables, she had a dislike of bending her back, and it was in fact Agnes Mayle, short and dumpy and quick-tempered, who worked the hardest and got things done. Agnes would scold Mrs Bessemer, who spent a whole morning cleaning the silver, and would chivvy her from place to place, thrusting a bucket and mop into her hands and doing her best to make her ashamed.

"How can you sit there, rub-rub-rub, when Mrs Wayman's slaving away, scrubbing and scouring for all she's worth? Get into that dairy and give her a hand!"

There were ding-dong battles between these two, and Agnes Mayle's rough tongue often prevailed where Gwen's civil entreaties failed. But on one score at least the two women were in accord, and that was in their devotion to the children. Agnes was an excellent cook, and during the school holidays, the children would sneak in repeatedly, sure of being given a tart or a rock-cake each, still warm from the oven. And Mrs Bessemer, not to be outdone, was a specialist in providing drinks. On cold winter days it was hot cocoa or beef-tea, and in summer-time, when the hot days came, it was ice-cold gingerade, the recipe for which was a jealously guarded secret.

"That's my Bert's favourite drink. He'd drink it all day, given a chance. He says nobody makes gingerade like me."

"It's not the only thing your Bert drinks," Agnes muttered, under her breath.

Mrs Bessemer's husband, Bert, was invoked every day at Holland Farm. His word was law, and it seemed he held very strong ideas.

"My Bert don't like me peeling onions. We never have them at home ourselves. He don't like me cleaning your silver by rights, on account of it spoiling my hands, and that's why I have to wear them gloves. He don't like me spoiling my hands. They're a woman's best feature, he always says."

Gwen wondered about this fastidious man.

"What does your Bert do?" she asked, and before Mrs Bessemer could reply, Agnes gave a snort and said: "He's a cowman at Outlands, same as my dad!"

"*Second* cowman," Mrs Bessemer said.

Gwen was careful not to smile.

"How is it that you both work here, instead of at Outlands, then?" she asked. "I've heard Mr Challoner say more than once that he needs someone to help in the house."

"My Bert wouldn't like me working there. Mr Challoner's a widower, as you know, and must be sixty if he's a day, but he's got a sweet tooth as the saying is. It'd never do, my going there. Agnes will tell you. She knows what he is."

Agnes, by her silence, seemed to concur, but Gwen, to avoid further gossip concerning a neighbour, began to talk of other things. She mentioned it to Stephen, however, later that day, and he was not in the least surprised.

"Challoner ought to marry again. The trouble is, he's gone up in the world, now that farming is prospering, and there's no woman in the district worthy of the honour he could bestow."

"I thought you liked him," Gwen said.

"He's been a good neighbour to me so far. I've got no

9

reason to complain. But as for the people who work for him, that's a different matter, I'm afraid. He talks of his men as though they were dirt."

"I'm disappointed," Gwen said. "I thought he was rather a nice man."

But, as Stephen said, he himself got on well enough with Challoner, and that was something to be thankful for.

At its central point, for a hundred yards or so, Challoner's land ran with Stephen's; but a lane came down from Puppet Hill, passed through the yard at Outlands Farm, and continued on down to the village; so for two thirds of the way down, the two farms were thus divided. This in itself brought problems sometimes, especially at harvest time, when a loaded waggon from Holland Farm, going down, might meet an empty one from Outlands coming up. But a friendly agreement already existed between the two farms when Stephen arrived, and, by talking things over beforehand, it was easy to avoid serious trouble.

When the men from Outlands did meet the men from Holland Farm, there was a great deal of swearing and argument between them, before one or the other gave way. But it was only a ritual and was much enjoyed on both sides. There were two tractors at Outlands; there were only horses at Holland Farm; and this meant a certain rivalry.

"When are you going to get mechanized?" Johnny Marsh would ask, jeering, and Bob Tupper as often would say: "When that there tractor drops a foal!"

Challoner himself often chaffed Stephen on this score.

"Even old Gould had a tractor, you know, and you're a young man of thirty-five. I'd have thought you'd be bang up to date, making us older ones open our eyes."

"I can't afford to buy tractors yet," Stephen said. "I want to get my mortgage paid. And I'm happy enough, using horses."

There were eight mares at Holland Farm; he meant to breed from them if he could; and one of the first things he did was to buy a Shire stallion at Capleton Mop. There were no good stallions in the neighbourhood, so it seemed a good idea to keep his own, even if it was something of an extravagance.

"Besides which," as he said to Gwen, "I've already had a few enquiries from farmers round about, who've got brood mares, so Lucifer will not only be earning his keep but making a profit on the side."

When the stallion arrived and Bob Tupper inspected him, he remained silent a long time. It looked as though he disapproved. The stallion's face was light grey: "white as moonlight," Gwen had said: but his neck and body were dappled and dark, and his hind quarters were iron-black.

"Well?" Stephen said, impatiently.

"Strikes me he's a different horse in front from what he is behind," said Bob.

"But what do you think of him?" Stephen asked.

"I suppose he'll do," Bob said.

He was not much in favour of keeping a stallion on the farm. It meant a lot of extra work, and who had time for coddling a horse that ate its head off, day in, day out, got the odd mare into trouble now and then, and never did a hand's turn in front of the plough?

"If that's all that's worrying you," Stephen said, "I'm quite happy to look after Lucifer myself."

But that was not right, either, and Bob gave a series of little grunts.

"I daresay I'll manage to fit it in."

And manage it he did, for Lucifer was always in tip-top condition, beautiful in every respect, and he soon had an excellent reputation with farmers who bred from their own mares. When the stud fees came in they were kept in a cashbox of their own, and every six months or so Stephen would give half the money to Bob Tupper, for him to divide among the men.

"Have a few drinks at The Rose and Crown – Lucifer's paying!" he used to say.

* * * * *

Stephen and Challoner both kept sheep and it was the custom, already established many years, for the two farms to share their shearing, both flocks being done at Outlands one year, Holland Farm the next.

11

That year it was Challoner's turn, and on a fine morning in May, the flocks were herded together at Outlands, and shearing platforms were set up in the big barn. The doors at both sides were open wide and a warm wind blew gustily through, bringing, now and then, a skitter of rain. One doorway had a row of hurdles across it, made to open like a gate; the ewes were let in, a few at a time, delivered into the hands of the shearers, and let out naked the other side, to join their bleating lambs in the fold. Stephen's shepherd, Henry Goodshaw, got on well with the Outlands shepherd, Arthur Thorne, and to see these two experts handling their clippers, sending the fleeces rippling back, was something that made the children stare. Chris, especially, watched by the hour, and Challoner's younger son, Gerald, older than Chris by eighteen months, brought him a ewe and some clippers to try.

"Go on, I'll hold her. Try your hand."

Chris wanted to try but he was afraid. Supposing he were to cut the ewe? Reluctantly he shook his head and watched as Gerald displayed his skill.

"Nothing to it!" Gerald said. "Any fool can shear a sheep!"

The two boys went to the same school, King Edward's in Chepsworth, but they were at home for Whitsuntide. All the children were on holiday and ran to and fro among the shearers. The older ones helped to tie up the fleeces, and little Emma pottered about, gathering up stray wisps of wool or stirring the warm tar in its pot.

"Come out of that!" said Morton George. "D'you want to get it on your pinny?"

Emma stared at him in surprise. Nobody ever spoke to her like that. She turned away without a word and walked to the far end of the barn, to swing on a rope that hung from the rafters. But after a while, feeling herself no longer observed, she slipped away out of the barn, into the house in search of her mother.

Gwen and Mrs Bessemer were busy in the kitchen with Kitty Cox, preparing luncheon for the shearers. Kitty was the stockman's wife and worked in the house six days a week. She was strong, cheerful, sturdy and rough, and stood no nonsense from anyone. She put a biscuit into Emma's hand and sent her out to the garden to play.

Gwen was surprised, knowing John Challoner's passion for improvements on the farm, to find they did not extend to the house. Admittedly there were carpets in the best rooms and velvet curtains at the windows, but there was no piped water supply and no adequate sanitation. Water for the house came from a hand-pump outside the door, and the privy was merely a filthy latrine in a tumbledown shed next to the dairy. The kitchen range was very old and the stovepipe so rusted that it constantly smoked, yet Kitty was expected to produce a feast for the hungry shearers, and by some miracle, produce it she did.

Baked ham, boiled beef, and three pressed ox-tongues were carried out to the smaller barn and set on the trestle table there. Pork pies, mutton pasties, and jellied brawn, with bowls of potatoes, beans, and green peas, were carried out and set down there. Spotted dick puddings, apple tarts, jam turnovers and egg custards: all these were carried out; and, last but not least, a whole cheese was set on the board.

"I wish their damned union could see them now!" Challoner remarked to Gwen. "Stuffing themselves at my expense!"

They were a merry party at the table that day. The two groups of workmen got on well and the barrel of beer loosened their tongues. They returned to work in high good humour and as the shearing recommenced the jokes were still flying from mouth to mouth.

"I ent got room for a ewe in my lap. My belly's too full with all that good food."

"It's the Chepsworth ale that's done *me* in. This ewe of mine has got six legs!"

"Anybody want a trim?" Tupper asked. His clippers went snip-snip in the air. "Short back and sides? Or maybe a bob?"

"Bobbed by Bob," said Billy Rye, and there was laughter all round as the men settled down to work again.

Later, however, towards the end, a quarrel blew up suddenly between Morton George on the one hand and an Outlands man named Jack Mercybright on the other.

"Call that shearing?" Mercybright said. "The moths could do a better job than that!"

Indeed the ewe was a sorry sight. She tottered away from Morton George with ridges of wool left on her sides and blood seeping from three or four cuts.

"It's these damned clippers, that's what it is! I never used such duddy things!"

"It's a bad workman that blames his tools."

"Supposing we swap, then, you and me? You take my clippers and I'll take yours."

"Supposing you deal with that ewe of yours before the flies get wind of her?"

"Don't you tell me what to do!"

George snatched up the pot of tar and angrily dabbed at the ewe's wounds. He sent her, with a kick, to join the rest. The two shepherds, Goodshaw and Thorne, watched and listened while they worked, but neither of them spoke a word. The other shearers were silent too. Mercybright was an elderly man with thick grey hair and a grey beard, and was tall enough, when he stood erect, to look down his nose at Morton George.

"Now what? You gone on strike?"

"Maybe I have. I've a good cause. Shearing ent my proper work. Why should I shear the bloody sheep?"

"It's everyone's work when it's there to be done."

"It's shepherd's work. It ent mine. Why should we help to do their work?"

"They help in the fields at harvest time. What's the odds for God's sake?"

"The shepherd gets a lot more pay. Lambing money, for a start. Ask them two just what they earn!"

Outside in the yard, loading fleeces into a cart, Stephen and Challoner heard most of this. Challoner swore and leapt down. Stephen followed him into the barn.

"What's going on?" Challoner bawled, but the two participants turned away, each seizing a ewe from the man at the gate and stooping to the work in hand. Challoner, after a glance round, led the way outside again.

"You need to watch that fellow George. He's a union man, he stirs things up. I've got three of them here, you

14

know, and the first chance I get they'll be out on their necks."

"I agree with what you say about George. The man's a slacker, I know that. But why shouldn't they belong to a union? *We* belong to the N.F.U.".

"That's different," Challoner said, but was unable to explain why.

That evening, when the shearing was done, Stephen and Gwen and the four children walked back home across the fields. The pockets of Emma's pinafore were stuffed with bits of sheep's wool and she carried a lamb's tail in her hand. Her small legs were soon tired, and Stephen offered her a pick-a-back ride.

"*I'll* carry her," Chris said. He crouched for his sister to climb on his back. Gwen had told her eldest son that his father must be saved from exertion whenever possible, owing to the pains in his chest and side, and Chris had taken the lesson to heart. "Hold tight, Emma! We're off!" he cried, and galloped across the fields towards home, leaving the others well behind.

"My hands are all soft with handling the fleeces," Joanna said, marvelling.

"So are mine," Stephen said.

"And mine! Have a feel!" Jamesy said, and they all had to feel one another's hands, to marvel at the softness of their skin.

"It's the lanolin," Stephen said.

"What's lanolin?" Jamesy asked.

"It's the natural grease in sheep's wool. It's used in the making of ointments for our skin."

"Is it good for freckles?" Joanna asked.

"It won't rub them out, if that's what you mean."

"What a pity. I wish it would."

"Silly thing," Jamesy said.

Over their heads, their parents smiled. The business of watching their children grow up was a strange thing full of queer little quirks. They knew each one so intimately; the physical bond was so very close, every thought and feeling could be divined; yet what could they know of the people these children would one day become? Each one so different, moved by an unknown force within, yet all bearing a common likeness. Not just the likeness of face and form, but the affinity created by small daily experiences shared, stored up as though in a bank, from which they could draw at will.

The four children would grow apart. As adults they might be scattered about the world. But the memory of this particular day, for instance, would always be shared by all of them, and however briefly they might meet, a word would be enough to bring it back. The warm gusty day with its little showers; the smells of sheep muck and wool and tar; the magical softness of their hands: the day would be one they would remember always, in future times, when they were old; and the sharing of such memories was a thing they could only experience together, as members of the same family.

"It's a queer thing, being a parent," Stephen said, and Gwen, laughing, took his arm, knowing how much he had left unsaid.

They walked on with Jamesy and Joanna, and soon saw that Chris, arriving first, had already been at work. Smoke rose from the kitchen chimney. The kettle would be on for tea.

* * * * *

It was a wet summer that year. Haymaking spun itself out and was not finished until late July. Stephen had other worries, too, for the government was regretting its policy on corn prices and was threatening to remove the guarantee. His harvest that year was good enough, considering the wet season, but in November, when he sold his corn, prices were already beginning to fall, giving warning of what was to come.

Just before Christmas Morton George came to him and asked for a rise of ten shillings.

"Don't be ridiculous," Stephen said. "You know what the present situation is."

"Yes, and I'm putting in now, before it gets worse. The union's behind me in asking for this rise. They gave it out at the meeting last night."

"The union needs to face facts."

"I've seen the corn prices in *The Gazette*. The farmers ent all that badly hit."

"I've got to look ahead," Stephen said. "The good days for farming are petering out. We've all got to face that fact and pull in our horns."

"You don't need to tell *me!*" George exclaimed. "It's what our speaker said last night. There's dark days in front of us, I know that, and who's going to suffer? – Men like me!"

Stephen knew that it was true.

Chapter 2

Just after Christmas that year, the mare, Nancy, gave birth to Lucifer's first foal. Emma, the youngest of the Wayman children, was allowed to choose the foal's name, and the name she chose was Phoebe.

"I bet you can't spell it!" Jamesy said, and all three older children rocked with mirth.

"Emma's quite good at spelling," said Gwen. "Miss Protheroe is pleased with her."

Emma, being only five, went to Miss Protheroe's "Little School", in the cathedral close in Chepsworth. It was the older children's task to call and collect her at four o'clock every day, and because of its tiny tables and chairs they scornfully called it the "Dolly School."

"Phoebe's a good name," Stephen said. "Emma has chosen very well."

Later, in March, at the Mare and Foal Show in Chepsworth, Nancy and Phoebe won first prize. Stephen lifted Emma up so that she could pin the red rosette on Nancy's headstall. Then Emma was put onto Nancy's back and with Stephen leading her by the rein, and with Chris leading the foal nearby, the whole family walked back home.

"My! But you must be tired!" Mrs Bessemer said to them. "You must be nearly ready to drop."

"*I'm* not tired," Emma said.

"*You've* been riding," Joanna said.

The spring was a dry and sunny one; the driest, it was said, for sixty-three years; and yet the nights were bitterly cold. Often during the Easter holidays, the children awoke to a world white with frost, and yet the days were bright and warm.

They were never at a loss how to fill their time. The

18

farm's secrets were known to them now, and they went in a kind of ritual from one marvel to the next, willing to share them with one another but guarding them fiercely from outside eyes. There were crabapple trees out in blossom along the hedges in Long Gains, and the moorhen had chicks on Copsey Pond, but few people were allowed to know. Cowslip places and bluebell places; squirrels' nests and foxes' earths; catkin bushes and wild cherry trees and the thrush that built in the pony's stall: only their parents and Agnes Mayle were allowed to know about these things; everyone else was kept in the dark.

And of course there was always the work of the fields. They watched the men ploughing and drilling; they watched the shepherd delivering lambs; and they poked their noses into the sheds, eager to know what was going on.

"What do *you* want?" said Morton George.

"Nothing much," Chris said.

"Take it and go, then, and shut the door!"

But the other men were friendly enough: Tupper and Hopson, especially, and the younger men, like Jenkins and Rye: the children were always welcome with them; and Chris, the eldest, now thirteen, was sometimes allowed to take the handles of Tupper's plough or ride on the step behind the drill, keeping the grain on the move in the box and calling out when it ran low.

Stephen's health was improving a lot. The tightness in his chest and the pain in his side, legacies of the poison gas, rarely troubled him these days. He was doing more and more on the farm: milking every morning and evening; hoeing the rootcrops, digging the drains; ploughing his quota with the men.

Sometimes the whole family were out in the field at the same time: working together in the sun and the wind; resting together, eating their food; returning home in the fading light, with the jingle of horse-chains and the rumble of wheels. They, as a family, were self-complete. They wanted no one but themselves.

"You live in a world of your own up there," John Challoner used to say. "Aren't you ever coming down?"

This was because Stephen never wanted to go to the

19

village whist drives; never joined the Crayle Hunt; never spent an evening at The Rose and Crown; never attended the N.F.U. "social evenings". Challoner liked to do all these things. He sometimes called Stephen a dull dog.

But Stephen did take some part in local affairs. Challoner had got him onto the parish council and the vicar, Mr Netherton, had voted him onto the board of managers of the village school. Stephen at first was against this. He felt it would be presumptuous of him to sit on the board of the village school when he sent his own children to schools in Chepsworth. But he was persuaded to change his mind. He already had a certain interest, for the school playground abutted on to his land, and he had agreed to the vicar's request that the little meadow of three acres, just behind the school, might be used by the pupils for their summer games. And Stephen, as the vicar pointed out, was a useful man on any board because of his knowledge of the law.

· Nevertheless, Stephen felt some embarrassment when he met Miss Izzard, the mistress-in-charge. "I feel an intruder, poking into your school's affairs when I've only lived here eighteen months." But she said, in a straightforward way he liked, "You let us use your meadow, Mr Wayman. That's passport enough as far as I'm concerned."

There was much news in the papers at that time of the hardships suffered by the coal-miners of England and Wales, who had been on strike for three months. Early in May, at a meeting of the school managers, the vicar reported that Miss Izzard wanted to hold a concert in the school, to raise funds for the miners' children. The vicar, who was in his early fifties, was a man anxious to move with the times but always uncertain how far he should go. He tended to lean on younger men, especially those who knew their own minds.

"I don't know that I approve of this scheme. It could well be argued that we were encouraging men to strike. But Miss Izzard, as you know, is an obstinate young woman, and she insisted that I put it before the board."

One or two of the managers shared the vicar's uncertainty, but Stephen took a firm stand.

"The miners are striking for a fair living wage. That's not

much to ask, it seems to me. Whatever the rights and wrongs of it, that's no reason why their wives and children should starve!"

So the concert was held and raised the sum of twenty pounds. Stephen took all his family, and Joanna was so much impressed by the young lady pianist from Cheltenham, who wore a long dress with net sleeves and played two pieces by Mendelssohn, that she went home filled with a new resolve to practise her scales before school every morning.

"When's your recital?" Jamesy asked, putting his hands over his ears. "If I buy a ticket, can I stay away?"

Joanna's ambitions, musically, were apt to alter with the wind. The spirit was willing but the flesh was weak, and her piano practice soon became as intermittent as it had been before.

* * * * *

The dry spring gave way to a dry summer. The days began to be very hot, and the children gloried in the sun. They shed their school clothes the instant they got home and ran about in cotton shorts until, as Henry Goodshaw said, they were "brown as eggs, the lot of them."

Often it was difficult to get the three older ones into bed, for the evenings never really grew dark. But there came a moment eventually when peace descended on the house, and Stephen and Gwen would walk out into the fields, glad to see the sun go down, after its fierceness during the day, and thankful for the coolness of the falling dew.

One evening it rained, a rain so light it was almost unreal, falling softly and silently from clouds so high they could not be seen. Stephen and Gwen walked out in this rain and stood with their faces upturned to it. They held out their arms and spread their hands and asked for the rain to soak the earth. The scent of it as it touched the grass; touched the hot surface of the soil; was a miracle of coolness and sweetness, and they drank it in through nostrils and mouth, greedily, with a kind of lust.

Gwen went forward into the rain, and her dark hair, with

21

its loose fronds, caught and held the droplets of light. Her eyebrows and lashes were speckled with them; her face, her throat, her naked arms, shone with the wetness of the rain; and her white cotton dress clung to her, showing the long shape of her thighs. She spun around and her wet skirts flared out. Then, suddenly, she was still.

"Why are you looking at me like that?"

"Can't I look at my own wife?"

"Only if you tell me what you're thinking."

"I was wondering what the children would say if they could see you twirling about."

"You think it's unseemly at my age?"

"It's my thoughts that are unseemly," Stephen said.

During the course of a busy day, Gwen was many things to him: a voice calling him in to his meals; a pair of eyes that saw things he missed; a pair of hands outstretched to help; mother of his children and mistress of his house. But at moments like this she was none of these things. He had time now to look at her; to rediscover the girl in her; to rediscover himself as a lover.

"You look even younger than when I married you. You might be eighteen, standing there."

"The light is fading, that's why."

But there was enough daylight left for her to see the look in his eyes, and for him to see the hint of warmth kindling under her clear skin.

"Whatever's the matter with us?" she said.

"It must be the rain," Stephen said. "It's making us drunk." Then, later, walking home: "It won't do much good, a sprinkle like this. What we need is a thorough soak."

"You don't think we'll get it?" Gwen asked.

"Not a chance," Stephen said.

In a few minutes more, the rain had stopped, a teasing promise unfulfilled. The next day was as hot as ever.

Hay harvest that year was all over within a week, but the hay was poor stuff, very light and dry. The aftermath of grass in the fields, instead of growing fresh and green, remained as it was, just short pallid stalks, with all its goodness burnt away. People began to speak of a drought.

During the summer of 1921, the newspapers made sorry reading. Famine in Russia; riots in Egypt; and in Germany terrible bitterness at the severity of the war reparations being exacted by the Allies. Republican atrocities in Ireland; continuing strife in industry at home; a decline in prosperity on the land. The threatened repeal of the Corn Act became reality in June, and John Challoner, along with every other farmer in England, felt that he had been betrayed.

"The same old story! We might have known! The farmer was a hero during the war. Now he can go and hang himself! Don't you mention Lloyd George to me!"

But Challoner found some crumb of comfort in the fact that the Wages Board was to be abolished, together with the power of the county council to enforce their own rules on cultivation.

"At least we can damn well *grow* what we please! And decide for ourselves what to pay a man when he's finished work at the end of the week. I shall have something to say to them, especially those union tykes, when we've finished with harvest this back-end!"

Stephen, however, was sick at heart. "We may be able to grow what we please, but shall be be able to sell it?" he said. And, walking with Gwen in the cornfields, with their bright illusion of riches to come, for the first time he began to have doubts of his wisdom in buying Holland Farm.

"It won't be too bad this harvest, I suppose, with the government paying compensation. But as for next year! – My God! What then?"

"Oh, we shall manage!" Gwen said. "We'll have to cut down a bit, that's all."

·"Maybe you're right," Stephen said, but he was more vexed than comforted by the cheerful way she brushed it aside. "Maybe you're right. Let's hope you are."

"Did you sell those weaners today?"

"Sell them? I practically *gave* them away! The market's glutted with pigs just now. You've read the papers, haven't you?"

"There's no need to bite my head off."

"Sorry!" he said, in a loud voice. But what in God's name,

23

he thought, did she expect?

The hot weather was getting him down. The drought, according to the national press, was "serious but not yet grave." Stephen fretfully disagreed.

"They should see Holland Farm!" he said to Gwen.

Water was low in ponds and wells, and the pastures were badly burnt up. The cows were sickly, swallowing so much dust as they grazed, and the heat was affecting their milk-yield. Turnip seed and mangold seed, three times sown in the Twelve Acres, had each time failed to germinate, and peas and beans in the Goose Ground were all shrivelled in their pods.

Even in the meadows, like Long Gains and Gicks, the ground had opened in terrible fissures, and Stephen gave orders that a close watch be kept on the cattle in case they should stumble into the cracks., Such an accident had happened at Lucketts, a farm on the other side of the brook, and the cow in question, having broken her leg, had had to be destroyed.

Everywhere it was the same, the parched land crying out for rain, sheep and cattle suffering, and in places the early slaughter of beasts because there was not enough food for them. On a farm near Peggleton, a man had been gored to death by a bull, never before known to be vicious. The heat, it seemed, had maddened it. On the railway at Bounds, sparks from an engine had set fire to the grass and broom on the bank, and the fire had spread into cornfields nearby, destroying thirty acres of oats. Fires broke out repeatedly on Springs Hill and the Burlows beyond, and when the fires had been put out, the burnt patches could be seen, like great black scars, as though the smooth green flanks of the hills had been branded by an enormous iron.

Fire was Stephen's constant dread. He kept a close watch on his men, for they were smokers, one and all. And sure enough, in the stackyard one day, a sudden whoomphing assault of flame! Bob Tupper was at work with his prong, clearing the yard of old hay and straw, ready for the building of the new cornstacks. The fire shot up from the loose hay as he was forking it into a cart. It leapt at him like an angry dog, and the searing heat, sucked quickly in as he caught his breath, burnt his mouth and throat and lungs.

He ran to the nearest drinking-trough, put his head into the water, and doused the rest of himself with a splash. Then he turned to deal with the fire. By that time Stephen and most of the other men were there and the flames were douted in a trice. Bob, much blackened about the face, with a sore throat and singed eyebrows, now gave vent to some choice language, and it seemed he knew where to lay the blame, for Jimmy Jenkins had passed through the yard a few minutes before, smoking a hand-rolled cigarette.

"Supposing the kids had been playing here?" Bob Tupper said to him, and Jimmy, who was only seventeen, looked at him in horror.

"I'll never smoke another bloody fag," he said, "until we've had some bloody rain!"

"If you break that promise," Stephen said, "I swear I'll sack you on the spot!"

* * * * *

Harvest was going to be early that year, but all the corn crops were woefully poor. Oats in the One-and-Twenty Field were so thin and light in the grain, they were not worth cutting after all, and Stephen folded the cattle there to eat the oat-crop as it stood.

The water shortage became acute. In the house there was strict rationing; every drop must be saved for the stock; but there was some slight relief when Stephen, poking about in the Bratch, where an old cottage had once stood, found a well full of brackish water and piped it to the pastures below. Most of the ponds had dried up, and even the deep dark Copsey Pond, shaded by surrounding trees, had been reduced to a mere puddle, six feet or so below its banks. Because of the steepness of these banks, and the low level of the pond, the sheep who came from the meadows to drink were in danger of toppling in and drowning, so Stephen gave orders to Bob Tupper that someone should be sent to fence it round.

Bob sent Morton George and Jimmy Jenkins. They put a roll of wire netting into a barrow, together with their tools and a bundle of stakes, and threw their luncheon-bags on top. This was a day in early July, a day as hot as any that summer so far, and the two men sweated in the heat. The pond had dried up completely now. The bottom was merely a black morass, and out of it stuck an old waggon-wheel, a few dead boughs from the trees around, and the grey skeleton of a pig. In one of the meadows next to the pond, sheep, grazing the stalky grass, stopped eating and stared at the men, ears twitching at the noise they made as they hammered the stakes into the ground.

Two thirds of the way round, their roll of netting came to an end. They would have to go back to the farm for more.

"It's almost dinner-time now," George said. "I'm just about dying of flaming thirst, so how about going up to the pub? We'll finish this when we get back."

They took their satchels from the barrow and tramped, melting, across the fields to where, on the edge of Huntlip Common, stood a small public house called The Black Ram. The landlord gave them his paper to read. They talked about Dempsey and the big fight. The pub, with its sunken stone-flagged floor, was cool. They stayed there, drinking, until it closed.

When they got back to Copsey Pond, Jimmy, the younger of the two, offered to go for the netting alone.

"Oh, sod the netting!" George said. "Seems to me it's a waste of time. No sheep is going to drown in *there*. How can they when the water's gone? If Tupper asks me about this job, I shall say it's a bloody waste of time."

He threw his satchel into the barrow and began trundling it away. Jimmy shrugged and followed him. Behind them, under the willow trees, one third of the pond remained unfenced. A moorhen emerged from her nest in the bank and picked her way across the mud. A wagtail perched on the broken wheel.

In the farmyard, when George and Jenkins returned, they were called upon to take a turn at the pump, with orders to fill the water-cart. The electric motor had broken down; the water had to be pumped by hand. Stephen was in the cartshed, overhauling the reaper-and-binder. He stopped work and called to George.

"Did you put that fence round Copsey Pond?"

"We ran out of wire," George said. "But the water's all dried away now. No sheep's going to drown itself in there. There's no need to worry until we've had rain."

Stephen gave an impatient sigh. The men had been gone since eleven o'clock. Now it was almost half past three.

"Oh, very well!" he exclaimed. "You'd better leave it for today. Get a move on, filling that water-cart. The troughs are empty in the top pastures."

He went back to work on the reaper-and-binder, feeling fretted and annoyed. The two men had wasted half a day, just when time was becoming precious, for Nate Hopson had broken his leg and was going to be laid up for some time, and harvest was getting under way. The fence round the pond would have to wait.

* * * * *

They started cutting in the Oak Field and then went on to the Eighteen Acre, and every day as they toiled in the heat, they were choked by the everlasting dust that rose and enveloped them like a cloud. Stirred up by the horses' hooves and the blades of the reaper going round, the dust seemed to blast itself into their skin. Their eyes were on fire with it; bloodshot, inflamed; and their throats ached intolerably.

"Oh for some rain!" groaned Billy Rye, and nobody there upbraided him for a prayer so strange at harvest-time. "God be good and send some rain!"

But no rain came. There was no relief. The pillar of dust towered above them, and all day long they followed it, toiling and suffering in their sweat. The sun was a tyrant over them, and their day of deliverance was not yet come.

Sometimes, in the distance, thunder could be heard, but the promise of a storm remained unfulfilled. The hot sky pressed on the earth. There was no breath of air between the two. There was only the weight of heat pressing down and the throbbing current of heat rising up, visible in its shimmering waves. And out of the heavy, sagging sky the tiny black thrips or thunder-bugs descended on all living things to crawl, minute but maddening, and add their torment to suffering skin.

Emma came running into the house, weeping because of the tiny thrips that crawled on her face, her scalp, her arms, and were clustered, black, on the front of her frock.

"Horrible dirty things!" she cried. "Mummy! Make them go away!"

Gwen removed them as best she could and rubbed the child's skin with lemon-scented oil, but the thrips came on her just the same, and Emma, gradually growing calm, would sit on the garden-seat by the hour, unable to think of anything but the tiny insects that plagued her skin.

"No," she would say, again and again. "No. No. I tell you *no*." And at each vehement syllable, one smaller finger would descend to rub out another of the tiny, creeping, hateful things that had dared to settle on her person. "No. No. I tell you *no*."

Often when Gwen had finished in the house and the dairy, she would join the men in the harvest-field. They were cutting a crop of dredge-corn now: oats and barley, winter sown; the best crop of the harvest so far. There were no delays in this weather. Long before the last sheaves were stooked, the waggons were lumbering to and fro, and a new stack was rising in the stackyard. Gwen helped to set up the stooks and then took a fork to help with the pitching. Stephen worked at the next waggon. He gave her a smile but said nothing. There were few words wasted by the harvesters toiling in the heat that year.

Gwen was wearing a printed frock, the pattern of which, in the course of that summer, had faded from a rich dark blue to a pale and ghostly shade of grey. On her head she wore a straw hat with a curving brim down over her eyes, and on her feet an old pair of sandals without any straps.

Stephen was aware of her constantly, without directly looking at her. They were so close in their intimacy, and knew each other in such a way, that whenever she took a sheaf on her fork and raised it aloft to the man on the load, it was like a movement of his own body. Knowing her lissomeness as he did; the grip of her hands and the curve of her arms; the shape of her shoulders, breasts, and thighs:

28

he felt her movements in himself and knew that she in turn felt his. He knew when she turned to fork a sheaf; knew when she lifted it overhead; and knew how, at the very last, she danced a little on her toes, reaching up as high as she could to deliver the sheaf to the man on the load.

She, as a girl on her father's farm, had been bred to this work. It was in her bones. He would never have the knack of it so well as she, digging into the sheaf just so, raising the fork and turning it, all in one motion, scarcely seen, yet so exactly right each time that the sheaf could be taken from the curve of the prongs without danger, without delay. He liked to see her out in the fields. It was another bond between them, that they worked together, side by side.

And yet he was anxious about her too. He felt that she asked too much of herself; went beyond her woman's strength. Today, for instance, as the load grew higher in the waggon, he wished she would stop and take a rest. With every layer of sheaves on the load, she had to reach higher and higher still, and he sensed the tremulous weariness in every movement of her arms. He could see the strain of it in her face, shaded though it was by her broad-brimmed hat, and could hear the shortness of her breath.

"Don't overdo it, will you?" he said. "It's most unwise, in this heat. I think it's time you went back to the house."

"But I've only just come out," she said. "Would you shut me indoors again?"

Gwen could be obstinate when she chose.

* * * * *

Mrs Bessemer came to the farm only in the mornings nowadays. She could only work two hours a day. The prolonged hot weather was making her ill.

"What about us?" said Agnes Mayle. "Ent we supposed to feel the heat?"

But Mrs Bessemer's illness was perfectly genuine. The heat reduced her in a terrible way, and sometimes she fell to the floor in a faint, eyes wide open and face pale as death. She stayed at home in the afternoons, and Gwen and Agnes managed alone.

"Shall I get another woman in?" Stephen asked.

"Good gracious no!" Gwen exclaimed. "Surely this weather will break some time?"

"Sometimes I wonder," Stephen said.

The heat was a burden on them all. Even the children, when they came home from school, sought whatever shade could be found and sat engaged in quiet games. The heat was a strain even on them.

And everywhere it was the same. The earth and everything that lived craved rain, but no rain came. The grass in the leys was so pale and dry that grassland and stubble looked alike. Even in the meadows the grass was brown. There was no greenness anywhere. The fruits of the earth were withering; the tiny apples fell from the trees; and the brown crinkled leaves were everywhere, crackling dead and dry underfoot.

"You know what I think?" Mrs Bessemmer said. "I reckon it's the end of the world."

"Don't talk daft!" Agnes said.

But Gwen, as she went about the farm, observing the suffering of the animals, sometimes shared Mrs Bessemer's fears. The earth was dying in the heat. Only a miracle, she felt, could ever bring it to life again.

In Huntlip church, as in churches throughout the country, prayers were offered up for rain. But still no rain came. The sky pressed closer upon the earth, and the beasts of the field were borne down, panting open-mouthed in the heat.

* * * * *

It was a day in mid-July, and Gwen was all alone in the house. Agnes had finished her day's work and had left early, to take some milk to Nate Hopson, still laid up with his leg in plaster. Stephen was with the other men, cutting thirty acres of wheat on the far side of Woody Holl.

Gwen went out into the garden to fill a basket with lettuces, radishes, and spring onions, ready for the children's tea. There was thunder in the air. The sky was yellow and deep mauve, mottled like an angry bruise. She was on her way back to the house when she heard the faint sound of a sheep bleating, and noted it as an unusual thing, for the sheep had been quiet all through the drought. Perhaps, today, the storm would break.

The air was so close she could scarcely breathe. She set her basket on the step and went across to the stable yard, to look in over the door of the shed, where an in-calf heifer lay in the straw, somewhat sickly and near her time. Having seen that the heifer was all right she stood for a moment, listening, and heard the sheep bleating again. The sound was remote, indistinct, but there was a querulous note in it, and a certain persistence that worried her.

She went through the gate into the Home Field and walked slowly across the stubble. She was wearing her sandals, without any straps, and the stubble scratched her naked feet. The sandals were soon full of dust and seeds and the needle-sharp barbs from the oat-flights that worked their way painfully into the skin. She stopped for a moment to empty them, then went on across the slope.

The sheep was no longer crying now. Gwen stood listening, but there was no sound. She put up her hand to shade her eyes and gazed out over the empty fields. The stubble lands were bleached and bare. Between the stalks, on the snuff-dry earth, the pimpernels were open wide. She was thinking of turning back towards home when the sheep began bleating again, and this time she heard in the drawn-out cry the unmistakable note of distress. She walked across the next two fields and down to the meadows in the dip, and so came to the dried-up pond with its incomplete fence and its circle of trees, and its waggon-wheel sticking out of the mud.

The flock was in the meadow called Gicks, and a ewe had gone down the bank of the pond for the sake of the coolness of the mud at the bottom. She had probably lain there, cool, for some time, and now, when she wanted to come out, her hindquarters were stuck in the mud. She was heaving about in it, clumsily, and her efforts had gouged out a deep rounded pit, in which the last of the moisture gathered, making a loud sucking noise as her haunches scrabbled and sank back.

31

The mud at the outer edge of the pond was dry, and had opened in fissures six inches wide. Gwen climbed over the wire netting and picked her way down towards the ewe. When she had gone five or six yards, the mud grew soft and covered her feet above the ankles. She trod carefully, slock-slock, and held her skirts above her knees.

When the ewe saw her coming, it made another frantic heave, trying to hump itself out of the pit. But it only sank back again as before. Gwen now let go of her skirts and they hung trailing in the mud. She leant forward, facing the ewe, and seized it at either side of its neck, gripping wool and flesh together. But when she leant backwards, using all her strength, the ewe began to turn away, heaving sideways instead of forwards, and Gwen was pulled to her knees in the mud.

"Stupid animal!" she said. "Can't you see I'm trying to help?"

She let go of the ewe and flung out her arms to keep her balance, struggling onto her feet in the mud and trying to climb onto firmer ground. But the ewe, on finding itself released, scrabbled about sideways and backwards, and Gwen was suddenly sucked down, into the centre of the pit. The mud yielded under her and in an instant was up to her waist, closing between herself and the ewe but dragging them both down together.

Suddenly she became afraid. There was a wellspring beneath her feet; she could hear it bubbling and could feel its surge; but surely the bottom of the pond could not be so deep as to suck her down? She gave a little scornful laugh. With her arms outstretched, she tried to move. Her feet trod the softness down below, seeking firmness; expecting it.

There was no firmness. Only liquid mud. And she was sinking all the time. She reached up to the willow trees; she reached out to the broken wheel; but branches and wheel were too far away. Only the ewe was close to her, unmoving now, supine in the mud. Gwen again took hold of it and tried to lift it out of the pit. If with her help it could clamber out, its momentum in turn would help her. But her strength was nothing. The animal's weight was mountainous. And the weight of the thick black viscous mud was pressing on her, squeezing her flesh, numbing her body from the waist down.

Her only chance was help from elsewhere. The essential thing was to keep calm. She opened her mouth and gave a loud cry. She put all her strength into her voice, and the cry travelled out across the fields, a long-drawn *hallooo* of desperate appeal.

But who was to hear her when she called? Agnes had gone to Rayner's Lane. The children were not yet home from school. Stephen and the men were harvesting in a field on the other side of the farm. There was no one to hear her when she called but the flock grazing in the meadow nearby, and the ewe beside her in the mud.

Her cry was a shock to the terrified ewe. It reared itself up in the mud beside her and began a violent scrabbling. Its two front feet came down on her, and the sharp cloven hooves scrabbled madly, cutting her face and tearing her frock, marking her flesh in several bright weals from her throat and shoulders down to her breasts. When she sought to protect herself, her hands and arms met the scrabbling hooves and were lacerated most dreadfully. And now, when she cried aloud for help, the cry was full of pain and fear.

"Surely not!" she said, sobbing. "Surely I'm not going to die like this? Please, God, make somebody hear!"

Panic got her by the throat. She cried out for help again and again, but nobody heard her, nobody came. And the ewe, with its marbled yellow eyes, its black nostrils streaming mucus, its heavy body against hers, was bearing her downwards all the time. It was leaning on her. It was taking her strength. Whenever she uttered her cry for help, it reared up and trampled her. When she was silent, it was still. But even then, very gradually, she was sinking lower into the pit.

In the heat the mud had a terrible stench. The ewe also stank, because of its fear. Gwen, breathing with painfulness, thought of it as the smell of death. Why had she tried to help the ewe instead of going to fetch the shepherd? What would Stephen say to her? And, thinking of Stephen, she began to cry, turning her face away from the ewe and yielding, exhausted, to the pull of the mud.

Then her fighting spirit revived. She tried yet again to struggle free. Her mind was clarified, sharpened by fear. She knew she was struggling for her life.

* * * * *

The children came home to an empty house. They sought out their father in the harvest field. He was surprised that Gwen was nowhere to be found, but he thought she would very soon turn up, He told them to get their own tea and to bring something up to the field for him.

While he ate, with the other men, the three older children set up some sheaves, and Emma sat in the shade of the hedge, plaiting a bracelet of cornstalks. They stayed with him until six o'clock and then, when three of the men went down to see to the evening milking, he sent the children back to the house. If their mother was not yet back, Joanna was to put Emma to bed, and when she and the others had done their school prep they were to go to bed themselves.

Stephen and the men worked until dusk. Most of the men then went straight home, but two of them returned with him, leading the horses, Boxer and Beau, with one loaded waggon which they put in the barn.

The house was in darkness, upstairs and down. Plainly Gwen had still not come home. Stephen could not understand it at all, and he was more than a little annoyed, for the in-calf heifer, placed in Gwen's care, was lowing distressfully from the shed.

"Where the devil's my wife, I wonder? I shall have to see into this!"

At that moment Henry Goodshaw came into the yard, having been the rounds of his flock in the meadows. He stood for a while deep in thought, and his look and manner were very strange. He asked to speak to Stephen alone. He had found Gwen's body in the mud of the pond. The ewe, by its bleating, had drawn him there. The ewe had trampled her to death.

34

Chapter 3

The silence that settled over the farm was something that had to be broken down. The men would stop talking when he came by, and would listen to him, when he gave his orders, with a kind of considerate gentleness that was almost more than he could bear. They would answer him in quiet voices, doing their best to be natural, but failing because of what they knew; because the knowledge filled their minds.

One day he came upon three of them in the field of barley at Long End. They were trying the grain in the palms of their hands, rubbing it till it broke from the husks. They had been talking until he came. Now they were silent, avoiding his glance. The field was not far from Copsey Pond.

"Well?" he said. "What do you think?"

"I think we should cut," Tupper said.

"Then for God's sake get started!" Stephen said. "Why stand about wasting time?"

Nobody blamed him for lashing out. They felt they deserved it, the three of them, because their lives were still intact, and their womenfolk were safe at home. They put themselves in Stephen's place. "If that was me – " Bob Tupper said. He had no need to say more.

They knew they ought to talk to him, but there was danger in every remark, and they wanted to spare him their clumsiness. And Stephen himself was unable to talk. The silence, though a burden, was refuge too. He could give his orders on the farm; conduct his business on market day; speak to Agnes about the children, and speak to the children when need be. But each of these was a separate task, and he came to each task with his mind prepared. Whenever one overlapped another, he felt as though he would go to pieces. How did men manage, who lost their wives? He could face only one thing at one time. When he gave himself up to the farm, and the children came to him with their worries, he felt he could hardly bear to look at them. And when, at certain allotted times, he gave himself up to his children completely, the work of the farm did not exist.

Only Agnes Mayle, taking charge of household affairs, had the courage to mention his dead wife's name.

"Mrs Wayman used to pay us on Fridays," she said, when Stephen mentioned the matter of wages; and always, whatever queries arose, she answered in the same forthright way: "Mrs Wayman dealt with the eggs," or "Mrs Wayman's poultry book is up on that shelf, behind the clock."

He got through those early days somehow: the nightmare of breaking the news to the children; the coroner's inquest; the burial; the reporters calling at the house; the sympathy and the good advice. "You must think of your children," the vicar said, and Stephen angrily turned away. "I don't need *you*," he said in his mind," to tell me what I have to do."

* * * * *

He got his children through those days: saw them off to school in the morning; made sure he was always there to meet them when they came home in the afternoon; set time aside to talk to them, and tried to wrap them round in love.

But soon the holidays would begin, and the prospect filled him with secret dread. He took the three older ones aside and told himself they were almost grown up: Chris thirteen; Joanna twelve; Jamesy eleven in two months' time.

"I'm worried about little Emma," he said. "She's only five and she's young for her age. Now that the holidays are nearly here, I want you to take great care of her, and see that she's never left alone. Will you promise me you'll look after her?"

Solemnly they gave their word, but when the three of them were alone, they looked at each other helplessly, eyes questioning, doubtful, afraid.

"What are we supposed to do?" Chris said. "Dad doesn't tell us what to *do*!"

Looking out through the kitchen window, they could see little Emma in the garden, following Agnes as she hung out the clothes, handing her the pegs from the raffia bag.

"Emma's all right," muttered Chris. "*She's* too young to understand."

* * * * *

A new stack, at the edge of the stackyard, was leaning dangerously to one side. Poles were needed to shore it up. Morton George was given the job and Bob Tupper said to him, "See that you do the thing properly! – *This* time!" George did the job and the stack was shored up safely enough. He went to Stephen, alone in the byre.

"I reckon you'd better give me my cards."

"Why now, suddenly?"

"It's all these remarks!" George said. "It's the way the others look at me. D'you think I don't know you hold me to blame?"

Stephen could never bring himself to look at George. He hated to see him about the farm. But the burden of blame could not be carried by this one man alone. It was too much for any man.

"You were at the inquest," he said. "You heard what the coroner had to say."

An element of negligence had been involved. That was what the coroner had said. But no single person could be blamed, and Mrs Wayman had met her death through a series of tragic circumstances, and because, in her concern for a helpless animal in distress, she had taken no thought for her own safety.

"I know what *he* said!" George exclaimed. "But it's what the chaps've got to say!"

"Do you *want* me to give you your cards?"

"If I've got to put up with all these remarks –"

"That's something you've got to sort out with them."

"And what about you, Mr Wayman, sir? I reckon *you*

37

blame me right enough!"

"Get back to work," Stephen said.

* * * * *

The holidays came; long hours to be filled; and once again
Agnes took charge. She chivvied the children about the
house until some order prevailed there each day, and she
found them a great many things to do.

"I can't do everything myself! Mrs Bessemer's having one
of her turns. So just you get busy and show some vim!"

There were chickens to feed and eggs to collect; there
were pans in the dairy to be scoured out, and the dairy floor
to be sluiced down and scrubbed; potatoes to be dug from
the garden for lunch, peas to be shelled and mint to be
chopped, and the carving-knife to be sharpened and
cleaned. And when the household chores were done she
would issue forth with them out of doors to help with the
harvest in the fields. She would make a game of it, ordering
them about, and they would work to some elaborate plan,
seizing the sheaves and setting them up and arranging the
stooks in such a way that they made a pattern across the
field.

"Damn and butter!" Agnes would say. "I ent got enough
to finish this star!"

The way she scowled and pursed her lips, and the way she
clumped across the stubble to snatch two sheaves from
Trennam's hands, made the children laugh aloud. They
ran about after her, snatching up sheaves from one place
and setting them down again in another, until the stooks on
the slope of the field formed an enormous six-pointed star.
And Stephen, seeing them at their game, hearing their
voices across the field, gave thanks for Agnes and such as
she, who kept things going and knew what to do.

"When is your cousin coming, daddy?" the children
asked almost every day.

"Not just yet," Stephen said. "It's a long journey from
India, you know."

He had cabled his cousin, Dorothy Skeine, telling her of
Gwen's death, and Dorothy had answered by return that

38

she would come at once to England, to keep house for him and look after his children.

"What's she like?" the children asked. "Is she young? Is she pretty? Is she nice?"

"I haven't seen her for fifteen years, but no, she's not young, not exactly," he said. He wondered himself what she was like. Fifteen years was a long time. "You'll see for yourselves in due course."

"Why can't Agnes live with us?"

"Agnes has got her father and brothers to look after, as you well know. She's working too hard as it is."

Their father's cousin was on her way. She was coming to England in a ship. They tried to picture her but failed.

"I wish she'd *come*," Joanna said.

"I'm not so sure," Jamesy said. "Supposing we don't care for her?"

"Supposing she doesn't care for *us!*" said Chris.

They were silent, sunk in thought.

* * * * *

Sometimes at night while the children slept, Stephen walked in the empty fields. Harvest was almost over now, the earliest harvest in many years. They would begin ploughing soon, if the plough could cut through the hard-baked earth.

"God! The ploughing!" he said to himself.

His mind veered away from it, rejecting it, unable to think. Yet he knew the ploughing would be done; the seed would be sown, the green blades would come; and the earth would tilt away from the sun, taking its quarterly season of rest.

How was it that he could work by day, as though he cared about what he did? How was it that he could walk the earth; could eat and drink and go to sleep; talk to people; put on his clothes; when he was filled with such a rage? Even on the night of Gwen's death, he had helped to deliver a new calf. The thing was hateful, unspeakable, and yet he did it just the same. Was this the way it would always be?

One night he walked in the harvest field, and there was a

moon very nearly full. The cornsheaves stood, leaning together in the stooks, and each stook had its long shadow, slanting towards him across the stubble. The air was hot and perfectly still but suddenly, as he walked in the field, there was a little flaw of wind that blew on the ground among the stubble and spiralled upwards into the sky, carrying with it dust and chaff and little bits of pale-glinting straw.

The play of the wind, and its rustling noise, were like a presence among the sheaves, and he came to a sudden startled halt. The earth had been so perfectly still that the wind touched him and took his breath. The rustling awoke something fearful in him. It seemed like the spirit of the earth, that moved on heedlessly, down the years, knowing nothing of the emptiness that death created in human hearts. The earth spirit would keep him alive even though he was dead within, and the knowledge of this made him afraid.

Two miles away, beyond Blagg, a motor car ground up the steep road and changed gear about half way. Its headlamps came swinging over the hill, marked the course of the road for a while, and vanished again down into the dip that held the village. This brief intrusion from the outside world seemed to leave a greater silence behind. The aloneness and emptiness were everywhere. And he asked himself yet again: What in God's name did a man do, who had had so much and then lost it all?

On his way homeward, down the field, his foot kicked something on the ground. It was a single sheaf of wheat, dropped by a careless harvester, and it lay on the ground, having burst from its bond. Stooping, he gathered the loose sheaf, and tied it securely together again. The cornstalks rustled and so did the ears, and the bunch of straws that made up the bond were dry and brittle between his fingers, breaking into tiny splinters that pricked and penetrated his skin. He took the rustling sheaf in his hands, carried it with him a few paces, and set it upright against a stook. The moon watched him from overhead as he followed his shadow down the slope.

* * * * *

40

One day when Stephen walked into the garden, he found his children close in a group, and in their midst, fawning, soft-eyed, a spaniel puppy three weeks old.

' "Mr Challoner sent it to us. Gerald brought it, it's ours to keep. We *can* keep it, can't we, dad?"

"Yes, of course," Stephen said. "Have you decided on his name?"

"We're calling him Sam," Jamesy said.

The puppy was everything to them. They took it with them everywhere. It gave some meaning to their lives. And Stephen felt a twinge of shame, because he had not thought of giving them a puppy, and John Challoner had.

People were really very good. Mrs Bessemer, although still suffering from the heat, had them to tea once or twice a week and allowed them into Bert's pigeon-loft, to see the pigeons and stroke their breasts. The children always had plenty to do. Everybody saw to that. Bob Tupper, in his dinner-hour, cut them each a pair of stilts, and they stumped about, up in the air, able to see over hedges and walls and to rat-tat-tat on the dairy window, making poor Agnes jump out of her skin.

Gerald Challoner came over sometimes, driving one of his father's tractors, and Chris was allowed to take the controls. Nate Hopson came over, with his leg in plaster, and challenged Joanna to a race, he on his crutches and she on her stilts, and the prize for Joanna when she won was Nate's old Army cap-badge, which she wore with great pride, clipped to her blouse.

But there were times, inevitably, when no one could fill the space in their lives. One day during piano practice, Joanna completed an exercise without any faults or hesitations, and swung round in triumph at the end, having heard someone come in at the door.

"Did you hear that, mummy?" she exclaimed, and of course it was Agnes standing there. The moment of triumph was splintered into bits. Joanna stared through hot surging tears. "Why did mummy have to die?"

"She didn't *have* to! She just did!" Agnes marched across to a chair and punched a cushion into shape. "As to the why of it, don't ask me! The why is always followed by zed, and zed is the end of it, that's what I say!"

Agnes would do anything in the world for the four children, but she had no comfort to offer them. Death was death. It took the best. There was no rhyme nor reason in the world, and her attitude rubbed off on them.

The vicar called at Holland Farm, and, waiting for Stephen to come in from the fields, sat with the children in the garden.

"You must miss your mother very much."

"Of course," said Chris, in a curt tone. "She happens to be dead."

The vicar was shocked. He himself never spoke of death. He felt he had a duty to these four children facing him.

"Don't you know where your mother is?" he asked, eyeing each of them in turn. "Surely, now, you can tell me that?"

Chris and Joanna looked away. The vicar's question embarrassed them. They knew what he wanted them to say, but they had no use for the life hereafter, even if its existence could be proved. He turned his gaze on Jamesy instead.

"What about you, young man? Can you tell me where your mother is?"

"Yes," said Jamesy, "she's in her grave."

When Stephen came, the vicar stood up. He would not stay more than a moment, he said. He knew how busy farmers were.

"I came to see if I could help. With a young family like yours, I know what problems there must be, and if there's anything I or my wife can do –"

"You're very kind," Stephen said. "But my cousin, Miss Skeine, is coming back from India soon. She's going to make her home here, and look after us all, my children and me."

"So glad, so glad," the vicar said.

Stephen went with him to the gate.

"I wish she'd come, this cousin of dad's, *if* she's coming," Jamesy said. "How much longer is she going to be?"

* * * * *

The day came when cousin Dorothy was expected. Stephen went in the pony and trap to meet her train at Chepsworth station, and the four children remained at home, under orders to be on hand ready to welcome her on her arrival.

When their father returned and drove into the stable yard, the children were at the kitchen window, where they could get the earliest glimpse. Emma stood on the kitchen stool. She was wearing her best blue cotton frock. Agnes, discreetly, was upstairs, but no doubt had her look-out post. The house was as clean as a new pin.

The woman who descended from the trap was thin and loose-boned. She wore a grey silk blouse and a grey worsted skirt that reached to the tops of her old-fashioned boots. Her brown-skinned face was narrow and long, with strong cheekbones and strong-jutting chin, and eyes set deep under bristling eyebrows. She had already taken off her hat, and her grey hair, cropped amazingly short, covered her head in a close frizz, tough and tight-curled, like steel wool. When she descended from the trap, it was with a little ungainly leap, revealing stockings of dark grey lisle, gathered in wrinkles about her knees; and as she stood in the stable yard, gazing at the house and the farm buildings, she flung out her long ungainly arms in a wild gesture of ecstasy.

"England!" she said, in a powerful voice that rang round the yard. "England again! Oh it does smell so good!"

At the kitchen window, the children watched.

"Is that *her* ?" Joanna breathed.

They eyed one another in dismay.

"I do think dad might have warned us," said Chris, lifting Emma down from the stool, and Jamesy said, resentfully, "Why do we have to have her here? We didn't ask her. She asked herself."

When cousin Dorothy came indoors, the children stood in a formal row. Their father introduced them to her, and she shook hands with each of them, vigorously, squeezing their palms. She treated each child to a long, hard look, and her eyes were unexpectedly blue, looking out keenly from under her brows.

"You needn't think you are strangers to me, just because

43

we've never met. I've seen your photographs, over the years, and had news of you now and then, *when* your father remembered to write. I know a lot about you, never fear, and what I don't know I shall soon find out!"

The three older children stood like posts. Looking at her, they were struck dumb. Only little Emma spoke and that was because, leaning towards cousin Dorothy, she was counting the tiny round black buttons sewn close together, dozens of them, down the front of the grey silk blouse. Stephen warningly cleared his throat, and Chris, with reluctance, began to speak. Sometimes he wished he was not the eldest of the four. All sorts of duties fell on him. He fixed cousin Dorothy with his scowl.

"It's very kind of you to come all the way from India. We hope you'll be very happy here."

"What a beautiful speech," cousin Dorothy said. "I shall be happy, I promise you."

"We've certainly got a lot to thank cousin Dorothy for," Stephen said, pointedly. "She's made a considerable sacrifice, leaving India to come here."

"Oh, don't tell them that, for goodness' sake! Do you want them to hate me from the start? Anyway, it isn't true. I was glad to leave India. Very glad." Once again she threw out her arms, striding about the big kitchen, looking around her with rapturous eyes. "Oh, to be in England now that April's there!" she said in her powerful, loud-thrilling voice.

Jamesy looked at her with scorn.

"It isn't April, it's August," he said, and, turning stiffly towards his father, he asked: "Can we go out now? We *did* wait in."

"Very well," Stephen said. "No doubt cousin Dorothy will be glad to excuse you."

In another moment the children were gone, the puppy yapping at their heels.

"I apologize for my children's lack of grace. I hope you will bear with them for a bit."

Dorothy raised a brown-skinned hand.

"They are the ones who must bear with me."

"It's very good of you to come. What did Hugh say to

44

your leaving him?"

"Oh, never mind Hugh!" Dorothy said. Her brother was dismissed in a single wave. "He's well established out there. Plenty of servants to run round after him. You need me more than he does now."

There was a pause. Dorothy stopped striding about and stood with her hands on the back of a chair. She began to speak of Gwen's death.

"Tell me about it," she said to him.

* * * * *

He realized, for the first time, that he had not fully faced the facts of Gwen's death. The manner of it. The horror, the pain. The fear she had suffered, perhaps for hours. In keeping the details from his children, he had succeeded in keeping them from himself. Even at the inquest he had not really faced up to these things: the need for control had shut them out; and in the weeks that had passed since then, his mind had sheered away from them.

He had faced the meaning of Gwen's loss: what it meant to him and his family; but not the agony of her dying. That he had pushed deep into his mind; into some dark forgetfulness; and now, as he talked to Dorothy, the horror was still too great to bear. It threatened him, deep in his soul. Even the war had not prepared him for such a death as Gwen's had been.

"And all for the sake of a damned ewe! The stupid brute lived, did I tell you that? It trampled my wife to death in the mud, and Goodshaw found her, all bleeding and torn!"

In his rage, he flung away. Dorothy watched him. She gave him time.

"Is he still employed here, the man who didn't finish the fence?"

"Yes," Stephen said, "he's still here."

"I hope I don't meet him, then, that's all."

"He's no more to blame than I am myself."

"You're talking nonsense, my dear boy."

"It's Gwen herself I blame!" he said. Again his anger overflowed. "She had no *right* to go down there, being so

45

careless with her life! Why didn't she fetch one of us? We were just up there, in the harvest field. We were less than half a mile away!" After a while, controlled, he said, "I wish we'd never come to this farm. If we'd stayed in Springs she'd still be alive."

Hands clenched in his breeches pockets, he stood in front of the open window. Out in the yard, under the elms, the children sat in the stationary trap. Chris had the ribbons in his hands, and Joanna was nursing the puppy, Sam. Jamesy, frowning, patient, intent, was removing a cleg from Emma's hair. Huddled together in the trap they looked forlorn the four of them, their faces wistful but lacking hope.

"My poor children!" Stephen said, but Dorothy Skeine, looking at him, knew that he would take longer to recover from the loss than they.

* * * * *

At first there was some uncertainty as to what the children should call her. They resolved it themselves and called her aunt Doe. Whether or not there was an element of derision in the name, as Stephen suspected, she accepted it without demur.

"I see you're looking at my hair, Joanna. Does it strike you as strange?"

"It's so short," Joanna said.

"Six months ago I had no hair at all. It's only recently begun to grow. Shall I tell you what made it fall out?"

The children said nothing. They merely stared. But she needed little response from them.

"Kala-azar! That's what it was. It's a nasty disease you get out there. India's a terrible place for diseases, you know. It's a terrible place for many things."

"Then why go there?" Joanna asked.

"Why indeed!" aunt Doe exclaimed.

Dorothy Skeine had a great sense of duty. Because of it she had gone to India in 1907 with her bachelor brother, a clergyman, and had helped him to run a mission school in a village outside Ranjiloor. Now duty had brought her home

46

again, but this time there was no hardship involved, and she made that clear right from the start. To be back in England was reward enough. She felt as though she had been reborn. Everything enchanted her. So that when Stephen talked to his children of the debt they owed to their aunt Doe, and the need for showing some gratitude, they were quite unmoved.

"Nobody asked her to come here. She came because she wanted to. She says so twenty times a day."

"It's very good of her all the same."

When aunt Doe's tin trunk arrived at the farm, there were presents for them from Ranjiloor: a soapstone model of the Taj Mahal; a pair of slippers with upcurled toes; a sandalwood box with a secret compartment; and a wood-wind pipe such as snake-charmers used when charming snakes in the market-place.

"No snakes, I'm afraid!" she said to them. "They would never have survived the journey to England."

The children thanked her with formal politeness, and carried their gifts away with them, up to their playroom in the attic. They examined them, but without any joy. Somehow the gifts were rather bizarre. They came from India, a place unknown, and there was a certain shoddiness about them. The soapstone model was chipped and cracked; the gilding on the slippers was flaking off; and the secret compartment of the sandalwood box kept springing open by itself. As for the snake-charmer's wooden pipe, it proved extremely difficult to blow.

"Here, you have a go," Jamesy said, pushing the pipe towards Joanna. "You're the one that's supposed to be musical."

After trying for ten minutes, all Joanna ever achieved was a few squeaks of piercing shrillness and an ache in the glands below her chin.

"Let me try," Emma said, and her efforts were so unexpectedly successful that the other children fled from her, leaving her alone in the attic, where she remained until supper-time.

"Where's Emma?" their father asked.

"She's up in the attic, charming snakes! Can't you hear

47

her?" Joanna said.

The children were bored by aunt Doe's stories of India. They listened with perfectly blank faces and changed the conversation as soon as they could.

"Who on earth cares," Joanna said to Chris one day, "how many annas make a rupee?"

"The mysterious east can remain mysterious as far as I'm concerned," said Chris.

But when she tried to talk to them about the farm, the fields and the woods and the district around, they were equally unresponsive.

"I'm hoping you'll take me for some walks. I thought we might go blackberrying."

"They're not worth picking, after the drought. And anyway, it's still too hot."

* * * * *

Aunt Doe took over the running of the household, and Agnes was glad to hand it over to her. She and Agnes got on well. They worked together as a team. And in dealing with Mrs Bessemer, still suffering from the heat, aunt Doe was brusque but sympathetic.

"It's hotter than this in Ranjiloor. But it's just as well for you to take care. Heatstroke can be a terrible thing."

The children resented the changes she made. When she wanted to wash their hair, Joanna led an open revolt.

"Agnes always washes our hair."

"Not any more, now that I'm here. Agnes has got enough to do."

"We're old enough to do it ourselves."

"I don't think Emma is old enough."

"*I'll* see to Emma's," Joanna said.

"Very well. It's just as you please. So long as you're clean, that's all I ask."

"We always *were* clean, before you came," Joanna muttered, under her breath. "*We* never suffered from kala-azar!"

Stephen, a witness of this behaviour, was worried by their hostility. He liked his cousin well enough. She had been a good friend to him during his youth. But she had altered in the past fifteen years, and sometimes, seeing her through his children's eyes, he had to admit that she made a ridiculous spectacle, with her outlandish clothes, much mended and patched, the hem of her skirt often hanging down or else fastened up with a safety pin, and her habit of groping inside her blouse, twisting herself into dreadful contortions as she searched for an errant handkerchief.

Her voice and her manner embarrassed them, especially when outsiders were present. They were barely civil to her face, and behind her back they mimicked her.

"Not *Skeine* as in *wool*," Chris would say, catching her intonation precisely, and the manner in which she used her hands, "but *Skeine* as *though* to *rhyme* with *bean!*"

Sometimes Stephen was on the point of breaking out angrily at them. Aunt Doe saw it and restrained him.

"If it doesn't work, my being here, I shall have to go," she said.

"They have no right to behave like this, when you've come all this way for their sake."

"They want their mother back again, and no one else will do," she said. "We must make allowances."

To the three older children she was a fool. They avoided her whenever they could. If they had any problems to be resolved, they went to Agnes, not to aunt Doe.

One afternoon, however, when Agnes was needed, it so happened that she was not there. She had gone in the trap on an errand to town and had taken Emma along for the ride. The other three were in the barn, hunting out old pieces of wood for the house they were building up in a tree, and during an argument between the two boys, a long shiny nail, sticking out of a plank, passed through one of Jamesy's fingers.

At first the boy felt nothing at all, but somehow the plank was stuck to him, and when he looked down to see why, there was the shiny point of the nail impaling the top joint of his finger and protruding two inches on the other side.

"Now look what you've done," he said to Chris, and his voice had the calmness of disbelief. "My finger's stuck on this duddy old nail."

Chris and Joanna were appalled at the sight. Neither of them knew what to do. Their father was miles away, up in the fields, and Agnes Mayle had gone into town.

"I'll have to fetch aunt Doe," said Chris. He dashed off quickly into the house.

Within a few seconds, aunt Doe was there. Jamesy, frowning, looked up at her, and his face, though calm, was deathly pale. No blood had come from the finger yet. Nor did he feel the slightest pain. The pain would come when the nail was removed.

"Look away," said aunt Doe, and her strong bony fingers closed over his. "Look away and take deep breaths. This won't take long, but you'll have to be brave."

Obediently Jamesy looked away. He fixed his gaze on the barn door and tried to think of other things as aunt Doe, without delay, eased the finger off the nail and wrapped a white handkerchief round his hand.

"There! It's done!" she said to him. "Now come indoors and we'll clean you up, and put a bandage on it, eh?"

Jamesy nodded, unable to speak. He went, under escort, into the house and through to the scullery, with its stone sink. The handkerchief was bloodstained now; his finger bore two bright red blobs; he saw them welling, and looked away. Aunt Doe turned on the tap and held his hand in the stream of cold water. Chris and Joanna stood and watched.

"It's a lucky thing the nail didn't go through the bone," said Chris.

"It's a lucky thing, too, that the nail was clean," said Joanna, "or he might have got lockjaw, mightn't he?"

"Fetch the first-aid box, will you, please?" Aunt Doe quelled them both with a frown.

Jamesy swallowed and said nothing. The injured finger was coming to life. He watched as the first-aid box was brought and a clean piece of lint was taken from it. Aunt Doe dried his hand, smeared the finger with antiseptic ointment, and bound it up with a gauze bandage, taken, new, from its paper wrapping. She snipped down the last ten inches of gauze, tied a knot between the two strips, and fastened them with elaborate care, round the finger, across the hand, and one last knot around the wrist.

50

"There, now, is that comfortable?"

"Yes, thanks," said Jamesy, in a husky voice.

But he was beginning to feel rather sick. The whole of his hand was full of pain. And aunt Doe, observing his pallor, sent the other two back to their games.

"Jamesy needs to rest a while. He can sit and watch me washing the eggs."

"Shall we go and tell dad?"

"Yes, go and tell him, certainly. But there's nothing for him to worry about. Jamesy'll be fine when he's had a rest."

The instant Chris and Joanna were gone, Jamesy, his face like candlegrease, turned and was sick in the scullery sink. He had always hated the sight of blood. Afterwards, when it was all over, aunt Doe gave him milk to drink and a lump of barley-sugar to suck. She took him into the living room and put him to sit in the big wing-chair, with his bandaged hand on a cushion to rest, and a favourite book for him to read.

"How do you feel now?" she asked. She leant over him, anxiously, and touched his forehead with her hand.

"All right, thanks," Jamesy said.

"It was a nasty thing to happen, and you were a very brave boy."

Jamesy's lip was tremulous.

"I don't call it brave, being s-sick!" he said, and, what with his shame and his self-disgust and the violent throbbing in his hand, he suddenly burst into childish tears and flung himself forward into her arms.

"Poor boy!" she said, holding him close, and his face was against her cool silk blouse. "I still think you were very brave."

In a little while, when he was more himself again, and all traces of tears had gone, he forced himself to meet her gaze.

"You won't tell the others I cried, will you?"

"Of course I won't! Whatever next?"

"You won't tell them that I was sick?"

"I won't tell them *anything*. Honour bright!"

And aunt Doe, as all four children were to discover, was a woman who always kept her word.

A little later that afternoon, Stephen came in with Chris and Joanna to see how Jamesy was getting on.

"I hear you've been in the wars, my son."

"Yes, but I'm all right now," Jamesy said. He showed his beautifully bandaged hand. "The puttee wallah bound it up."

"Puttee wallah?" Joanna said.

"That's what they say in India. A puttee's a bandage, did you know?"

Later still, after supper that evening, Chris and Joanna were out in the yard, helping their father to shut up the hens.

"Aunt Doe's all right, you know," Chris remarked, poking a chicken down from a tree.

"Of course she's all right! What did I tell you?" Stephen said.

In his heart he was much relieved.

* * * * *

So aunt Doe was accepted by them. When the house in the tree had been completed, she was their first visitor, and she brought with her an old salt-stained telescope that had once belonged to her uncle John, a seafaring man from Deal, in Kent. As she climbed the ladder up to the house, Chris watched anxiously from behind, one hand holding her by the skirts.

"I'm sorry about the missing rungs."

"It's better to have a few missing rungs, to baffle the enemy coming at night."

Exploring the inside of the house, she poked into corners here and there, and gave them unexpected advice.

"You want a few handy rocks, you know, for repelling invaders when they come. And you want some hard tack to store in that chest in case you need to withstand a siege. I'll let you have some biscuits and nuts."

On leaving she made them a present of the telescope.

Aunt Doe, they discovered, was always ready to take part in whatever scheme they had in hand: to bowl a few overs in a game of cricket; stand by with a watch to time their races; or hunt out a couple of old twill sheets for them to erect a tent on the lawn. Once she took part in a game of rounders and hit the ball right over the barn, into the yard on the other side, where it hit Reg Starling on the skull. And once when a sow got into the garden, she flung herself astride its back, caught hold of it by its flapping ears, and rode it through the open gateway, back to the stockyard where it belonged.

Whatever she did she did with verve and then, suddenly, recalled to a sense of domestic duty, she would give a cry and throw up her hands and hurry off, with her long mannish stride, back into the house again.

"I've got six beds to make before lunch," she would say, or: "The egg-man is coming at twelve o'clock."

She got through a great deal of work in a day, and she was a stickler for perfect detail. Her linen-cupboard was a model of tidiness and organization; beds were made most beautifully, with "hospital corners" and unwrinkled sheets; and all four corners of every pillow had to be insinuated meticulously into all four corners of the pillow-case, clean and white and stiff with starch.

"Aunt Doe's beds," Joanna said, "are a lot better dressed than aunt Doe herself."

She was also an excellent cook. They enjoyed the curries she made for them. Only Mrs Bessemer disapproved.

"I could never eat that. Oh dear me no. What'd my Bert have to say to me if I went home to him smelling of that?"

"What does he smell of," Agnes asked, "after his evenings at the pub?"

"She needn't eat it," aunt Doe said. "Chris and Jamesy will soon scoff that."

She enjoyed cooking meals for these young cousins of hers, with their hearty appetites, but one thing she could not abide and that was waste. If any food was left on a plate, she would point at it with a bony finger, and would fix the offender with a stern blue gaze. "The people in Calcutta would be glad of that!" she would say, and the phrase became a family joke, so that someone had only to leave a tiny morsel, such as a single green pea, to provoke the inevitable chorus.

One morning at breakfast, their father was the guilty one; he left some bacon-rind on his plate; but when the expected chorus came: "The people in Calcutta would be glad of that!", he looked around with a bland smile. "Oh no they wouldn't! – It's pig meat!" he said, and aunt Doe, clicking her tongue, snatched the plate away from him.

"I don't know who's the worst," she said, "you or these four scallywags here."

The household, under her influence, was gradually coming back to life. There was laughter in the house again; a sense of purpose, a meaning in things; a feeling that everything mattered again. It was not that aunt Doe had taken their mother's place with them: nobody could ever do that; but she was there, and they leant on her. She gave herself willingly to their needs, and allowed them to draw on her woman's strength.

Stephen, finding that this household of his went on the same though his wife was dead, was sometimes filled with hurt for her. Hearing laughter about the place, or aunt Doe's voice as she called to the hens; seeing the baskets of new-laid eggs, and remembering Gwen's pride in them; watching Joanna in the dairy, skimming the cream off the pans of milk in exactly the way Gwen had taught her: he would sometimes stand, arrested by pain, overcome by the sense of his loss.

But he was moved to wonder, too, and gave thanks for such as aunt Doe, another like Agnes, a giver of life.

By the time term began, aunt Doe had been at the farm almost a month. She was accepted. She was part of their lives.

* * * * *

Aunt Doe had been born in Sussex, but she was happy in Worcestershire, and one of the happiest things she did was to buy a second-hand bicycle. All through the tropical autumn that year, she rode about on it everywhere, eager for every sight and sound, and speaking to everyone she met. She was soon well-known all around Huntlip, riding her old ramshackle machine, and sometimes, in the fields at Holland Farm, the men while working would see her go by, rattling down the steep snakey lane, and would joke about it among themselves.

"There goes Miss Skeine on that warhorse of hers. Better keep off the roads today, if you value your lives, all of you."

It was certainly true that aunt Doe on her bicycle constituted a danger to the public at large, for her lamp battery was always flat, and her brake-blocks were worn to "no more than a cheese-rind" as Bob Tupper once said. One evening at dusk, careering at speed down Holland Bank, she passed so close to the elderly retired schoolmaster, Mr Quelsh, as he stepped from his gateway into the lane, that she knocked his Panama off his head.

"Dammit, woman, where are your lights?" the old man shouted after her.

"Next to my liver!" aunt Doe called back, and rode on merrily down the lane, tinkling her bell now and then lest anyone else should be fool enough to get in her way. As always, on a Sunday evening, she was late for evensong.

Aunt Doe's bicycle, with its sit-up-and-beg handlebars and its broken mudguards tied up with string, was a great embarrassment to Chris and Jamesy and Joanna. They knew how people laughed at her whenever she rattled through the village, and they heard the remarks of the men on the farm, and, since aunt Doe herself had no sense of the fitness of things, they decided to take the matter into their own hands.

One Saturday afternoon, when she was busy making jam, they wheeled the bicycle into the barn, lugged it up the ladder into the hayloft, and hurled it out of the hayloft door, down into the stackyard below. There, with relatively little noise, the wheels parted company from the frame, bounced a few times on the straw-littered ground, and at last lay still, buckled and broken beyond repair.

"Well!" said Chris, brushing his hands. "She'll never ride *that* old thing again!"

They were not present when Aunt Doe discovered the mangled remains. They were up in the fields with Tupper and Rye. But when they went to the stackyard again, the bits and pieces had all gone, and they found them later on the farm's golgotha, the rubbish heap behind the cartshed, among the old bits of harrows and ploughs.

"She may not know it, but we've done the old girl a good turn," Chris said as they walked away. "Sooner or later she'd have killed herself, riding that thing down Holland Bank."

"What do you think she'll say to us?"

"Oh, there'll be the deuce of a row, I daresay."

But in fact aunt Doe said nothing at all, and her sad silence in the days that followed somehow spoilt the splendid joke, bringing a feeling of anticlimax. The three children followed her example; they resolved to stay dumb as long as she; but after three days of this, poor Jamesy lost his nerve.

"Where's your old bike, then, aunt Doe?" he asked.

"I'm afraid something happened to it," aunt Doe said, looking at him sorrowfully.

"What sort of something?" Jamesy asked.

"As to that, I'm not quite sure, but I think it must have fallen from a very great height."

Jamesy gave a nervous snort. Chris and Joanna looked away. And little Emma, helping aunt Doe to make sausages, looked up at her sister and brothers accusingly.

"Aunt Doe's bike is all smashed in bits. There's nothing to laugh about in that."

"Who said there was?" Joanna asked.

Aunt Doe went everywhere on foot now. The children's father noticed it.

"Why no bicycle?" he asked.

"It needs a few repairs," she said.

The children met in the tree-house to discuss what they felt they ought to do.

"You know what I think?" Chris said. "I think we should buy her a new bike."

They were agreed. They fetched their money-boxes and tipped the contents onto the floor. Between them they had eleven-and-six. But before their discussion could go any further, a noise drew them to the window, and there was aunt Doe, riding triumphantly into the yard on another ramshackle bicycle, just as shabby as the first; bought, she announced when they gathered round, from a man with a junk-cart at Otchetts End.

"He wanted ten shillings but I got it for five. I haven't

shopped in the market-place at Ranjiloor all these years without learning a thing or two!"

Watched by the children, whose feelings were mixed, she rode round and round repeatedly, ringing her old rusty bell with such brio that Stephen came hurrying from the piggery.

"What do you think of my new bicycle?" she asked.

"New?" he said, incredulously.

"I think," she said, with a glance towards Chris and Joanna and Jamesy, "I shall have to keep this one chained up."

"Why?" said Stephen. "Does it bite?"

* * * * *

The long drought ended at last, and rain fell on the tired earth. Suddenly the weather was cold. The nights especially were sharp. But because of the heat stored in the soil, as soon as the rain soaked the ground, there was a quick growth of grass, so that brown parched meadows and brown leys were all a fresh bright green again before winter came to check their growth. The first sowings of wheat were up, green enough to cover the ground, and oats, sown as the first snow fell, were up in flag when the snow had gone.

By the end of November, water ran in the ditches again, and Copsey Pond was brim-full. Stephen went to the pond one day and stood at the edge, under the trees, watching a moorhen swimming across to vanish, darkly, among the reeds.

He had had the wire fence removed, so that cattle and sheep could drink there again, and had had the fletchers all cleaned out. But he himself had kept away. Now he had come, in secret, alone, to look at the place and test himself. But the pond, having filled with water again, was not a place of fear for him. He looked at it and was perfectly calm. It was the drought that had killed Gwen, and the word *drought*, with all it meant, would always strike terror into his heart and fill him with the sickness of hate. The pond itself was innocent. It was a place where moorhens lived; where the farm animals came to drink; where alders grew, and willows and oaks; and where, in the springtime every year, the martins collected mud for their nests.

Stephen turned and walked away. He was meeting his shepherd in Long Gains, to overlook the flock of ewes. The rams would be put in to run with them soon, so that the lambs would be born in May, and the flock be renewed. Rain fell on him as he walked. He drew his collar up to his ears.

Chapter 4

Early in the new year, the threshing tackle arrived. For days its smoke and smell filled the stackyard, and its noise could be heard all over the farm. John Challoner strolled over one afternoon. He was next on the list for the threshing team. He had come to see how long they would be.

"I can lend you a man or two if you like. Get done that much sooner, what do you say?"

"We can manage, thanks," Stephen said, pausing in his work of pitching the sheaves.

Challoner went to the grain-shute and took a handful of grain from the sack. He allowed it to run between his fingers.

"I hear you've got two horses sick. I can lend you a tractor if you like, to get this lot into town when you're done."

"We can manage, thanks," Stephen said.

"Suit yourself! Suit yourself!" Huffily, Challoner walked away, pausing only long enough to speak to the man in charge of the tackle. "You know your way up to my place by now? I'll expect you on Tuesday evening, then."

Stephen, on the stack, resumed his work, pitching sheaves down onto the drum. Tupper, beside him, gave a snort.

"He's in one of his lending moods. I wonder what he wants in exchange."

One morning at the end of the month, the hunt met at The Black Ram, up on the edge of Huntlip Common, and the chase led across Holland Farm. Billy Rye's son, a boy of thirteen, earned himself a shilling by opening the gate into Turner's Piece, and the hunt, trampling the soggy ground, ruined five acres of young tender rape.

The next day was market day. Challoner and Stephen met at the pens.

"I heard you were looking for two new tups. I think I can do you a favour there. A friend of mine from Porsham way —"

"There's just one favour you can do for me. You can damn well stop hunting across my land."

"Eh? What's that? Did we damage your rape? Hang it, man, you must send in a claim! We always pay for damage done."

"I don't want paying," Stephen said. "I only want you to keep off my land."

"You ought to join us," Challoner said, clapping Stephen on the shoulder. "Then you could get your own back a bit, hunting across the other chaps' land!" But, seeing that Stephen was not amused, he said: "I'll have a word with the M.F.H.. He's a reasonable chap. We *all* are. I'll tell him you lost that field of rape."

A few days later, half a dozen bottles of port were delivered at Holland Farm, with a message written on a card: "Apologies. The Crayle Hunt." Stephen was somewhat irked by the gift, but to send it back would be churlish indeed. He walked over to thank Challoner straight away.

"Think nothing of it," Challoner said. "I told you we always paid our debts."

"There is just one thing," Stephen said. "I still don't want hunting across my land. I've given orders to my men that no gates are to be opened for you."

Challoner went very red in the face.

"That's hardly sporting of you, man!"

"Then the port *was* intended to buy me off?"

"Dammit! Of course not! I never said that! We merely thought, the Master and I, that a show of goodwill on either side —"

"I made my feelings clear to you when I first came to Holland Farm."

"But it cramps our style no end, you know, to have your land out of bounds to us."

"The answer's still no," Stephen said.

"Well, Wayman, I'm disappointed, I must admit. I never thought you'd hold out like this. That port came from the Master's own cellar —"

"Maybe I'd better send it back?"

"No, no! Good God, that's absurd!" Challoner made a mighty effort and managed to laugh away his chagrin. "I'll come over and help you drink it if you like!"

"Yes, do," Stephen said.

Although he and Challoner got on quite well, Stephen could never really like the man, and later that year, in the middle of June, something happened that renewed his mistrust.

The sheep-shearing, shared as always between the two farms, took place at Outlands that year. Challoner's ewes were shorn first, and the fleeces were stacked at the end of the barn. Then Stephen's ewes were shorn, and the fleeces were loaded into his cart, drawn up in readiness out in the yard. When the first of his fleeces came, and Stephen went forward to pick them up, Eddie Templer, one of Challoner's men, spoke to him in an undertone.

"I'd count them fleeces if I was you."

Stephen stared. He was taken aback. The year before, and the year before that, his fleeces had gone uncounted to market and been sold there according to weight.

"Why should I need to count them?" he asked.

"It's the best way of making sure they're all there."

So Stephen, when he loaded the fleeces into the cart, kept a careful count, and at the end of the afternoon, instead of the ninety there should have been, there were only seventy-five.

"Seems I'm a few short," he said, as Challoner came up to him.

"Short? By how many?" Challoner asked.

"Short by fifteen," Stephen said.

"How the hell did that happen? Someone's been careless! I'll have his guts!" Challoner strode into the barn and called to his shepherd, Arthur Thorne, to bring fifteen fleeces from the heap. "Mr Wayman's fifteen short. Whose fault is that, I'd like to know? It's all this chatting and larking about! That's how these mistakes are made. If I'm not around to watch you men —"

The fifteen fleeces were brought out and thrown up into the cart. Challoner stood and counted them, in a loud

61

voice, for all to hear. Eddie Templer was one of those who helped to bring the fleeces out. He took good care to avoid Stephen's eye.

"There! All correct?" Challoner asked.

"All correct," Stephen said. "I think I'll drive them down straight away."

"Before they can vanish again, eh?" Challoner gave a great hearty laugh. "I hope you don't think I'm to blame?"

"No, of course not," Stephen said.

Driving the load of fleeces home, he pondered over the incident. Although he had always mistrusted Challoner, he now found it difficult to believe that the man would stoop to such an act, merely for the sake of a few pounds' worth of wool. It could just as easily have been a trick, played out of spite by Eddie Templer, to cause his employer embarrassment. Challoner, as Stephen knew, was much disliked by the men he employed. Whatever the truth, it would probably never be known, for Challoner's manner gave little away and his greeting when Stephen met him again was as bluff and hearty as ever before.

But aunt Doe, it seemed, shared Stephen's mistrust.

"What was all that I heard about fifteen fleeces?"

"A misunderstanding," Stephen said. "They got in with Challoner's by mistake."

"By mistake? I wonder!" she said.

* * * * *

All through the spring and summer that year, when Stephen walked about the fields, it seemed to him there was always a wind. It whispered in the green corn and ran like the ghost of a grey-green hare through the long grass in the leys and meadows. Under the sunlight, under the wind, the green blades of grass and the green blades of corn bowed themselves down in humility, while the green stalks stood upright in their pride, flowering and coming to seed.

Every year, this miracle. A green excitement possessing the land; touching everything; sparing nothing. Stephen stood in the Home Field, and the green corn came surging up to his feet. He saw how the sheath at the top of each stalk was beginning to open, split by the ear, and he felt the excitement in spite of himself. He walked in the fields of mowing-grass, and the grassflowers touched him, blown by the wind. They left their coloured dust on him. He saw it, golden, on his hands.

By the middle of June the corn stood so high in the Home Field that Emma, creeping between the rows, could stand upright and not be seen. The cool green blades touched her bare arms, and the tall green stalks, with their green ears of grain, towered up above her head. She liked the cool greenness of the corn, and the whispering of the wind among the blades.

Once when she walked in the corn like this, she suddenly came on a hare in its form: a soft-furred doe, nursing her young, her ears drawn back and her eyes protruding as she crouched in her hollow in the ground. Emma stared at the crouching doe, and the doe stared through her with unblinking eyes; without so much as a twitch of a whisker. Child and hare were stillness itself, confronting each other in the green swaying corn. Then Emma turned and tiptoed away. Leaving the corn, she danced and ran. The hare was a secret that had to be shared.

But when she led Chris and Joanna and Jamesy there, creeping, small, between the rows, the hare and her young were not to be found.

"Are you sure this is the place?"

"I *think* it is," Emma said.

"You must have scared her away, then."

"No, I didn't. She stayed quite still."

"Well, she's not here now, is she?" said Chris.

"*If* she was ever here at all," Joanna said, walking away.

"She *was* there, I saw her," Emma said. "She had two babies suckling her."

"Well, I haven't got time to search the whole field. I've got better things to do. You can go on searching if you like."

The three older children went away. Emma was left alone in the corn. But although she searched up and down the rows, that day and on other days, she never saw the hare again, and the others often teased her about it.

"Seen your hare today, Emma?"

"Next time you see her, put salt on her tail."

"Or make a noise like a lettuce leaf. She'll follow you home if you do that."

Sometimes when Emma walked in the corn, she would hear aunt Doe calling to her from the garden, or her father calling across the fields. She would hear them saying to each other: "Where's Emma? Is she with you? Then she must have gone off with Chris and Joanna."

Hearing their voices speaking so close, Emma would laugh without sound to herself, knowing that she was hidden from them, although she walked upright in the corn. Gathering poppies and corncockles, or looking for larks' nests full of brown eggs, she would wander the corn-rows by the hour, while aunt Doe went searching everywhere, calling her name again and again.

* * * * *

"Where have you been?" Stephen asked, as Emma appeared in the cowshed doorway.

"I've been in the corn," Emma said.

"I hope you didn't trample it down."

"Of course I didn't. I walked in the rows."

"The others not back yet?" Stephen said. But he knew they were not. It was a Saturday afternoon; the two boys were playing in a school cricket match; Joanna was camping with the Girl Guides at Springs. "What about helping me wean this calf?"

The calf in question was six days old. Stephen had a pail of its mother's milk and was trying to persuade the calf to drink. He held his hand under the milk, his upturned fingers breaking the surface, but the calf ignored this enticement and nibbled the edge of the pail instead. Emma came close and watched, dark-eyed.

"Supposing you try," Stephen said. "Put your hand in under the milk and let him lick it off your fingers."

"No, I don't want to," Emma said. She put her hands behind her back.

"You're not afraid of a little calf?"

"Yes, I am. They always nip."

"That's not the reason," Stephen said.

"What is the reason?" Emma asked.

"You don't want to get your hands in a mess, that's your reason," Stephen said.

"How do you know it is?" she asked.

"I know my Emma!" Stephen said.

The calf was beginning to suck at last, curling its tongue round Stephen's finger. Gradually, he withdrew his hand, and the calf supped the milk till the pail was empty. Raising its head, it shook itself. Emma stepped back to avoid being splashed. She watched the calf as it licked its lips.

Nearby, in the straw, the farm cat, Maisie, also watched, waiting to lick up any milk that might be spilled over the cobbles. Emma went and picked the cat up, but it struggled free and leapt away, leaving a scratch on the palm of her hand. She licked away a drop of blood.

"Did she hurt you?" Stephen asked.

"Yes," Emma said. She showed him her hand. "But I forgive her. She's only a cat."

Stephen let the calf out into the paddock, to join the other, older calves. It lowed a little, wanting its mother, and the cow answered from the pasture behind the barn. Stephen turned back and looked at Emma, who was tying a handkerchief round her hand.

"I've got to go up to Blagg," he said. "Would you like to come with me and see Mr Maule?"

"No, thank you," Emma said.

"What are you going to do with yourself, then?"

"I'm making a sweetshop," Emma said.

"Well, aunt Doe's around if you want her," he said. "She's in the garden, hoeing the beans."

Sometimes it worried him that Emma, being so much younger than the other children, was often left to play by herself. Yet she never complained of loneliness. She would watch the others getting ready to go out: the boys assembling their cricket gear, Joanna dressing up in her Guides uniform and packing her rucksack to go to camp; and, waving to them as they set out, she looked a sad little figure indeed. "Can't I go to the cricket match? Can't I go camping?" she would ask.

65

But she never moped, once they were gone. She would play by herself for hours on end, heaping up empty flower-pots in the old garden shed, or painting the slatted garden-seat with a pot of white paint and a tiny brush, or scraping the moss from the farmyard walls. And when, at the end of these self-chosen tasks, she found that her smock had somehow become stained and grubby, she would run indoors to find aunt Doe.

"Can I have a clean pinny? This one's not nice!" she would say.

Today, when Stephen left her, she was already dragging a box across the yard to set up her "sweetshop" in the shade. She scarcely bothered to wave him goodbye. So long as he was about the farm, she would come to him many times in the day, to show him some prize or watch him at work, and it was the same with her sister and brothers. But once they were gone and she was alone, she became self-absorbed, in a world of her own, occupied until they returned.

The sweetshop was set up close to the door where the boys, coming home from their cricket match, were bound to see it. In little glass dishes, set out on the counter, were coloured pebbles, coloured beads, and small chips of stone wrapped in coloured papers. In front of each dish stood a carefully printed price-ticket.

"What's this? said Chris, easing his cricket-bag from one hand to the other; and Jamesy, his cap on the back of his head, his blazer slung over one shoulder, said: "Our little Emma is after our money."

"I'm selling sweets," Emma said. "The shop is still open, if you want anything."

"Have you got a licence for running a shop?" Chris enquired, with a solemn frown. "You'll get into trouble with the police if you haven't got a licence, you know."

"It's only pretending," Emma said.

Chris, with a nudge, drew his brother's attention to one of Emma's price-tickets: "Penny each or two for twopence." The two boys rocked on their heels at this. Emma surveyed them uneasily.

"Have I got the spelling wrong?"

"No, not the spelling," Jamesy said.

"Why are you laughing, then?" she asked.

"Because you're a cough-drop," Jamesy said. "Got any cough-drops by the way?"

"I'm afraid not," Emma said. "I'm expecting them in any day."

"What about bull's eyes?" Jamesy asked, and took a round pebble from a dish. He put it into his mouth, sucked it noisily for a while and then, apparently, swallowed it. "Went down like a stone!" he said to Chris.

Emma looked at him in dismay.

"It *was* a stone! You know it was!"

"I thought you said it was a sweet?"

"Only pretending," Emma said.

"Oh, cripes, I shall die!" Jamesy said. He clutched at his throat and gave a cough, turning despairingly to Chris. "Do something, quick, or it's all up with me! I've swallowed a stone! I shall die! I shall die!" His eyes were bulging hideously. He gave a horrible choking gasp. "Too late! I'm sinking!" he said with a moan.

Suddenly Emma burst into tears. The boys were all contrition at once. Jamesy stopped acting and spat the pebble into his hand. He held it out for her to see.

"I didn't really swallow it!" he said. "Laws, what a goose you are, to be sure! There, there, I'm not going to die. No need for weeping or gnashing of teeth."

"Tell you what, Emma!" Chris exclaimed. "We won our match like billy-oh! Two hundred and eight to their ninety-six. What do you think of that, eh?"

"Chris made forty," Jamesy said.

"Jamesy made twenty-three. Aren't you proud of your brothers, eh?"

Emma nodded. Her tears were gone. She straightened the bowl on her "weighing-machine" and flicked a beetle from her counter.

"I knew he hadn't really swallowed it."

"Of course you did. So did I."

"Jolly good sweetshop you've got here. I must come and buy your bulls' eyes again."

"Penny each or two for twopence!"

Spluttering with laughter, the boys went in. The joke

67

would last them a good many days. Emma, left alone, dismantled her shop. She returned the glass dishes to the kitchen cupboard, and threw the price-tickets into the stove.

"Where's your shop?" demanded aunt Doe. "I was coming to buy some sweets."

"It's closed for today," Emma said.

* * * * *

One day the children came home from school and found the hay in the Long Meadow cut, lying in its curving swaths, wave upon wave of dark seagreen rippling over the light bright green of the aftermath. They knew at once that the hay had been cut, for the smell of it came to them on the warm wind as they toiled homeward up the track. They ran to the meadow, drawn by the scent, and were just in time to see the machine, driven by Trennam in his haymaking hat, cut through the last long strip of grass and lay it sideways on the ground, completing the last long rainbow curve.

"You started without us!" Chris exclaimed. "What a dirty rotten trick!"

Chris was fourteen in July that year. He was tall, square-shouldered, sturdily built: "every inch the young farmer," as aunt Doe said; and Chris had no fault to find with that. The farm was his passion, first and last. School had become irksome to him. If only his father would let him leave!

"At fourteen years old?" Stephen said. He would not hear of such a thing. "There are all sorts of careers open to you. You could take your pick, the headmaster says."

"Farming's the only career I want."

"You're too young to decide that yet. You may change your mind in a year or two."

"I shan't," Chris said. "I know I shan't."

"Yes, well, we'll wait and see."

Haymaking days were the longest days. The sun seemed reluctant to leave the sky. Field after field of mowing-grass fell to the blades of the mowing-machine; grass became hay in the wind and the sun; and was carted home, swaying and creaking, to be built into stacks or stored in the barn.

All through the busy haymaking days, in the fields around the green corn grew tall, rustling dryly in the wind, the wheat striving upwards, spearlike, erect; the barley bowing its feathered heads; the oatsprays dangling, never still. The greenness faded, under the sun, and a luminous pallor took its place. The pallor went and colour came, deepening to a dusty gold.

But where was the wisdom, Stephen thought, in growing so many acres of corn? At market now, as he well knew, prices were falling all the time. His harvest that year was going to be good, but afterwards, when he threshed his grain, what price would it fetch in the market-place, competing against imported corn? He knew that cuts would have to be made. The men's wages, reduced once, would have to be reduced again, and one of the women, Agnes or Mrs Bessemer, would have to go. It would not be easy, even then, to pay his mortgage, tithes, and costs.

It was aunt Doe's idea that one of the two women should go, and Stephen gratefully agreed.

"Which one will you keep? Agnes, I suppose?"

"No, Mrs Bessemer," aunt Doe said. "It seems her Bert is losing his job when harvest is over at Outlands this year. Agnes's menfolk are all in work."

So Agnes Mayle left and Mrs Bessemer remained. There was more work than ever for aunt Doe, and Stephen, talking things over with his children, won a solemn pledge from them that they would help her whenever they could: in the house; the dairy; the poultry yard. He talked to them on equal terms and explained the need for economy.

"You could say I made a hash of things, taking up farming when I did. It's not going to be easy in the next few years, and I thought I ought to let you know. There won't be much money for luxuries. On the other hand, if I were to give up the farm and go back to practising the law –"

"But you can't do that! You simply can't!"

They were appalled. They cried out against it with all their heart. They would sooner go hungry all their days than think of leaving Holland Farm.

"It won't come to that, I hope," he said, turning the

matter off with a smile. "There's always plenty to eat on a farm."

"If I could leave school –" Chris said.

"Next year, perhaps, but not before."

"Think of the money you'd save on my fees."

"Why, would you work for nothing, then?"

"Anything to keep the farm!"

So Stephen knew that, whatever his folly in buying Holland Farm, his children at least would never reproach him. They would sooner remain on the farm, poor, than live in riches anywhere else.

"You have your answer," aunt Doe said.

"So it seems," Stephen said.

It was puzzling for them, even so, with the wealth of the growing corn around them, to understand the difficulties. At harvest time, when they helped in the fields, Joanna took up a sheaf of wheat and examined the fat, round, plumped-up grain. She took it to Tupper, building the stooks.

"Is it good, the corn we grow?"

"Best in the world," Tupper said.

"Then why doesn't it fetch a good price?"

"There's corn coming in from abroad, that's why, selling cheaper than what we grow. Canada, America, places like that."

"Why is it cheaper?" Joanna asked.

"On account of the way it's grown out there. Thousands and thousands of acres of it, and great big machines to harvest it. Don't ask me how or why, Miss Jo. I dunno. It's a mystery to me."

"There's something wrong somewhere," Joanna said.

"I reckon there is," Tupper said.

"What is it, exactly, do you think?"

"If I knew that —" Tupper said.

"Yes?" said Joanna. "What would you do?"

"I'd write a letter to *The Times!*"

"I'll tell you what's wrong!" Chris said, having listened impatiently while his sister displayed her ignorance. "It's this blasted government! That's what's wrong!"

"Ah," said Tupper, shaking his head. "You may be right,

Master Chris. Though speaking as one man to another —"

"Yes?" said Chris suspiciously.

"— there ent much to choose between none of them!"

* * * * *

"Mrs Bessemer pulling her weight, is she?" Stephen asked.

"Oh, we get done, eventually!" And aunt Doe added, with her keen blue glance: "You can see to read a book in the brasswork when Mrs Bessemer's finished with it!"

Aunt Doe herself was tireless. She kept on the move from morn to night. But she always made light of the housework and the gardenwork, and never wasted a moment of time. If she had to go from one part of the big roomy house to another, she would take a feather duster with her, to flick at the cobwebs on the way; and whenever she had to cross the garden, she would pull up a handful of weeds on the way or nip the dead heads from the daffodils.

No job dismayed her, however unpleasant. When Mrs Bessemer refused to clean out the kitchen drain, aunt Doe did it herself, plunging her arm in up to the elbow until it was coated with black greasy sludge.

"Oh! The smell!" Mrs Bessemer said, but aunt Doe retorted, with a curl of her lip: "I've smelt worse than that in Ranjiloor!"

One day, alone in the house, she fired Stephen's shotgun up the chimney, to bring down the soot. She then went, with a blackened face, to answer a knock at the back door. A red-faced farmer stood there. Behind him, in the yard, stood a sweating black mare.

"I hear you've got an entire," he said.

"An entire what?" aunt Doe enquired.

"An entire horse!" the farmer said. His face grew more red than it had been before.

"Oh, you mean the stallion?" aunt Doe said. "Certainly. Follow me."

She led the way to the stable yard and the farmer followed, bringing his mare. Aunt Doe was quite without fear or prudishness. She led the stallion out of his stall. The farmer, however, kept hanging back, although pulled about by his eager mare.

"Ent there a man about the place?"

"Oh, yes, there are plenty of those!"

She perceived the farmer's embarrassment, and tethered Lucifer to the fence. She went off in search of Bob Tupper. But over her shoulder she gave vent to her scorn.

"I've seen worse than that in Ranjiloor!"

* * * * *

One day towards the end of September, Stephen called the men together and warned them that their wages would have to be cut, from forty shillings to thirty-five.

"We knew that was coming!" said Morton George. "It's one damned reduction after another, ent it, now that the Wages Board is gone?"

"You see the papers," Stephen said. "I've got no choice as you well know."

"Seems to me we've done pretty well," Tupper said, in his quiet voice. "Wages been down a month or more on some of the other farms around. What can't be altered has got to be borne."

Stephen nodded and walked away. Morton George rounded on Tupper.

"Sucking up as usual? The old battalion? Toeing the line?"

"Shut your mouth," Tupper said. "If you was at Outlands instead of here, you'd have a lot more to skike about. There's men been turned off up there, you know, and it's much the same on other farms."

"The farmers need to be shown what's what. At the union meeting the other night –"

"What can the union do to them?"

"Sweet bloody nothing! I know that. There's not enough membership, that's why! Take all you lot here for a start –"

"Here we go!" Hopson said. "The music goes round and round, ooh-ooh-ooh-oh, and it comes out here! For God's sake let's get back to work!"

"Ah! Sweating our guts out!" George exclaimed. "And all for thirty-five bob a week!"

"Sweating?" said Tupper. "What, you? That's against the union rules, ent it?"

As harvest that year came to an end, and the first teams were out, ploughing the stubbles, Stephen discussed with Bob Tupper what sowings they would make that year. Less corn than hitherto, more grass and clover leys, more grey peas, more beans, more rape; and twenty acres of sugar beet, a crop much promoted by the government. Stephen also talked to his shepherd, walking with him in Long Gains. Sheep were a safer investment at times like this, and Stephen planned to increase his flock.

"It's always the way," Goodshaw said. "When farming is high, it's nothing but corn wherever you look. But when things is low, as they are now, grass comes back into fashion again and the shepherd is Somebody all of a sudden. Still, I ent complaining. Oh, no, not me!"

"Can you manage another hundred ewes?" Stephen asked in a tentative way.

"Is that all you're getting?" Goodshaw asked.

The other men were inclined to resent the growth in the number of sheep on the farm. When the first batch arrived, driven up the track by Goodshaw and his two collie dogs, the men stood watching over the fence. Hopson, in a voice loud enough for Goodshaw to hear, spoke to Reg Starling, at his side.

"Which do you dislike the most, Reg, sheep or shepherds?"

"Which is which?" Starling asked.

One day Challoner came over for his customary chat. He walked with Stephen about the fields, and noted the changes everywhere.

"What about this sugar beet they're telling us to grow now?"

"I mean to try it, in the spring. Twenty acres. That field up there. And you?"

"I'm not so sure. I had enough of that in the war, the government telling me what to do. But if you're going to try it up here –"

"Don't go by me, for God's sake. You've been farming all your life. I've been at it for three years."

"You made a mistake, giving up the law to try farming, eh?"

"No, I don't think so," Stephen said.

"What, all the money solicitors make, and you mean to say you've no regrets?"

"No, no regrets," Stephen said.

They walked in silence for a while, picking their way through a field of swedes.

"You know, Wayman," Challoner said, "it's time you thought of marrying again."

Stephen said nothing. He looked away. Gwen had been dead less than eighteen months.

"You're a young man," Challoner said. "Thirty-six is no age at all. It's no good trying to live in the past. You take my advice and look for a wife. I'd do the same, given the chance, but it's not so easy at my age. The market gets tricky when you're pushing on."

Stephen came to a sudden halt and turned to look Challoner in the eye. The man's coarseness offended him. The big handsome face, with its ready smile, was quite suddenly loathsome to him. He felt he could strike it with his fist.

"Am I speaking out of turn?"

"Yes," Stephen said, "I think you are."

"I know exactly how you feel. When my wife died, six years ago, I said I'd never marry again. I had my two boys John and Gerald, and for their sake I carried on. John's in a farm of his own now. Gerald will take over Outlands one day. They're good boys, both of them, and Gerald is company for me. But a man gets lonely all the same. Once you've been married, it's just no good. The loneliness gets into your bones."

Stephen felt guilty. His rage had gone. Challoner, whatever his faults, was just an ordinary feeling man.

"Supposing we talk of other things?" He resumed his walk down the edge of the field, to the pasture where Goodshaw was marking his ewes. "You can tell me what you think of my new flock."

* * * * *

74

One Saturday morning, during the winter, the children turned out in their oldest clothes to whitewash the inner walls and roofs of the farm buildings. Tupper showed them how to mix the lime into a wash, with a lump of fat floating in it to give it an extra stickiness, and, armed with big brushes, they transformed cowstalls, stables, piggeries, sheds, into dazzling white palaces, sweet-smelling and pure. They took pride in their work and Chris especially was a perfectionist. The lime must be scrubbed very thoroughly into every grain in the wood, into every crevice and pore of the ancient brickwork.

"The whitewash is meant to cleanse," he said. "It's no good leaving little cracks for the dirt and vermin to collect in."

Emma, wearing a clean white smock, stood watching Chris at work in the byre.

"Why can't I do the whitewashing too?"

"Don't be silly. You're too small."

"I want to try it," Emma said.

"Well, you can't, and that's flat!" Chris said. "You'll splash the lime into your eyes and that'll burn you and make you cry."

Emma, driven out of the byre, took refuge in the stables instead. Joanna and Jamesy were working there. Their stiff-bristled brushes went splish-splash, splish-splash, and Emma took care to sit out of reach, perched on the ladder leading up to the loft. Sitting there, she plaited her straws. She was making a workbasket for aunt Doe. And all the time, as her fingers worked, she sang to herself, in a monotone, the hymn she had learnt from Mrs Bessemer.

> "Jesus loves me, this I know,
> For the bible tells me so –"

Splish-splosh, splish-splosh, went the whitewash brushes on the wall, and Emma, above, plaiting her straws, returned for the umpteenth time that day to the chorus of her favourite hymn.

> "Yes! Jesus loves me!
> Yes! Jesus loves me!
> Yes! Jesus loves me!
> The bible tells me so!"

Jamesy, with a scowl, looked up at her, whitewash brush poised in his hand. He was sensitive to sound.

"Jesus doesn't love you!" he said. "Nobody loves you when you make that noise!"

After the whitewashing of the sheds, there were the farm implements to be painted. The boys set to work with loving zeal; a pot of blue paint, a pot of vermilion; and hay-turner, horse-rake, reapers, ploughs, were made to look as good as new. But Chris was not content merely to smarten the implements up: he wanted to know how everything worked; every tool and every machine must yield its secrets up to him, and he must learn to master them all.

And so it was with the tasks of the farm. He would talk to Tupper, Goodshaw, Rye, and pick their brains without shame. But he also read a great deal and kept up with new developments. The farm was his life. He wanted no career but that. He was determined to prove to his father in every way that this was not a boyish craze, but a man's decision, made for good.

Jamesy, on the other hand, though he loved the farm, had set his sights on a different future. He wanted to be an architect. Already, although only twelve, drawing was not just a hobby with him, but a thing that possessed him heart and soul. He saw everything in terms of design. Whatever he was talking about, he was sure to reach for a pencil and paper. "Here, I'll show you," he would say, and the mystery, whatever it was, would be resolved in a diagram.

"Even a cow chewing the cud!" Chris said to Joanna once. "Ask Jamesy how it works, and he'll do you a drawing, exactly to scale!"

Jamesy made drawings of all the great buildings in Chepsworth: the cathedral, the guildhall, the market cross; exteriors and interiors; exact in detail and true to scale. He made drawings of every building on Holland Farm: the house, the barns, the cottages; and when Hopson's cottage was renovated, and a lean-to extension was built on, Jamesy drew up the plans for it, and Mr Hake, the Huntlip builder, used them with only one òr two minor alterations.

"So you want to be an architect, building houses and such, eh?"

"What I'd really like to do is to build a cathedral," Jamesy said.

Mr Hake stared. He gave a laugh.

"Well, if I hear of anyone wanting a cathedral putting up, I shall be sure to mention your name."

"Oh, I shan't build cathedrals until I'm old!"

"How old is old, if I might ask?"

"When I'm forty," Jamesy said.

The two boys, then, had already settled where their futures lay. But what of Joanna, now thirteen? Joanna varied with the wind. Doctor; dancer; courtesan; the model in a painting by Augustus John: Joanna yearned to spread her wings.

Early in 1923 a gipsy woman called at the farm and sold aunt Doe a dozen pegs.

"There are children in this house, I know, and one of them has a gift for music."

"Is that a fact?" said aunt Doe.

"A great gift for music. You mark my words."

She had no doubt looked in at the parlour window and seen the piano against the wall. Aunt Doe told the tale to the family as a joke, but Joanna, on hearing of the gipsy's words, felt sure that they referred to her. She resumed her piano lessons at school and practised assiduously at home. Everything else was quite forgotten. Music was the only thing. She saw herself, in her mind's eye, on the concert platforms of the world. She would always wear crimson, she told herself, for her school-friend, Elaine, said it suited her.

Often during the dark winter evenings aunt Doe would get out her violin, and, riffling through her music, brown with age, would find some piece that she and Joanna could play together. The family enjoyed these times. Stephen was very proud of his daughter, and the two boys, although they teased, were impressed by the progress their sister had made.

But one Sunday evening in late March, when she and aunt Doe were playing together, Joanna suddenly heard herself as though for the first time. It was the Bach Minuet, a piece they had played as a duo before, but she heard with sudden clarity that aunt Doe, on the violin, was carrying her and bearing her up. There was nothing there, in her own performance. She played the right notes and that was all. The music was coming from aunt Doe.

"It's no good, is it?" she said at the end, swinging round on the music-stool, and, although there were tears in her eyes, she was laughing at the same time. "I shall never really be any good! That gipsy was talking through her hat!"

"Come, now, Joanna," Stephen said, "Rome wasn't built in a day, you know."

Joanna still looked towards aunt Doe.

"Tell me what you honestly think."

"It all depends what you want to do. Your music will always give you a lot of pleasure –"

"But as a career! Have I got what it takes?"

"What does your teacher say at school?"

"My teacher says the same as you."

"Well, you're surely not going to give it up?"

"Oh, I shall play just the same, of course. But I know I shall never do great things." Joanna was perfectly matter-of-fact. She folded her music and rose from the stool. "Whoever it is in the family who has a great gift for music," she said, "it certainly isn't going to be me."

"Well, don't look at me," Chris said.

"No, nor me," Jamesy said.

There was a silence in the room.

"Perhaps it's me," Emma said.

Such a shout of laughter came from Joanna and the boys that Emma stared in frowning surprise. She had been sitting crocheting. The piece of work was in her hands, and the bright green wool was round the hook. Now she bent over it again and counted the stitches along the edge.

"Emma – musical!" Chris exclaimed.

"Now I've heard everything!" Jamesy declared.

"Poor little Emma," Stephen said. He drew her close to him, on the settee. "How do we know she's not musical? She may be. We shall have to see."

Emma resisted him, drawing away. She was trying to rescue a slipping stitch.

"I don't care if I am or not! Silly old music!" she said to him.

"Emma singing!" Jamesy said.

"Emma playing the snake-charmer's pipe!" Joanna said, with a grimace.

"That's enough!" said aunt Doe, putting away her violin. "Emma is very fond of music. She may surprise you all yet."

One afternoon, when aunt Doe went into the parlour, Emma sat at the old piano, frowning at the music on its stand. The keyboard was open, as it always was – the ivories would turn yellow otherwise – and Emma's hands hovered over the keys. But she snatched them away when aunt Doe came in and folded them in her lap instead.

"You could have piano lessons if you like, you know, and learn to play as Joanna does."

"No, I don't want to," Emma said.

"I could start you off at home."

"No," Emma said. She shook her head.

"What about the fiddle, then? Would you prefer to learn that?"

Emma was fond of the violin. The sound of it, when aunt Doe played, would always bring her into the room. And now, as aunt Doe took it out of its case and played a few bars of "Annie Laurie", there was a gleam in the child's dark eyes.

"Here," said aunt Doe. "You have a try. I'll help you to hold it while you start."

"Shall I be able to play a tune?"

"Not straight away. That takes time. But you'll soon learn, if I show you how."

"No, I don't want to," Emma said.

"Why won't you try it?" aunt Doe asked. "There's no one around to hear you try. The others are all out in the fields."

"I don't care if they are or not. I just don't want to, that's all."

"Very well," aunt Doe said.

She laid the instrument back in its case, but left the lid open, invitingly. She went out of the room and closed the door. Emma slid from the music stool and went to look at the violin. She put out a hand and touched the strings, and a little tremor broke the air, causing a shiver in her skin. She drew her finger, delicately, over the warm red varnished wood; she touched the bow where it lay in its clips; she felt the satin that lined the case. Then, suddenly, reaching up, she brought down the lid with a sharp little click.

Out in the dairy, scouring pans, aunt Doe saw Emma leaving the house; running across the stable yard, skipping and dancing in the wind.

"Where are you off to?" she called from the door.

But Emma pretended not to hear.

Chapter 5

Emma was very small for her age. Chris could carry her for miles; it was nothing to him, being so strong. He would run with her at high speed, pretending that he was a galloping horse, and Emma would bob up and down on his shoulders, shrieking with laughter when he neighed.

"You're just like a little doll," he would say. "I forget you're up there until you yell."

Emma at seven was so small she could scarcely reach the snecks of the doors. She had to stretch herself, up on her toes, and this was a joke to the other three.

"Poor Little Tich!" Jamesy would say. "Let me open the door for you."

They would reach things down for her from high shelves and would unscrew difficult jars for her. They would lift her when crossing a ditch on the farm.

"No! I can jump it! Leave me alone!"

"All right, let's see you," Jamesy said.

"She's bound to fall in," Joanna warned.

"Oh no I shan't!" Emma said.

"Very well. Go ahead and jump. But don't blame us, you silly thing, when you get yourself all black with mud."

Emma retreated a few yards and prepared to make a little run. But the ditch seemed wider, suddenly, and somehow the spring went out of her feet.

"There! You can't do it!" Jamesy said.

"Yes, I can. I've done it before."

"Then why don't you do it and not so much fuss?"

"Because you're watching," Emma said.

"Oh, all right, we'll look away."

But it made no difference whether they looked away or not. So long as they stood there, close by the ditch, Emma knew she would surely fall in, and the knowledge paralysed

81

her legs.

"Come along, little un!" Chris said to her. "You may as well let me give you a hand."

And Emma, yielding herself to him, was swung across to the other side.

She *could* jump the ditch, when she was alone, but they would never believe that.

Sometimes aunt Doe was cross with them, because of the things they did for Emma. When Jamesy fastened her shoes for her, or Joanna offered to cut up her meat, or Chris completed her jig-saw puzzle, aunt Doe reproved them, severely displeased.

"Emma is not a baby now. It's time you allowed her to grow up."

They only laughed at the idea. To think of Emma growing up! The sight of this tiny sister of theirs, coming behind the herd of cows, tapping her little stick on the ground and calling out, "Get over, old cow!" made them feel protective to her. She was so tiny; such a doll. They felt very big and strong beside her, and Chris especially, hoisting her up to sit on his shoulders, felt himself a man of great power.

"Emma's our mascot," he said once.

"That she is not!" declared aunt Doe. "Emma's a person, the same as you."

"Are you a person?" Chris teased the child.

"Yes," Emma said, "you know I am."

"First person singular, I suppose?"

The older children enjoyed the joke, but Emma herself was unsure, glancing at each of them in turn, and saying nothing.

"Take no notice of them," said aunt Doe. "They're not so smart as they think they are."

"Who's not so smart?" Stephen asked, coming into the room just then.

"These three children of yours," she said.

"I thought I had four," Stephen said.

He, according to aunt Doe, was just as bad as the rest of them. Emma was still a baby to him. He spoilt her and made a pet of her, for she was the one who was most like Gwen.

"There's plenty of time for growing up," he said, with his hand on Emma's hair.

At Easter, during the holidays, Chris spoke to his father again on the subject of his leaving school.

"If I'm to leave at the end of next term, we need to tell the headmaster soon."

"Are you sure it's what you want?"

"Absolutely. A hundred-per-cent."

"You're still very young," Stephen said, "to decide the course your life will take."

"Hang it all. I'll be fifteen by then. Gerald's been farming for nearly a year. So have Jeff Twill and David Mapp."

Stephen was not much impressed by this. He did not care for Challoner's son, nor for the other two sprigs thus named, and just lately, as he knew, Chris had been much in their company.

"I don't need to tell you that farming is in a bad way. There's not much scope for ambitious men."

"It'll get better in time. It must."

"I don't see much hope in the next few years. You'll get little joy but the work itself."

"It's still what I want. Honestly."

"Very well," Stephen said. "I'll write to Mr Priestman immediately."

"Thanks, dad!" Chris exclaimed. Jubilant, he shook Stephen's hand. "You won't regret it, I give you my word."

"I hope *you* won't. That's the main thing."

"I shan't," said Chris. "I know I shan't!"

The decision was taken; the headmaster informed. Chris would leave school at the end of July. Stephen still worried, all the same. He talked about it to aunt Doe.

"I hope I'm doing the right thing."

"Chris knows his own mind. His heart is in farming, there's no doubt of that."

"I hope his heart won't be broken by it. Older men's have been, these past two years."

"Why not look on the bright side? Four lots of school fees are a drain. Be thankful you'll soon be saving one."

"It *will* be a saving, certainly."

A few days later he heard that Miss Protheroe's Little

School, which Emma attended, was to close down at the end of the summer term. Emma would have to go elsewhere.

"Why not send her to the village school? You'd be saving two lots of school fees then."

"Is Emma's education to suffer, merely to save me a few paltry pounds?"

"I don't see why it should suffer at all. What does she learn at Miss Protheroe's that she wouldn't learn at the village school?"

"What would she learn at the village school that was better not learnt?" Stephen said.

"I've always heard it's a particularly good school."

"Yes. It is. Or so I believe."

"You ought to know. You *are* on the board of managers."

"It has a high standard, certainly. In fact it has the reputation of being one of the five best village schools in the three counties."

"In that case, I don't see what you've got against it."

"I've got nothing against it," Stephen said.

But the idea was new, and new ideas were hard to digest. His little Emma at Huntlip school, in the rough-and-tumble of that noisy playground, with labourers' boisterous daughters and sons? Cold-shouldered, perhaps, because she was different from themselves. If she had gone there from the first. . . .

"She'll soon get used to it," aunt Doe said.

"But will she be happy?" Stephen asked.

"She's made no friends at Miss Protheroe's. Perhaps she'll do better, nearer home."

"Labourers' children?" Stephen said.

"She talks to the labourers on the farm. Why not to their children, for goodness' sake?"

"I'm not being snobbish, you understand."

"No, of course not," aunt Doe said. There was a dryness in her tone,

"I only want what's best for Emma."

"You're afraid she'll be roughened, perhaps, down there, hobbing and nobbing with the villagers?"

"Isn't it possible?" Stephen said.

"That Miss Izzard, the mistress-in-charge. . . I was talking to her at the jumble sale the other day. She doesn't strike me as being rough."

"Of course she's not," Stephen said.

"She's a reasonably well-educated woman, isn't she?"

"I can see where you're leading me, you know."

"An intelligent woman, would you say?"

"Intelligent, yes, certainly."

"Yet she is a product of that village school, I understand."

"Very well. You've made your point. I shall think about it, I promise you."

So in time yet another decision was taken. Stephen went down to the village school and arranged that Emma should begin to attend there in September. As to the wisdom of the decision, only time would tell on that, but Emma herself was well pleased. She thought of the village school as her father's school, because it stood below the farm, and because the children who went there were allowed to play their summer games in her father's meadow, just behind.

"When am I going to daddy's school? Will they ring the bell for me? Shall I go down across the fields?"

As far as Emma was concerned, September could not come soon enough.

* * * * *

The flocks on the two farms were too big now to be shorn together on the same day. The two lots of shearers banded together as usual, but on different days, first at Outlands and then Holland Farm. And that, as Billy Rye remarked, meant two shearing-feasts instead of one.

"Shearing-feasts!" said Morton George. "They starve us all through the bloody year and give us a feast at shearing time! Are we supposed to be grateful for that?"

Wages were cut again that year. They were down to thirty shillings now. This was in accordance with the recommendations of the local "Conciliation Committee", set up to deal with such matters, but there was resentment all the same, and it showed in the faces of the men when, on a Saturday in July, they came to the office to be paid.

"Is that all I'm worth to you, Mr Wayman? Thirty

shillings?" Nate Hopson said.

"The slump hits all of us," Stephen said. "We've all got to make economies."

"God! I could spit!" said Morton George. He snatched up his money and walked out. His loud voice could be heard in the yard as he talked to Starling and Billy Rye. "Economies! Sweet Jesus Christ! What economies does *he* make, I'd like to know?"

The rest of the men said nothing at all. They took their money and slouched away, each one avoiding Stephen's glance. Their sullenness irked him; it got on his mind; and yet they had his sympathy. They were the ones who suffered most. It was their children who would go hungry when harvest was over and winter came.

All through the summer and autumn that year, there was a constant stream of men, most of them strangers to the district, calling at the farm in search of work. Aunt Doe would give them something to eat and perhaps put a shilling into their hands. But there was no work for them on the farm.

"Surely there must be something?" they would say. "Especially now, at haymaking time? Surely you need an extra man?"

But Stephen refused them, one and all.

"Any extra work I have goes to the local men," he said.

He made it a rule, and kept to it. He hardened his heart to these ragged strangers and watched them trudge towards Outlands and Blagg. Challoner, he knew, sometimes employed these casual men. He paid them less than their work was worth and, as he said to Stephen once, it kept his own men on their toes.

"They know, if they monkey with me, that I've got two or three chaps at my gate, ready to step straight into their shoes. That gives them something to think about, and keeps them from too much idling around!"

One man who called at Holland Farm was Eddie Templer from Outlands, the man who, at shearing time the summer before, had urged Stephen to count the fleeces.

"Challoner's given me the sack. I'm a union man and he hates our guts. It's been in the wind for a year or more. I've

86

come to ask you for a job."

"I've got all the labour I can use."

"I done you a favour once, remember, when Challoner was trying to cheat you."

"Is that why you did it?" Stephen asked. "Against the day when you might want a favour in return?"

"What if I did? What's wrong with that?"

"Did Mr Challoner really try to cheat me that time? Or was it just a trick of yours?"

"Seems you've got a suspicious mind."

"You haven't answered, yes or no."

"Are you going to give me a job or not?"

"I've already told you, there's nothing here. I'm sorry, Templer, but I can't *make* work."

"Never mind the apologies! I can't keep my wife and kids on *them*! Seems I backed the wrong bloody horse!"

Less than half an hour after Templer had gone, aunt Doe came running up to the hayfield to say that the cattle were in the corn, in the twelve acre piece above Long Gains. Chris, coming home from school just then, was quick to believe that Eddie Templer was to blame. He had passed the man coming up the track.

"He's a bolshevik, one of the worst. Mr Challoner's well shot of him. Thank goodness you didn't take him on."

"We don't know for sure that he let the cattle into the corn."

"They're all the same, these unemployed. *Good* working men don't get the sack. They're either shirkers or bolshies or both and they ought to be put to mend the roads."

"Is that what Gerald Challoner says?"

"I do have opinions of my own."

"And no doubt they coincide with his."

"Yes, on the whole, I think they do."

"I think that's a pity," Stephen said.

"Dammit, dad! Gerald's my friend!"

"Yes, I know," Stephen said.

And that was a pity, too, he thought.

* * * * *

It was not only corn prices that had fallen so low. It was the same with cattle and pigs: the prices they fetched at market now hardly covered the cost of rearing them; and Stephen, going over his accounts, read the sad story on the page. Only the sale of fat lambs showed a worthwhile profit there. Sheep were keeping the farm alive. Sheep and aunt Doe's poultry yard.

Aunt Doe had savings in the bank, which brought her in fifty pounds a year. She wanted to remove her capital and give it to Stephen to pay off the mortgage on the farm. He would not hear of such a thing.

"Why not?" she asked. "I spend hardly anything on myself."

"Then it's high time you did," Stephen said, and he looked critically at her shoes, the laces of which were bits of string.

"You can talk! Just look at you! Ragged old jacket and that awful cap!"

"You'll want that money for your old age. I'm paying the mortgage gradually. Another two years should see it through. There's nothing for you to worry about. We're keeping our heads above water – just!"

"And *you* are wearing yourself to a shade."

Stephen's angular, loose-knit face, with its high cheekbones and long lean jaw, had a tired look in it these days. She wished there was something she could do to smooth away the deepening lines and ease the burden of anxiety. But he would not take the money she offered, and she knew he would never change his mind. All she could do, she told herself, was to try and save him in every way.

Nothing was wasted in the house. Meatbones were boiled to make stock for soups; potatoes were always cooked in their skins; all manner of fruit was bottled and jammed. Used tealeaves were kept for cleaning the carpets, and soft soap was made at home. Cough-cure was made by baking onions with brown sugar, and all sorts of garden herbs were kept, for whatever ailments might come to the family. No one dared be ill in that house, for fear of aunt Doe's remedies, but her home-made wines were popular, especially the plum and the walnut-leaf.

Stephen would sometimes smile to himself, seeing her carefully hoarding the scraps that would go to make a curry for lunch the next day. Food, as he often reminded her, was the one thing that was plentiful on the farm.

"I like to think I'm helping you, even if you don't think my efforts are worthwhile."

"Of course you're helping me," he said.

* * * * *

One afternoon at the end of July, Chris left school for good. He celebrated in true Chepsworth style by hurling his "boater" from King Richard's Bridge, into the swirling river below, and watching it float away downstream.

"Poor old Wayman! He's a farmer now!" A school-friend stuck a straw in his mouth. "Don't forget to set your alarm."

"Or wind up the cockerel," another boy said.

"We'll think of you Wayman, milking the cows at four o'clock!"

"I'll think of *you* next term," Chris said, "sweating blood over Shenstone's impots!"

He and Jamesy ran for their bus.

A week later harvest began, and when the first field was cut, Chris was there in the first dim light, taking his place among the men, working beside them with his scythe. To his surprise nothing was said. There was no banter of any kind. The men worked in silence, in a row, cutting a way round the edge of the field so that the reaping-machine could get in.

The sun was not yet visible, and the men were shadowy, featureless shapes, mowing their way through the milk-white mist. Then the sun began to rise, burning over the earth's edge, touching the oats with its molten redness. The men's faces were crimson-flushed. Their scythe-blades, at every returning stroke, appeared for an instant to drip red fire. Only then did the mowers speak.

"Who's this new chap here with us, Billy?"

"That's the young master," Billy said.

"What, him what was only last week at school?"

"The very same," Billy said.

"Well, I'll say this for him, at any rate – he's no slug-abed, that's for sure. Nor he don't yap too much, neither, first thing. Seems to me we'll keep him on."

Chris, though he smiled to himself at this, said nothing in reply. He needed every ounce of breath if he was to keep pace with the other mowers.

The day came at last when Emma was to start at the village school. Stephen, as it happened, was attending a sale. He had to leave home at six o'clock.

"You'll take her down?" he asked aunt Doe.

"*I'll* take her down," Chris volunteered.

But when, at a quarter past eight, Chris came in to eat his breakfast, Emma was nowhere to be found. Her shoe-bag had gone from its place on the dresser. So had her luncheon, packed by aunt Doe. Emma had slipped off to school alone, and nobody had seen her go.

* * * * *

On ordinary mornings, Betony Izzard walked the mile from her home to the school, but today, the first morning of the new term, she asked her brother for a lift and rode with him in the workshop cart, sitting beside him on the box, with her big canvas hold-all on her lap. It was not yet eight o'clock. She liked to be early on the first day of term. And behind her, in the cart, among the timber and the carpenter's tools, stood two big baskets full of apples. The apples were her reason for wanting a lift.

When they arrived at the school, Dicky carried the baskets in and set them down as she directed, one in each of the two classrooms.

"I dunno what great-grumpa will say when he finds you've been at his precious apples. Nor dad and mother, come to that. They won't be best pleased if you ask me."

"They needn't know if you don't tell them."

"They'll notice the apples is in short supply."

"I shall say the mice have been eating them."

"Ah, two-legged mice!" Dicky said, glancing round at the empty desks. "You spoil them kids. You do, that's a fact."

Betony hung up her coat, closed the cupboard, and went

90

to her desk.

"One apple a day for each child! Do you call that spoiling, Dicky?" she asked. "For some of them – those whose fathers are out of work – that apple will be all they have to eat between coming to school in the morning and going home in the afternoon."

"And what they thieve in the fields on the way!"

"Do you grudge them a slice of raw turnip?"

"*You* can't feed all the poor of the parish and it's no use your trying," Dicky said. "But I ent got time to stop chatting here. I'm meeting dad at Mr Twill's. We're building him a summer-house to go with his brand-new tennis-court."

"And farmers complain that they have no money!"

"Seems to me I'd better be off, before you get on your hobby-horse."

The door closed and Dicky was gone. She heard him turning the cart in the playground. Stillness and quietness stole on her. She liked the hour between eight and nine, when she had the building to herself, and on the first morning of term, especially, there was always much to be done.

Out of her big brown canvas bag she took a roll of coloured posters, bought on a recent visit to London. She began pinning them up on the walls. They depicted people in history and were painted in bold lines and colours. Alexander taming his horse. Stephenson watching the boiling kettle. Captain Scott at the South Pole. Nurse Cavell, facing her captors. And others not so instantly recognizable, such as Ptolemy and Caractacus, William Willett and John Brown, to stir her pupils' curiosity. In the course of the term the children would come to know them all as intimately as they knew one another.

Next she took out a spray of hops and hung it above the classroom door. The scent of the flowers, and their stickiness, remained on her fingers and her palms. She wiped them clean on a piece of rag. She took out sprays of hips and haws, oakleaves and acorns, ashleaves and keys, and put them into a stoneware vase, up on one of the window-sills. The morning sunlight shone on them: scarlet rose-hips and crimson haws; acorns beginning to turn

91

yellow; ashkeys already parchment-brown. She fetched a jug of water and filled the vase.

The school was really one large room. It was divided into two by a sliding partition of wood and glass. When Betony had first been made headmistress, there had been a hundred and nineteen pupils, but now, when the children reached the age of eleven, they went to the school at Middle Cross. There was more room at Huntlip now. When attendance was at its peak, there were sixty-seven children in all.

* * * * *

At half past eight Sue Vernon arrived. She was Betony's sole assistant. Small, neat, dark-haired and dark-eyed, she walked in with a sharp briskness as though impatient to start the day's work. She enquired after Betony's holidays and answered a query about her own, but her glance kept straying to the basket of apples standing beside Betony's desk.

"I brought them from home," Betony said. "There's another one in your room. The children can have one apple each when they stop for the morning break."

"How generous you are. I hope they appreciate it, that's all."

"The apples won't last long, I'm afraid. Not unless attendance is low."

"No doubt it will be, seeing the harvest is still going on. I saw some children in the fields as I cycled past Moat Farm just now. I nearly stopped and spoke to them, but I know your feelings on the subject, and I thought I'd better leave it to you. I can give you the names of three of them."

"No, there's no need," Betony said. She set up her easel and put in the pegs. "I shall know about it soon enough."

Sue Vernon's gaze was critical.

"Mr Pugh says it's a downright disgrace, these absences at harvest time. He says we teachers are to blame. We delay in reporting them to him."

Mr Pugh was the school attendance officer, a personal friend of Sue's family. He lived in the house next door to theirs, in one of the better parts of Chepsworth.

Betony reached for the blackboard and lifted it up onto the easel. The argument was an old one between them. It varied little from year to year.

"The parents need the extra money. This year, perhaps, more than ever before."

"Well, I think it's very wrong indeed, that the children's schooling should be neglected just for the sake of a few coppers."

"What's the use of filling their heads if their bellies are empty?" Betony said. She took chalk and duster from the cupboard and placed them in the tray pegged to the easel. "A few coppers are not to be sneezed at, to a labourer with a family."

Sue Vernon walked away, into her own classroom next door, and laid her small suitcase on her desk. Miss Izzard's use of the word "bellies" was really rather typical. Sometimes she seemed to set out to offend. Or was the coarseness ingrained in her? Something that could not be overcome?

Miss Vernon, not for the first time, took herself severely to task. For she was the daughter of a church organist, a man of standing and refinement, and she had enjoyed advantages denied to such as Betony Izzard, whose father was a village carpenter. A good enough man in his way, no doubt – even well-to-do, in fact, for the family business was a flourishing one – but a countryman of no education: slow, simple, unlettered, uncouth, and almost laughably broad in his speech.

"Really," Miss Vernon told herself, "one must make allowances, after all."

Acting on her good resolution, she took a piece of paper from her case and carried it in to Betony.

"I've drawn up a list of hymns for the term. I thought you'd like to see it first."

One of Miss Izzard's disadvantages was that she could not play the piano. As mistress-in-charge she must feel it keenly. Miss Vernon therefore deferred to her whenever it seemed reasonable to do so. Betony took the neatly written list.

"Not three-three-one. At least not today. It's not very

93

cheerful, is it?" she said. "Let's have 'To be a pilgrim' instead. The children like it. So do I."

Miss Vernon drew a deep breath. Her good intentions were draining away.

"I haven't practised it, I'm afraid."

"I'm sure you can play it, even so."

"Oh, I can play it, certainly. But it won't be up to a high standard."

"The children won't mind. Neither shall I. We'll do our best to drown you out."

"Oh, how true!" Miss Vernon said, with more than a touch of bitterness. But when she met Betony's glance, she was gradually obliged to smile. "Oh, how true!" she said again, and the truth of it made them laugh together, with real amusement on both sides. "As for that dreadful piano in there – !" She returned once more to her own room.

Betony Izzard went to her desk. She took out pen-tray, inkwell, register. She opened the register out on her desk and wrote the date at the top of the page: Tuesday, September the 4th., 1923.

Her watch, which was pinned to the front of her dress, told her that it was five-and-twenty to nine. She stepped up onto a wooden form and looked out of the high window. The playground below was still deserted. No children had come to stir the dust. Only a movement in the "back-house" showed where the cleaner, Mr Miles, was filling a bucket at the tap.

Betony was proud of that tap. Not many country schools had a piped water supply indoors. It had taken three years to get it installed. But she was not so proud of the school privies, housed in a hut among the trees. How many years would pass, she wondered, before the managers would admit that four latrines were inadequate for sixty-seven children, girls and boys?

She was about to step down from the form when she saw a child in the playground. It was Emma Wayman from Holland Farm. For her first day at the village school Emma evidently meant to be in good time, but, finding herself alone in the playground, she stood uncertainly at the gate, swinging her shoe-bag on its string. A tiny thing, very small for her age, she wore a plain blue cotton frock and a clean white pinafore, crisply starched. Except that she carried a change of shoes, there was nothing to set her apart from the rest of the village children; nothing to show that hitherto she had gone to a private school in the town and mixed with the daughters of professional men. She was dressed like any Huntlip schoolchild. Plainly her aunt, Miss Skeine, had sense. Betony went to fetch her in.

* * * * *

"Didn't anyone bring you, on your first day?"

"No," Emma said, "I came by myself."

"Are they busy up at the farm?"

"Yes, they're harvesting," Emma said.

Betony took the child's hand and led her into the school porch. She showed her where to hang her bag, and watched while she changed into indoor shoes. Emma's movements were slow and precise. She looked about her curiously.

"I expect it seems strange to you after Miss Protheroe's," Betony said. "But you'll soon get used to it, you'll see. I'll take you into your classroom now, and you'll meet your teacher, Miss Vernon."

But Miss Vernon, in the smaller room, had removed the lower panel from the piano and was on her knees in front of it, tightening the pedals with a screwdriver. She looked fraught, and her hair was dishevelled. Betony tactfully withdrew.

"You'd better wait with me for a while, at least till the other children arrive. You can give me a hand with my morning chores."

Betony sat the child at a desk and gave her a box full of broken pencils. She gave her a sharpener shaped like an egg, and an empty carton to catch the shavings. And while Emma sharpened the pencils, Betony went to and fro, taking exercise books from the cupboard and sorting them into separate piles.

"Did you come down across the fields?"

"Yes," Emma said, "it's the quickest way."

"Are there still mushrooms in Cowpark Meadow? There

95

used to be when I was a little girl like you."

"I didn't see them," Emma said.

"Perhaps it's too early in the year."

Betony climbed onto the form and looked out of the window again. There were children in the playground now: six of them chasing an old rubber wheel; their booted feet kicked up the dust, and their voices shrilled with merriment. Betony got down again.

It made Emma smile to her see her headmistress bob up and down from the wooden form. Miss Protheroe would never have done such a thing. Miss Izzard was younger; she was light on her feet. She was fairer, prettier, more full of life.

"The children have begun to arrive now. Would you like to go out and play with them?"

"I haven't finished the pencils yet."

"That doesn't matter. You've done a lot."

"I'd sooner finish them," Emma said.

She liked this little task of hers, sitting at a desk in the sunny classroom, while her new headmistress passed to and fro. The pile of sharpened pencils grew, each one pointed beautifully, and the curly shavings filled the carton, tinged with yellow, red, and green. When she had finished, she sat quite still. She looked at the hops above the door; the hips and haws and the autumn leaves, catching the light on the window-sill; the coloured posters on the wall. She watched Miss Izzard, secretly, as she wrote on the blackboard with a chalk.

Outside, in the playground, the noise of playing children grew. From the classroom next door came a heavy thud as Miss Vernon replaced the front of the piano. She came and opened the connecting door.

"I'm going out to the playground now. There's a bit of a rumpus going on. The Tillotson boys, as usual. Goodbye to peace for the next three months!"

A few minutes later she was back, entering by the main door and ushering in, very formally, a young woman and a small boy.

"Miss Mercybright to see you," she said.

The young woman had auburn hair. It showed like

copper, gleaming bright, under her rather shabby hat. The little boy, on the other hand, was dark-skinned and had black hair. Yet there was enough likeness between them to show that they were mother and son. Miss Vernon's glance was shrewd and sharp.

"You did say *Miss* Mercybright, I believe? I'm sorry if I made a mistake –"

"Thank you, Miss Vernon," Betony said.

Miss Vernon withdrew, flushing slightly, and closed the door. Betony put her chalk away and wiped her hands on a clean duster. She moved between the rows of desks. Smiling, she stooped to the little boy, and lifted him up to stand on a form.

"Well, Robert, and how are you? I haven't seen you since ever so long. Not since we went to the Whitsun fair. Have you still got the fairing you won at the stalls?"

The little boy's hand went into his pocket. He held up the fairing for her to see. It was a tiny tumbler bell and he jingled it on the end of its string. Then he put it away again. Betony, laughing, looked at him.

"You look very smart in your corduroys. Are you glad to be starting school?"

Robert gave a little nod. A slight smile touched his lips. His mother reached up and removed his cap. She tried to smooth his straight black hair.

"He's very young to be starting school. He isn't even four yet. But I've got this job at Tinkerdine, doing the cleaning for old Mrs Frail, and dad said Robert should come to school."

"Robert will soon settle down with us. There are others here just as young, you know. It'll do him good to have company."

"He's always had company," Linn Mercybright said. "He's never been left alone in his life."

"But he's had no other children to play with. It's lonely out there in Stoney Lane."

"I suppose you think I've been too protective. But he *is* my son. Remember that." Linn, avoiding Betony's glance, pulled a thread from Robert's sleeve. "You and your family have been very kind. You've helped us for his father's sake –"

"We've *tried* to help," Betony said. "Tom was brought up with my family – is it so strange that we should want to help his son?"

"Robert is all I've got left of Tom. If Tom had lived, we'd have shared him together, but I'm not going to share him with anyone else."

"Why should you indeed?" Betony said. "Except in those ways that are best for him?"

"I'm the one to decide what's best."

"Well, at least you've allowed him to come to school."

"As to that, I have no choice, if I'm to work for Mrs Frail. We need every penny we can get."

Linn's tone had an edge to it. There was a coldness in her face. If it had been any other school she would have found it easier, but Betony, being the little boy's godmother, had a special claim on him, and Linn would have given anything rather than yield him up to her. Betony apprehended this. She sought to set Linn's mind at rest.

"Robert will be in Miss Vernon's class. He won't come to me until he's eight. There's nothing much to worry you."

"Oh, I'm not worried!" Linn said. She turned it off with a little shrug, pretending not to understand. "He'll soon settle down, I'm sure of that."

All the time, while the two women talked, the little boy stood on the form, watching them with a deep dark gaze. Once he turned his head and looked at Emma, sitting primly at her desk, but otherwise he scarcely moved.

"I hope there won't be any trouble from the other children."

Linn spoke carefully, with some hesitation, but Betony knew what she meant to say. Robert was illegitimate. In a village like Huntlip, this would be known to everyone.

"He's not the only love-child here. There may be remarks from time to time, but that's something that's got to be faced, isn't it?"

"So long as it isn't worse than that."

"I shall watch over him, never fear."

"Yes," said Linn, "I'm sure you will."

Suddenly she coloured up. The tartness this time had

been unintended. Confused, she turned to her son again, straightening his collar and tightening his tie. She forced herself to meet Betony's gaze.

"Do you see Tom in him?"

"Yes, in his stillness," Betony said. "And because he's so dark, of course. But he's got a look of your father, too, especially about the eyes."

She gave the little boy her hand and encouraged him to jump from the form. She walked with him and Linn to the door.

"How is your father nowadays?"

"His leg is giving him trouble," Linn said, "though he'll never admit it, needless to say."

It was time for her to go. She found it hard to leave her son. She forced herself not to touch him again, but looked at him with severity.

"Be a good boy on your first day at school. I'll call for you at three o'clock. And do remember what I said! – You mustn't say 'aunty Betony' – you must say 'Miss Izzard' like everyone else." And, turning to Betony, she said: "I hope it doesn't slip out, that's all. I've told him about it often enough."

"It won't be the end of the world if it does. He is my godson, after all."

At the outer door, Linn turned to wave. Robert answered by waving his cap. Then suddenly she was gone, and a shadow flickered across his face. Betony gave his hand a squeeze.

"Come along, Robert. I'll find you a friend."

She took him to Emma, who sat with folded hands in her lap.

"This is Robert, my godson," she said. "He's never been to school before. Will you be his special friend?"

Emma nodded. She and Robert exchanged a stare. When she stood up, small though she was, she felt herself tall compared with him. Shyly, she took his other hand.

"It's not worth your going out to play now," Betony said. "They're all coming in in a minute or two. I'll take you into your own room."

"Can't we stay in here with you?"

"No, Emma, I'm afraid you can't."

Emma was in Standard I; Robert was in the Infants' Class; they had to go into the smaller room, and Miss Vernon was the teacher there.

Betony went to ring the bell. Half a dozen peals, and then a hush. But within a short space of time, the school resounded to the trampling of feet, the slamming of desk-lids, the shifting of forms. Fifty-eight children, girls and boys, stood in their places in the sunlit room; the panelled partition was slid back half way; and Miss Vernon sat at the ancient piano. Gradually the noise subsided. Betony said the morning prayer.

"Give to thy children gathered here a day of peace, Oh Lord, and strength to be dutiful in thy sight."

When the opening bars of the hymn were played, she spared a thought for Sue Vernon. The piano was indeed old. Two strings were broken and many were loose. But fifty-eight pilgrims, undismayed, lifted their voices to the roof and sang with all their might and main.

> "He who would valiant be
> Gainst all disaster –"

* * * * *

Emma sat at the back of the room; Robert with the "babies" in the front.

"Silence, everyone!" Miss Vernon said. She tapped with a ruler on her desk.

The first day of term was always like this. The children were slow to settle down. The basket of apples drew all eyes.

"Miss Izzard has kindly brought them for you. One apple a day for everyone but *not* until eleven o'clock."

Through the glass-panelled partition, now closed, Emma could see Miss Izzard in the room next door, the sunlight on her smooth fair hair as she stood talking in front of her class. Emma sat very straight and still. *She* would wear a little watch pinned to the bosom of her dress, when she grew up, she told herself.

"Pay attention," Miss Vernon said.

Out in the playground, during the break, Robert was surrounded by older children, who wheeled him about in the gardener's barrow. Emma sat under the chestnut tree, on one of the knobbly outcropping roots. Florrie Ricks came and sat by her.

"Ent you going to eat your apple?"

"No, I'm keeping it," Emma said.

"You can't be very hungry, then."

"No. I never said I was. I've just had my elevenses."

"Lucky thing," Florrie said. "I ate all mine on the way to school."

"What did you have?" Emma asked.

"Bread and scrape," Florrie said.

The two were silent for a while. Emma waved away a wasp. Florrie picked at a hole in her sleeve.

"Where's your father? Is he dead?"

"No," Emma said. She looked away. "He's gone to Wales."

"Your mother's dead, though, isn't she? Hilda Bowers said she was. You've got an aunt looking after you."

Emma made no reply. She breathed on her apple yet again and polished it on her pinafore. Florrie gave a little sniff.

"You won't have no apple left if you keep on rubbing it like that."

"Oh yes I shall."

"If you don't want it, you should ought to put it back."

"Back where? Back on the tree?"

"Back in the basket, clever dick."

"Well, I'm not going to, so there."

"I knew you wouldn't," Florrie sniffed.

"I'm going to keep it," Emma said.

But the apple, placed on her desk during the rest of the morning's lessons, had somehow vanished by dinner-time.

"What have you lost?" Miss Vernon asked.

"I've lost my apple," Emma said. "Somebody must have taken it while I was giving out the books."

"That's not a very nice thing to say."

"*Somebody* took it. They must have done."

"Perhaps when you have your apple tomorrow it will

teach you to eat it up at once instead of hiding it away just to tease the other children. Now run along home, child, or you'll be late for lunch."

When Emma reached the Brooky Field, Chris was waiting at the stile. He put her to sit astride his shoulders and jogged home with her up the steep track.

"Somebody slipped off to school by herself and never said nothing to nobody!"

Because it was Tuesday, there was curry for lunch. Aunt Doe was filling a bowl with rice. Joanna and Jamesy were both there because school had not started for them as yet.

"How's our little Emma, then, and what did she think of the village school?"

"Put her to sit in dad's chair. She likes that when he's away."

"What are the children like down there?"

"Were the teachers nice to you?"

"What sort of lessons did you have?"

"Ordinary lessons," Emma said. "We did our arithmetic on a slate."

"Do you like it? asked aunt Doe.

"Yes, it's all right," Emma said.

When she returned to school after lunch, one of the children, sniffing her breath, made a face of great disgust.

"What've you been eating, for goodness' sake?"

"Curry, of course," Emma said.

Emma shared a desk with Jenny Quinton, a child with wire-rimmed spectacles and a bulging forehead that shone like wax. When Jenny broke the point of her pencil she took Emma's from its slot in the desk and put the broken one in its place. She raised her hand to gain attention.

"Please, miss! Emma Wayman's broken her pencil."

Emma was allowed to sharpen it, while Miss Vernon waited impatiently.

"You mustn't be so careless next time."

"*I* wasn't careless," Emma said.

"Don't answer back, if you please."

Breaking your pencil was a grave sin in Miss Vernon's eyes. It was also a sin to allow your chalk to squeak when writing with it on your slate.

"Really, Emma! Must you make that dreadful noise?"

"It isn't me, it's the chalk," Emma said.

There was a titter from the other children, and Emma looked round at them in surprise. Miss Vernon's irritation grew.

"Were you allowed to make that noise when you were at Miss Protheroe's?"

"We didn't have slates there."

"Emma, my child," Miss Vernon said, "I'm aware that you've been to a *better* school, but we do our poor best here in Huntlip, you know, and you will have to get used to us."

Emma did not understand what she meant. The village school had a bell on the roof, a playground with a chestnut tree, and stained glass windows in the porch. It was a much better school than Miss Protheroe's.

Stephen came home from the sale in Brecon, bringing gifts for all of them. A sleepy Emma sat on his lap, nursing a doll in Welsh national costume.

"How did you get on at your new school?"

"All right, thank you."

"She won't tell you much," Chris remarked. "We know. We've already tried."

Emma removed the doll's tall black hat and then put it on again.

"Winnie Aston's got a loose tooth."

"Has she, now? Fancy that."

"She's got a hammer toe as well."

"The things one hears at a village school!" Joanna said disdainfully.

Jamesy leant forward and tweaked Emma's hair.

"You're a cough-drop. That's what you are."

"Oh no I'm not!" Emma said. She nestled against her father's chest. "I'm not a cough-drop, am I, dad?"

"You're a little girl who should be in bed and I'm going to take you there," Stephen said. "Come along, sleepy head! Up the Wooden Hill to Blanket Street!"

Later that night, sitting alone with aunt Doe, he spoke to her about the child.

"Is she going to be happy there?"

"Give her a chance. It's only one day."

Certainly Emma seemed happy enough. She was ready for school betimes in the morning and glanced repeatedly at the clock.

"What would you like for elevenses?" aunt Doe asked.

"Bread and scrape," Emma said.

* * * * *

Emma and the boy, Robert Mercybright, stood in a warm patch of sun, leaning against the toolshed wall. He was eating the last of his apple. When he had finished, she offered him hers. He refused it, shaking his head.

"Don't you want it?" Emma asked.

"I mustn't take things from anyone."

"Did your mother tell you that?"

"Yes, and I promised her," Robert said.

"Go on, have it. She won't know."

But Robert again shook his head. He could not be persuaded, small though he was. Emma ate the apple herself.

"Can I see your little bell?"

He held up the bell for her to see, and jingled it on the end of its string. He put it into his pocket again. Emma took a bite out of her apple.

"Tell me about when you went to the fair with your auntie Betony," she said.

While they stood by the toolshed wall, a group of children, forming a ring, danced up to Robert, surrounding him, and began to draw him into their game. Emma hung on to him, by the sleeve. She tried to push the others away.

"No!" she said. "You leave him alone!"

"He can play if he wants to, bossy thing!"

"He doesn't want to. He's talking to me."

"Bossy old thing!" said Evie Wilkes. "You ent his sister or anything!"

"I'm his *friend*."

But the children had hold of Robert's arms, and he was pulled from Emma's grasp. In another moment he was part of their ring, dancing with them across the playground.

Emma sat on the toolshed step. Winnie Aston joined her there.

"I dreamt my tooth came out last night and when I woke up it really had." She drew back her lip and revealed the gap. "I planted it in the garden," she said. "It'll grow to be twopence in a day or two."

"How will it?" Emma asked.

"Mum will put the money there." Winnie sucked at the space in her mouth. "Do you ever dream much, Emma?" she asked.

"Sometimes I do," Emma said.

"What sort of things do you dream about?"

"All sorts of things, the same as you."

"Yes, but what? Can't you remember?"

"Once I dreamt about aunt Doe's violin."

"Yes? What happened?" Winnie asked.

"I dreamt I could play it, that's all."

"You can't really, I don't suppose."

"No," Emma said, "it was only a dream."

Her apple was just a core now. She threw it into the nettles nearby.

"Can *you* play the violin?" she asked.

Winnie Aston gave a shrug.

"I could if I wanted to," she said.

At home these days, when Emma talked, they noticed a change in her way of speech. Working out a sum aloud, "It's fivepence-three-fardens!" she announced, and, talking of the spaniel, Sam, who was sick, "He's off his fettles," she explained.

Chris and Jamesy were much amused.

"Our little Emma is getting quite broad."

"Broad your own-self!" Emma said.

The two boys were beside themselves, but Joanna fiercely disapproved.

"Don't encourage her!" she said. "She shouldn't be allowed to talk like that. 'Coal-skiddle' and 'cloe's-hoss'! That's what she's picking up at school!"

"If she picks up no worse than that," said aunt Doe, "I for one will not be too worried."

And Stephen, taking his cue from her, smiled at Emma

105

across the table.

"Emma's doing well at school. She got ten out of ten for Scripture today and nine out of ten for composition. She's quite a good scholar, aren't you, Emma?"

He worried about her, all the same, because he had thrust her into a school where the children were an unknown quantity. He would have to keep an eye on her, especially in these early days.

But this was September, and he was busy. The weather was open so far, and ploughing was going on apace. Often, with the other men, he ploughed from first light to mid-afternoon, and sometimes, with a fresh team, carried on until darkness fell. He was putting more and more land down to grass; growing more rape, more kale, more swedes; and planning to grow more sugar-beet. The open weather could not last for ever. There was much to be done before it broke.

"If we had a tractor," Chris said, "we could get done in no time at all."

"I can't afford one," Stephen said.

On Chepsworth Fair Day the weather broke and from then onwards there was endless rain. All landwork was at a halt and Stephen had time for other things. He had time to think of his little daughter, setting out for school every morning, dressed in her oilskins and rubber boots. Was she happy at the school? It was difficult to tell.

"Next year when I'm eight," she said to him, "I shall be in Miss Izzard's class."

Chapter 6

Joanna had a new ambition. She thought she would like to be an actress. Aunt Doe was inclined to approve; she had had some experience of amateur theatricals in her youth; and she suggested that the children should put on a play for Christmas, inviting all the men from the farm, with their wives and families. Joanna was taken with the idea, but what play could they perform with the limited cast that they could muster?

"When I was a girl," said aunt Doe, "we always used to write our own."

Once again she had sown a seed, and this was how Joanna and Jamesy, one Saturday morning in November, came to be sitting in the attic, biting their pens. It was a dark and dreary day. The little lamp had been lit on the table. Emma was trying to knit a scarf.

"Am I going to be in the play?"

"No, you're too small," Joanna said.

"Can I help to write it, then?"

"Don't be silly. You wouldn't know how."

"I would if you showed me," Emma said.

"Do be quiet! I'm trying to think."

Chris, who had a few minutes to spare, found his way up to the attic.

"What's it about, this play of yours?"

"Pirates, for one thing," Jamesy said.

"Oh no it isn't!" Joanna said.

"Well, the bit I've written is, so there!"

"What's it going to be called?" asked Chris.

"'Captain Terror'," Jamesy said. He had been to the cinema recently, and Douglas Fairbanks was his god.

"Really! I ask you!" Joanna said, spreading her hands to Chris in dismay. "How can I act in a play about pirates?"

107

"That's easy," Chris said. "You'll be the plucky heroine, held to ransom on the high seas. A proud, beautiful haughty girl —"

"Why don't you join us and write it down?"

But Chris was a man now; he worked on the farm; the writing of plays was kids' stuff. What little leisure time he had was spent upon more robust pursuits.

"I'm waiting for Gerald as a matter of fact. I only looked in for a moment or two. But you're quite welcome to use my ideas —"

"Rats to you!" Jamesy said.

He threw his bunjy at the closing door and went back to biting his pen. Joanna by now was making notes. Emma, on her knees under the table, was disentangling her ball of wool, which had rolled around the legs of her chair.

"Do stop jogging!" Joanna said. "Can't you see I'm trying to write?"

Emma put her wool on its needles, dropped her knitting into its bag, and slipped quietly out of the room. The other two hardly heard her go.

*　*　*　*　*

There was an old disused quarry between Holland Farm and Outlands. Thorn trees and rowans grew from its sides, with clumps of bramble and gorse and briar, and water collected in its bottom. Up on the rim, against the fence, a spindle tree grew, leaning over the edge.

Emma had to climb onto the fence and stand on the topmost rickety bar, leaning out over the quarry, before she could reach the spindleberries. The tree shook when she broke off the sprays, and a shower of raindrops fell on her. The fence creaked under her and one of its bars, breaking with a crack, let her down suddenly. Her arms and legs were badly scratched, but she had her sprays of spindleberries, and she was well pleased. She walked along the path skirting the quarry and down into Stoney Lane.

There was a cottage in the lane. A tiny place, in need of repair. One of its windows hung awry, and its roof was patched with a piece of tin. The little boy, Robert Mercybright, stood perched on a ledge inside the gate, leaning over it, dangling his arms. Emma stopped and stared at him.

"Is this where you live?" she asked, surprised.

Robert answered with a nod.

"Is your mother indoors?" she asked.

"No, she's gone to the shop," he said. "Granddad's at work. The thresher's come."

The noise of the threshing machine could be heard, throbbing away over at Outlands, and smoke could be seen among the trees. Emma looked at the little boy and showed him the sprays of spindleberries, coral-coloured, waxy, smooth, breaking from their rough pink husks, among the russet-coloured leaves.

"I'm going down to the village," she said. "You can come with me if you like."

"No, I mustn't," Robert said.

"Come just a little way, down the lane."

"No," he said, "I dussn't dare."

"Your mother won't mind. I'm sure she won't. I shall look after you, little boy."

"Mother always says to stay."

"I daresay we'll meet her, if we go down. We'll be able to help her to carry things. She's probably nearly home by now."

It took a long time to persuade Robert to open the gate and step out into the lane with her. He looked at her with anxious eyes. But Emma took him by the hand and he went with her down past the farm; then up the track to the wicket gate; and out onto the open hill.

He really was very small, and the way he put his hand into hers, tiny fingers finding their way, stealing in warmly and clinging to hers, made her feel very grown-up. She looked down at him from a greater height, and he looked up at her, dark-eyed and grave. She liked his dark eyes and straight black hair, and she liked his small features, so neatly made. Her only wish was to see him smile.

"They used to have Punch and Judy shows up here. That's why they call it Puppet Hill. A long time ago, my father says."

"I want to go back now," Robert said.

"Come just a little way further on."

"How much further on?" he asked.

"Down to those chestnut trees in that lane."

Kicking through the leaves in Cricketers Lane, Robert forgot about going back. He became absorbed in watching his feet, moving forward so rapidly, stirring up the damp dead leaves so that their colours were constantly changing, a red-brown flurry around his legs. Emma too kicked up the leaves, and they danced together along the lane, the wetness soaking the front of their clothes.

All the way across the village playing-field, they saw no sign of Robert's mother, nor was she coming along the road. They stood outside the gate for a while, but the road was empty in both directions. The village lay to the left of them. Emma turned towards the right.

"No!" Robert said. "I want to go home."

"You can't go home by yourself," Emma said. "Don't be silly. Come along."

"This ent the way to the shop," he said. "We should've gone the other way."

But Emma's strength was greater than his. She was able to pull him along. And soon they stood at two tall gates, peering through the bars into a yard, stacked up high with timber planking. To the right of the gate, above the hedge, stood a large wooden notice-board, painted boldly in black on white. Tewke and Izzard, carpenters, est. 1850; and beyond the great square stacks of timber, stood the old carpenter's workshop, backed by bushes and nut-trees.

This was Saturday, nearly lunch-time. There was not much activity in the workshop; only the sound of a man sawing wood and the jaunty whistling of a tune. Emma and Robert moved on, turned left down a narrow lane, and stood at yet another gate. Beyond stood a big old timbered house. It had enormous twisted chimneys. Smoke rose from one of them.

"Do you know this place?" Emma asked.

Robert nodded. He looked at her.

"Whose house is it?" Emma asked.

"Auntie Betony's house," he said.

"Does anybody else live there?"

110

"Uncle Jesse. Auntie Beth."

"Anyone else besides them?"

"Uncle Dicky. Granna Kate." Robert thought for a moment or two. "Great-grumpa Tewke, he lives there too."

Emma stood and frowned at the house. A great many people lived in it. Were they all at home today? Its windows, shadowed, gave no clue.

"Why don't you go and knock on the door?"

"No," Robert said. He resisted her shove.

"Are you frightened?" Emma asked.

Robert's gaze was deep and still.

"I ent frightened. No, no not me."

"Why won't you go and knock, then?"

"I don't want to. I want to go home."

"Don't you want to see your auntie Betony?"

"I seen her yesterday, in school."

Emma, reluctantly, turned away. She took the little boy's hand again.

* * * * *

Betony had spent the morning in Chepsworth, selling poppies from door to door, raising money for Earl Haig's Fund founded to help ex-servicemen. For today was the eve of Armistice Day, when people everywhere would remember their dead, and some would spare a thought for the living.

At one house, in Albion Square, a well-dressed woman of middle age sighed as she searched her purse for a coin.

"Five years afterwards," she said, "and we're *still* paying for that dreadful war!"

Across the square, on the other side, two old soldiers stood in the gutter, one on crutches, the other blind. The blind man played an accordion, the man on crutches played a flute. A collection box stood on the ground and on it the one word "Passchendaele."

"*They* are the ones who are still paying," Betony thought as she crossed the square.

Just before lunch-time she was driving through Huntlip on her way home. She had passed over Millery Bridge when she saw the two children, Robert and Emma, coming towards her along the road. She stopped the trap and spoke to them.

"You're a long way from home," she said. "What are you doing right out here?"

"We've been for a walk," Emma said.

"Just by yourselves, the two of you?"

"Yes. We came over Puppet Hill."

Betony looked at the little boy and saw the anxiety in his eyes.

"Does your mother know where you are, Robert?"

"His mother wasn't there," Emma said. "She'd gone out and left him all by himself."

"So you decided to take him for a walk?"

Emma nodded. She looked away. Her small face was blank, abstracted, still.

"You shouldn't have brought him away like that," Betony said quietly. "His mother will worry when she gets home."

"His mother's gone to the shop," Emma said. "We thought we'd meet her on the way." She looked directly at Betony. "You said I was to be his special friend."

"Yes, that's right. So I did."

"I brought him to see you. We went to your house. But Robert was shy. He wouldn't knock."

"Why did you bring him to see me?"

"I don't know. I just thought I would."

"Well," said Betony, hiding a smile, "I think it's time you were both back home."

She took them up into the trap and turned back into the village. There was no sign of Linn on the way. The shop, when they passed it, was closed for lunch. She drove out to School Lane and turned off up Holland Bank. The two children sat close to her, Emma with her sprays of spindleberries cradled in the crook of her arm.

"What beautiful spindleberries – where did you find them?" Betony asked.

"Up by the edge of the old quarry."

"Isn't it dangerous up there?"

"Oh, no," Emma said.

When they reached the track leading off to the farm,

Betony stopped and let the child down.

"Wait, you've left your berries," she said.

She picked up the sprays from the seat of the trap and leant down to give them to the child. Emma refused them. She shook her head.

"I don't want them. I picked them for you."

She turned and went dancing up the track.

Betony, as she drove on, put her arm round the little boy and gave him a reassuring squeeze. His face was still puckered with anxiety and when, on nearing Lilac Cottage, he saw his mother out in the lane, his hand crept into Betony's.

"Where have you *been*, you naughty boy? How dare you disobey me like that?" Linn's angry gaze switched to Betony. She stood accusingly by the trap. "What do you mean by coming here, waiting until my back is turned, and taking my son away with you? I've been worried out of my mind. Coming home to an empty house! Nothing to tell me where he'd gone! If such a thing ever happens again –"

"I didn't take him," Betony said. "He went for a walk with Emma Wayman. It seems she passed here, earlier on, and persuaded Robert to go with her."

"Emma Wayman?" Linn said.

"One of the children from Holland Farm."

"She had no right to do such a thing!"

"They took the pathway over the hill. They thought they'd meet you on your way back from the shop."

"I didn't come across the hill. I had a lift in Ricks's cart."

Linn reached up to her small son and lifted him down with a show of roughness. She leant over him, straightening his clothes.

"You're a naughty boy, going off like that! I've always trusted you before and now you've gone and let me down! I'm disappointed in you. It seems I can't trust you after all."

Robert was silent. He hung his head.

"You'd better go in now and wash your hands." She sent him on his way with a gentle push. "I'll have more to say to you presently."

"Don't be too hard on him," Betony said.

"He really must be made to obey."

"I'm sure it'll never happen again."

"What about this Wayman child? Why should she come and entice him away?"

"I suppose she wanted company. She knows Robert at school, you see, and I asked her to be his special friend."

"What are her family thinking of, letting her wander about like that, right away from her own home?"

"Lots of children go out alone. It isn't so very far after all."

"She's only a little thing, isn't she? Supposing something had happened to her?"

"Nothing did happen," Betony said. "I've just delivered her at the farm."

"But things *do* happen. You know they do. Mr Wayman's wife, for a start. She was suffocated in the mud of a pond, in broad daylight, on a summer's day, and no one around to hear her call. There's a lot of carelessness, if you ask me, up there at Holland Farm."

"You may be right," Betony said. She thought of Emma, out alone, picking sprays of spindleberries from a tree that grew by the edge of the quarry. "Things do happen, as you say."

"Thank you for bringing Robert back. I'm sorry I snapped at you as I did."

"Don't be too severe on him."

Because of the difficulty of turning the trap in the narrow lane, Betony drove straight on and so went homeward by Outlands and Blagg.

* * * * *

On her way down Craisie Lane, she stopped to speak to Fred Cox. Fred worked at Outlands Farm. He was an honest, intelligent man and was secretary of the local branch of his union. Betony knew him and his wife, for they had three children at the school and the eldest boy, Billy John, would almost certainly, next year, win a free place at the Grammar School in Chepsworth. Fred was on his way home from work, his dinner-satchel over his shoulder, a can of milk in his hand. He walked with a heavy, slouching, tread.

"You look down-hearted," Betony said.

"How many people, nowadays, ever look anything else?" he asked.

"Not many, if they work on the land."

"We've had an Irishman's rise this week. That's the second time in six months." He meant that his wages had been reduced. "We're down to twenty-seven-and-six. I feel I could just about jump in the brook."

"What about the local Conciliation Committee? Surely they'd have something to say to that?"

"My master, Mr Challoner, he don't take no account of them. Nor don't Mr Twill of Dunnings neither. Wages there is even worse. They're down to twenty-five bob there."

"Oh, but that's infamous!" Betony said. "Can't your union do anything?"

"Not many chaps belong any more. They can't afford fourpence for the fee. There's only two of us left at Outlands and our days is numbered, I daresay." Fred's voice had tears in it. He was a man at the end of his tether. "What sort of winter's it going to be? No bloody Wages Board any more! No bloody union left to fight! We'll just about be starved off the land!"

Shrugging, he apologized. He made an effort to cast off his gloom. He spoke of the coming General Election.

"We've got a man putting up for Chepsworth. A union man, one of our own. He's worked on the land since he was a boy. Now if *he* could get in we'd be getting somewhere, cos he knows our problems inside out. I want him to hold a meeting here in Huntlip, but with no village hall nor nothing, he says it wouldn't be worth his while. Folk won't stand about out of doors, not in this weather, after dark. Nor they won't trouble theirselves with travelling into Chepsworth neither."

"What about holding it in the school?"

"Should we be able to, do you think?"

"I don't see why not."

"Your board of managers, that's why not! Tories, every one, I bet!"

"Leave it to me," Betony said. "I'll speak to the vicar as soon as I can. You'd better see your candidate and let me know what date you fix. You'll need some posters putting up –"

"I'll see to that! There's no problem there!" Fred's face was quite transformed. Hope had brought him back to life. "Christ, Miss Izzard, you're a brick! Just supposing our man got in?"

"That I can't promise," Betony said. "I haven't even got a vote." She would not be thirty for another two years.

"You would have, by God, if I had my way! If women had the vote at twenty-one, we'd soon see a change of government, and Labour once in would be in for good."

"You seem very confident, anyway."

"If you can get us the use of the school –"

"I shall certainly do my best," she said. "I'll be in touch when I've got some news."

She saluted him and drove away.

When she reached home and drove through the archway into the fold, her father and brother were at the pump, splashing their faces and hands in the trough. They had come from the workshop, covered in sawdust.

"You're late, my blossom," her father said. "Did you bring the paper like I asked?"

"Yes, I've brought it," Betony said.

"I hear there's some Labour chap putting up. He's got a nerve, putting up round here. Why, we've had a Liberal man for Chepsworth ever since never, practically. We've never voted for nobody else. Nobody else ent never stood."

Dicky, going to see the pony, gave his sister a broad grin.

"Dad's not the only one who's got it, you know. It's spreading like wildfire everywhere."

"What are you talking about?" she asked.

"Election fever!" Dicky said.

In the kitchen, when Betony went in, her mother was taking a pie from the oven and granna Kate was mashing the swedes.

"Did you bring my buttons?" Beth asked.

"And my lozenges?" granna asked.

"Yes, I brought them," Betony said. "And great-

116

grumpa's nasal drops."

"Did you sell all your poppies?" Beth asked.

"All except a handful, yes."

"That there Earl Haig!" granna said. "Strikes me he's doing a proper job. I reckon they ought to make him a Sir."

Beth and her daughter exchanged a smile. Granna's sayings were all of a piece. At seventy she was full of her years, and was always a little out of touch with what was going on around. Great-grumpa Tewke, on the other hand, although he was turned ninety-two, was just as astute as granna was vague. He might be stiff in his joints these days; short of breath when he climbed the stairs; but not much escaped his memory. He came into the kitchen now as Dicky came in at the other door.

"Did you finish them trestles for Edgar Mapp?"

"Yes, I finished them," Dicky said.

"Did you take them down to him?"

"I took them down at ten o'clock."

Dicky was rather pleased with himself. He did not always emerge so well from the old man's catechisms. Betony took the opportunity, now that great-grumpa Tewke was there, of mentioning a troublesome fault in the trap.

"That offside tyre is still loose. One of the rivets is nearly out. The tyre was rattling all the way home."

Great-grumpa's head came round at once.

"Ent you fixed that rivet yet? You get it done this afternoon! If need be, take it down to the forge, and get Will Pentland to deal with it."

Dicky, swearing under his breath, took his place at the table, next to Betony.

"There goes my afternoon off!" he said. "Did you have to mention that damned tyre?"

"I wanted it done," Betony said. "I'll be needing the trap in the next few days."

The tyre had been loose for a week or more; Dicky and her father would let things slide; any old day would do for them; it was great-grumpa Tewke who got things done. Although "retired" from the carpenter's business, he always knew what was going on, in the workshop and in the house, and a word from him would still be obeyed.

117

The family sat down to their meal. Beth began to cut the pie. Jesse was still immersed in his paper. He put it away reluctantly and took his place at the foot of the table.

"There's all sorts of chaps putting up this time. Liberal, Conservative, Labour, the lot. Poor Mr Crown will have to fight. I reckon that's hard on a man of his age, after being our Member all these years."

"He'll get in just the same, you mark my words," said great-grumpa Tewke.

"How do you know that?" Betony asked.

"The Liberals have always held Chepsworth, that's why, and that ent a town to change its coat."

Great-grumpa Tewke voted Liberal, as every right-minded person did, and the outcome to him was therefore unquestionable.

* * * * *

"I'm afraid not, Miss Izzard," Mr Netherton said, when Betony called at the vicarage. "The Labour candidate? Oh dear me no! Such a thing would never do."

"What about the other candidates? Will they be allowed to use the school?"

"The matter hasn't arisen," he said. "No one's approached me on that score."

"Supposing they do? How will you answer them?" Betony asked.

"The only promise I can make is to raise the matter with the managers and see how they react to it. But I'm quite certain they will refuse."

"If they disagree with Labour principles, they can always come to the meeting themselves, to voice any criticisms they have."

"Well, speaking for myself, as a Liberal –"

"You would naturally want to hear both sides. Will you come to the meeting if it is held?"

"No, I think not," Mr Netherton said. "As vicar of the parish, you know, I'm afraid my attendance at such a meeting might influence my parishioners."

Secretly Betony doubted it. Mr Netherton had been vicar

of Huntlip for two and a half years and the only effect he had had on his parishioners was to cause them intense irritation. In the pulpit he had great eloquence, but out in the parish he was weak. He tried too hard to please all men and was therefore destined to please almost none.

"If you were to forbid a Labour meeting in the school, however, you might be influencing them in the other direction."

"I neither forbid nor accede, Miss Izzard. The decision is not just mine alone."

"But you could influence the board."

"I'm not sure that I want to do that."

"Mr Netherton," Betony said. "When the General Election is held, the school will be used as a polling station. If people can go there to vote for the Labour candidate, surely they can go there to hear him speak beforehand?"

"I will raise the matter with the managers. That is as far as I will go."

Betony knew he was stalling her. He would leave the matter until it was too late. She therefore went to see Fred Cox and together they planned their course of action. Four days later the posters arrived. She had them put up throughout the village. The vicar met her after school.

"Really, Miss Izzard, I must protest! I did not consent to this meeting of yours –"

"Have you seen the managers?"

"No, not yet, I must admit."

"Would it be better if I saw them myself?"

"You've left it rather late, haven't you, seeing these posters are everywhere?"

"It would certainly be very awkward if the meeting had to be cancelled now. People would say – and there would be some truth in it – that a man had been denied freedom of speech."

Mr Netherton was annoyed.

"You've deliberately forced me into this position, Miss Izzard, and it's no good looking to me for support. It seems I'm obliged to yield to you, but let me say categorically, that I don't for one moment approve of it, and when the managers tackle me – as they surely will – I will make my

119

position clear to them. Furthermore, I hold you personally responsible for the conduct of the meeting in the school, and everything connected with it."

"Yes, of course," Betony said.

Within a few days, many more posters had appeared. The day of the meeting was announced on them as Friday November the twenty-fourth. Tea and refreshments would be served.

One of the posters was nailed to a tree in Rayner's Lane. Chris, who was taking two horses to be shod, stopped in the rain to read what it said, and Gerald Challoner, out shooting, came across the field to him.

"I suppose you'll be going?" he said with a grin.

"What, to hear some socialist spouting rot?"

"Might be fun in it," Gerald said.

"Are you thinking of going, then?"

"There's two or three of us going, my boy. We've got some ideas for making the meeting go with a swing. Coming with us or are you too young?"

"Just try and keep me out, that's all!"

When Chris had gone, leading the horses down the lane, Gerald reached for the rain-soaked poster and pulled it from its nail. He screwed it up into a ball and thrust it into the nearest ditch. It was the third he had dealt with that day.

Chapter 7

The night of the meeting was cold and wet. When Chris arrived at The Black Ram, up on the edge of Huntlip Common, Gerald was there waiting for him, with Jeff Twill of Dunnings, Jackie Franklin of Lucketts End, and David Mapp of Letts. They drank outside, keeping away from the lighted windows, for all of them were under age and their drinks were passed out to them by the maid. When their glasses were empty, Gerald took a look at his watch.

"Eight o' clock! Let's go!" he said, and the five of them set off down the hill, boots pounding the rough stony road.

Chris was among his equals tonight. The five of them, as they strode together, were united by a common bond. They were all farmers' sons, and each boy's father owned his farm. They were little lords of the land, and the knowledge gave them a fine swagger. Laughing and joking, they descended on the village school, where lights shone in the high windows, and where the doors stood fastened back, open to welcome all who came.

* * * * *

Inside the schoolroom, the panelled partition had been removed, and so had all the children's desks. Betony, helped by Fred Cox, had carried everything out to the playground and covered the pile with a canvas sheet. Wooden benches had been brought in, mostly from the workshop at Cobbs, and a table and chairs had been set in front for the speaker and his supporters. On the wall above hung a printed poster: Vote for Bob Treadwell: Vote for Action and Employment. Of the school furniture, only the cupboards and piano remained, and these had been pushed into a corner. Because the night was wet and cold,

121

Betony had kept the stoves alight, and beside each stove stood a scuttle of coals. None of Betony's family were there. Dicky had come, bringing the benches, and had helped to carry them into the school. After that he had gone away.

"Politics is nothing to me. You can have my vote for half-a-crown!"

By half-past-seven, when the candidate arrived, there were fifteen people gathered in the schoolroom, mostly labourers from the farms around. By eight o' clock, when the meeting was timed to begin, a few younger labourers were drifting in, having come, it was plain, from The Rose and Crown. Three of these were dressed in their best and wore Tory blue favours in their coats. Others wore the Liberal yellow and one or two the Labour red.

Betony, standing inside the door, surveyed the assembly. She knew all the people there by sight, and could put names to most of them, especially those who had children at school. There were three men from Holland Farm, two from Outlands, and two from Letts. Fred Cox had brought his wife, and there were three other women there.

"Not much of a turn-out," Fred remarked. "Not for a village the size of Huntlip. Most of these youngsters ent got a vote and as for the rest – Bob'll be preaching to the converted."

"Let's wait a few minutes," Betony said. "Perhaps there'll be some late-comers."

But the only late-comers were the five fresh-faced young farmers' sons, led by Gerald Challoner, who arrived just as the doors were closed and hammered loudly for admittance. They swaggered in, these corduroy lordlings so full of themselves, and stood for a moment glancing about, eyes narrowed against the light. Then they shouldered their way to the front and slumped together on the foremost bench. They were well aware of the pause in the hum of talk around, and the many eyes that were turned their way, and they glanced at each other, smirking and winking, pleased with the stir their arrival had caused.

"Any of your lot here, Chris?" Gerald asked in an undertone. "There's two of ours, needless to say, but I knew *they'd* be here, they're union mad."

Chris looked over his shoulder and counted three of his father's men. Only two of them sat together: Reg Starling and Billy Rye; the other man was Morton George and he sat with Tommy Long of Letts.

"There are three of ours," Chris said. "But only one is a union man. The other two are all right."

"They could still vote Labour, couldn't they?"

"Yes, well, I suppose they could."

At twenty-past-eight the meeting began. Fred Cox, in the chair, introduced the candidate, Bob Treadwell, who arose to the sound of ragged applause.

"Ladies and gentlemen!" he began, and a few young labourers booed at him. He bore it all with a friendly grin and when it was over he began again. "Comrades, I'll say, if you prefer it –"

"Get away!" said a voice from the back. "Get back to Moscow where you belong!"

"Friends, then!" the candidate said.

"We'll have to think about that!" said the voice. "We"ll have to take a vote on it!"

But the candidate made his start at last and spoke for a while without interruption. He had a good voice and a sense of humour and he made his audience of farm-workers laugh by explaining the blue-black mark on his cheek.

"Not, as you might think, a heckler throwing a rotten egg, but a cow I was milking early this morning who was rather careless with her tail!"

Soon, however, he became serious, talking of conditions on the land and unemployment in particular. Something would have to be done, he said, and a Labour government, once elected, would soon show that they knew the answers to the problems.

"Don't we all!" Gerald said, in a tone of heavy sarcasm.

The candidate merely carried on.

"The disgraceful treatment by employers of men, and most especially on the land, where conditions are worsening all the time –"

"Who pays their wages?" Gerald asked.

"Wages?" the candidate replied. "Down to thirty shillings a week and in some cases even less! Does the young

123

gentleman call that a wage?"

"Where would the labourers be without it? You tell us that!" Gerald exclaimed.

"Wages in 1919 were forty-six shillings a week –"

"Prices were higher then," Gerald said. "Now where are they? Down the drain!"

"I know what problems the farmer has to face –"

"The labour problem for a start!"

"The flaming union!" shouted Jeff Twill. "That's one of his problems, to name but a few!"

"If the young gentlemen will hear me out –"

"Yes, let him speak!" said Billy Rye's wife. "He's the one we came to hear, not you half-grown bits of lads!"

"Aren't we allowed to air our views?"

"We know your views! We hear nothing else! The farmers get their say all the time. The papers is full of what they say! So you pipe down and let the man speak!"

"Yes, let the man speak!" Gerald said. "Let's hear what he's got to say about solving our problems for us. How he's going to stop foreign corn –"

"I will come to those things," the candidate said, "but first I want to deal with the labourer –"

"Let's deal with *him* by all means!" Jackie Franklin said with a sneer.

"No problems are going to be solved while conflict continues to exist between the farmer and his men."

` "Who causes the conflict?" Chris demanded. He felt it was time he had his say. "The union causes it by sowing discontent! The average labourer would be happy enough if it weren't for the union stirring him up."

"Happy be blowed!" said one of the men from Lucketts End. "It's up to us to say whether we're happy or not!"

"You're still wet behind the ears, young fella," said an elderly man, just behind Chris. "You want to go back home to your dad and wait till you've growed up a bit before you start talking on our behalf."

After a while, order of some sort was restored, and the candidate began again. But he had not proceeded far when Gerald, turning to his friends, spoke out in a loud voice.

"Not much of an audience here, is it, in spite of all the

posters about? I expected a lot more folk than this. It's hardly worth the poor chap's trouble."

"If I could perhaps be allowed to proceed –"

"Just a minute!" Gerald said. "Two of my friends don't feel too well."

He nudged Jeff Twill and Jackie Franklin, and the two of them lumbered to their feet. Each held a handkerchief to his mouth, and, making a great deal of noise and fuss, left the schoolroom and slammed the door.

"Where have they gone?" whispered Chris.

"You'll see in a minute," Gerald said.

"My object in coming here tonight," the candidate went on in a ringing voice, "is to offer some hope, some ray of light, to those who are groping in the darkness and gloom enveloping our country at this time." Pausing, somewhat surprised at the silence, he took the chance of a deep breath. "My party *is* that ray of light. . . ."

* * * * *

Betony, at the back of the room, sitting with Billy Rye and his wife, listened with only half an ear. She was worried about the two young men who had just gone out.

"I don't think we've seen the last of them. I think I'll go out and lock the porch door."

Billy half rose to accompany her, but Betony motioned him to stay. She walked quietly to the door and passed through into the porch, which was lit by a single hurricane lamp hanging from a beam in the roof above. The outer doors were still fastened back, but before she had time to loosen the hooks, there was a sudden scurry outside and three wet sheep pattered into the porch. They were quickly followed by five or six more and coming behind them, urging them in, were the two young men, Twill and Franklin.

"Get these animals out at once!" Betony cried furiously. She stood in the way, trying to turn them. "Do you hear me? Get them out!"

But Jeff Twill, ignoring her, was already opening the inner door, and Jackie Franklin, wielding a stick, was driving the sheep into the schoolroom. They lolloped in, confused and frightened, blinded by the glare of light, their ears back and their eyes rolling. Seeing the people gathered there, they came to a halt, defensively, and one or two of the older ewes stamped with a fore-foot on the floor. Gerald Challoner and David Mapp now sprang up with a loud halloo. They darted forward with arms outstretched and sent the sheep lurching around the room.

"That's more like it! Here they come! Are they all good union members? Make way for them, it's only fair! They've got a right to have their say and bleat along with the rest of you!"

The frightened sheep went careering about, and most of the audience rose at once, trying to shove them towards the door. The benches, thus vacated, were sent toppling in all directions, and one of them, sliding along the floor, struck two young men behind the knees, bringing them down together in a tumbled heap. Angrily they scrambled up and lunged towards Chris and Gerald. Chris got a stinging blow on the mouth and Gerald was hurled against the stove. Bellowing because he was burnt, Gerald rushed towards his attackers, but was knocked down and winded by one of the ewes. David Mapp and Jackie Franklin were wrestling with two young labourers and were getting the worst of it by far. Chris mopped the blood from a cut on his lip and reluctantly went to their aid. The noise by now was terrible. The whole of the schoolroom was in an uproar.

The older men, such as Fred Cox and Billy Rye, were doing their best to catch the sheep and hurl them out through the open door, and their womenfolk were trying to help by driving the sheep in the right direction. But the younger men were out of hand. They had formed themselves into two camps, one at either end of the room, and were pelting each other with coal from the scuttles. One young man, Leslie Smith by name, having snatched up a chair that came flying his way, had seated himself at the school piano and, in the manner of a cinema pianist, was playing a spirited accompaniment to the mêlée around him.

The battle raged across the room, and there was a crash of splintering glass as a lump of coal went through a window. The music came to a sudden stop, and the young pianist looked down in surprise as blood dripped into his lap from a cut in his forehead, neatly opened by flying glass. Chris, during a lull in the battle, saw the pianist's bloodied face and watched as a woman led him away. The sight of the blood made him feel sick. He wished he had never come to the meeting. Gerald and Jeff Twill, he saw, had opened one of the school cupboards and were hurling inkwells across the room.

The sheep were driven out at last. Three men went with them across the playground to drive them down to the village pound. Billy Rye sent his son to fetch the constable from Slings, and the candidate, on hearing this, thought it was time he slipped away. His motor car was brought to the door.

The coal-slinging battle was at its height when someone shouted: "The constable's coming!" Hostilities ceased miraculously. The opposing factions skeltered away.

"Come on, let's go!" Gerald said, and his fellow lordlings, with blackened faces and hands and clothes, joined him in a rush for the door. Chris for a moment hesitated. Then he too followed the rest, taking to the fields in the wind and the rain.

By the time the constable arrived, only the older men remained, with Betony and three of the wives. The constable opened his little book and listened to the story he was told.

"There was five of the young sods altogether, but my young master from Outlands, like, he was the ringleader," Johnny Marsh said.

"It was the young chap from Dunnings, though, that went and brought in the bloody sheep. Him and that cross-eyed lout from Letts."

"They all came together, the five of them. You could see they meant mischief the moment they walked in at that there door."

"Ah, and my master's son was one of them, the cheeky young swine!" said Morton George.

"Names, if you please," the constable said.

He knew well enough who the culprits were, from these

127

remarks bandied about, but he had to observe the formalities and write in his notebook as informed. So the five names were given to him: Gerald Challoner; Jeffery Twill; Christopher Wayman; Jackie Franklin; David Mapp.

"All farmers' sons," the constable said. "And these are the ones you say are to blame?"

"They are the ones that started it, there's no doubt of that," said Fred Cox. "We was having a quiet meeting here and they was determined to break it up. They're the ones to blame all right. No two ways about none of that."

But Betony, when they had all gone and she stood alone in the empty schoolroom, surveying the wreckage and the dirt, knew that as far as the vicar was concerned she and she alone would be held to blame for what had happened there that night.

She put on her hat and coat and scarf, turned out the last of the lamps in the room, and quietly let herself out of the school. She locked the door on the chaos within and walked away towards the village. She went at once to the vicarage.

* * * * *

Mr Netherton heard her through with an angry tightening of his lips and a gathering of colour in his cheeks. He sat without moving in his chair.

"I was against it from the start. I don't have to remind you of that, I hope? And now you see the sad result of flying in the face of my opinion."

"You can't have foreseen what would happen tonight?"

"I lay no claim to such a thing, but a Labour meeting such as this –"

"It was those who support the opposite side who caused all the trouble," Betony said.

"The inescapable fact is that if you had regarded my views on the matter, none of this would ever have happened."

"I shall of course take full responsibility for all the necessary repairs."

"I'm afraid the matter will not end there."

"No. I didn't think it would."

128

"As soon as this regrettable affair is known to the school managers, they will come to me for an explanation, and I shall have no alternative but to tell them the truth: that you went against me in this matter and allowed the school to be used for this meeting without my approval or my consent. I have no doubt that the consequences for you will be very grave."

"How grave?" Betony asked.

"I'm very much afraid, Miss Izzard, that after what has happened tonight, the managers are bound to feel that you should be asked for your resignation."

"And what if I refuse to give it?"

"The chances are that you will be dismissed."

"Will that be the course you recommend when meeting the managers?" Betony asked.

"I certainly don't feel that I can speak up on your behalf, either to the managers or to the education secretary when I see him. How can you expect such a thing when you went against me so wilfully?"

Betony rose and drew on her gloves.

"I don't expect it, Mr Netherton, and I wouldn't dream of asking it."

She said goodnight and took her leave.

When she got home it was past ten o' clock, and the faces of her family, waiting up, told her that they had heard the news. The incident, apparently, was all over Huntlip. Dicky had heard of it at The Rose and Crown. Jesse, her father, was much disturbed.

"Whatever possessed you, my blossom," he said, "to let that Labour chap speak in the school?"

"Why shouldn't he speak?" Betony said. "He speaks for the hungry, the unemployed."

Jesse shifted in his chair.

"I know there's a lot of talk these days about poverty on the land and that, but I dunno that it's really so bad as some of these Labour chaps make out."

"Don't you, father?" Betony said. "Haven't you seen those half-starved men tramping the lanes hereabouts as they go from one workhouse to the next? Haven't you had them in the yard, offering to do a day's work for a bite of

129

bread and a bowl of stew? Even those who *are* in jobs – have you any idea how much they earn? Have you seen their wives, as thin as laths, old and grey before their time? I've got children in my school whose only breakfast before they leave home is a slice of bread dipped in the water that has boiled an egg for their father's dinner!"

"All right, girl!" great-grumpa said. "No need to get in such a lather about it. There's always been poverty in the world. Hungry folks ent nothing new."

"You'd better tell my father that. He seems to think it's a fairy tale."

"About this meeting," Jesse said.

But Betony had had enough. She made her excuses and went to bed.

* * * * *

Chris, going home after leaving the school, loitered for a time in the cartshed, watching the windows of the house. He waited until they were all in darkness before he stole quietly in to his bed. The following morning, at five o' clock, he arose after a sleepless night and took himself off across the fields, lit only by a sprinkling of stars. He still had a lot to think about but when he returned, an hour later, his mind was not much clarified.

News of the incident at the school reached the farm just before six, when the men arrived at the milking-sheds. Morton George spoke to Stephen about it, and Stephen went in search of Chris. He found him in the kitchen, drinking a cup of hot sweet tea.

"Have you got something to tell me?" he asked.

"I daresay you've heard it from Morton George!"

"It would have been better if you'd told me yourself."

"I needed time to think things out."

"I hear you behaved disgracefully, you and young Challoner and the rest. A pack of hooligans, raising Cain! If it was only half as bad as Morton George says it was, you've got some explaining to do, my boy."

"It *was* pretty bad," Chris said. He stared miserably into the fire. "Everything somehow got out of hand."

"Was there much damage done to the school?"

"I don't know. I daresay there was. Somebody let the sheep in, you see, and after that there was hell to pay."

"Were you a party to all this?"

"I had nothing to do with the sheep, but I'm naming no names," Chris said.

"I know all the names. Be sure of that."

"We only intended it as a lark. We went to heckle, and what's wrong with that? You should have heard that Labour chap and all the rot he talked last night!"

"There's only one thing to be said for these piffling excuses of yours! – At least they show you have some sense of shame!"

Stephen was angry, a rare thing when dealing with his children, and he looked at Chris with hot, hard dislike.

"Had you been drinking at all?" he asked "Morton George seemed to think you had."

"One pint, that's all, outside The Black Ram."

"I won't have you drinking at *any* pub, inside or outside or anywhere else! You're only fifteen. It's against the law."

"It's a damn silly law, if you ask me."

"I am *not* asking you!" Stephen said. "I'm not interested in your views on *anything* till you show some signs of maturity. And as a first step towards that end, you can go in due course and call on Miss Izzard, and apologize for your behaviour last night."

"But I can't do that! I simply *can't!*"

"Oh yes you can. Indeed I insist."

"Well, I'm not going to!" Chris exclaimed.

"Then I must do it for you, that's all. I shall have to see her in any case, but it seems I shall also have to explain that my eldest son, although fifteen, is too much of a coward to make his own apologies."

Stephen returned to the milking-sheds and worked there until eight o'clock. He then went in to his breakfast; washed and shaved with extra care; and changed out of his working-clothes. Chris had taken himself off again. The younger children were eating their porridge. Aunt Doe saw Stephen as far as the door.

"What's all the atmosphere about?"

131

"I haven't got time to tell you now. I'll tell you later, when I come back. Or, if my eldest son comes in, you can ask *him* what it's all about!"

But aunt Doe did not have to wait for Chris. She heard the story from Mrs Bessemer.

* * * * *

Because it was Saturday, Stephen intended to walk out to Cobbs, expecting Miss Izzard to be at her home, right at the farthest end of the village. On nearing the school, however, he saw that the doors were wide open and that chairs and benches stood outside. So he crossed the playground and went in.

Inside the schoolroom, Betony, with a broom and shovel, was sweeping up the coal that littered the floor and putting it back into the scuttles. Most of the coal was dust by now, trodden into the wood-block floor, with the sheep-dung and the broken glass and the bits of broken inkwells. Stephen looked round, grim-faced. He saw the black marks on the white-painted walls, where the flying lumps of coal had exploded, and he saw that the coloured posters and maps and the pictures painted by the children had been taken down, torn and blackened, to lie in a pile on the teacher's desk. Betony stopped what she was doing and turned to face him. Her eyes in the light from a nearby window were a very clear bright shade of blue.

"I hardly know how to start," he said, "except that I've come to apologize."

"On behalf of your son?"

"I hope, when he's had time to think, he will come and apologize for himself. At the moment he's too ashamed. But I'd like to make it quite clear that, whatever the cost of the damage done, I expect to pay the bill."

"Your son wasn't the only hooligan involved, Mr Wayman. He was merely one of a group. As for the damage done here, my brother is coming in to paint the walls and replace the window-pane, but thank you for offering all the same."

"Isn't there anything I can do to ease my conscience in

132

this matter?"

"I'm more concerned with my own feelings at the moment, Mr Wayman, rather than giving relief to yours."

"I share your anger, I assure you, especially now that I see this mess."

"Your son is very young to be taking such an interest in politics."

"Much too young, I quite agree."

"He's against socialism and the union. It seems he's against free speech as well. Does he take his stand from you?"

"If he does," Stephen said, "he much mistakes my attitudes."

"You're not against the union yourself?"

"The one union man I've got on my farm is a poor advertisement for the rest. You must make allowances for my son if he takes a somewhat jaundiced view."

"On some of the farms in this district, men run the risk of losing their jobs if they join the union, so I'm told."

"There's bound to be prejudice, I suppose."

He knew there was truth in what she said, but he did not wish to be drawn into an argument concerning his neighbours' actions, and he therefore looked for another subject. He turned to the pile of children's paintings lying, tattered, on the desk.

"Will they be upset, seeing their pictures spoilt?" he asked.

"They will no doubt be puzzled," Betony said, "at the strange behaviour of their elders and betters."

"Is there anything of Emma's here?"

"No, there's nothing, I'm afraid. She did have a picture put up in class, but she took it down and threw it away."

"Why did she do that?"

"She told Miss Vernon that it wasn't good enough."

There was a pause. Betony looked at him absently. She leant her broom against the wall, and dropped her shovel into the scuttle. With her hands in the pockets of her pinafore, she turned again, considering him.

"You are interested in Emma's school work, then, Mr Wayman?"

"That's a strange question to ask, isn't it, seeing that I'm her father?" he said.

"You were not at our Parents' Day last Friday. That's why I ask."

"I didn't know it was Parents' Day."

"Every parent was sent a note. The children wrote them out themselves. They copied the words from the blackboard."

"I never had mine. I must ask the child what became of it."

"Would you have come, if you'd known in time?"

"I might have done, certainly. A lot would depend on the work of the farm –"

Stephen broke off, looking at her. He saw that her smile was sceptical.

"Miss Izzard," he said in a gentle tone, "are you taking me to task?"

Betony chose her words with care.

"Emma seems a lonely child. She doesn't seem to have any friends. It's all right while she's in school . . . She talks to the other children here . . . but out of school it's a different matter and she seems at a loss for something to do. Forgive me for saying so, Mr Wayman, but I don't think she ought to be allowed to wander about by herself so much."

Stephen's feelings were beginning to change. Amusement was yielding to irritation.

"I don't think I neglect my children, Miss Izzard, if that is what you are trying to say."

"Perhaps neglect is too strong a word –"

"Use whichever word you like so long as you say what you really mean!"

"Seeing that your eldest son is running wild, it shouldn't be too difficult to understand what I mean."

"Running wild?" Stephen said. "That is something of an exaggeration! Chris as a rule works very hard. He works a full day on the farm with me. Last night was the first occasion of its kind and if the Labour candidate who addressed your meeting had not been so provocative –"

"What he said was only the truth."

"Part of the truth, but not the whole."

"How do you know? You weren't there."

"I've heard Bob Treadwell speak in the town. He neglects the farmer's point of view. The prices we're getting for our produce now –"

"Do you know what wages are paid at Outlands these days?"

"My neighbour, Mr Challoner, –"

"Do you know what they are at Dunnings?"

"I know what they ought to be," Stephen said.

"They're down to twenty-five shillings."

"How do you know about these things?"

"I make it my business to know!" she said.

Once again there was a pause. They looked at each other, and each drew breath.

"I've always heard you were a firebrand, Miss Izzard, and now I begin to see it's true."

"Then it may satisfy you to know that because of what happened here last night I may well lose my job."

"What?" Stephen said. He was appalled. "What in heaven's name makes you think that?"

"The vicar made it plain to me when I went to see him last night. And now, if you will excuse me, I do have rather a lot to do."

"But this is unheard-of!" Stephen said. "I really must get the matter clear."

"I'm sorry, Mr Wayman, but I haven't got time. My brother is coming in at ten and I have to get this room clean enough for him to start work." She took up her shovel and her broom. "Thank you for coming on your son's behalf. It was kind of you to take the trouble."

As she began to sweep again, the coal-dust rose and hung on the air, the particles glistening in the pale sunlight. She was intent on what she was doing. Stephen felt himself dismissed. He stood for a moment, watching her, then swung away and left the school.

* * * * *

He went straight to the vicarage and was shown into the vicar's study.

"What's all this about Miss Izzard losing her job? You

surely can't be serious. Where's your good sense?"

Mr Netherton was taken aback. He drew up a chair for Stephen to sit.

"I feel that Miss Izzard acted irresponsibly in allowing the meeting at the school. She chose to ignore my considered advice. I knew the managers would be incensed when they heard about the disgraceful affair and I warned her last night what the probable outcome would be. I've already had Major Jeans here this morning, with Mrs Talbot of Crayle Court, and they both insisted that I should call a special meeting of the managers for Monday next at twelve o' clock. Miss Izzard will be required to give an account of herself and as she is quite unrepentant I'm afraid they will ask for her resignation."

"I am one of the managers," Stephen said, "and I shall ask for no such thing."

"The major made his feelings plain. So did Mrs Talbot, needless to say. And some of the other managers, I'm sure, will feel that Miss Izzard ought to go."

"Then it's up to us to change their minds!"

"Is it?" said the vicar, doubtfully.

"She's good at her job, isn't she?"

"Well, of course, there's never been any question about that."

"Then we should be foolish to let her go."

Stephen sat quiet for a while, watching the vicar as he polished his glasses. Then he spoke again with vehemence.

"If Miss Izzard is dismissed I shall resign from the school board and make known my reasons for doing so. I may tell you also, speaking from my knowledge of the law, that Miss Izzard might well have grounds for bringing an action against the managers for wrongful dismissal. The education secretary would probably support her in such a course. *I* certainly would!"

"Wrongful dismissal?" the vicar said.

"I shall go along and see Mrs Talbot straight away and do my best to talk some sense into her. I shall see Major Jeans and the other managers, too, if need be."

"It would appear that you feel very strongly about this matter, Mr Wayman."

"My son was one of the troublemakers. No doubt you've heard who the others were. Is Miss Izzard to lose her job because of the bad behaviour of a handful of boys? No, Mr Netherton, it will not do!"

"Yes, well, I begin to think you're right," Mr Netherton said. He rather liked Stephen Wayman because Stephen, alone of the farmers in the parish, never grumbled about paying his tithes. "I will certainly speak for her at Monday's meeting and that, together with your eloquent representations, should sway the rest of the board, I think."

"I should damn well hope it does indeed!"

"Nevertheless, there are still grounds for criticism, I think, in that Miss Izzard allowed the school to be used for a political meeting without obtaining the board's consent. I feel therefore that when she is called before us on Monday she should receive a reprimand."

Stephen got up and went to the door. He had a full morning in front of him.

"Reprimand her if you must but I will not be present at the meeting to witness such a piece of flummery."

Walking through the village, out towards Crayle, he smiled to himself in a wry way. His concern for her feelings at Monday's meeting was probably quite unnecessary. It would take more than the vicar's reprimand to put *that* young woman out of countenance, he thought.

* * * * *

In the attic at Holland Farm, Joanna and Jamesy were trying on costumes for their play. Chris, with his hands in his breeches pockets, sat on a corner of the table, watching them as they flounced to and fro.

"What's the good of choosing the clothes when you haven't even written the play?"

"We've written some of it," Jamesy said. "It's the Second Act we're stymied on."

"If you're so clever," Joanna said, sweeping Chris with a swirl of her cloak, "why don't you help with writing it?"

"I've got better things to do."

"Such as smashing up poor Emma's school?"

137

"Sssh!" said Jamesy, with a warning glance, but Emma, rummaging in aunt Doe's tin trunk, gave no sign of having heard.

Chris slid from the edge of the table and slouched about the room. He picked up Jamesy's cardboard cutlass, gruesomely stained with crimson paint, and tried on Jamesy's three-cornered hat. More than once he glanced at his watch. It was almost eleven o' clock. He went to one of the barred windows and stood looking down over the fields. His father was coming up the track.

"Where are you off to?" Jamesy asked.

"Never you mind," Chris said.

He left the playroom and hurried downstairs. He met his father in the yard.

"Well, I've had a busy morning of it, thanks to you," Stephen said. "I've seen the headmistress of the school. I've seen the vicar and three of the other managers, and I've seen the young man whose face was cut by glass last night. I've also called on the constable."

Stephen looked pointedly at his son. Deliberately he paused, waiting, and Chris at length muttered his thanks.

"You'll be relieved to know that the young man with the cut face is recovering from the shock and bears nobody any grudge," Stephen said. "You'll also be relieved to hear that no summons will be brought against you for the damage you did to the school. The constable will be calling on you to give you a piece of his mind, but otherwise there will be no action from the law, because no one intends to bring any charge."

"What about the headmistress? I bet she had plenty to say!"

"She said nothing that wasn't deserved. She called you a hooligan, and so you are. But you may be interested to know that she blames me as much as you. She thinks I neglect you and let you run wild."

"Oh, what rot!" Chris exclaimed.

Hands thrust into his pockets, he stood without speaking for a while, kicking a stone with the toe of his boot.

"I've been thinking over what you said, about making my apologies to her. There's no sense in putting it off. I'd better get it over with, hadn't I?"

"If you go straight away," Stephen said, "you'll probably find her still at the school."

Chris went swinging away down the track. Somehow his mood was lighter now. He felt he could do almost anything. Phrases were forming in his mind.

As Stephen turned towards the house, little Emma came running out.

"I've been talking to your headmistress," he said. "She says you had a note for me, about the Parents' Day last week. What happened to it, I wonder?"

Emma frowned. It seemed she had trouble in remembering.

"I must've lost it on the way home."

"That was careless, wasn't it? But why didn't you tell me about the note? You could easily have remembered what it said."

"It was only about the Parents' Day."

"Didn't you want me to come to it?"

"I didn't want aunt Doe to come."

"Why ever not?" Stephen asked.

But it was easy to guess why not. Aunt Doe was a figure of fun. Fond though the children were of her, she was a source of embarrassment to them. They would grow out of it in time.

"Very well. You run along. But mind you take care of any notes you have for me in future."

When he had gone, Emma went across the yard and let herself into the little orchard, where the rows of hen-coops stood and the chickens were pecking about in the grass. She opened the lid of a nesting-box and looked inside it in search of eggs.

* * * * *

Standing outside the school door, Chris could hear voices from within, and the sound of a scrubbing-brush in use. For an instant he thought of turning back; he hadn't bargained for an audience; but while he stood indecisively, watching the smoke from a pile of rubbish burning on the waste-ground by the sheds, Betony came out of the school with a bucket of water to throw down the drain. Seeing the boy, she came to a halt. She knew who he was. She left him to speak.

"I say!" he exclaimed, swallowing. "I'm terribly sorry about all this! Last night and everything, I mean, and all the mess!"

"So you should be sorry," she said.

"I'd no idea it would turn out like that. If I'd known beforehand about the sheep –"

"Would you have stopped it?" Betony asked.

"Yes! I would most certainly! It was a rotten thing to do!"

"I suppose your father sent you here?"

"I know I ought to have come before but I was in a bit of a state and I wanted to think out what to say."

"At least you have come. None of the other hooligans have. Not so far, anyway."

No, nor would they, Chris thought. Gerald, David, Jackie, Jeff: *they* would never apologize; and he suddenly felt himself better than they. Though younger in years, he was more mature. He had learnt a few things about himself during the course of his sleepless night. He knew that Gerald and the rest were not the friends he really wanted.

"I would like, if I may, to make an apology on their behalf." Words were coming more fluently now. He sensed that he had her sympathy. "I would also like to say that I think it's jolly decent of you to take it all so well as you have."

Betony inclined her head. A smile hovered about her lips. Chris sent a glance towards the school.

"I wondered if I could give you a hand with clearing up the mess in there."

"I've got plenty of helpers, thanks, mostly people who were here last night. The cleaning is very nearly done."

"I'll be getting along, then. I've got a few more calls to make and a lot more apologizing to do."

"You'll find it easier," Betony said, "now that you've had a bit of practice."

Chris gave a grin and walked away. Then he stopped and retraced his steps.

"We're doing a play at Christmas time. My sister and

brother and I, that is. I suppose you wouldn't care to come?"

Betony hesitated, thinking of the angry words that had passed between his father and herself, earlier that morning. She thought, too, of the threat to her job. But clearly the boy knew nothing of that.

"Thank you," she said, "I will certainly come."

"That's really very decent of you. I'll let you know when we've fixed the date."

He walked away with a jaunty step. An unpleasant duty had been accomplished and had not been so difficult after all. Next on the list, he told himself, was a visit to the village constable.

Close upon lunch-time, when he got home, he sought out Jamesy and Joanna, who were still busy up in the attic, painting an old calico sheet as a backcloth, all sea and sky and black scudding clouds.

"I say, you two! We've got to get our skates on, you know, if we're to put on that play for Christmas. I've invited someone to come and see it."

"Who?" said his sister and brother together.

"Miss Izzard, that's who," Chris said.

"Cripes!" Jamesy said, making a face. He splashed white paint on his foaming green sea.

Joanna handed Chris her notes.

"It's up to you to write Act II."

* * * * *

The schoolroom was filled with the smell of wet paint. Dicky worked quickly and with skill, disguising the smudges and scars on the walls. Betony's other helpers had gone. The wood-block floor had been scrubbed clean, and she was on her hands and knees, with a brush, a cloth, and a tin of polish.

At one o'clock they stopped for lunch. There were sandwiches and cherry cake. The day was reasonably mild, and they thought they would eat their lunch outside, sitting on one of the benches there.

"Hello, what's this?" Dicky said. "Someone's been in and

we never heard."

On the table in the porch lay a tiny spray of winter jasmine, just beginning to come into flower, and beside it three brown chicken's eggs, lying in a nest of crumpled paper.

"One of your kids, who wishes to remain anonymous?"

"I know who it is, though, all the same."

"Teacher's perks, eh?" Dicky said. "You'd better make the most of them if you're going to get the push next week."

* * * * *

By Monday morning, the schoolroom was restored to order again, and a few new pictures hung on the walls. Miss Vernon, smelling the new paint, had to be given an explanation, and her pupils, who had heard all about the rumpus at the meeting on Friday night, were able to fill in the details for her, which they did with some embell-ishments.

Betony approached Emma in the playground to thank her for the eggs and the spray of jasmine.

"How did you know it was me?" Emma asked.

"Ah, now, I wonder!" Betony said.

At twelve o' clock, in the course of her luncheon break, she presented herself at the vicarage and stood before a meeting of the school board, specially convened for the purpose and chaired by Mr Netherton. The managers had plenty to say and Betony heard them through in silence. To her surprise, the vicar spoke in her defence, and nobody asked for her resignation. When she emerged at a quarter past twelve, she was still headmistress of Huntlip School.

"How did it go?" Miss Vernon asked, coming to meet her in the playground.

"I was given a reprimand," Betony said.

Chapter 8

It was Saturday, the First of December, a day of keen winds and sharp stinging showers. From the steps of the Corn Exchange the Member of Parliament for Chepsworth, Mr James Crown, was addressing a gathering of some three score of his constituents, reminding them that in five days' time they would be asked to cast their votes. Mr Crown had been Member for Chepsworth for seventeen years. His election campaigns had been smooth and painless. He had never had to fight for his seat, and he was unused to the cut-and-thrust, the pertinent question, the jeers and abuse and derisive laughter that were coming his way from the crowd this morning.

And the one person who had started it all was a young woman, apparently alone, dressed in a bottle-green coat with a high collar and a pillbox hat trimmed with fur. Being only of medium height and surrounded mostly by men, she had climbed onto the edge of a horse-trough, and was thus head and shoulders above the crowd, looking stright across at the Member for Chepsworth. Her questions rang out across the town square and Mr Crown had the greatest difficulty in following the speech he had prepared. It was pretty much the same speech he had made in previous election campaigns. His simple beliefs were embodied in it. It had always been heard with respect until now.

"Would the fair-haired young lady in dark green – who is wearing a very entertaining hat – be good enough to repeat her question?"

And the young lady, quite unmoved by the compliment, was only too willing to oblige. The questions came, thick and fast, and Mr Crown was kept busy. Would he say that the coalition government, during its term of office, had done well by the unemployed? Was he reasonably well

143

satisfied with the sight of ex-servicemen begging their bread in the town's gutters? And could he promise, if returned to his seat again, that these atrocious conditions would be maintained and that perhaps a new and even worse record might be achieved?

Stephen stood at the back of the crowd, having come from some business in Millichip Street. James Crown was known to him: he owned an estate at Newton Childe and farmed six hundred acres of it himself; Stephen had sometimes bought sheep from him. Crown was a good enough man in his way; he scarcely deserved his fate here today; and Stephen, smiling to himself, braced his back against the wind and settled down to watch and listen. Betony Izzard was now asking questions about conditions on the land.

"Why is there no national insurance for farm workers?"

"Because they don't need it," the Member said. "There is plenty of work on the land."

"Take us to it!"a man shouted, and a few others took up the cry.

"You are a landowner, Mr Crown," Betony said in her clear-ringing voice. "Will you give these men a job?"

"I already employ more than twenty men."

"How much do you pay them?" Betony asked.

"They don't complain!" the Member said.

"It seems to me you're evading the question. What are the wages on your farm?"

"I think we're getting away from the point —"

"Why don't you answer?" Betony asked. "Is it because the wages you pay your men would not satisfy the Conciliation Committee?"

There was a ripple in the crowd, and a dozen voices began to chant, "Answer her! Answer her! Answer, answer, answer her!" The Member suddenly became aware of the cold; he hunched his shoulders and buttoned up his coat; and at that moment the rain came down, cold and white and saturating, dispersing the crowd to the shelter of doorways, here and there about the square.

Stephen, as the crowd thinned, ran across to the Corn Exchange and sheltered under its portico, with James

Crown and his canvassers.

"Take courage, man!" he said. "The elements are on your side!"

Betony Izzard, he could see, was sharing an elderly man's umbrella, between two buttresses of St Winifred's church.

"That young woman!" Crown exclaimed. "I wish the rain would drive her off home!"

"Has she got you rattled?" Stephen asked.

"It's all very well for you to jeer. I've never had much of this before. It's always been a clean, straightforward affair, and I've always been allowed to say my piece."

"I can see she's been giving you a rough ride."

"Young woman like that! You'd think she had something better to do. If I had a daughter as troublesome as that, I'd keep her at home under lock and key!"

"I happen to be acquainted with her. I'll see if I can take her off your hands."

"Do that," Crown said, "and I'll send you a couple of brace of pheasants."

"Right, it's a bargain," Stephen agreed.

As the shower eased, and people emerged again into the square, Stephen went across to St Winifred's and met Betony coming away.

"Miss Izzard!" he said, raising his cap. "This is a very pleasant surprise."

"Is it?" she said, sceptically.

"For me it is, anyway. Will you come and have coffee with me?"

"I'm sorry, Mr Wayman, I don't think I can. There are certain things I want to do."

"Perhaps you're still out of charity with me. We exchanged some sharp words the last time we met. But our argument was cut short and I'll be glad of the chance to pick up the threads."

He could see the reluctance in her face. She was glancing across the town square to where James Crown, on the Corn Exchange steps, had a crowd in front of him again.

"I would also be glad of the chance to talk about Emma."

"What about her?" Betony asked.

"Come and have coffee," he said again, and this time she

agreed.

* * * * *

"The thing about places like this," he said, looking around the tiny teashop, "is that they are citadels of femininity and men are only allowed in on sufferance."

"Women will not be satisfied, however, until they have stormed and taken a few of the citadels guarded so jealously by men."

"You are a socialist, Miss Izzard?"

"I don't have a vote yet, Mr Wayman, so it hardly matters what I am. But in fact I haven't made up my mind."

"You held a socialist meeting in your school."

"It was a meeting of *people*," she said. "Anyone was welcome – even farmers."

Stephen smiled.

"It's a great pity I didn't come. But I take little interest in politics."

"You vote, however, I daresay."

"Surely you don't grudge me that?"

"You grudge it to *me*," Betony said.

"*I* do?" he said, much astonished. "It's hardly my doing that women can't vote till the age of thirty."

But the truth was, as he had to admit, that his thoughts on the subject had never been clarified, even to himself. It amused him to think of women having the vote; he couldn't understand why they wanted it, since men took care of things like that; but in fact he had more respect for women than many men did who were loud in support of equality. His own attitude to women was such that he didn't see why they should want more freedom than he already extended to them. He tried to explain this to Betony.

"My household is ruled by women," he said. "By my cousin, Miss Skeine, on the one hand, and by Mrs Bessemer on the other. But I don't storm *their* citadels. I merely take refuge in the barn."

Betony smiled. She was used to this kind of chaffing patronage. But she would not make the mistake, as some women did, of pursuing the subject in seriousness merely

146

that men might be amused.

"Most women don't want to rule their menfolk, Mr Wayman. They ask only to rule themselves."

"I'm glad you agreed to have coffee with me. It shows you bear me no grudge, after all, for my son's behaviour at the meeting last week."

"I have no reason to bear you or your son a grudge. I am not to lose my post after all. But, as one of the managers, you must already know that."

"As one of the managers, and the father of a child at the school, I am extremely glad to hear it."

He did not mention his own part in influencing the rest of the board. In fact it hardly crossed his mind. He was watching her as she poured the coffee.

"I've been thinking over what you said about Emma being neglected," he said. "I've got three other children, as you know, and Emma is very much their pet. She gets her fair share of spoiling, I assure you, but she's a lot younger than the others and she does get left out of their games, I'm afraid."

"That's why she wanders off alone."

"I asked her about the note you mentioned and she said she lost it on the way home." He helped himself to sugar and stirred it round in his coffee. "I don't think she wanted any of her family to come to the Parents' Day. I get the feeling that she wants to keep her new school all to herself. Don't ask me why. It's a mystery to me. You probably understand her better than I do."

"Emma is not yet in my class, but I keep an eye on her, of course, and Miss Vernon talks to me about her. Emma, like all children, wants attention, but sometimes, when she's got it, she retires into herself."

Betony drank the last of her coffee and set down her cup.

"I feel I should withdraw that charge of neglect, Mr Wayman. It was made somewhat hastily and I apologize."

"You spoke as you found," Stephen said. "I hope you will always do that."

There was a pause, and he drank his coffee. Betony refilled his cup and when he took it from her she noticed for the first time that the fingers and thumb of his right hand were twisted and scarred.

"I was hit by shrapnel," he explained. "But the hand still works reasonably well. There aren't many jobs I can't do on the farm. It's a bit stiff in winter, unfortunately, and then the cows don't like me milking them. The milk comes out crooked, my cowman says."

"Where were you, in the war?"

"Flanders, first, and then the Somme. Sezerincourt and Mametz Wood. I was gassed a bit at St Hélène. It left me with a husky voice."

Betony nodded. She had heard that huskiness in men's voices before; had seen many scars like those that puckered Stephen's hand; and had seen that tiredness which even now, six years afterwards, was like a shadow at the back of his eyes. And suddenly she remembered, with a cold sense of shock, that this was the man whose wife had died in a tragic accident, less than half a mile from home.

"How long were you out at the front?"

"Only ten months in all. But – I was glad not to have to go back again."

Across the small table, with its coffee cups and its plate of biscuits, they looked at each other and were silent a while. He rather liked her straight, calm gaze, but something was nagging at the back of his mind.

*   *   *   *   *

There was a story he had heard, of her jilting her fiancé on the wedding day. How could a woman do such a thing? There must be some hardness in her, he thought, although it was not to be seen in her face. And, looking at her, he wondered about her, wishing he could read her mind.

Outside the teashop, when they left, they met the Member, James Crown, who, with a group of laughing attendants, was just coming in in quest of lunch. He raised his hat with exaggerated politeness to Betony and gave Stephen a broad wink.

"Much obliged to you, Wayman, I'm sure. I'll do the same for you some day. Though half an hour in such pleasant company was no great sacrifice, I don't suppose?"

148

"Quite the reverse," Stephen agreed.

The rain had died out altogether now. A pale, unwarm sun was struggling forth. He walked with Betony to The Plough, where she had left the pony and trap.

"What did Mr Crown mean?"

"He was thanking me," Stephen said, "for having taken you off his hands while he said his piece to the crowd in the square."

Betony faced him.

"Was that your object in asking me?"

"Not exactly. It was a joke."

"You are easily amused, Mr Wayman."

"Come, now, Miss Izzard! You're surely not hipped?"

"Nobody likes having their time wasted."

"It wasn't wasted as far as I am concerned. As Crown just said, half an hour in such pleasant company –"

"No gallantry, please, Mr Wayman. I've had enough masculine patronage for one morning. Thank you for the coffee. I'll bid you good-day."

She nodded coolly and turned into the livery yard. Stephen made his way to The Revellers in Lock Street. Had his "gallantry" been patronizing? Well, yes, perhaps it had. It was certainly not his usual style. But did the young woman have to take herself so seriously? He decided to put it out of his mind.

On the way home, however, he caught up with Betony on the road and drove behind her for about a mile. When she looked back and saw who it was, she pulled over onto the grass verge and stopped, signalling to him that he was to pass. Instead he drew up close beside her and they looked at each other, glimmeringly, while the two ponies, the black and the grey, leant together, nose to nose.

"Really, Miss Izzard, don't you think this is absurd? I asked you to have coffee with me because I wanted to talk to you. That I did Crown a favour at the same time was just a joke and nothing more. I certainly wouldn't have asked you merely on his account alone."

"And yet you will vote for him, probably."

"In the absence of someone better, yes, I daresay I shall."

His answer, somehow, was unexpected. It brought a

149

smile to her lips. In another moment they were laughing together and all her frostiness was gone. He spoke again.

"My son would never have forgiven me if I had seriously offended you. Neither would Emma, come to that. I hope there'll be peace between us from now on."

"I don't see why there shouldn't be."

The two traps kept shifting a little. The ponies, having become bored with each other, were growing restive between the shafts. Betony drew in the slackened reins.

"Will you go ahead, Mr Wayman?"

"No, I'm waiting for you," he said.

So Betony pulled out into the road again and touched the pony to a trot. Stephen followed close behind, rather enjoying the advantage it gave him, of watching her and the way she drove. You could learn quite a lot, he told himself, from the way a person handled a horse, and as far as her driving was concerned, he had no fault to find in her. But there was something else as well; something he admired even more; and that was her easy naturalness. Plainly the girl was conscious of him: she would not have been human otherwise; but there was no affectation in her; she felt no need to act a part merely because he was watching her. She had a clear view of the world. Whatever happened, she would be herself.

At Rider's Cross, knowing that he would be turning right, she looked round and nodded to him, raising her whip in a little salute. He responded by raising his cap. And all the way home along Rayner's Lane he carried in his mind an image of her, sitting erect in the pony trap, her fair hair, in the old-fashioned style, twisted in a knot at the nape of her neck, under the fur-trimmed pillbox hat.

When he got home, aunt Doe was in the garden, cutting broccoli for lunch. He leapt from the trap and went over to her.

"What was that tale about Miss Izzard, jilting her fiancé on the day of the wedding? – Do you remember it?" he asked.

"Yes, I remember it," aunt Doe said. She stood erect and turned to him. "It was something to do with her foster-brother, a boy brought up with her family. I believe he was blinded in the war. The day Miss Izzard was due to be married, he was in trouble with the police. She put off her wedding to go to him. Her fiancé couldn't forgive her for it, so the wedding never took place at all."

"And her foster-brother? What happened to him?"

"It seems the poor boy was desperately ill. That's why Miss Izzard was so concerned. I believe he died that very day." Aunt Doe looked at Stephen's face. "I don't remember the ins and outs. But Mrs Bessemer's sure to know. If you want the details, you'd better ask her."

But Stephen, although he was interested, had no intention of gossiping with Mrs Bessemer. It was enough for him to know that, whatever the details of the story, Betony Izzard had not jilted her finacé out of caprice or out of wilful cruelty. He said something of this to aunt Doe, and she gave a little impatient shrug.

"You could tell she wasn't *that* sort of girl, just by looking at her, I would have thought."

"Perhaps you're right," Stephen said.

* * * * *

There had never been a general election like this one. Huntlip was full of fluttering posters, and slogans were chalked up everywhere. On polling day, at eleven o'clock, Mr and Mrs Talbot of Crayle Court drove up to the school to cast their votes, and behind them, in a huge brake drawn by four horses, came their employees from the estate. Mr Talbot wore the Tory colours in his lapel, and Mrs Talbot, who was very young, wore a hot-house carnation, dyed blue, pinned to the bosom of her coat. When they emerged from the school and drove away, the estate employees stood and cheered. They then went in to cast their own votes, and five of them at least voted for the opposite party.

Betony was busy throughout the day, driving about in the pony trap, fetching voters from outlying places. She wore no colours about her person; sported no posters on the trap; she was no more than a ferryman and observed a strict neutrality. She did not stop for lunch, but ate her sandwiches as she travelled about, and at three o'clock, when darkness fell, she lit the two lamps and carried on.

At six o'clock, as arranged, she returned home to Cobbs. Her father and mother and great-grumpa Tewke, dressed in their best as befitted the occasion, stood waiting in the fold, and Betony, jumping to the ground, relinquished the trap in her father's favour. Granna Tewke was not going to vote, but she had come out to see them off.

"I'm too old for that caper, driving out in the cold," she said. "And so is some others that I could name." She gave great-grumpa a prod in the back. "Gadding about at your age and you so comical these past few days!"

The old man had not been too well. The doctor had warned him against exertion. But he was determined to cast his vote, and, helped up by willing hands, he heaved himself into the trap.

"Where's Dicky?" Betony asked.

"There's no room for him in the trap. He says he'll go later when he's finished work."

Betony followed granna indoors, and granna gave her a cup of tea.

"You ent going out again, I hope? Not on a nasty night like this?"

"Yes, I am, when the trap comes back. But there aren't many more calls now."

"I pity that pony," granna said.

At half-past-six the trap returned, and Betony went off again. It was cold and wet, but she wore a mackintosh cape and hood, and had goloshes on her feet.

Beth Izzard went indoors, but Jesse and the old man went to the workshop, where, beneath the hanging lamps, the carpenters were still at work. There were eight men there, besides Dicky, and eight faces now looked up, wearing a bright expectancy. Great-grumpa Tewke spoke to them.

"I suppose you're hoping I'll say you can leave early, on account of the polling, eh?"

"It'd be a great kindness, gaffer," said Albert Tunniman.

"All right. You can go. But mind you all vote for the right man!"

The eight carpenters reached for their coats. In three minutes they were gone. Great-grumpa Tewke went into the house. Dicky remained at the bench, working.

"Ent you going to vote?" Jesse asked.

"I'll go when I'm finished," Dicky said.

"The polling shuts down at eight o'clock. Do you think you'll have finished that job by then?"

"It don't take *me* a month of Sundays to put a new floor in a damned tumbril!"

Dicky, it seemed, was in a bad mood. He did not often sneer at his father. But Jesse, aware that he was slow, and a poor craftsman compared with his son, took it all in good part.

"I reckon I'll leave you to it, then. It ent worthwhile my starting again, seeing I've got my best suit on and all. I reckon I'll follow your great-grumpa in."

But before he reached the door of the house, Beth came hurrying out to him, to say that great-grumpa had collapsed.

"All right, wife, keep calm!" Jesse said. He himself was far from calm. "Is it bad, do you suppose?"

"Yes," Beth said, "he's slumped in his chair."

"Laws!" Jesse said. "Oh, glory be!"

He returned to the workshop and shouted for Dicky to go for the doctor. Dicky set off, white-faced, at a run.

When Jesse entered the kitchen, Beth was loosening great-grumpa's clothes. His collar and stock were very tight and she had trouble removing them. His face was a dark and terrible colour and there was a wetness on the skin. He was making a noise as he fought for breath. Granna stood weeping on the hearth. She had her pinafore up to her face.

"Silly old obstinate man!" she said. "I knew he shouldn't have gone to the poll. He's done for hisself, he has, that's a fact. He won't never recover now."

Beth and Jesse exchanged a glance.

* * * * *

News always travelled fast in Huntlip. Betony heard of the old man's collapse from a group of voters outside the school. She drove home immediately. By the time she arrived, great-grumpa Tewke was conscious again, and he

153

had been got upstairs to his bed; and he had enough of his old spirit left in him to have ordered the doctor out of the room.

"You're not taking me to no hospital and that's all-about-it, young fella-me-lad! If I'm going to die – and I surely am – I'd sooner do it in my own home!"

Dr Day was with the family in the kitchen when Betony arrived.

"It's probably better for him to be at home. Rest and care, that's what he needs, and he'll have them here."

"He ent going to die, is he, doctor?" Jesse asked anxiously.

Dr Day spread his hands.

"Anno domini, Mr Izzard. He's a wonderful age, you must admit. I'll call in again tomorrow morning."

"There!" said granna, when the doctor had gone. "As good as done for! What did I say?"

The others were silent, lost in their thoughts. The old man was ninety-two; he had had a good innings certainly; yet the thought of his death was hard to accept. House and workshop would seem very strange without William Tewke to order the comings and goings there. Jesse Izzard looked at his wife. Dicky looked at Betony. Dicky felt the need to be occupied.

"I'll go and see to the pony," he said, "and there's lamps to be douted in the workshop too."

Betony went upstairs and quietly entered the old man's room. She sat in a chair beside the bed and after a while he opened his eyes. His face was now as pallid as yeast, and his voice when he spoke was just a whisper.

"I know you're there, child, watching me."

"Is there anything I can do?"

"You can tell me how the voting went."

"From what people say, it looks as though Mr Crown will win, but we shan't really know until tomorrow, of course."

The old man closed his eyes. His breathing, though heavy, was regular. Betony sat in her upright chair and kept watch over him while he slept, and at ten o'clock, quietly, her mother came and took her place.

The next morning he was better. When Betony left for

154

school, he was eating a breakfast of porridge and milk. Janie, her married sister, had come and was sitting with him, pouring his tea. At eleven o'clock the doctor came and pronounced himself pleased with the old man's condition. He advised him, however, to stay in bed.

Jesse gave orders that no noisy work should be done in the workshop that day. There was plenty of painting the men could do. But the old man missed the hammering; the noise of the saw at work in the sawpit; the voices shouting in the yard.

"What's the matter with them all down there? Why ent they working?" he said to Beth.

Only with the customary sounds coming from the workshop and the yard could he lie peacefully in his bed.

After lunch the vicar called.

"Are you in a hurry to bury me?" the old man demanded with a scowl. "I see you've brought the books along."

"I thought perhaps a short prayer. . . ."

"Can't do much harm, anyway. But don't expect me to join in. I've got things to think about."

The vicar read the eighty-fourth psalm, followed by a prayer for the sick. The old man sat propped against his pillows and listened patiently to the end. Abruptly he spoke.

"What worries me is them gates!" he said.

"Gates?" said Mr Netherton. His mind being full of piety, he thought of St Peter and the gates of heaven. "What precisely do you mean?"

"The churchyard gates, of course, what else? You've been needing new ones these two years past. Have a word with Jesse while you're here. Better still with his boy Dicky. He'll let you know what that'll cost."

* * * * *

He would not have granna in the room. "Her long face makes me sick," he said. Only Beth was allowed to sit with him, and Betony when she came home; and by then he was weak again; he was beginning to talk to himself.

"Better to bring the old tree down, once the rot's got in at

155

the roots. Put a couple of wedges in . . . and bring it down, clean and straight . . . out of the way of them bits of saplings."

Betony looked at her mother's face. Was the old man wandering? – Talking of the oak in the workshop yard, felled in the autumn of 1913? No, he wasn't wandering. After a lifetime working with timber, he saw himself as an old tree. He had stood like a stubborn oak for years. No one had ever seen him yield. And now, when he knew his time was come, the woodman had no fears for him.

At three o'clock, Dicky came into the house with a newspaper, fetched hot-foot from Jeremy Rye's. It contained the latest election news. In Chepsworth, as Betony had said, the Liberal member had kept his seat, but in the country as a whole, there had been a swing to the left. The next government would be a Labour one.

"Laws!" Jesse said. He was much upset. "A Labour government! I dunno! I'd have thought the country had more sense!" He dropped the paper in disgust. "Your great-grumpa Tewke won't care for that. He won't care for it at all."

And then Betony came in to them, to say that great-grumpa Tewke was dead.

* * * * *

On the day of the old man's burial, the carpenter's shop was closed all day. The carpenters attended the funeral and six of them, with Jesse and Dicky, bore the coffin to the grave. The vicar prefaced his address with words from Ecclesiasticus: "Let us now praise famous men, and our fathers that begat us." For William Henry Tewke, carpenter, had been a famous man in his way, as the many mourners gathered in the church testified. He had lived to a great age, and before he died there had been five generations of his family living in the parish. Now he was gone and the four generations remaining sat in the church to honour him. . . .

As Dicky said afterwards, the vicar might not be much of a mucher outside his church, but in the pulpit there was no one to beat him.

Later that day, at Cobbs, when the last of the mourners had left the house, Dicky went to the workshop yard and walked about, his hands in his pockets, among the criss-crossed stacks of timber, good oak and elm, ash and beechwood, and the softwood planks of foreign deal. He was gazing into the sawpit when his father came looking for him.

"At least we can get rid of this lot now." Dicky kicked at a baulk of timber, so that it toppled into the pit. "We can get all our stuff from the sawmill now, instead of sawing it all by hand as though we was Noah building his ark."

Jesse looked at his son in horror.

"That ent no way to talk, boy, with your great-grumpa Tewke hardly cold in his grave."

"He wouldn't care," Dicky said. "He was no humbug, I will say that. The living came first with him all along. He wasted no time on 'em once they was dead."

"You should show some respect all the same. Your great-grumpa Tewke, he started this place. He was its founder, as they say."

"The business has got to carry on."

"Ah. But you was talking of making changes."

"Shall we be keeping the sawpit, then, just cos great-grumpa started it, way back in 1850? Shall we still be sawing by hand in another ten or twenty years?"

"I never said that," Jesse said.

"There's got to be changes, you know, dad."

"H'mm, and it seems you've decided how, where, and when!"

But Jesse, in fact, was quite content to allow Dicky to take the reins, and Dicky knew it. Jesse rarely asserted himself. His wife, his daughter, and his son, could impose on him just as they pleased. His wife knew best in everything, and he trusted her. His first-born child, Betony, was always the apple of his eye. And Dicky, shedding his youthful feck-lessness, was already showing signs of the drive that would keep the business flourishing.

In the days following the funeral, the changes were already showing themselves. When Joe Kyte called, to discuss the repairs at his granary, Jesse at once summoned

157

Dicky.

"My son is the chap you need to see. He'll come along with you to the farm and give you an estimate of the cost. You'll find there's a lot of old Mr Tewke in him. He's got a better business head than I'll ever have in a hundred years."

* * * * *

But there was one small business matter, not connected with the workshop, which Jesse always dealt with himself. He owned a cottage known as the Pikehouse, which stood three miles out, on the old Norton road. It had been left to him by his mother; he was its owner, and he alone; and the ownership gave him a certain importance. He let the Pikehouse, for a weekly rent of one-and-sixpence, to a stonemason named Horace Nash, and every Friday on his way home from work Nash called at Cobbs to pay his rent.

Jesse always looked out for him and made a fuss if he was late. The money went into a small cashbox, which was carefully locked afterwards, and the rent-book was signed with immense pains: always in ink, never in pencil; always carefully blotted dry, and breathed upon for good measure. It was a family joke at Cobbs and Beth said once to Betony: "Your father can sign a rent-book more slowly than anyone else in the world."

It happened one night that Nash came early, in Jesse's absence. Beth took the money and signed the rent-book. And Jesse, coming in, was almost angry. He looked at the money as though it were defiled.

"That's *my* job to sign for the Pikehouse rent. It ent no one else's, I'll be bound."

"How could you sign it when you wasn't here?"

"Nash could've waited, couldn't he? You knew I'd be in by seven o'clock."

"It doesn't matter who signs the book. It's just a sort of formality, that's all, to show that the rent has been paid."

But Jesse was not to be persuaded. He returned to the matter again and again. His Friday evening had been quite spoilt.

"It's *my* job to sign for the Pikehouse rent. If Nash comes

158

early another time, you make him wait."

Every two or three months or so, Jesse took the money out of the box and paid it into the post office. This was another great day in his life, and for some time beforehand, whenever he went to the cashbox, he would give it a little shake and say, "That's beginning to get fuller again. I'll soon have to go to the Huntlip bank." Once he said to Betony, "That's twenty-one shillings in there. It's amazing how quickly it all mounts up."

"Seeing that you're so rich," she said, "why not give it to the Fund?"

There was a scheme afoot in the village to raise money for a parish hall, and Betony was on the committee.

"Oh, no!" Jesse said. "That's Pikehouse money, and it goes in the bank, cos I never know when that might be needed to pay for repairs. But I daresay I'll find something for your Fund."

He gave her ten shillings the very next day, but the rent-money must never be touched. It was sacred, Dicky said.

On December the fourteenth, there was a concert in the school, to raise funds for the parish hall. Jesse was rather shocked that Betony should join in the entertainment, less than a week after great-grumpa's funeral, but all the rest of the family went, even granna, and Jesse as always was over-ruled.

"It'll be a good thing if Huntlip gets a parish hall," Dicky said when he got home. "I spoke to the vicar about it tonight and he promised that we should have the job of building it."

"Laws!" Jesse said. "Did you ask him outright?"

"I don't believe in passing things by."

Dicky, as foretold, was treading the path great-grumpa had trod. Doing business was in his blood.

Chapter 9

On December the twenty-first, when the village school broke up for Christmas, the children were given those pieces of work which they had done during the term and were allowed to take them home. Emma had a small raffia basket, a peg-doll dressed in blue paper, and a knitted kettle-holder. But out in the playground, before going home, she gave these things to Winnie Aston, who gave her a pear-drop in exchange.

"Surely you want your little doll? I think she's nice, all dressed in blue."

"No, you can have it," Emma said.

"I shan't give them back, once I've took them home."

"Nobody's going to ask you to."

Emma, twirling her shoe-bag on its string, walked backwards to the gate. Miss Izzard and Miss Vernon stood outside the school porch, wishing their pupils a happy Christmas. Miss Izzard wore a dark blue suit, and had a black band of silk sewn to one sleeve. She had worn the black band for a fortnight now and Emma knew, having asked Florrie Ricks, that it was because Miss Izzard was in mourning for her great-grandfather, William Tewke.

"Happy Christmas, Emma!" Winnie said.

"Happy Christmas, Winnie!" Emma replied.

Emma walked up Holland Lane. It was too wet to go by the fields. The weather just lately had been very bad. When she was half way up the lane she stopped and took something from her pocket. It was her end-of-term report. She took it from its envelope and read her marks. She then read the sentences at the bottom, written by Miss Vernon in a large clear hand. "Emma must try and concentrate. She is too much given to day-dreaming." Emma tore the report to bits and scattered them in the dark puddles. Swinging her shoe-bag, she went on her way, sucking the pear-drop Winnie had given her.

* * * * *

All over Christmas the weather was cold, with sleet and snow showers coming by turns. This was the hated time of year, when the farm became a sea of mud, and the men as they squelched about the yards were inclined to be surly and quarrelsome.

"I hope it's cheerful, this play of yours," Stephen said to his older children. "We could do with cheering up a bit, especially the men."

"D'you think they'll come?" Chris asked.

"I don't see why not. They've received their invitations, I understand. I heard Tupper and Rye talking about it this morning."

"What were they saying?" Joanna asked.

"Tupper was wondering," Stephen said, "whether he ought to wear white tie and tails!"

Up in the attic with Jamesy and Joanna, Chris gave a reading of Act II, which he had completed on Boxing Day.

"The curtain rises on the posh drawing-room of a house in Kent –"

"Posh?" shrieked Joanna, outraged. "You can't say *posh*, for heaven's sake!"

"I don't see why not. The audience won't see the stage-directions."

"If we are going to do this wretched play, at least let us do it properly." Joanna spoke with a touch of hauteur. She was already feeling her way into the part of her heroine, the Lady Rosina Cavendish.

"Oh, very well," Chris agreed. He altered the word in his exercise book. "The curtain rises on the *elegant* drawing-room –"

"That's better," Joanna said. "But whereabouts in Kent exactly?"

"Cripes!" said Jamesy impatiently. "When are we going to start rehearsing?"

Rehearsals brought new difficulties. Joanna, as the

161

haughty heroine, having been abducted by the wicked pirate, Captain Terror, and thrown into the hold of his ship, *The Scourge,* was there to find the hero, Chris, lying unconscious on the floor, bleeding from a wound in his right temple.

"A goodly looking youth but *reeks* of garlic!" Joanna cried tragically. "How am I to bandage his wounds?"

"*Bind* his wounds, not bandage them!" Chris reminded for the seventh time. "They didn't have bandages in those days."

"You're supposed to be unconscious."

"I can still hear you making a muff of your lines."

"Order! Order!" Jamesy said, bringing his cutlass down, smack, on the side of his gumboot. "Or I'll have you marooned, you mutinous dogs!"

Downstairs, in the bedroom she shared with Joanna, Emma stood in front of the wardrobe, looking at herself in the long mirror. She wore a black silk band on her arm and a tiny tin watch, taken from a Christmas cracker, pinned to the bosom of her frock. She folded her hands in front of her and bowed her head.

"Lighten our darkness, we beseech thee, O Lord, and by thy great mercy defend us from all perils and dangers of this night. . . ."

Below, in the hall, a door closed and aunt Doe's voice called up the stairs. Emma pulled the black band from her arm and threw it into an open drawer. She unpinned the watch and set it aside.

"Emma, where are you?" aunt Doe called. "I've got a little job for you."

"All right, I'm coming!" Emma replied.

* * * * *

New Year's Eve was cold and wet. All day at the farm, fires burnt in the sitting-room and dining-room, and the children were busy with their preparations. With the connecting doors removed, the two rooms became one, and when all the inessential furniture had been removed, there was space enough for six rows of chairs. The "stage," at one

162

end, consisted of two shearing-platforms, and drawstring curtains hung in front from a wire fixed to a beam in the ceiling. At the back of the room, behind the rows of seats, a trestle table had been set up, covered with a clean white sheet, and by seven o'clock in the evening aunt Doe, with Mrs Bessemer's help, had filled the table with all sorts of food.

At seven o'clock, the farm-hands arrived with their wives and children, all dressed in their best clothes. Only Morton George stayed away and, as Chris remarked, who cared about him? The vicar was there with his wife and daughter; Agnes Mayle was there with three of her younger brothers and sisters; so were some friends of aunt Doe's from the Women's Institute; and a few of the neighbouring farmers came, including John Challoner and his son Gerald.

Aunt Doe, in a brown woollen dress, ran to and fro without pause, showing people to their seats and going "backstage" now and then to help the actors with their costumes, their lines, and their last-minute nerves.

"My gosh!" said Jamesy, having peeped through the curtains at the audience. "There's no end of a crowd! Where the deuce is my three-cornered hat?"

Chris had no nerves. Although in a state of some excitement, he was in command of himself. He was even brave enough to walk out into the hall, wearing his costume, to welcome Betony when she arrived.

"I'm so glad you could come, Miss Izzard, and after my behaviour at the meeting that time, I think it is more than I deserve."

His welcoming speech was well-rehearsed. He had spent some days perfecting it. And, dressed as he was in his best fawn breeches and the "cutaway" coat aunt Doe had made him, with white lace ruffles at throat and wrists, he delivered his lines with a certain panache. But his smile and his look were genuine enough and Betony responded to them.

"I wouldn't have missed it for the world."

"It's only a bit of a lark, you know. It's something Joanna and Jamesy dreamt up and I got roped in to give them a hand."

He took her coat and hat and hung them up. He ushered her in to a seat at the front, specially reserved with her name on it. He treated her as the guest of honour.

"I'm afraid I shall have to leave you now, but you will excuse me, won't you?" he said.

He walked away down the side of the room and there was a little round of applause from the Holland Farm men and their families before he vanished behind the curtains. Betony, turning in her seat, looked round at the rest of the audience. They were all known to her, especially the children, and she exchanged greetings with them. When she turned back again, she found Emma sitting beside her.

"Aren't you going to be in the play?"

Emma said nothing, but shook her head.

"Oh, well, never mind. I expect you'd sooner watch, like me."

A voice called out and the lights were dimmed. The audience stopped talking and applauded instead. The curtains parted to reveal the stage, lit by a single hurricane lamp, carried by Jamesy as the villainous pirate, clad in striped pyjama trousers, a shirt painted with the skull and crossbones, and a scarlet bandana round his head.

"Easy does it, you lubberly rogues!" he snarled to an imaginary crew behind. "Belay there and hold your noise! Easy on the tiller, you fool! Now! – Fire a shot across her bows!"

Stephen, outside the sitting-room window, set off a charge of gunpowder in an old iron stovepipe to simulate the cannon's roar. He was then able to go indoors and take his place at the back of the audience, glad of the room's enveloping warmth after the wind and rain outside. He could see Betony, six rows in front, sitting next to his youngest daughter.

* * * * *

All through rehearsals, Chris had taken the play very seriously, and had often been vexed by Joanna's carelessness with her lines. But now, tonight, there was a change. Aware of the audience watching him, he suddenly

164

saw the play for what it was, and an imp of mischief got into him.

"A goodly looking youth – " Joanna cried, remembering to project her voice; and Chris, who should have lain still, being unconscious, gave a little modest cough and put up a hand to straighten his cravat; " – but reeks of garlic!" Joanna said, reproving him with a sharp kick.

Chris however was unrepentant and when, later on in the same act, his part required that he should lift Joanna into his arms, he deliberately allowed his knees to buckle and staggered with her across the stage.

"Fear not, my love! You are but a sylph!" he gasped. "I could carry you to the end of the world!"

The audience responded with a cheer. The play was giving them a good many laughs. And when Chris, setting Joanna down at last, knocked over the "ship's table" and it was seen to be a box stencilled with the words "Hardy and Hawker's Binder Twine", there was another loud cheer. Joanna by now was furiously angry. She set the box upright again, with the treacherous words hidden from sight.

Exits and entrances were through a door to the right of the stage. In the last act, due to a shortage of actors, aunt Doe made a brief appearance as one of the pirate crew. Wearing a scarf tied over her head and a black patch over one eye, she opened the door with such force that Jamesy's cutlass was knocked from his hand. She fixed him with her one ferocious staring eye and delivered her only line in the play.

"What orders, Captain?"

Her voice was immense. It took the principals by surprise. Chris and Jamesy got the giggles and Jamesy for a while was quite unable to answer her.

"What orders, I say?" aunt Doe bellowed.

"H-hoist the mains'l!" Jamesy said.

"Splice the main-brace and batten the hatches!" Chris shouted, carried away. "Weigh anchor and man the oars!"

These lines were not in the written play. Nor were many of the others that flew across the stage in the next few minutes. But the story moved to its appointed end and the wicked pirate met his desserts.

"See where he hangs from yonder yard-arm!" And Chris pointed to where poor Jamesy, hooked to a rope hanging from the rafters, was brandishing a puny fist. "England is safe from one black-hearted villain at least!"

"Let me down!"Jamesy piped, forgetting to pitch his voice to a growl. "Let me down, you mutinous swabs, or I'll have you keel-hauled, every man jack of you!"

"*I* am the captain now!" Chris declared. He danced a hornpipe, whistling the tune. He at least was enjoying himself, but Joanna, crimson in the face, looked as though she could murder him. "The skull and crossbones fly no more from yonder masthead! Instead I have hoisted the flag of St George! We sail for England – and Holland Farm – where this fair maid shall be my bride!"

"Stop it, you're spoiling everything!" Joanna hissed.

Chris merely took her into his arms. Reverently he kissed her cheek.

"Are you happy, my Lady Rosina?"

Joanna's answer was inaudible. Secretly she was pinching him, twisting the flesh at the back of his neck. He bore it bravely and kissed her again.

"What did you say, my shyest one?"

This time her answer was audible, but only to him, and he, with the greatest aplomb in the world, turned to face his audience.

"She's blissfully happy and I'm standing on her foot!"

There was loud applause from the audience, and a great deal of stamping of feet. The stage curtains began to close but became stuck half way across. Aunt Doe, still in her eye-patch and bandana, tugged at the drawstrings and broke them off. She went and closed the curtains by hand, swearing at them in Hindustani.

* * * * *

"I suppose," said Bob Tupper, enjoying a plateful of cold ham and pickles, "our young master here will be going on the films next."

"Tomorrow morning," Chris said, "I shall be out with you in the Bratch, making a start on that sugar-beet."

"What, in them clothes?" said Billy Rye.

Chris was still wearing his stage costume. He grinned at the men and moved away. Joanna and Jamesy, with their father, were standing talking to the vicar.

"I'd no idea your children had such a comic talent, Wayman."

"Neither had I," Stephen said.

"As for the beautiful heroine –"

"When I've got time," Joanna said, "I intend to write a *proper* play."

Emma had a plate of hot mince-pies and was offering them to Betony. But Betony's plate was already filled with sausage-rolls and sandwiches. She was talking to Mrs Billy Rye. She smiled at Emma, and the child went away. Chris, too, was hovering. Mrs Rye gave way to him. He carried a bottle of ginger wine and he refilled Betony's glass.

"At least the food and drink are all right, Miss Izzard, even if the play was not up to much."

"The play went down very well," she said, "and now the food is doing the same."

She rather liked this boy of fifteen. Tonight he was gay and debonair; the occasion had filled him with ebullience; but underneath this evening's mood, she thought, there was seriousness of purpose and great resolution. He would not be slow in growing to manhood.

"The idea was to cheer everyone up a bit. Things are rather gloomy on the land just now."

"And elsewhere."

"Do you think the new government will mend matters, Miss Izzard?"

"I'm not a crystal-gazer, I'm afraid. All I can do is hope for the best."

Chris was called away by John Challoner. He excused himself with great politeness. Betony, still with her plate in her hand, went to speak to a group of children, gathered where the table was most full of food. She saw that two of the Starling boys were cramming their pockets with apples and nuts. She spoke to them and they put the things back. She returned to where she had left her glass.

From across the room Stephen watched her, although he was talking to Arnold Twill. A little while later he came to her. The hubbub around them was very loud. He had to speak up to make himself heard.

"It was kind of you to come, especially on such a bitter night. Can I get you another drink?"

"Thank you, no, I've got plenty."

"I was sorry to hear of your great-grandfather's death. I only met him once or twice, but I knew his reputation as a craftsman, and as a man of forceful character."

Betony smiled.

"You will hear people say that he was a hard, unyielding man, and there is truth in what they say, but a piece of old Huntlip has died with him, I think, and perhaps a piece of old Worcestershire."

"Do you regret its passing?" he asked.

"Most things take on a special colour, once they are in the past," she said.

"Will the present bad times do the same, do you think, when we look back on them in years to come?"

"It depends how long the bad times last."

"Let's drink to the future, anyway," he said, and raised his glass. "I wish you good health, Miss Izzard, and a happy new year."

"A happy new year!" Betony said.

When she left Holland Farm it was close upon midnight, and by the time she got home to Cobbs the hour had struck. It was 1924.

* * * * *

The following morning, Chris started work on the sugar-beet, in the fifteen acres known as the Bratch. He worked with Starling and Morton George, Harry Ratchet and Billy Rye, and cold wet dirty work it was too. The sugar-beet, loosened in the ground by the plough, had to be pulled up by hand and knocked together to shed the soil. The green tops were then cut off and the beets were thrown into the waggon. But the beets were too wet to shed the soil. Icy cold and covered with slime, they stung the men's hands until they ached. And the language heard in the field that day sometimes reddened Chris's ears.

Once Stephen came into the field and took a turn at lifting and topping. But with his badly twisted fingers he was less deft than the other men, and after an hour his hand was useless, the fingers seized up in a painful cramp. He threw down his bill-hook and walked away, and as soon as he was out of earshot, Morton George gave a grunt.

"That's a great help, I must say, his doing that! How many beets did he throw in? We should get on famously if we all done as much as the master done!"

Chris, though angry on his father's behalf, went on with his work and said nothing. Morton George was beneath his contempt. Chris never spoke to him if he could help it.

At Outlands, when they lifted their beet, it was left in great mounds beside the road, to await collection by motor lorry. Chris thought this a grand idea. He wanted his father to do the same. But Stephen wouldn't hear of it. Each load must go to the factory as soon as lifted.

"Hang it all!" Chris protested. "Think of the time we should save."

"No," Stephen said, "I want that beet taken in straight away."

Three days later the hard frosts came. Chris was at Outlands on an errand one day and Gerald showed him their sugar-beet crop, heaped by the roadside, ready to be taken to the factory. Gerald kicked at it savagely. The rotten pulp was all over his boots and the sweetish carroty smell of it was very strong on the frosty air.

"So much for the Ministry's precious beet! I'm damned if we'll grow that stuff again!"

"You should've carted it straight away, the same as we did," Chris said.

He did not often get a chance to score off Gerald. He went home whistling up the hill.

There was a friendly rivalry between the two boys as they went about their work on the two farms. If they met at the boundary, they would stop for a chat. But Chris was much less in Gerald's company these days, and much less inclined to repeat his opinions. Stephen noted it and was glad.

In the middle of January there was a heavy fall of snow. Then the rain came again and washed it away. It was bitterly cold on high ground, and in the valleys there were floods.

At the village school, children who came from outlying places arrived soaked and shivering. Their faces were pinched, their hands and feet numb. At such times as these, Betony set routine aside. Coats and shoes were put to dry; forms were drawn up around the stoves; and the children sat as close as they could, steaming dry in the heat of the fires and drinking the cocoa that Betony had heated for them on the hob.

The first lessons of the day were taken round the stove, but instead of following the timetable, the children were encouraged to talk about the terrible weather and the things they had seen on their way to school. In the smaller room, Miss Vernon did the same with her younger ones, who soon lost their shyness as the game went on.

"I seen one of Mr Franklin's turkeys swimming for his life when I came by. The brook was up as far as his barn."

"I seen a dog with a fish in his mouth, running along Withy Lane."

"Old Mrs Tarpin at Collow Ford, she'd got a great mattress in front of her door, to stop the water getting in. But it *got* in all right. She was upstairs hollering at the window and the blacksmith was reaching her up her milk."

All the children had something to tell, even the "babies" of three and four. Only Emma Wayman remained silent.

"Well, Emma, and what about you?" Miss Vernon said cheerfully. "What did you see on the way to school?"

"I didn't see anything," Emma said.

Rain continued all day, and Betony decided to cut the afternoon short, but already, at two o'clock, word was coming in that the Derrent brook had burst its banks and had flooded the road at Slings Dip. Eighteen children used that road and Betony went down with them to see for herself how matters stood. Sure enough, the road was impassable for two hundred yards or more, the water being

170

a good two feet deep. She was herding the children back to the school when a cart came down from Holland Lane and drew up beside her. Stephen Wayman leapt to the ground.

"Tupper told me the road was flooded. I thought maybe you might need help."

"Indeed we do!" Betony said. "These children would have a three mile walk if they had to go round by Lippy Hill."

Stephen wasted no time. He began lifting the children into the cart, and Betony helped him. The bigger ones clambered in by themselves. There was a lot of laughter among them as the cart, creaking, began to move. Their journey through the swirling waters became a mighty joke indeed. The mare, Phoebe, splashed her way through and, reaching the unflooded ground beyond, gave vent to a thankful whinny. The children, once they had been set down in safety, stood watching as Stephen, with some difficulty, turned the horse and cart in the road. They watched it make its return journey, then they scampered off towards home, some to Steadworth and some to Bounds.

Betony stood outside the school gate. Stephen stopped to speak to her.

"Is that the lot living out that way?"

"Yes. And I can't tell you how grateful I am."

The rain had stopped for a little while, but the gale still blew ferociously, whipping the words from Betony's lips. She had to lean forward into the wind to keep her balance against its buffets. She had to hold on to the skirts of her coat to keep them wrapped close about her legs.

"What weather!" she said, looking up at him, and she laughed because of the rollicking wind that threatened to knock her off her feet.

"Would you care to be driven home?"

"No, thank you, I've got things to do."

"Then I'll bid you good-day," Stephen said.

She returned to the school. He drove up the lane. The afternoon sky was very dark, the black clouds rearing up thick and fast, blown by the wild north westerly wind.

After the floods, there were frosts again. One morning when Betony arrived at school, she found the stoves still unlit, and the caretaker, Miles, waiting to see her.

"Seems we're out of coal," he said. "A skiddle of slack, that's all there is."

"But we had half a ton not long ago! The heap was up to the back-house window."

"That's just the trouble," Miles said. "Anyone can get at that coal. They've only got to climb the fence. It ent the first time we've had thieves in here in the cold weather."

"It's the first time they've left us without any coal whatsoever! Do they want the children to freeze to death?"

Betony went to the post office and sent a wire to the coal merchant, ordering half a ton of coal to be delivered at once, that very day. She returned to the school and, with Miles and Miss Vernon to help, moved the desks to the back of the room. When the children arrived, they were told to keep their coats on, and Betony, standing in front of them, led them in a game of "O'Grady Says." After an hour of this, Miss Vernon played the piano and the children sang songs of their own choosing, for singing too helped to keep them warm. At eleven o'clock, however, a telegram arrived from the coal merchant to say that the coal could not be delivered till the following Monday. The maximum temperature in the school was thirty-eight degrees. Betony had to admit defeat. She sent the children home and closed the school.

As she and Miss Vernon were leaving, Stephen and two of his men arrived, with twelve sacks of coal in the back of the cart, brought from his own stock at the farm.

"Emma tells me you're out of coal. She's very upset at being sent home. Will this see you through till your order comes?"

Certainly it would see them through. Betony unlocked the gate again to let the horse and cart drive in. She watched the three men unload the coal.

"If you have trouble with your order, let me know," Stephen said, "and I'll send in to town to fetch it for you."

By twelve o'clock the stoves were lit. By half-past one the rooms were warm. The desks were all back in place again, and Betony rang the school bell, to tell her pupils throughout the village that the school was open after all. Miss Vernon came and stood by her.

"Mr Wayman is very kind. That's the second time he's come to our rescue. He never used to take such an interest in the school. Not such a *personal* interest anyway. But now he can't do enough for us."

Betony pulled on the bell-rope and the bell rang out in its turret on the roof.

"Not so surprising as all that, now that he has a child here with us."

*　*　*　*　*

There were outbreaks of foot-and-mouth disease in the area that spring. A farmer at Stamley lost his pedigree herd. Everywhere, throughout the district, precautions were taken against the infection, so mysterious in its ways, and the movement of cattle was controlled.

At Holland Farm, as on other farms, there were buckets of antiseptic fluid at every entrance, and anyone who had been beyond its boundaries had to dip his booted feet in this and sluice the wheels of vehicles. Stephen was in the cartshed one day when Morton George drove straight through the gateway without stopping, although he had come from Steadworth Mill.

"It's all a waste of flaming time!" he said when Stephen challenged him. "How do we know it does any good?"

"How do we know it doesn't?" Stephen said.

He made the man dip his boots in the bucket and sluice the axles and wheels of the cart.

"If you disobey me again over this, you'll get your cards without delay!"

The outbreaks died away at last. Stephen and his neighbours breathed again. The weather improved in April, although not much, and the ploughs were able to get out on the land.

"If we had a tractor," Chris said, "we should soon catch up on all this lost time." He was bitterly jealous of the two tractors so busy at Outlands, crawling about the green and brown fields. "Surely now that you're saving on my school fees –"

"But I shouldn't be saving them," Stephen said, "if I spent the money on a tractor instead."

"It would pay for itself in no time at all if you were to sack one of the men."

"I prefer to keep men in work."

"Even Morton George?" said Chris.

"Look," Stephen said, somewhat curtly, "I said you could come and work on the farm, but I didn't say you could take over!"

But he smiled to soften his words a little, and passed *The Farmer and Stockbreeder* across to the boy, open at a page on beet-growing.

Chris tried to enlist Bob Tupper's support, but Bob was a horse-man through and through.

"Don't speak to me about tractors," he said. "A tractor ent human, like a horse. And it don't seem natural to me, neither, to hafta look back on your work all the time instead of forrards, the proper way."

"At least a tractor doesn't eat its head off when it's not working."

"No, nor it don't manure the land, neither."

"Hah! Manure!" Chris said in disgust. "We're up to our ears in it on this farm!"

"You speak for yourself, young master," said Bob.

Chris was very keen to plough. He wanted to do every job on the farm. Once he and Bob were in the same field; Bob was ploughing with Beau and Bonnie; Chris with the geldings, Spick and Span; while over on the other side of the hedge, in an Outlands field, Gerald on his tractor lurched to and fro, completing four furrows in less time than Chris could do one. Once he came to the hedge and shouted.

"How're you peasants doing up there? Have you ever heard of a thing called progress?"

Chris took no notice but ploughed on, his young face tight-set under his cap.

"Peasants!" he said, later, to Bob. "That just about hits the nail on the head! Why not use oxen and be done with it?"

But, as Bob remarked to Stephen one day, in spite of the

boy's bitterness, his work in the field was always good, whether ploughing or drilling, and he was improving all the time. He might look down on the use of horses but his team was always well turned out and he worked them with as much patience as Bob did himself.

Sometimes Stephen had worried about Chris, coming so young to the work of the farm, without having seen the outside world. He feared that the boy would become cloddish. But Chris had a busy, adventurous mind. He read a great deal; kept abreast of new things; he was outward-looking, ambitious and keen. He was the sort of young man who would build the future of agriculture – if only he were given the chance. Stephen wished he could give in to him and bring modern methods to Holland Farm, but he felt that the bad times had come to stay and his instinct counselled cautiousness.

"Take John Challoner," he said. "He spent big while the going was good. Now he needs to pull in his horns and he's finding it difficult to do."

"At least he's got tractors," Chris said. "At least he's got electricity." Then, after a moment, he said: "At least he keeps hunters and rides to hounds."

"Do you want to ride to hounds?" Stephen asked.

"I'd like to be able to afford it, that's all."

"That's just it, Challoner *can't* afford it," Stephen said.

* * * * *

The weather turned wet again. Very little ploughing was done. The two war veterans, Tupper and Hopson, were heard singing the hymn-tune, "Holy! Holy! Holy!" as they went about the farm. But the words they sang were those they had so often sung in Flanders: "Raining! Raining! Raining! Always bloody well raining!" And Tupper said to Morton George, "I don't think it's stopped since this ruddy government of yours got in!"

The lambing season was bad that year. Stephen was out at all hours, helping his shepherd, Henry Goodshaw, but their losses were heavy all the same, and he grew quite hardened to the task of burying dead lambs.

175

One day in the pasture at Wood End, he found three dead lambs in an old disused well. Morton George had thrown them there.

"I didn't think it'd hurt," George said, "what with the weather being so cold."

"Have you smelt them?" Stephen asked.

"It ent my job, anyway. It's the shepherd's job to bury his lambs."

"Then leave them where he can see them, man, and don't go flinging them into holes."

This was a trying time for Stephen. He was suffering from lack of sleep. He knew he must keep a check on his temper whenever he dealt with Morton George, for the man was growing more slovenly and every day brought cause for complaint. Pig-swill inadequately boiled; barn-doors left swinging in the wind; coils of barbed wire thrown down and left where cattle could entwine their legs.

"If that was me I should sack him as soon as look at him," said Chris. "He's more trouble than he's worth."

"I've never had to sack a man yet and I hope I never shall," Stephen said.

Round about the middle of April, however, something happened that changed his mind. The mare, Tivvy, was in foal. It was a month or so to her time, and she was therefore excused from work. Yet Morton George, with a heavy load of manure to cart, put Tivvy into the shafts and drove her uphill to the Eighteen Acre. It happened that Tupper was in the field. He unyoked the mare and led her home. But the harm was already done by then. Tivvy miscarried and the foal was born dead. Bob Tupper was beside himself. He threatened to take Morton George apart.

"Bloody lazy pigging sod! He took the mare because she was nearest! It saved him fetching Beau from the meadow. You'd better keep him away from me, Mr Wayman, cos I'm in the mood to break his neck!"

But Stephen himself had had enough of Morton George. The man was useless. He was given his cards.

"You think I don't know why you're sacking me? It ent on account of a bloody horse! It's because I'm a union man, that's why it is! You bloody farmers is all the same!"

176

"There's an extra thirty shillings there. That's instead of a week's notice. You can go this minute, without delay."

"I shall see my union about this!"

"Just be sure and tell them the truth!"

"What about my cottage? Are you putting me out in the road?"

"You can stay in the cottage till the end of the month. Then I'll want it for a new man."

In fact Morton George was gone by Easter. He left the district with his wife and three boys and was seen driving a cart towards Capleton. When Stephen went to the empty cottage, he found that the place was no more than a shell. Doors and floorboards had been removed and burnt on a bonfire in the garden. Some of the rafters had been sawn through and the glass had been broken in all the windows. The kitchen range had been smashed; so had the copper in the scullery; and in the overgrown garden behind, fruit trees and lilacs had been cut down.

But there was a worse discovery still, for in the pasture behind the cottage, an in-calf heifer was found dying, and the vet said she had been poisoned by eating yew. There were bits of it still in her mouth, and a yew tree grew in the cottage garden. There was nothing the vet could do. She died while he was examining her.

Chapter 10

At Easter the weather improved for a while. The nights were frosty but the days were fair. There was a bustle on the farm and all possible teams were out, ploughing, harrowing, drilling seed, busy wherever the ground allowed. Chris was in a fever from dawn to dusk. He thought and talked of nothing but work. And Jamesy, home for the holidays, followed his brother everywhere.

Joanna was in the grip of a different fever. Her schoolfriend, Elaine, was staying at the farm for the Easter week-end, and the two girls were writing a novel. They shut themselves away in the attic and played the gramophone all day, mostly Mozart and Mendelssohn.

"Music enables me to think," said Joanna. "It makes me aware of life and death."

Did Elaine know what she meant?

"I think," said Elaine, her eyes half-closed: "I think Persephone will die when she thinks Julian has forsaken her."

"But Julian, of course, comes back a rich man."

"Having intended all along to marry her . . ."

"He goes to the churchyard and sees her grave . . ."

Mendelssohn had come to an end. Joanna reached out and changed the record. She put on the Mozart Sonata in D.

Emma, attracted by the music, climbed the steep stairs to the attic playroom, but found the door locked against her.

"Go away!" Joanna shouted. "We're very busy. We need to think."

"I want to come in and listen to the gramophone."

"Well, you can't!" Joanna said.

Emma, having rattled the door-knob in vain, turned and went downstairs again. She slipped past aunt Doe and Mrs Bessemer, who were busy swilling out the dairy, and left the house by the side door.

Outside, in the barnyard, Jamesy was helping Chris to load sacks of grain onto a trailer. They were sowing barley in the Goose Ground.

"Can I come with you?" Emma asked.

"Don't be silly," Jamesy said.

"I want to ride behind the drill."

"You run along in, there's a good girl, and aunt Doe will find you something to do."

"No," Emma said. She turned away.

"Where are you off to?" Jamesy asked.

"Nowhere in particular," Emma said.

"Well, whatever you do, don't go down to the bottom yard."

"Why, what's in the bottom yard?"

"Never you mind what's there," said Chris. "Just do as you're told and keep away."

"Is it a surprise?" Emma asked.

"No, it isn't. It's nothing at all. Now mind out of the way or you'll get run over."

When they had gone, with their load of seed, Emma went into the barn and climbed the ladder into the hayloft. There was much to be seen from the hayloft door. Half the farm lay spread below. She could see her father, with Spick and Span, harrowing the green winter wheat on the slopes of the One-and-Twenty. She could see three ploughs at work in the Freelands. She could see the shepherd and his boy, moving about the lambing-pens, and could even see a hint of steam rising from the backs of some of the ewes.

When she climbed down the ladder again the spaniel, Sam, came running to her, wagging his little stump of a tail.

"Rats?" Emma said. "Have you seen any rats? You come with me, I'll find you some rats."

She left the barn, with the dog at her heels, and walked down the track to the bottom yard, a place used for stock in wintertime, on three sides enclosed by shelters and stalls. She opened the gate and went into the yard. The spaniel chose to remain outside.

"Rats? Any rats?" she said to him, but although he wagged his tail again, he made no move to follow her. "Oh, very well, you please yourself."

She pushed the gate and it latched shut. Sam stood peering at her through the bars. Then, with a whimper, he ran off home. Emma stood alone in the empty yard.

Lately, the muck had been carted away, and the concrete ground had been scraped clean. The open-fronted shelters had been mucked out and the cobblestones had been hosed down. There was nothing to see in the shelters or stalls. There was only something in the middle of the yard; something bulky, rounded in shape, covered by a stack-cloth weighted with stones. Emma went closer, two steps at a time. She removed one of the big stones and lifted a corner of the cloth.

The dead cow's eyes were open wide, but were covered by a thick clouded film. Its black tongue hung curling out of its mouth; its lips and nostrils were covered in slime. Emma shrank back with a little cry, letting the stack-cloth fall again.

She ran to the gate and climbed over, tearing her pinafore on a nail. There was a hedge at the side of the track, and when she had pushed her way through the thorns, she ran across the pasture into the coppice. From there she passed into Stoney Lane; ran full pelt past Lilac Cottage; and squeezed through the gate onto Puppet Hill. She couldn't run up the steep track because of the terrible stitch in her side, but once she was over the brow of the hill, she ran like the wind down the other side, scattering sheep in all directions. Her feet went twinkling over the turf. She ran as though she would never stop.

* * * * *

In the old walled garden at Cobbs, Betony was working with her mother, putting in sticks to support the peas.

"We've got company," Beth remarked, and Betony, following her mother's glance, saw the child at the garden gate. "Is it the gipsies as usual?"

"No, it's Emma Wayman from Holland Farm."

"What's she doing, flitting about?"

"I think she's probably looking for me."

The moment Betony opened the gate, Emma turned as though she would flee, but Betony caught her by the arm and drew her inside. The child's dark brown hair, usually so neat, was utterly wild and had lost its ribbon; her dress and pinafore were torn, her face and hands were covered in scratches, and she was muddy from head to foot.

"Whatever's happened to you, my child?"

"Nothing! Nothing!" Emma said. Then, suddenly, she was in tears. Her face was pressed against Betony's apron. "I don't like it at home any more! Can I come and live with you?"

"Poor little girl," Betony murmured. Her hand was on the child's hot head. "Let's go indoors, anyway, and do something about those cuts."

Her mother spoke from across the garden.

"Do you want me to come and help?"

"No, there's no need," Betony said.

Talking cheerfully all the time, she led the child into the kitchen and sat her in a chair under the window. She fetched warm water, iodine, lint, and bathed the bleeding cuts and scratches.

"How do you come to be in this mess?"

"I don't know," Emma said. She squinted down at herself in surprise and tried to brush the mud from her pinafore. "I ran and ran, right down the hill. I couldn't stop and I fell in the mud."

"Why were you running down the hill?"

"I wanted to run away from home."

"Did something happen to you there?"

"Yes, it was horrible," Emma said.

"Won't you tell me what it was?"

"The cow was after me," Emma said.

Betony, smiling, turned away. She busied herself with the iodine.

"Well, it's always as well to keep out of their way, especially if they happen to have calves."

"She didn't have a calf, she was dead," Emma said. "She was all black and slimy and she smelt bad."

"Oh! That *is* horrible!" Betony said. She folded the lint and put it away. "But dead cows don't chase you over the

181

hill."

"I thought she was going to," Emma said.

Soon, with her face and hands washed clean, and her hair put to rights, brushed and combed, she appeared less of a wild wan waif, and Betony, looking into her eyes, saw there was no real terror there. Indeed, Emma sitting by the fire, enjoying biscuits and warm milk, while her muddy boots dried in the hearth, looked on the whole well-pleased with herself, as Beth, coming in from the garden, remarked.

"No bones broken nor nothing like that?"

"Cuts and scratches, mostly, that's all, and a bit of a fright."

"And rather enjoying it, I should say."

"Yes, perhaps," Betony said.

Emma's only tragedy, now, was the state of her clothes. Whenever she glanced down at them and saw the terrible muddy stains, she wrinkled her nose in disgust.

"I need a clean frock and pinafore."

"I can't help you there, I'm afraid. There's nothing in the house small enough."

"Aunt Doe will see to it, when I get home."

"I'll walk back with you," Betony said. "They will be wondering where you've got to."

"Oh, *they* never worry," Emma said.

* * * * *

But the child had been missed for an hour or more, and Stephen was out looking for her. He came across the turnip field as Betony and Emma walked into the yard. He spoke to the child with severity.

"Where have you been, all this time? You promised aunt Doe you'd stay within call." And, to Betony, he said: "Where did you find the wretched child?"

"It was one of those days for running away from home, apparently and Emma got as far as Cobbs."

"It might be one of those days when somebody got a smacked bottom," he said. "It seems to me it's what they deserve."

Emma was quite unmoved by this threat. She showed him

the mud and dirt on her clothes.

"I need clean *everything!*" she said.

"Yes, I can see you do, my girl. You'd better go in to your aunt Doe and say you're sorry for causing her so much anxiety."

The child went skipping into the house. Never once did she glance back at them. She was intent on the need for clean clothes. Stephen looked at Betony.

"It seems my children are determined to be a nuisance to you. You'll be sick of us Waymans before long. What's all this about running away from home?"

"It was mostly to do with seeing a dead cow, I believe."

"Damn and blast!" Stephen said. "All the farm to play about in and that child has to choose the bottom yard. I thought the carcass was safe enough there."

"Surely it would have been safer still if it had been buried?" Betony said.

"I can see what you must think of us, Miss Izzard, and of course you're quite right. The cow died two days ago but what with our landwork being behind – "

"And a shortage of labour perhaps?"

"Shortage? No. I wouldn't say that."

"I heard you'd got rid of one of your men."

"Ah. Yes, I see. That was Morton George." Looking at her, he considered her. He knew her well enough by now to guess what was passing in her mind. "I suppose you've heard gossip of some kind. Victimization. Is that it?"

"George was a member of the union, I understand."

"That's not the reason he was dismissed."

"He thought it was," Betony said.

"Did you know him?" Stephen asked.

"Only slightly, I must admit, but one of his boys was in my class."

"Do you know what kind of man he is?"

"Surely no man, whatever his shortcomings, deserves dismissal at such times as these?"

"The times are bad for all of us, not just for those like Morton George."

"You can't deny it's worse for them?"

"That dead cow," Stephen said. "It was Morton George

who did that. He poisoned her by giving her yew."

There was a pause. She frowned at him.

"Have you any proof of that?"

"Enough to satisfy myself. I don't have to satisfy anyone else."

He could see from her face what impression his words had made on her. She thought him high-handed, that much was plain.

"Have you got a few minutes to spare?"

"What for?" Betony asked.

"I'd like to show you something," he said.

He took her to Morton George's empty cottage and showed her the damage that had been done there. He showed her the fruit trees and lilacs cut down, lying on the grass in the back garden.

"I know it's no proof that he poisoned my cow, but it's proof of the kind of man he is. And there's the yew by the gable there. The cow couldn't get at it by herself."

"I would never have thought," Betony said, "that a man could stoop to such spitefulness."

"The cottage will take some time to put right. I've been meaning to come along to your place, to ask if your father will do the repairs. I shan't take another man on just yet, but when I do he will want the cottage."

"My father will see to it certainly. I'll ask him to come and call on you." Betony, turning, met Stephen's gaze. "I'd like to apologize," she said. "I was speaking in ignorance, defending Morton George as I did."

"You are a champion of the unemployed, Miss Izzard, and it means the employers get all your blows. But not every farmer is a despot, you know, and I'd like to think I'd convinced you of that."

He looked at her and she smiled at him. Her hair in the sunlight was smooth and bright; her eyes reflected the spring-blue sky. He found he enjoyed looking at her. There was serenity in her face. He stood with his hands in his jacket pockets and watched her move away from him, walking about the overgrown garden, among the fallen apple trees.

"It may seem unfair, bringing you here to see all this,

when George is not here to defend himself, but – I happen to mind what people think of me."

"Will you try and prosecute him?"

"I doubt if he could ever be found. He'll take good care to cover his tracks. And he certainly won't be writing to ask me for a reference!"

Together they walked across the pasture and out through the gate into the lane. In the ten acre field on the other side, Tupper and Hopson were drilling oats, and Tupper's quiet voice could be heard as he spoke to his team. The air was full of the scent of spring.

"Will you come to the house for a cup of coffee?"

"No, thank you," Betony said. "I've got a jumble sale after lunch. It's high time I was getting home."

"Then you'd better take the right of way. It'll save you half a mile from here. I'll come with you as far as Blake's Wood."

* * * * *

The right of way lay across part of Challoner's land, crossing two pastures and skirting a coppice. Betony had not been there since childhood.

"I thought Mr Challoner had closed this path."

"He's tried to close it a couple of times. He doesn't like people crossing his fields. But the parish council directed him to take his barbed wire down."

John Challoner, however, determined to discourage "trespassers", had allowed his hedges to overgrow the stiles, and Stephen, with a stick, had to beat aside the brambles and briars before he and Betony could climb over. Even so, a sharp briar caught her face and a spot of bright blood squeezed from the scratch, like a glistening red jewel on her cheek. Stephen watched her brush it away.

"I'm sorry about this," he said. "It wasn't such a good idea after all, taking the short cut, was it? I must speak to my neighbour about his thorns. If he doesn't cut them back, the parish council will do it for him, and he won't like *them* trampling over his land."

Betony laughed.

185

"It must be useful, having practised the law. Do you ever miss it at all?"

"No, not really. I always wanted to farm. I went in for the law to please my father."

The second field they had to cross was steeply humped in the middle. Once they were over the top of the hump, they were walking beside a fenced coppice, which ran down to the foot of the slope and filled the whole of the hollow below. There were horses in this field: Challoner's hunters, his pride and joy; and as Stephen and Betony walked down the path skirting the coppice, two of these horses, a black and a roan, came thundering down the slope behind them.

Stephen knew the black horse: he had a bad name for tormenting his fellows; and today his victim was the roan. Both horses were highly excited, the black with devilment, the roan with fear, and they came careering down the slope, ears back and eyes rolling and the breath coming in visible spirts out of their widely dilated nostrils.

Stephen and Betony turned to face them. Caught as they were in the angle formed by the fenced-off coppice, they had no room to step aside. The horses bore down on them at a gallop, sweat and foam splattering off them and bits of turf flying up from their heels. Betony stood, paralysed, sure that she and the man beside her were going to be trampled under the hooves. But Stephen stepped forward a pace or two and spread his arms in front of the horses. He spoke to them in a loud voice.

"Whoa, there! Steady, now! Get over, you brutes! Whoa! Whoa!"

His last words were lost in the thundering of hooves. Then, a miracle, the horses were past, veering away at the last instant. They passed so close in their headlong career that as Stephen stepped back a pace, one flying hoof snicked the shin of his boot, and the roan's tail caught him full in the face. Drawing breath, he watched them go. They gradually slowed as they circled back up the slope again and in a moment they had stopped, leaning over the fence of the coppice to pull at the leaves on the hazel trees. The roan kept a watchful eye on the black but otherwise, as they browsed together, they looked the picture of peacefulness.

"Whew! That was close!" Stephen said. He wiped away the dirt that had spattered his face and turned towards Betony. "Are you all right?"

"Yes, I'm all right. Or I *think* I am!" She gave a little tremulous laugh. Her voice was not quite under control. "But I really thought . . . just for an instant . . . that we were both going to be killed."

"No thanks to Challoner that we're not!" Stephen said angrily. "He's no right to keep such mischievous brutes on this public right of way. I must certainly see him and warn him about it." Pausing, he looked more closely at her. "Are you sure you're all right?" He put out a hand and touched her arm.

"Except that my bones seem to have melted, yes, thanks, I'm fine," Betony said.

Her voice was perfectly steady now, and she gave another self-mocking laugh. She had passed from a moment when violent death seemed inevitable to a moment when she was immortal again. But only the pallor in her face showed what that moment had done to her. Otherwise she was herself. Her eyes were steady, calm, amused. Stephen admired her self-control.

He opened the gate and they passed through it into the wood. There were primroses growing under the trees, and the pathway was starred with celandines. The wood smelt of moss and new green growth, and the sunlight, finding its way through the scrub oak and ash and the hazel boughs, lit the greenness on the ground.

"This business of Emma running away from home . . ."

"I don't think it's very serious."

"Not another example of my neglect?"

"I retracted that charge, if you remember."

"I'm not sure that it wasn't deserved. The child does wander about a lot. I must keep a closer watch on her."

"Remembering my own childhood, I know how difficult that can be. I was always running away from home. I never got any further than Emma did today, but it must have been very worrying for my parents, all the same."

They glanced at each other, silent a while, and the sunlight, shining through the straight ash poles, flickered on their faces as they walked. They came out at the end of the wood and leant together over the gate, looking down on the straggling village.

"You're no longer given to running away from home, Miss Izzard? You seem pretty settled nowadays."

"Too much so," Betony said. "I've hardly been away from home since the war ended. I've been at the school for four years."

"Is that such a bad thing?"

"Sometimes I feel perhaps it's wrong to be settled so comfortably into one's rut."

"I hope you're not a puritan, Miss Izzard, courting discomfort for the good of your soul."

"You make it sound reprehensible."

"I don't see why life should not be enjoyed."

He opened the gate and she passed through. He closed it again, remaining inside. This was as far as he meant to go.

"I'll call at Outlands on my way back and see Challoner about those horses. I'll make it quite clear that they gave us a fright. Thank you for bringing Emma back. It was kind of you to take so much trouble."

"I enjoyed the walk," Betony said.

He watched her until she had gone from sight.

* * * * *

In the schoolroom, when Betony arrived after lunch, the stalls had already been set up and money was already changing hands. Her sister Janie, selling produce from her own dairy, was doing the briskest trade of all.

"Thank goodness you've come! I really can't manage both stalls at once. You're nearly twenty minutes late."

Betony had a rummage stall. Everything on it was priced at twopence. The coppers rattled into the tin, and she was kept busy until four o'clock. The afternoon's sale raised four pounds seventeen shillings and sixpence.

"Ah, well, every little helps!" said one of the stall-holders cheerfully. "We shall have our parish hall by the time I'm eighty!"

Afterwards tea was served from a big copper urn. Betony

and Janie sat together, drinking out of enamelled mugs. Janie looked at Betony's hair.

"Isn't it time you had it cut?"

"Whatever for?" Betony said.

"Nobody wears it long these days."

"Oh, yes, they do," Betony said, looking around her at the other women in the room. "I can see five or six at least."

"So old-fashioned you are still!"

"Am I? Yes, perhaps I am." Betony, although the elder of the two, was used to Janie's criticisms. She listened to them and laughed them off. "I certainly can't compete with you."

Betony was not much interested in fashion. She took trouble with her clothes, but once they were on she forgot about them. As for her thick straight flaxen hair: her mother had coiled it into a bun for her on the day she had left school, and she had worn it like that ever since.

"That was ages ago," Janie said. "Aren't you ever going to change it?"

Janie herself was passionately interested in fashion. "I may be a farmer's wife but I don't have to look like one!" she would say. "Besides, Martin likes me to look nice." Janie had been married for ten years. She felt sorry for Betony.

"It's high time you found yourself a husband. *He'd* soon make you mend your ways."

"Would he indeed!" Betony said.

"Haven't you ever thought of it?"

"Not in so many words, no. Not since breaking with Michael, that is."

"Then it's high time you did!"

"I'm perfectly happy as I am."

"You certainly look it, I must admit."

It was something Janie could not understand. Her husband and children were everything to her. To be twenty-eight, as Betony was, and not yet married! – How could she bear such a wasted life?

"Mother once said to dad that you'd find it difficult to give yourself heart and soul to a man."

"How do you know she said such a thing?"

"Because dad mentioned it to me, that's how." Janie drank the last of her tea. "I've often wondered if it's true."

189

"I don't know. I haven't thought." Whether it was true or not, Betony was reluctant to discuss it with her sister, close in affection though they were. "Mother says a lot of things."

"Surely you *want* to get married some time? You'll leave it too late if you don't watch out."

"When you've found someone suitable, I promise to give it my consideration."

"I wish you'd be serious once in a while."

"I'm getting myself another cup of tea. Shall I get you one as well?"

Janie, with a look that admitted defeat, handed Betony her empty mug.

*   *   *   *   *

The school reopened on April the twenty-fifth. The weather had turned bad again, and every morning the two rooms were filled with the smell of wet boots and overcoats drying around the two stoves. The sky was so dark that the lamps were kept burning all through the day. It was just like wintertime. Emma, coming down the lane through the rainy darkness, liked to see the lights shining out from the schoolroom windows, and would run the last two hundred yards, drawn by the brightness and bustle within.

"No one is to sit down in their places until they have shed their wet boots or shoes," Miss Vernon would say every morning, and there was always much jostling and noise before her order had been obeyed.

"Whew! What a smell!" said Florrie Ricks, holding her nose between finger and thumb, and the other children all did the same.

But Emma, although she held her nose with the rest, rather enjoyed the smell of hot wet wool and mackintosh and leather drying by the stove. She liked the bustle and noise of the wet mornings; the flickering of the lamps and the smell of the oil; the red glow of coals in the iron stove and the mugs of cocoa, steaming hot, handed out by Miss Vernon.

It was difficult for the children to settle down after these preliminaries. They were restless; excited; full of naughty glee. Three little boys, in the dinner-hour, hid Miss Vernon's pinafore behind the stove-pipe, where she discovered it, black with soot. They were sent to Miss Izzard, who kept them in for ten minutes of their playtime, sitting with their hands on their heads.

The next day, Miss Vernon's galoshes were filled with mud, and the two culprits, Emma Wayman and Winnie Aston, received the same punishment. And, on yet another day, in the middle of a scripture lesson, Emma leant across to Betty Trennam and yanked her hair-ribbon undone. Miss Vernon witnessed this incident, and Emma spent the afternoon break sitting under Miss Izzard's eye, writing out twenty times. "I must behave better in class." The following morning, Emma threw a lump of plasticine at Festubert Wilkes, and was sent to Miss Izzard yet again.

Betony looked at the dark-eyed child standing before her and wondered at this burst of naughtiness.

"Well, Emma? You're always in trouble nowadays. Why is that?"

"I don't know," Emma said. She stared at the watch on Betony's bosom.

"This is the third time you've been sent to me in a week. Aren't you ashamed?"

Emma dutifully hung her head.

"Well, run along, then!" Betony said. "Go back to Miss Vernon and be a good girl."

Emma's head came up at once.

"Aren't you going to keep me in?"

"No, not today. It's stopped raining for once in a while and you will be better taking your playtime out of doors."

Emma went off, out to the playground, and stood with her feet in a dirty puddle. Nobody came to scold her for it. After a while she moved away.

* * * * *

May was almost as wet as April. Landwork was halted everywhere. Rootseed rotted in the waterlogged ground and young cabbages, yellow-leaved, were washed out into the furrows, which ran like rillets continuously. The derrent brook broke its banks again and many people's homes were flooded; part of the road at Slings Dip had been washed away; and, at the little village school, fires were still being lit in the mornings, six weeks after they had usually stopped.

On May the twenty-sixth, the school celebrated Empire Day, and the morning began without rain. In Miss Vernon's room, after prayers, each child in Standard I was given a sheet of paper and told to paint a union jack, copying the flag draped over the blackboard.

"Don't try to hurry. There's plenty of time. Be sure to let each colour dry before commencing with another."

In spite of the warning, Emma's colours ran together, and the more she tried to put matters right, the worse mess she made on her paper. The smaller children were using crayons. Even their work was better than hers. She hid her flag inside her desk.

Miss Vernon stood before the class.

"Is your paint dry, Standard I? Then take the two pins I've given you and pin your union jacks to your chests. When you've all done that, you can help the little ones with theirs."

The children became extremely busy; all except Emma, who sat quite still.

"What's the matter?" Miss Vernon asked, coming and standing beside the desk. "Why aren't you wearing your union jack?"

"It's gone all runny," Emma said.

"And whose fault is that, if I might ask?"

"It's her own silly fault," said Florrie Ricks.

"Show it to me, Emma, please."

Emma took her painting from the desk and laid it on top. She could not bear to see it. She looked away.

"Stand up, Emma. I'll pin it on."

Emma stood up, her face hot and red. Miss Vernon pinned the flag to her chest. The other children were looking at her.

"There! It's not so bad as all that. Now get into line, everyone, and march out of the school in an orderly fashion."

But Emma, looking down at her union jack, knew it was very bad indeed, and as she marched out in her line, she removed the odious thing from her chest and tore it into pieces. She dropped them into the wastepaper basket as she passed.

Miss Vernon was cross. Emma was taken before the head and asked to give an account of herself, while the rest of the school marked time in the playground, under a sky that threatened rain.

"Why did you tear up your union jack?"

"It had gone all runny," Emma said. "It's a silly idea, anyway. Who wants to wear a union jack?"

The upper standards were wearing rosettes. They were beautiful, Emma thought.

"Well, get into line," Betony said, "and when we all get to the green, I shall expect to hear you singing all the more heartily, to make up for not wearing your red white and blue."

Thus the school, as always on Empire Day, marched out to the green and assembled there. They heard the vicar's brief address and sang "O God, our help in ages past." They then saluted the union jack, hanging bedraggled on its pole, and marched back into school again, just in time to escape the rain.

Afterwards, when the children had all gone home, Sue Vernon discussed Emma's behaviour with Betony.

"All this naughtiness!" she said. "It's only to gain attention, you know. *Your* attention, to be precise. It will be better in future, I think, if I deal with her bad behaviour myself instead of sending her to you."

Betony, however, disagreed.

"I think it's time she came into my class. She's forward enough for Standard II. She'd be moving up anyway next term."

"But that's exactly what she wants. It's most unwise to give in to her."

"Sometimes children are much improved by getting what they want," Betony said.

"Well, it's your decision, of course," Sue said. "You are the head."

Privately, she thought her own thoughts. Was Miss Izzard a bit of a snob, favouring this gentleman farmer's daughter? Or were her motives more personal? She seemed on good terms with Stephen Wayman. Perhaps there was something brewing there.

The following morning, when school began, Emma had a place in the big room, with the four boys and seven girls of Standard II. She shared a desk with Hilary Slewton. Hilary helped her to do her sums.

At home, when Emma announced her news, the family made a great fuss of her.

"Why have you been moved up? Is it because you're a good scholar?"

"No, it's because I was naughty," Emma said.

Joanna and the boys laughed at her.

"It must be a jolly funny school!"

"Trust our Emma to be the opposite of everyone else!"

"Our little Emma naughty?" said Chris. "I don't believe a word of it!"

"I *was* naughty," Emma said. "I did all sorts of naughty things."

"Then I'm sorry to hear it," Stephen said. He frowned at this youngest child of his. "I shall have to speak to Miss Izzard about you."

But, meeting Betony soon afterwards, he heard that Emma was now a model pupil.

"She gives me no trouble," Betony said.

* * * * *

Although promoted to the big room, Emma did not forget Robert Mercybright, left behind in the infants' class. Sometimes she sought him out in the playground and gave him a sweet or a piece of chocolate or half the banana she had brought for her elevenses. One day, as they sat together on the toolshed step, she gave him a share of the small blue-black berries she had taken from a bush in the garden at home. Robert, on chewing them, made a face. He gave a shudder and spat them out.

"Aren't they nice?" Emma said. She tried one herself and

194

found it bitter. It made a roughness on her tongue. She too spat it out. "Oh, they're nasty, horrid things! Here, have a peppermint instead, and that'll take away the taste."

That afternoon Robert was sick. His mother was sent for, from Mrs Frail's, and came at once to take him home. By then his lips were swollen inside, and he complained that his tongue was sore.

"What have you been eating?" Linn demanded.

Robert was silent, looking at her. His face was pale and miserable.

"Did you eat anything?" Betony asked. She knew that Emma gave him sweets. "Don't be afraid to tell us, Rob."

They were standing together in the school porch. The boy was reluctant to answer them, but the story of the berries came out at last, and Betony went to fetch Emma.

"What sort of berries were they that you gave Robert to eat?"

"They came off a jumper bush," Emma said.

"Jumper bush? What is that?"

"It's just a bush in the garden at home. I picked them on the way to school."

"What did they look like?" Betony asked.

Emma put her hand into her pinafore pocket and took out the berries remaining there. She dropped them into Betony's palm.

"Juniper berries! Thank goodness for that!" Betony showed them in her palm to Linn. "You've nothing to worry about," she said. "They're perfectly harmless. Just bitter, that's all."

"How can you be so sure of that?"

"For one thing, they're used in flavouring gin. For another, I've chewed them up myself – long ago, when I was a child. They taste nasty but they do no harm."

"I wouldn't say they were harmless, myself. Look at the state of Robert's mouth. *And* you say he was sick as well." Linn, in her anxiety for her son, rounded angrily on Emma. "How dare you make him eat things like that? You're a very wicked, naughty girl!" She disliked the child's remote, calm gaze. She wanted to see some fear in her; some awareness of her own wrongdoing. "His lips are all swollen and sore inside. You should be ashamed, a girl of your age, forcing a little boy like Robert to eat bad things that make him ill."

"*I* wasn't sick," Emma said. "*My* lips aren't swollen inside."

"Perhaps if they were," Linn replied, "you might be a bit more sorry, child!"

Emma looked at the little boy, leaning against his mother's side. Then she looked up at Betony.

"Is he going to die?" she asked.

"No, of course not," Betony said. "Juniper berries aren't poisonous. You've just heard me say they're not. But I want you to promise me, faithfully, that you won't ever eat strange berries again or give them to other children, either."

"We didn't eat them. We spat them out."

"Will you promise me, anyway?"

"Yes, I promise," Emma said.

Betony sent her back to the classroom.

"She doesn't care twopence, does she?" Linn said. "Doesn't she realize the harm she could have done?"

"She's only a child," Betony said.

Linn was now preparing to leave. She laid a hand on Robert's forehead.

"I shall take him to the doctor before I go home. I'd sooner be on the safe side. I don't like the look of his mouth at all."

"Yes, I should do that," Betony said. "It will set your mind at rest. But I'm sure there's nothing to worry about. He's beginning to look better already."

She was sufficiently anxious, however, to walk over to Lilac Cottage that evening and find out how the little boy was. She found him in the garden, watching his grandfather Mercybright, who was up on a ladder, repairing the roof. The soreness and swelling had gone from his mouth; he had eaten his tea without being sick; and there was some colour in his cheeks. The doctor had said there was no reason for concern.

"Well, Robert!" Betony said. "I'm glad to see you're yourself again."

"Linn fusses too much," Jack Mercybright said. "She wraps the boy in cotton wool. If he comes to no worse harm than that, he'll be a lot more lucky than most."

Linn herself appeared in the doorway.

"Will you come in for a cup of tea?"

"No, thank you, I'll be on my way."

But Betony paused long enough to gaze up at the sunken roof, where four or five of the tiles were missing, leaving a gap some two feet wide. Jack was inserting a piece of tin, edging it under the upper tiles, spreading it over the lower ones. Elsewhere the roof was similarly patched.

"Won't Mr Challoner do those repairs?"

"I've been asking him since the year dot."

"At least he could let you have some tiles."

"The laths is gone under this tin. The whole roof's as daddocky as a sponge. We shall have it in on us one of these days. Challoner's got no money to spare for roofs. It goes on his hunters and his motor cars and paying his tailor to make him look thin."

"Yes, I know," Betony said.

And she walked away from the damp, dilapidated cottage, angry at the truth of what Jack said.

Next she went to Holland Farm. Aunt Doe answered the door and Betony told her about the berries.

"I thought I ought to warn you," she said, "in case Emma suffers some ill-effects."

"Silly child! She ought to know better!" aunt Doe said. "She certainly hasn't been sick so far. Is the little boy all right?"

"Right as rain now," Betony said.

"It's very kind of you to come. Emma's gone with her brothers up to the woods. Will you come in for a little while?"

"No, thank you, I'm on my way home."

"Stephen's over in the barn there. He's doctoring a sick cow. Won't you wait while I fetch him in?"

"No, please, don't call him away. I really must be getting home."

On her way back across the yard, she heard a rustling in the straw in the barn, and the quick loud snorting of a cow in distress. She heard Stephen's voice as he spoke to it; soothing it; calming it down. For a moment she paused, listening to him, thinking that perhaps she would look in on him after all. Then some strange shyness came over her. She had second thoughts and went on her way.

Chapter 11

That summer was the wettest for thirty-six years. In Chepsworth, in June, the three rivers overflowed and the town was flooded. Swans swam down the High Street and people went to and fro in punts. Many roads were badly damaged, and part of the railway embankment collapsed. The agricultural show had to be cancelled, for the first time in its history. On every farm throughout the district there was deep gloom. Haymaking was held back for weeks on end. Corn crops were beaten down and lodged.

"You were a lot wiser than me, cutting back on your corn crops so hard as you did," John Challoner said to Stephen. "The wet won't harm you the way it will me. I shall damn well go bankrupt if this goes on. I'll be coming to ask you for a loan!"

This was his refrain all through the summer. Stephen grew somewhat irritated. Once he said something sharp in reply.

"You could always send your new billiard table back!"

"Ah, you think that's extravagant, I suppose? But damn it, man, you wouldn't deny me a bit of fun?"

Stephen said nothing more. It was none of his business, obviously. But Challoner, spending up to the hilt, was a worried man, and he took it out on his labourers. The bad weather made loafers of them. Why should he pay them a full wage just to watch the rain from inside his barn?

"They've got to live, whether it rains or not," Stephen said.

"So have I!" Challoner said.

He reduced his men's wages yet again. He paid them twenty-four-and-six. In this he was ignoring the recommendations of the local Conciliation Committee, but he knew they had no power as a body. He scarcely gave them a passing thought.

"Another flaming cut in our pay?" said Bill Mayle, when pay-day came.

There was a seething among the men. They crowded close against Challoner's desk.

"You ent playing fair with us, master. It ent our fault the weather's bad."

"Twenty-four-and-six! Hell! How'm I going to feed six kids?"

"It ent even enough to starve on, by God!"

"I've got a sick wife at home. It'll just about kill her when she hears about this!"

"If you cut our wages much more, Mr Challoner, you'll soon be paying us in threepenny bits!"

There was a double barb in this, for Challoner carried a collection of silver threepenny pieces in his waistcoat pocket, and would dole them out, when the mood took him, to any children he happened to meet. He made himself popular in this way. There was always someone to speak well of him.

"That's enough of your lip, Cox!" he said. "If you don't like it, you know what to do. There's plenty of men only too willing to step into your shoes for that wage."

"How are we supposed to live?"

"You'll have to cut down a bit, that's all."

"Ah, we'll have to cut down on the luxuries, such as food and drink!" said Jack Mercybright, witheringly.

"That'll be the day!" Challoner said. "*You're* no stranger to a pint pot!"

"I'm a stranger to a decent living wage."

Later that day, when Jack left work, five of his mates were at the farm gate, waiting to have a word with him. Two of these were union men. They were keen for Jack to join.

"I'm reporting this cut in our wages," said Cox. "I'm going along this afternoon to see Harry Davids straight away."

"What good'll that do?" Jack asked.

"If the union was stronger, we'd soon get things done. There's talk of the Wages Board coming back. We shall press for that at the next meeting. Why don't you join us?

We need your sort."

Jack merely shrugged his way through the group.

"I prefer to fight my own battles."

"Ah, fight 'em and lose 'em!" Cox retorted scornfully.

Jack took no notice, but walked on. His bad knee, injured more than forty years before, gave him pain when the weather was wet. His only thought was to get home.

Linn, when she put his supper in front of him, saw at once that something was wrong.

"Another Irishman's rise this week!" He planked his money down on the table. "The way things are going with Challoner, I reckon *we'll* soon be paying *him* for the privilege of slaving on his land!"

Linn sat down wearily. She had her own story to tell, for her work at Tinkerdine, skivvying for Mrs Frail, would come to an end in another week. Mrs Frail had been displeased because Linn had left at two o'clock on the day Robert had eaten the berries. Now that a replacement had been found, Linn had been told that she could go. But the bad news would keep until after supper. Her father, she saw, was in pain with his leg. She leant across to her little son and dropped a knob of margarine into the centre of his mashed potatoes.

The day was already growing dark. It was raining heavily again. Overhead, in the room above, there was a rapid thud, thud, thud, as the rain dripped through the cottage roof, into the bucket placed to receive it.

* * * * *

When, a few weeks later, the Wages Board was reinstated and the minimum wage for a farm labourer was set by law at thirty shillings, Challoner promptly sacked two men. For him the issue was simple enough. "I can't afford you at that wage." His choice of two men was also simple: he sacked those two who belonged to the union, Fred Cox and Johnny Marsh.

Betony, shopping at Jeremy Rye's, met Fred Cox coming away, and they stood talking for a while. Fred was in a bitter mood. It was the day he had been dismissed.

201

"Funny it's always us union chaps. It was the same at Holland Farm, with the chap that was sacked at Easter time. The only union man on the farm and *he* was the one that got the push. You don't mean to tell me it's just by chance!"

"That wasn't the same," Betony said. "Morton George was a bad lot. He was an idler and a mischief-maker. Mr Wayman had no choice but to dismiss him."

"That's what all the farmers say. No doubt Challoner says it of me! Am I an idler, I'd like to know?" Cox's wrath and bitterness brought a hint of tears to his eyes. "It ent only me. It's Kitty as well." His wife cooked and cleaned for Challoner. — She also was losing her job. "And of course we've got to quit our cottage. We've got a week to find some place else. Jesus, what a bloody life! No job! No home! No bloody dole! Is this what I fought in Gallipoli for?"

"Can't the union do anything?"

"What can they do? They can't make jobs!" Cox took out a newspaper, some days old, and showed it to her, open at an advertisement in bold black type: "There is NO unemployment in Canada. Men and women are wanted here."

"Are you thinking of going?" Betony asked.

"When I got home, after the war, I swore I'd never leave England again. But what is England doing for us? It's treating us as if we was dirt. It can't be no worse in Canada."

"What about Billy John?"

Fred's eldest son, as expected, had won his free place at the Grammar school and was due to take it up in September.

"Where's the sense of his going to a good school if his dad's a pauper begging his bread?" Fred took the paper and pocketed it. "I wonder, if I was to apply to emigrate, whether you'd write me a character?"

"Yes, of course," Betony said. "If it's what you really want."

But it made her sad to think of men like Fred Cox being driven from their own country to seek a living elsewhere.

* * * * *

In a field of oats lying behind Jack Mercybright's cottage, he

202

and the other Outlands men were at work with their scythes, for the corn had been badly lodged by the rain and could not be cut by the reaper-and-binder. Challoner came down to see how the work was going on. He picked up a musty sheaf here and there and threw them from him in disgust.

"Not even fit for the pigs!" he said. "I shall soon be bankrupt at this rate!" He stood beside Jack and watched him at work. "Your leg playing you up?"

"Not so's you'd notice," Jack said.

"How old are you now, Mercybright?"

"Why do you want to know?" Jack asked.

"Strikes me you'll soon be putting in for your pension."

"Well, I ent the only one, come to that."

Challoner glanced at him narrowly, but Jack seemed intent upon his work, and his bearded face gave nothing away. The weather was humid; close and warm; Jack sweated as he worked with his scythe, and the sweat ran down into his beard. The other men worked some way away; they were keeping clear of Challoner.

Linn came out of the back of the cottage, carrying a mug of beer for her father. She faltered when she saw Challoner there, but then she came on, through a gap in the hedge, and so up the field to where Jack stood. Robert followed close behind, dragging a horseshoe on a piece of string. Jack took the beer and drank it half down. He wiped his mouth with the back of his hand.

"Good morning, Mr Challoner," Linn said.

John Challoner gave her a nod.

"You got a holiday from your work?"

"I don't go to Mrs Frail any more."

"Can't say I blame you," he said. "A bit of a Tartar, from what I've heard."

Jack finished his beer and she took his mug. Challoner watched her as she walked down the field. The dress she wore was too big for her; it hung in ugly folds round her hips. Her shoes were badly trodden down and a piece of brown paper, lining one sole, had worked its way up at the back of her heel. Challoner noted all these things. He also noted her shapeliness; the set of her head on her smooth

203

slim neck; the roundness and whiteness of her arms; a certain something in the way she walked. If she had money to spend on clothes. . . . He pictured the stir the girl would cause, arriving, perhaps, at the Hunt Ball. It was a pity she had red hair, and yet it was striking in its way; and he wondered, not for the first time, how Jack Mercybright, a common labourer, had come to produce such a beautiful daughter.

The following morning, when Jack arrived at the farm for work, Challoner met him in the yard.

"I need a woman to come in and cook and clean for me now that Kitty Cox is going. What about that daughter of yours? Would she be willing to come in?"

"You'd better ask her," Jack said.

"Can't you ask her when you get home? It's not too much trouble for you, is it?"

"All right, I'll ask her," Jack said, "but I dunno that she'll want to come."

He was against the idea from the start. He made that plain when he spoke to Linn.

"But why shouldn't I take the job? It would be so convenient, being close at hand."

"You'll have no peace if you go to that house. He's got a bit of a name, you know, and I've seen the way he looks at you."

"Oh, what nonsense!" Linn exclaimed. "Mr Challoner's always treated me very politely. You do exaggerate sometimes."

"You know the man better than I do, no doubt!"

"You want me to turn down a pound a week when we are as hard up as we are nowadays?"

"Whose fault is it that we're hard up? It's Challoner's fault and don't you forget it!"

"We need that money," Linn said.

"We can manage without it if we try. At least I'm back to thirty bob."

"No, father, I'm taking the job."

"All right. You suit yourself. But you'll have trouble with that man as sure as God's in Gloucestershire, and then you'll wish you'd listened to me."

Jack's tone was so earnest that Linn for a while experienced some fear. But later that evening, mending her small son's shabby clothes, she thought of the things she needed to buy, and the fear receded to the back of her mind. She went to the farmhouse on Sunday morning and told Mr Challoner she wanted the job.

"There is just one thing, however," she said. "I shall have to bring my little boy."

"Isn't there someone you could leave him with?"

"I'd sooner have him with me, Mr Challoner, at least until he goes back to school."

"My house is not a nursery, you know," Challoner said, in his jocular way. "I'll be paying you to cook and clean for my son and me, not to be coddling that boy of yours."

"The work will be done, I promise you, and I'll see that Robert gives no trouble."

"Very well. You bring him along. We'll fit in together, I daresay."

It was agreed. Challoner shook hands with her and saw her to the door. Linn looked at his good-humoured face and was sure that her father must be mistaken.

"I wonder if I might ask you something, Mr Challoner?"

"Ask away! I'm all ears!"

"It's the roof of our cottage," Linn said. "I know you're a very busy man, but it is in rather a bad condition, and what with the weather we're having now – "

"Leaking, is it? Well, that won't do. I'll get a man to come along and see what wants doing as soon as possible."

"Oh, if you could! I'd be ever so grateful, I really would."

Linn felt rather pleased with herself. She went home to her father and repeated Mr Challoner's promise.

"'As soon as possible'?" Jack said. "And when is that, I'd like to know? The roof's been leaking for nearly three years. I've asked him and asked him a hundred times but it ent made no difference that I can see."

"Perhaps you went the wrong way about it. You can be very surly sometimes."

"And *you* went the right way, I suppose?" Jack raised his newspaper and shut her out. His anger rose with the smoke from his pipe. After a while he spoke again. "Is it all fixed up, then, that you're going there to molly for him?"

"Yes, father, it's all arranged. I start tomorrow at seven o'clock."

Thus Linn went to work at Outlands Farm, and Robert went with her every day. She thought her father's fears were groundless, but if by any chance he was right, Robert would be her best protection.

"So this is young Master Mercybright?" Challoner said, on the first morning. "He's a solemn little chap, isn't he? And dark as dark! I can't see that he's much like you, so I take it he favours his father, eh?"

Challoner knew, as everyone in Huntlip did, that Linn had not been married to Robert's father. She glanced at him, suspecting some slyness in the remark, but he was still looking at the little boy, and was pressing a coin into his hand.

"Robert's father is dead," she said.

"I know that," Challoner said. "Chap called Tom Maddox, wasn't it? A carpenter down at old man Tewke's? But *does* the boy take after him?"

"Yes, there's a likeness," Linn said. She was shedding her mackintosh. "Where would you like me to start work?"

* * * * *

Within a week, Linn knew she had made a mistake. Challoner was in and out of the house all day. He hung about while she cooked the meals. Sometimes he came and stood by her, looking over her shoulder, into the pans, as she stirred a thickening into the stew or prodded the potatoes to see if they were done. He would lean against her, thigh to thigh, his body pressing hard against hers. He would take the wooden spoon from her, and would taste the broth, looking at her through the rising steam.

"A bit more salt!" he would say to her, and when she was putting the salt in, his big hand would clamp down over hers, squeezing her fingers very hard till the salt-lump was crushed and sprinkled in. "Don't be afraid to bung it in! We're both salt-herrings, my son and me. Let's try it again and see if it's right. Here, you have a taste and see what you

206

think."

Sometimes, when she was down on her knees, scrubbing the flagstones, he would stand in the doorway, watching her, eyeing the shape of her bent body. Although Robert was in the room, his presence was no protection to her, for the man made remarks to the little boy, playing upon his innocence.

"She's got a fine figure, this mother of yours. She's worth better things than scrubbing floors, don't you think so, young Mercybright?"

More than once, as he made these remarks, he stooped over Linn and touched her body, his hands going over the curve of her hip or tracing the slender course of her spine as she stooped to her work. And each time, when she squirmed away, pushing at his hand with her scrubbing-brush, he would step back, laughing deep in his throat, and would stand for a while in front of her, watching the colour that rose like a fire in her fair-skinned face. Once when he laid his hand on her, Robert ran forward and pushed at him, looking up at his face with a dark-eyed frown.

"Don't do that, my mother don't like it!" the little boy said.

"How do you know what your mother likes? You don't know everything, young fella-me-lad!"

He was always trying to catch Linn's eye. His admiring glances were meant to please. But Linn found it hard to look at him. In the past she had thought him a handsome man, but now his big face and easy smile and the meaningful softness in his eyes had become disgusting and loathsome to her. She knew that if she met his gaze her loathing would be betrayed at once.

Challoner's admiration for Linn was not confined to her looks alone. She was a cut above the rest of her kind. Her speech was less broad and her voice itself was pleasant to hear. Her work in the house was full of little touches that took him by surprise. When laying the table for a meal, she put out the cruets and serving-spoons that had long lain idle in their black bags, and when serving the meals, she made use of the gravy-boats and soup-tureens and saw to it that they were hot. The meals themselves were excellent. She took trouble in making savoury sauces to go with the carrots, the marrow, the swedes; and her light fluffy pancakes delighted him.

"Where did you learn to do these things?"

"I was in service at Meynell Hall."

"Seems to me we're in clover, my boy," Challoner said to his son Gerald. "We haven't been so well looked after since your mother was alive."

Gerald agreed. The house was a pleasant place these days. It was clean, comfortable, cheerful, and bright. There were fresh sheets on the bed every week; there were beautifully ironed shirts to put on; clothes were mended, boots were cleaned, and messages were got from the shop. There were even flowers in a bowl on the hall table.

"Why not ask her to come full-time?" Gerald suggested to his father one evening.

"What, come and live in?" Challoner said. "I doubt if she'd leaver that father of hers."

"She might if you made it worth her while."

"I'm not sure that I know what you mean."

"If you were to marry her," Gerald said, "that would make it worth her while."

"You're jumping the gun a bit, aren't you, my boy? She's only been here a couple of weeks!" But the thought was not new in Challoner's mind, and he saw that Gerald suspected as much. Casually, yet choosing his words, he said: "What would you really say, I wonder, at having a stepmother in the house?"

"I'd say good luck to you," Gerald said. He was already courting a girl at Blagg and hoped to marry her in the spring. As he was only nineteen, he was bent on winning his father's goodwill. "You could do a lot worse than marry the Mercybright girl, I reckon, though the boy'd be a nuisance, I suppose."

"I wouldn't say that. He's a nice little chap in his funny way. I've taken quite a fancy to him."

"Well, so long as you don't go and leave him the farm!"

"What, another man's child, and a bastard at that? Don't talk rubbish!" Challoner said.

But the thought of marriage, endorsed as it had been by his son, began to take firmer root in his mind. He began to watch Linn in a different way; weighing her up; all the pros and cons. He would be marrying beneath him, of course. He could hear what some of his neighbours would say. "One of his own labourers' daughters, and with an illegitimate child at that!" But he had no taste for marrying a woman of his own class, for that meant some widow, nearer his age. He would prefer a young wife like Linn; someone he could cosset and spoil; someone who would be grateful to him for lifting her up out of poverty; someone he could dote on and enjoy.

Linn was a very beautiful girl. He saw her, in his mind's eye, dressed in good clothes and some jewellery, presiding at his table when friends came to dine. He saw her accompanying him to whist drives and dances and the N.F.U. social evenings. He saw her wearing smart little hats, coming to him from the hairdresser's in town, smelling of scent and face-powder, her golden-red hair set in rippling waves.

One morning he woke with his mind made up. He would soon be sixty-two. He had been a widower for eight years. Where was the sense in hanging back?

* * * * *

The harvest weather was terrible. Most of the corn had to be cut by hand. And all day, across the fields at Outlands, came the tseep-tsawp-tseep-tsawp of the mowers sharpening the blades of their scythes.

Linn, when she took her father's dinner up to him in the Big Piece, found him wearing sacks tied like gaiters round his legs, and some of the other men the same. The corn as they cut it was sodden and heavy; the grain was sprouting in the ear; the straw was blackened and smelt of mould. There was no harvest jollity in the field. Jack took the basket with scarcely a word. She noticed that he was limping badly.

"Is granddad cross with us?" Robert asked, returning with her to the farmhouse.

"His leg is hurting him," Linn said.

One day when she had been picking beans in the garden at Outlands, she suddenly found that Robert was missing.

She went into the house, calling him, but only Challoner was there. He stood in front of the kitchen range, booted feet wide apart, hands deep in his breeches pockets.

"The boy's not here," he said to her. "I sent him to the village to buy some sweets."

"But he never goes to the village alone! And I don't like you giving him money to spend, Mr Challoner. I mentioned it to you once before."

"Don't be a spoilsport. He'll come to no harm. I wanted the chance of a word with you, without little pitchers listening, all ears."

"I'd rather you didn't, Mr Challoner."

"You haven't heard what I've got to say."

"I don't think I want to hear it," she said.

"You'll soon change your mind when you know what it is."

Challoner was deeply amused. He watched the movement of colour in her face and wished she would look him straight in the eye. He had arranged things pretty well; he meant to savour this courtship of his. The girl's show of modesty did her credit; it was only what he expected of her; and he would enjoy breaking it down. He was going to be very gentlemanly. He meant to treat her with perfect respect. He was going to show her, in fact, what marriage to a man of his sort would mean for a woman such as she.

But Linn, alone in the house with him, was filled with a sudden choking fear. The way he stood seemed to threaten her. His broad bulky body filled the hearth. She set down her basket and turned towards the door. Challoner quickly followed her. He took her by the shoulders and swung her round and when, more by chance than by design, one of his hands caught the front of her blouse, he thrust it inside to cover her breasts, squeezing her flesh most painfully between his big fingers, rough-skinned and hard. It was not what he had intended, but, once having touched her, he was inflamed. He spoke to her in a thickened voice.

"What're you running away for? Why don't you stop and give me a chance?"

"No, let me go, for pity's sake!"

As Linn writhed away from him, freeing herself, her fear

and disgust were so extreme that they blazed out of her, uncontrolled.

"Don't touch me!" she cried in a shrill voice. "Don't touch me with your big ugly hands!"

Challoner stared. He became very still. He saw the loathing in her eyes.

"My God," he said, incredulously, "I wonder what you think you are?"

"I may be your servant but I'm not your whore!"

"You can't always have been nice! That boy of yours is proof of that!"

"Oh, I knew very well enough what was in your mind!"

"You lived with Tom Maddox, didn't you? Brazenly, for all to see? You made yourself the talk of the place! – Do you think I don't remember it? And what were you then, living with him? Were you his servant or his whore?"

"I loved him," Linn said. "You'll never make me ashamed of that."

"You were never his wife, though, were you, by God? You were never any man's wife so far. Well, let me tell you something, madam! You with your talk about being a whore! If you hadn't been so quick off the mark – if you hadn't jumped to the wrong conclusion – if you hadn't shown yourself up for what you are – I was going to ask you to be *my* wife! Yes, madam, you can stare! That's brought you up short a bit, I can see."

"Your wife? You must be mad!" Linn said. At another time she would not have believed him. Now she hardly knew what she said. Her physical revulsion against the man gave her tongue a cruel edge. "Did you really think I would marry you? A man of your age with grown up sons? Did you think I was yours just for the asking, because I'm a servant in your house?"

"I hope you've finished now!" he exclaimed. "I hope you've said all you've got to say."

Challoner's face was an ugly red. His rage brought a wetness to his eyes. But Linn, as she recovered herself, saw that he was deeply hurt. She saw him as a foolish, self-deceived man, and fleetingly she was sorry for him. She wished she could call back some of the things she had said to him. But it was too late; she knew he would never forgive her now; and a new terror arose in her for, having offended him like this, her own job and her father's would be at stake.

"Mr Challoner," she began. "Mr Challoner, I'm sorry it's all turned out as it has."

"Sorry, are you? I can well believe that!"

"Do you want me to leave the house?"

"It's up to you. You can please yourself."

"I don't want to lose my job."

"No, nor lose your father his!" Watching her, he became sly. He knew what fears tormented her. There was a sneer in his voice. "You need the money, I daresay, and I shouldn't like to see you starve. You've got your boy to think about. Your little love-child. Your little mistake."

Abruptly he made towards the door.

"You can stay on by all means, and when you're doing your bits and bobs of chores about the place, you can be thinking this to yourself. – You could have been mistress of this house if only you'd played your cards the right way. Your little boy could have had my name. I could have done a lot for him and sent him to a good school. You just think what you've thrown away!"

The door slammed, and he was gone. Linn sat down, trembling, in a chair and rested her elbows on the table, but before she could yield to the threatening tears, Robert returned from the village shop. He had not spent his threepence on liquorice laces; he had bought a small tortoishell comb for his mother to wear clipped in her hair.

* * * * *

Challoner never touched her now, but he kept a close watch on her just the same, and whereas before he had been full of praise, now he found fault with everything.

"Do you call these clean?" he said, flinging his boots down in front of her. "You'll have to do better than that, by God, before they're fit for market wear."

There was far more washing to do now. Challoner changed his shirt every day. And whereas before, on washday mornings, the young lad Godwin had brought in

212

the coal, now she had to do it herself. She had to pump all the water and carry it in, and chop her own sticks to light the fire. Gerald soon noticed the change in his father's manner to her. He wanted to know what was wrong.

"Never you mind!" Challoner said. "The girl is a bitch, I can tell you that. I was never so taken-in in my life."

"She can't be as bad as all that, surely?" It was easy enough for Gerald to guess what lay behind the change. "You'll drive her away if you treat her like this."

"Hah! Not her! She wants the money too much for that. She said so herself."

Out in the fields, as wet as ever, harvest progressed with dreadful slowness. The sight of the sprouting, smut-blackened corn, mouldering as it stood in the shocks, did nothing to improve Challoner's temper. Once he came into the farmyard when Linn was carrying buckets of kitchen-waste to the boiler-house next to the piggery.

"Kitty Cox always used to give a hand out in the harvest-field," he said. "I suppose you're too refined for that?"

"I can't do everything," Linn said.

She bore his treatment as best she could. He would surely not keep it up for long. But his spite was not so easily assuaged; instead of lessening, it grew; he was determined to have his revenge. One day he took her out to the barn and set her to pluck two dozen fowls. They had to be ready by seven o'clock, he said, and it was then just after two. It took her till eight to pluck them all, and her hands by that time were red and raw, the finger-tips bleeding, too sore to touch. Robert played outside in the yard. He came into the barn when she was trussing up the fowls. Her hands were so sore she could hardly bear to handle the string. Robert helped her to tie the knots.

At home that evening, preparing supper, she wore a pair of cotton gloves.

"What's wrong with your hands?" Jack asked.

"It's some kind of rash," she said, shrugging, and to her relief he asked no more.

He took little interest, apparently, in the work she did for Challoner. He never asked her how she got on. He rarely

213

mentioned it at all. But once he said sarcastically: "When's he sending someone to fix up the roof? I thought you'd arranged it, you and him."

Whatever Challoner told her to do, she did without a word of complaint. But what caused her anguish, secretly, was that Robert should witness the humiliations heaped upon her. It was nothing that he saw her scrubbing floors, but that he should see her emptying the latrine, struggling to carry the big slopping bucket across the yard and down the track, to tip it into the piggery midden: she hated Challoner for this. That in front of the little wide-eyed boy the man should fling his gaiters at her and send a tin of saddle-soap rattling across the table to her, and should say in his loud contemptuous voice, "You won't take all day at that job, I hope? – I'm going out at ten sharp!": she hated Challoner for these things.

The depth of the hatred she felt for him sometimes shocked her and made her afraid. Following him out to his motor car once, carrying a hamper filled with game, she was shocked at the picture that filled her mind, of the motor car skidding on the wet road and the man lying dead across the wheel. What sort of woman had she become, that she could wish someone dead? she thought. But her greatest fear of all was that Jack should learn of the way Challoner treated her.

"Don't tell your granddad that I empty the privy up at the farm," she said to Robert one day. "It's better for him if he doesn't know. Promise mummy you won't tell?"

Robert nodded, giving his promise. She knew she could trust him, young as he was.

*　*　*　*　*

But it so happened, the following day, that as she was carrying the latrine bucket across the yard, her father came through the gate from the pasture, leading a horse that had gone lame.

"What's this?" he said, coming to her, and she set down the bucket to ease her arm. "Where's the lad that does these jobs?"

214

"I don't know," Linn said. She looked round the yard in a vague way, as though expecting Godwin to come.

"How long have you been doing jobs like this?"

"Father, don't make a fuss!" she cried, for the look in his face was frightening, and she knew that Challoner was in the barn. "It's no concern of yours what I do. Just leave me to manage my own affairs."

"That bastard's been putting on you, by God! D'you think I ent seen it in your eyes? D'you think I ent seen you dwindling away to a nottomy streak these past few weeks? D'you think I'm going to let it pass?"

"Dad, do be quiet!" Linn said. "Get back to your work and leave me to mine."

"That's no work for you!" Jack said. "Not after today, it's not, by God! Where's the swine hiding hisself? I'd like to have a few words with him!"

Challoner came out of the barn and stood with his hands in his breeches pockets. His voice rang out across the yard.

"You asking for *me* by any chance?"

"I'm glad you know which swine I meant!"

"You must be drunk, Mercybright, if you think you can talk to me like that!"

"What do you think my daughter is, that you get her to empty your stinking slops? Slavery's been done away with this good long time since! Are you aiming to bring it back?"

"If she doesn't like it, she knows what to do! She can clear off and leave the job to someone else!"

"She's going, don't worry! I'll see to that!"

"You can take yourself off at the same time! You think because you're an old man – "

"Old man be buggered!" Jack said. "At least I know what age I am! I don't make a fool of myself trying to get young women half my age to warm my bed for me and then turning nasty cos I don't get my way!"

"Have you finished, Mercybright?"

"I'll have finished when I get to the end!"

News of the quarrel had gone round the farm. The harvesters had come from the nearby field and were loitering about the yard. The two cowmen had come from the sheds. Gerald Challoner now appeared and stood with a

215

spanner in his hand, having come from repairing one of the tractors. His handsome round face was darkly flushed. He raised his spanner in a threatening way.

"We've heard about enough from you, Mercybright! You can come to the office and get your cards!"

"Lead the way!" Jack said. "I've been on this farm for ten years. That's ten years too long, so let's not waste time!"

Ten minutes later Jack and Linn and little Robert walked away from the farmhouse. Challoner's voice followed them.

"I want you out of your cottage by the end of next week! I'll serve an eviction on you, else! Do you hear me, man?"

Jack made no answer. He merely walked on. He was trying hard to disguise his limp.

"I knew this would happen!" Linn said. "Why, oh why, couldn't you leave me be?"

Again Jack said nothing, but walked on. His bearded face was grimly set. His mouth was a single tight-closed line. Robert, walking with one hand in Linn's, looked up at her anguished tear-stained face. She began to sob uncontrollably.

"I knew it would end like this!" she said. "If only people would leave me alone!"

Chapter 12

There was more heavy rain again in September. The Derrent burst its banks again and the roads were flooded for days on end. When the waters at last went down, Jesse Izzard with his son Dicky and three of the other carpenters from Cobbs were out working for eighteen hours, repairing the ruined sluice-gates. Then there were more thunderstorms and the Derrent was in flood again. But at least the sluice-gates were working now. The floods could to some extent be controlled.

"Them sluice-gates should hold till domesday now," Jesse said to Beth, his wife, "with all the good timber we've put into them."

Jesse was very important these days, now that great-grumpa Tewke had gone. Although his wife and son had more say than he in how the carpenter's shop was run, it was nevertheless a great thing for him to go to the sawmill at Capleton Wick and order timber in huge supplies. He had a little notebook for it. He talked of "invoices" and "delivery notes" and "credit charges". His lips were stained blue from sucking the tip of his indelible pencil. "All this paper-work!" he would say. "Seems there's no end to it, don't it, eh?" But he enjoyed it all the same.

"Dad's never happier," Dicky said, "than when he's walking to and from with a bit of paper in his hand."

There were other things, too, on Jesse's mind. The little Pikehouse, which he owned, out on the lonely Norton Road, was about to become empty again. Horace Nash was giving it up and going to live with his son at Blagg. Jesse, as landlord, had much to do.

"There's one or two been after me, to let them have the Pikehouse," he said, "and I reckon there'll be more as well."

"You can only let it to one," said Beth, with a glance

towards Dicky and Betony.

"That's what I said to them. My very words! 'I can only let it to one,' I said, 'and I need time to decide just who.' "

Betony and Dicky exchanged a smile. Their mother pretended to frown at them, over her spectacles, which were new.

"It's a great responsibility, being a landlord," she said to them. "You should treat your father with respect."

"They don't seem to realize," Jesse said, "that that little house will be theirs one day."

"That'll be useful," Dicky said, "when we need a kennel to keep a dog in!"

Jesse's face showed that he was hurt.

"I was born at the Pikehouse," he said. "Your two sisters was born there too. It ent just a matter of bricks and mortar and a bit of thatch. Your mother and me was married from there. We lived there two years of our married life."

"Sorry, dad! It was only a joke!"

Jesse looked at Betony, who was counting money on the kitchen table.

"Do you want me to take you in to the station, blossom?"

"No, I'm getting a lift with Jeremy Rye."

Although September was well advanced, the village school had not yet reopened, due in part to the late harvest, in part to the flooding of so many roads. Betony had decided to go away for a week, to see an old school-friend, Nancy Sposs, who now lived in Birmingham.

She left the house at eleven o'clock. That afternoon, at about three, Jack Mercybright called at Cobbs, having heard that the Pikehouse was falling empty. Jesse, as landlord, saw him alone. He led him into the best room.

"So you've come about the Pikehouse, then? The news soon gets round, my word, it does!"

"Is it right that Nash is going?"

"Moving out on Friday next."

"Then what about it?" Jack said.

"That needs some repairs doing first," Jesse said. "I was out there the other day and –"

"Never mind that," Jack said. "I don't mind doing a bit of repairs. The Pikehouse will just about suit us fine."

218

"It's the landlord's job to do the repairs."

"Ah, I know," Jack said. "I've seen 'em scrambling to get it done!"

"You won't find *me* neglecting the place. As soon as there's anything leastlike wrong –"

"Then you'll let us have it, Friday next?"

"Glory be, you're in a hurry!" Jesse said. He took out his pipe and began to light up. It was a thing that took some time. "How come you're looking for a house all of a sudden?"

"I've lost my job, that's how," Jack said, "and that means I'm losing my cottage too."

"Laws! You as well! Wherever will it end? There's any event of men out of work, coming to ask me for jobs and that –"

"D'you think I don't know it? I ent blind!"

"The same with the Pikehouse," Jesse said. "There's two or three been after me, wanting me to let them have it, and that's none too easy to decide."

"It's easy enough, I should've thought. Just a plain yes or no."

"Then there's the question of the rent."

"I can't pay no rent for a week or two. Not until I've found some work."

"Laws!" Jesse said. "As bad as that? Now Bert Smith was here on Monday night and offered me two shillings a week. That's sixpence more than the mason paid, and sixpence is sixpence, after all."

"So you're letting him have it, is that what you mean?"

"I never said so. Not in so many words."

"Well, I reckon my need it greater than his, so how about it?" Jack said.

"That's what they all say," Jesse said. "Please one and offend another – that's how it is when you're letting a house."

"Can I bloody well have it or not?" Jack said. "All I want is a straight yes or no."

"There's no need to swear," Jesse said. "It ent so simple as all that. You've got to give me time to think –"

Suddenly Jack could stand no more. He swung on his

219

heel and left the house. Jesse followed him as far as the kitchen and stood staring at the outer door, still vibrating on its hinges. Beth came in from the scullery, wiping her hands on her pinafore.

"What did he want to see you about?"

"He wanted me to let him have the Pikehouse."

"You surely didn't refuse him, I hope?"

"Of course I didn't!" Jesse said. "He gave me no time to think myself out."

"Then you'd better go after him, hadn't you?"

"Laws!" Jesse said. "He *is* a queer chap! Fancy flying off the handle like that, before I had time to say a word!"

"Are you going after him or am I?"

"All right, all right, I'm on my way."

But when Jesse caught up with him, Jack refused to stop and talk.

"You can keep your Pikehouse and be damned to you!" he said, brushing Jesse aside. "All I wish is I'd never asked!"

"Don't be a fool," Jesse said. "It's yours for the asking. You should know that."

"I ent asking! Not any more!"

"Then what'll you do?" Jesse said, calling after him anxiously.

"I'll do what I've always done!" Jack replied. "I'll fend for myself!"

Jesse returned home to his wife.

"Laws! But he *is* a funny chap! He threw my offer in my face."

"You should've stuck out," Beth said. "You must go to his cottage and try again."

"It won't do no good. You know what he is. He looked as though he could murder me."

"I don't blame him. I could do it myself."

"Oh, it's bound to be *my* fault, I know that!"

"What about Linn and the little boy? Didn't you ever think of them?"

"It's Jack's place to think of them. I said he could have the Pikehouse, didn't I? If he don't take it, that's his fault, not mine."

"I'll go and see him myself," Beth said. She took her coat

from the back of the door. "It's the only way to get things done."

But when she went to Lilac Cottage, neither Jack nor Linn was at home. And although she went twice the next day, each time there was nobody there. She pushed a note under the door and hoped for the best.

"I don't know what Betony will say to you when she gets home," she said to Jesse afterwards. "Such a mess you make of things!"

* * * * *

Betony returned from Birmingham on Friday night. It was after ten and the family were in bed. The next morning, as soon as she heard the news about Jack, she drove to the cottage in Stoney Lane. She found him and Linn in the act of moving out. He had borrowed an old hand-cart and was loading their furniture onto it. Linn was carrying out the bedding. Robert sat on a wooden hutch. He had a tame rabbit in his arms.

Betony tried to reason with Jack. She offered him the Pikehouse and work at Cobbs. But Jack, grim-faced, would have none of it.

"I've already got myself a job."

"On a farm?" Betony said.

"No. Sweeping the roads for the council at Springs."

"You'd sooner do that than work at Cobbs?"

"I'd sooner do *anything*," he said, "than be beholden for what I do."

"What about a place to live?"

"We've got the loan of a couple of rooms."

"Springs is a long way away from here."

"The further the better, where I'm concerned."

He lifted the bedding Linn had brought out and piled it on top of the furniture. Betony turned and took Linn's arm.

"What about you, do you feel the same? Can't I persuade you to change your minds?"

"I reckon dad's right," Linn said. "It's better for us if we fend for ourselves." She drew away from Betony's grasp. "I must get on. There's a lot to do."

221

"Yes. Very well. I'll give you a hand."

"No, there's no need," Linn said. "We can manage by ourselves."

Betony watched them helplessly.

"All this stuff on a hand-cart!" she said. "You'll kill yourselves, pushing that to Springs. Why not borrow our horse and cart?"

"No favours, thanks," Jack said. He hoisted a clothes-basket onto the load. "I asked one favour. I'll ask no more."

"You know my father meant no harm. It's just that he's so slow in his ways. He's very upset that you slammed out like that. He'd far rather *you* had the Pikehouse than anyone else in the world. Surely you must know that?"

"I don't know nothing of the kind."

"Won't you give him another chance?"

"I've just told you. We've got fixed up."

"At least let me take Linn and Robert in the trap. It's nearly fourteen miles to Springs."

"Robert can ride on the hand-cart," said Linn. "I shall be helping dad to push."

"Good God, but you're obstinate!" Betony said. "You'll kill yourselves, the pair of you!"

Neither Jack nor Linn answered her. They busied themselves, loading the cart. She saw that further argument was useless.

"You'll let me come over sometimes and see my godson?"

"Yes, of course," Linn said; but there was no hint of warmth in her tone, nor in the brief glance of her eyes.

"Can you tell me the address?"

"We're not quite sure where it is ourselves. We have to enquire when we get to Springs. The council foreman will take us there."

"Then I hope you'll write to me later on."

"Yes, of course," Linn said again.

Betony turned to the little boy. She stroked the white doe rabbit he held in his arms. He looked at her with deep, dark eyes.

"You won't forget your auntie Betony?" she said.

The little boy nodded, but she knew he meant "no". She laughed at him and touched his face.

"You *will* forget me? What a shame!"

"No," he said. He shook his head.

"I'll be over to see you as soon as I can. As soon as your mummy sends your address. If she forgets, remind her for me. Otherwise how shall I know where to find you when the Whitsun Fair comes round again?"

Reluctantly she left them and drove away. She was filled with anger at their plight, but she knew there was nothing she could do.

"Don't blame *me*!" her father said, meeting her when she got home.

"I *do* blame you!" Betony said. But, seeing the stricken look in his eyes, she relented at once. "No, I don't blame *you*. – I blame the world."

* * * * *

The world was growing old, she said to herself, and God was beginning to feel his years. In ancient times, or so we were told, whenever disorder came to his people, God put out a hand and pointed a finger accusingly, and men were brought to their senses again. Now, it seemed, he no longer cared.

On the third Sunday in September, the vicar of Huntlip, in his sermon, touched on the chaos in the world and took his text from the Book of Judges: "In those days there was no king in Israel: every man did that which was right in his own eyes."

People liked to hear Mr Netherton preach. His eloquence stirred them and woke them up. They felt cleansed and scoured after hearing him. And his sermon this Sunday touched on matters that were near home for many of the members of his congregation. Men had lost sight of those things in life that had the most value, he said. In agriculture, in industry, indeed throughout the world of commerce, there was a breakdown in hope and trust. On the land, especially, those who lived by the sweat of their brow were filled with sullenness and resentment. Who could have faith, who had been so betrayed? Was it any wonder that the faces of men and women everywhere were empty

223

of hope, who had looked for guidance and found it not? Our politics, our economy, our morals and our religious feeling, were in disorder throughout the country, and there was no one to point the way. . . .

Outside the church, after the service, Betony stopped for a word with Stephen Wayman. He was there with Joanna and aunt Doe.

"Were you suitably chastened by the vicar's sermon, Miss Izzard?" he asked. "We none of us escaped his lash this time. Employers and employed, rich men and poor! – We were all treated roughly here today!"

"The only one who escaped was God himself," Betony said. "Yet I think perhaps it is he who really needs to be taken to task."

Joanna, looking at her, was shocked. She had recently been confirmed and had entered into a pious phase. Aunt Doe merely smiled. But Stephen gave a little laugh.

"I'm inclined to agree with you, Miss Izzard, and I can think of no one better fitted for the job!"

He caught the quickening of her glance and saw her expression alter a little. He realized how uncouth his joke had sounded. But before he could say anything more, Betony's sister came up with her children, and she was surrounded by nieces and nephews. They were all going back to Cobbs for lunch: Stephen saw her borne away; and he swore to himself, under his breath. Why was he always so inept whenever he met her and talked to her?

Walking through the village with Janie and the children, and listening to their chatter, Betony forgot his remark. She remembered it only when she got home, and then it lodged like a burr in her mind. She looked at herself in the hall mirror as she hung up her coat and hat on the stand. Was that how he saw her? she asked herself. Officious? Admonitory? Self-satisfied? The quintessential school-marm ready to scold even God himself? She laughed at herself, because it hurt.

"There is no king in Israel," she said, speaking to the face in the hall mirror. "Only a handful of schoolmarms like me!"

There was a restlessness in her these days. Janie

remarked on it that afternoon.

"Are you busy hatching something?"

"What sort of something?" Betony asked.

"That's exactly what I want to know."

"I was only thinking, that's all. Perhaps it's not God that's set in his ways. Perhaps it's me after all."

"What do you think you're talking about?"

"I think I'm settling into a rut. I feel it's time I shuffled out."

"Then you are hatching something? I knew you were!"

"No. No, I'm not. It's only a thought. I've got no plans of any kind. At least not yet."

But it so happened that the very next day a letter came to her by post from her old school-friend in Birmingham. Nancy was working in politics. She was chairman of the local Women's Socialist Group. "You seemed interested when you were here, and I thought you might like to know that we shall soon be needing a new assistant secretary. Not much money but plenty of work. The job is yours if you care to take it." Betony wrote asking for details, and a fat package came by return. There was plenty in it for her to read. It occupied her mind for three days.

* * * * *

The weather continued very wet. At Holland Farm, as elsewhere, the harvest dragged on eternally. Although Stephen was growing less corn these days, it seemed it would never be gathered in. They worked in the fields wearing gumboots and macks, so wet was the corn as they handled it.

Betony, driving in the trap down Holland Lane, found her way blocked by a loaded waggon, its front axle lodged on the hump of ground between the deep ruts. There were three or four men gathered about the front of the waggon, and from the field higher up on the left, where barley was being cut and stooked, aunt Doe, helping the harvesters, was calling out unheeded advice.

Stephen came to Betony and raised his cap. He wore a brown tweed jacket, much patched with leather at the

225

elbows and cuffs, and tied round the waist with a piece of string. His gumboots and breeches were coated in mud.

"I'm sorry to hold you up like this. Tupper's gone to fetch a spade. You haven't got an appointment anywhere, I hope?"

"Luckily, no," Betony said. She would not have been able to turn in the lane, because of the terrible depth of the ruts. "The pony is wanting her manger, that's all. Otherwise there's no hurry."

"I'll give her something to stay the pangs."

He groped in the pocket of his shapeless jacket and gave the pony a couple of knobs of cow-cake. Rosie ate them and blew through her nose. She nuzzled his jacket in search of more, her lips exploring the knotted string. She then leant her forehead against his chest, and Stephen, stroking the smooth dappled neck, looked at Betony with a smile. His angular face, with its strong cheekbones and long jaw, looked somewhat drawn and tired, she thought. This was a worrying time for farmers. It had been the worst harvest for forty-six years. But his slow smile was cheerful enough; there was humour in his eyes when he looked at her; and when he came to the side of the trap, to stand with one hand resting on the ledge, he seemed at ease, unhurried, relaxed.

"A dry day for a change, thank God. Overhead at least, though not underfoot."

"Is your harvest very much spoilt?"

"I'm a lot luckier than some. I've increased my stock in the past year or two and most of this – " He pointed to the heavy load of corn towering up from the rut-bound waggon " – will be fed to the cattle in the sheaf."

"What about the years to come?"

"We hold tight and hope for the best."

"You are preparing for a siege?"

"It's what it amounts to, yes," he agreed. "Only a miracle can stop the recession getting worse, and I don't hold out much hope for miracles."

"You don't seem too desperately worried," she said.

Stephen gave the matter some thought.

"For myself and my family, no, I'm not. I paid off my mortgage a month ago. – We've got no debts of any kind

226

now. So I think we shall live to tell the tale. But for many others it will be worse. Some poor devils are going bust. A farmer near Kitchinghampton last week went and hanged himself in his barn. The rest of the breed are frightened men and fear makes them hard on those they employ."

"Your neighbour, Mr Challoner, for one."

"Yes," Stephen said, "I'm afraid that's true."

While he and Betony were talking together, Hopson, Starling, and Billy Rye were talking together on the far side of the waggon, and now, as Bob Tupper came up, bringing mattocks and spades, there was some teasing and laughter among them. Stephen went to see how the work was getting on. He returned and stood by the trap as before and his right hand, with its twisted fingers, rested on the narrow ledge.

"Shouldn't be long before we get it moving now. We'll pull into that gateway lower down so that you can get past without more delay."

"There's no hurry," Betony said. "I'm perfectly happy sitting here."

As soon as these few simple words were spoken, their implication came home to her and she wished them unsaid. She felt a hotness in her face and she stared, frowning, at the pony's ears. She knew that Stephen was looking at her. She turned her head and their glances held. With an effort she spoke again.

"I think perhaps you're right," she said. "It would be better after all."

Stephen stared at her absently.

"What would be better?" he asked. For a moment his mind had gone quite blank. "Oh, you mean if we pulled off into the field?"

"If it's not too much trouble," Betony said.

"None whatever. Certainly not. We've got to take a bit off this load, anyway. We've overdone it, I'm afraid. – We'll never get it home stacked up like this."

The axle was got free at last. The patient horses leant to their task. The wheels began to roll in the ruts and the waggon began to move down the lane. Creaking and swaying, it was driven left through the next gateway, onto an empty field of stubble. The way was now open and Betony, raising her whip in thanks, drove past the gateway and down the lane. Stephen raised his cap to her. He watched her until she had gone from sight.

When he turned to go into the field, he found that aunt Doe was watching him. She had come down the lane from the field above to share her flask of tea with him.

"Was that Miss Izzard you were talking to?"

"Yes. I'm afraid we held her up."

"Did she say when the school would be opening again?"

"No, and I didn't think to ask."

That evening at home, when he and aunt Doe were alone together, he found her thoughtfully studying him.

"Is there something on your mind?"

"When the day comes that you think of getting married again, just say the word and I'll be off. I'll get a little cottage somewhere. You needn't think I'll be in the way."

"Have you someone in mind for me?"

"Goodness, no! I leave that to you."

"Thanks a lot. You're very kind. I'm glad I'm to have same say in the matter."

Stephen was amused, and yet not amused. Had his thoughts been going that way? Well, yes, perhaps they had. But only as an exercise of the imagination. He had been a widower for three years. The thought of Gwen still brought him pain. But for some little time now, he had to admit, he had been looking at Betony Izzard as any unattached man looks at an unattached and pretty woman: with pleasure; curiosity; speculation; sometimes even with a certain longing. But marriage as a serious proposition? That was something else again. He was ten years older than she was; he was set in his ways; and she would not be a docile wife by any means. There were also his children to be considered.

And what about Betony herself? What was her attitude to him? She was aware of him certainly: her blush that day had shown him that; but how deep did her interest go? She appeared self-sufficient; self-complete. She seemed to have arranged her own life to her own perfect satisfaction.

He would have to give the matter some thought; dwell on it and give it time; see how his feelings worked themselves out. Did he want to fall in love? He, a man nearly thirty-nine? He remembered the wonderful singing pain of falling in love as a young man and he answered firmly, No, he did not. He remembered the blinding horror of loss and he felt a dreadful shrinking inside. No, not again. Still, the longing was there, and he recognized it. He would have to give it some thought. Dwell on it, and then decide.

But he was busy on the farm, getting the last of the harvest in. There were a good many things on his mind. Emma, starting her new school term, caught measles and had to be put to bed. Chris fell from a cornstack and twisted a ligament in his foot, and Hopson had jaundice for a couple of weeks, which meant more work for everyone.

He did not have a great deal of time for thought, but Betony had a place in his mind, and her presence there, constantly, was like a gentle kind of warmth: pleasurable, but as yet unexplored; so that now and then he would say to himself: "Yes, oh yes, I know you're there. But do you know you're in my mind and would you care twopence if you did?"

One Saturday morning when the weather was bad and there was a lull in the work of the farm, he walked out to the carpenter's shop to pay for the repairs that had been done on Morton George's cottage. He spent twenty minutes with Jesse and Dicky, chatting with them about this and that, and when he left he stood for a while at the workshop gate, gazing across at the old house. Had he come in the hope of seeing her? No, not really, he told himself. Yet he went away home feeling disappointed.

"You should have called if you felt like that," said a scoffing voice at the back of his mind. "No, I haven't had time to decide how I feel," said another, more cautious, voice in reply.

* * * * *

Purely by chance, Betony had seen him from her bedroom window, where she sat with her portable desk on her lap, writing a letter to Nancy Sposs. She had seen him looking up at the house; she had even begun to rise from her chair,

229

thinking that she would go down to him; but then he had suddenly turned away, and she had gone back to writing her letter.

Later that day, between the showers, she thought she would venture out to the post. Her father was just coming in from the fold.

"Mr Wayman was here earlier on. He paid for the work we done on that cottage."

"Yes, I saw him," Betony said.

"He seems a nice gentleman," Jesse said. "He pays his bills on the nail, anyway, and there ent so many that does that these days." He noticed the letter in her hand. "Have you decided, then?" he asked.

"Yes, I've written to Nancy to say I want the job."

"Gadding about again?" he said. "I thought last time you was home for good."

Betony laughed. What nonsense he talked!

"It's nearly eleven years," she said, "since I went away from home before."

"Is it, by golly?" Jesse said. "Don't the years go flying by?"

"Yes, they go much too fast," Betony said.

She went out to the village to post her letter.

Afterwards she called on the vicar to say that she was resigning her post as mistress-in-charge of the village school. He was much incensed.

"May I ask why you wish to leave?"

"I've decided it's time I had a change."

"Well, really, Miss Izzard, I *am* surprised! Why, only last year, let me remind you, when we had that disgraceful incident at the school, you came very close to losing your job. You were far from happy at the prospect of leaving then."

"That was nearly a year ago," Betony said, "and being dismissed is a different thing from deciding to resign for personal reasons."

"Very different indeed! And in view of the managers' lenience on that occasion, I consider it most ungrateful of you to throw our kindness back at us, after such a short interval."

"Must I stay at the school for ever, then, to pay off my

debt of gratitude?"

"Oh, you're perfectly within your rights, Miss Izzard, I don't dispute that. But I'm bound to admit that I am extremely disappointed in you and I'm sure the other managers will feel the same. You would almost certainly have been dismissed if it hadn't been for Mr Wayman speaking so strongly in your defence. Why, he even threatened to resign from the board, and he went to a great deal of trouble on your behalf, persuading the other managers that you should be allowed to stay."

"Did he do that? I didn't know."

"Had he known then that in less than a year you would be resigning your post so capriciously, I doubt if he would have been so zealous on your behalf."

"No, perhaps not," Betony said.

"You realize that your notice should have been given in before the beginning of term?"

"Yes, and I'm sorry about the delay, but it should be easy enough to find a replacement, I think. Teachers are two a penny these days."

"I don't know what the Education Secretary will say about this, but speaking for myself and the managers, Miss Izzard, I am extremely displeased and disappointed."

"I'm very sorry," Betony said.

* * * * *

She had heard nothing of Linn and Jack and little Robert; no letter had come, telling her of their address; so she drove in the trap to Springs one day in the hope of finding out where they lived. She enquired at the Scopton council offices but no one could tell her anything. A man named Mercybright *had* been employed by them for a while, sweeping the roads, but now he had left and nobody knew where he had gone. Betony returned home, feeling depressed. She thought of Linn and the little boy, shunted about from place to place, and she feared she would never see them again. She felt she had failed them in their time of need.

On nearing Huntlip, she decided to call at Holland Farm.

231

She had a duty to fulfil, and it had been weighing on her mind. Today she felt a certain detachment; nothing seemed to matter much; she was facing up to the prospect of change. When she drove into the farmyard, Stephen came out of the barn to her. He was dressed in his shabby working-clothes and the pony, knowing him at once, nuzzled the string that tied his jacket. He gave her a handful of cow-cake and stroked her nose.

"Your pony regards me as a friend."

"Mr Wayman," Betony said. "It appears that when the school board came close to dismissing me last autumn, you were responsible for changing their minds. I didn't know till a week ago. The vicar happened to mention it."

"The managers' threat was ridiculous. I'm sure they'd have realized that themselves. But, seeing that my son was one of those who caused the trouble, whatever I did was little enough."

"I'd like to thank you all the same."

"Did you come especially? It was kind of you to take the trouble. But I've earnt no thanks, I assure you."

"There is one other thing," she said. "I wanted to tell you – the news will be pretty general soon – that I'm leaving Huntlip at the end of the term."

"Leaving?" he said. "What do you mean?"

"I'm giving up teaching, at least for a while. A friend has offered me a job, helping the Women's Socialist Group, and I have decided to accept."

Stephen stared at her, feeling afraid. Her news had hit him like a blow and the shock of it, coming so casually, had told him something about himself. It had woken him out of a timeless dream.

"But you can't!" he said in a harsh voice, and they stared at each other, silent, shocked.

He had given himself away completely. He knew it and he no longer cared. Betony sat, very straight and still. His expression and tone had shaken her, and she found herself unable to speak. He saw the confusion in her face, and it brought him some degree of calm. He went to her and put up his hands.

"For God's sake get down from there!" he said. "We've

got to talk."

He helped her down out of the trap, and they walked together across the yard. He opened a gate and they passed through, into a narrow grass-grown lane, lined on each side with sycamores. It was not raining that morning, but the trees dripped moisture onto them, and they had to walk carefully, skirting the puddles.

"What are you trying to do to me?"

"I'm not sure that I know what you mean."

"Dropping by so casually! 'Oh, by the way, I nearly forgot! – I'm going away in a couple of months!' And where to, I should like to know? – The end of the world?"

"Only to Birmingham, actually."

"Don't joke with me! I'm not in the mood. As a matter of fact I'm seething mad."

"Yes, I can see you are," she said.

"Can you?" he said, his voice still harsh. "Then no doubt you can see something else? I've given myself away plainly enough!"

He came to a halt, confronting her. He knew they were hidden from the house. Betony met his accusing gaze.

"Well?" he demanded. "And what do you see?"

"I don't know. I can't be sure."

"Then you must be a fool, that's all I can say!"

The way he looked at her held her fast. It frightened her, yet she wanted him.

"Stephen –"

"Yes?"

"You have only to ask."

"For God's sake, I'm asking, aren't I?" he said, and took her angrily into his arms, holding her in a burning stillness, a terrible weakness in his flesh as he thought how easily he might have lost her. He hid his face against her hair. "I'm the one that's a fool," he said.

So much for those calm deliberations of his! He *might* just consider marrying her or he might just put her out of his mind. . . . As though he had had any real choice in the matter! His body had known better than he, and now it ached against her unbearably, recognizing that she was his. His eyes had known, ages ago, dwelling on her as they had

233

done at every opportunity; taking pleasure in her looks. His hands had known, certainly, and had found excuses for touching her. Only his mind had held aloof and even that had yielded now. Capitulation was complete.

After a moment he looked at her. Being in love at thirty-nine was not so very different, he found, from being in love at twenty-two. He wanted assurance. He wanted some pledge.

"Do you love me, Betony?"

"I think I do," Betony said.

"Only think? Aren't you sure?"

"Yes. I love you. Are you satisfied?"

But there was no answering smile from him, and when he kissed her she understood why: his longing for her was too intense: although he had only now yielded to it, his surrender was swift, free of doubts, complete. And, being a man and unreasonable, he demanded the same surrender from her. She had much to learn of what it meant to be loved and desired. His lips gave her warning of what to expect and she was almost overwhelmed. She withdrew a little, breathlessly, and looked at him, touching his face. They walked together along the lane, and the sycamores dripped on either side, splashing into the dark puddles.

It was a strange thing, this relationship between a man and a woman. They could circle around each other in thought, each aware of the other's interest, sometimes admitting it in a glance; sometimes even going so far as to laugh together in a certain way. But, being unspoken, lacking a sign, it could all be erased in the fraction of a second. Each or both could decide to draw back: the glance would grow cool, the laughter be withheld; and that would be the end of it. But perhaps, instead, came the overt sign: the word was spoken and the secret out; and once this had happened, it could not be recalled. There was a sense of inevitableness in it. Every glance and every word became charged with significance, and when the two people touched each other, there was a new confession in each caress.

"Betony."

"Yes?"

"You're certainly not going to Birmingham."

"Aren't I? No. Perhaps I'm not."

She was almost twenty-nine. She was used to making her own decisions. Could she give herself up to this man? Once again their glances held. The choice was not hers, any more than his. They had need of each other, in their bones.

* * * * *

One of the first things Betony did was to send a telegram to Nancy Sposs: "Sorry. Changed my mind. Getting married instead." And back by return came Nancy's reply: "Treachery! But good luck all the same!"

Betony's family were well pleased, especially her father. "You'll be staying in Huntlip after all." And Janie, her sister, somehow managed to take the credit for it all. "That you should marry a farmer too! I must have talked some sense into you!" Her mother said little, but welcomed Stephen into the house by reaching up and kissing his cheek, a thing which he took to be natural in her but which Betony found astonishing. Dicky was pleased, but had a little worry, too, which he divulged to her in private. "Four kids you're taking on! Have you thought what that'll be like?" he said. "I daresay I'll manage," Betony said.

Stephen's children were filled with dismay when first he broke the news to them. They stared at him in numbed silence. But then Joanna, who prided herself on her quick perception, said: "I knew there was something in the wind!" and somehow the ice was broken with them all.

"I knew it too!" Jamesy claimed.

"So did I," Emma said.

"I'm hanged it *I* did!" Chris said, and there was a bleak, precarious moment when he hung between anger, disapproval, and disbelief, all of which could be seen in his face. "I'm hanged if *I* did!" he said again.

"Well, now that you do know," Stephen said, "I'm hoping you will give me your blessing and wish me well."

He made it clear to his eldest son that the blessing was very important to him, and when he offered Chris his hand, the boy remembered that he was a man. The difficult moment passed away.

"I *do* wish you well! I wish you all the luck in the world!" He clasped Stephen's hand with a son's loyal warmth. "Both of you! I should think I just do!"

When Betony met the children for the first time after they had heard the news, there was shyness on both sides. But Joanna, who was nearly fifteen, had been reading a great many books lately, and she knew the mature way to behave. It was her duty to make Betony feel at ease, and, encouraged by aunt Doe, she made herself spokesman for the rest.

"The main thing as far as we are concerned is that you should make our father happy."

"I will do my best," Betony said.

"It's a great comfort to all of us, to know that when we begin leaving home, dad will not be left alone."

"I hope that won't be for a long while yet. I'd like a chance to get to know you first."

"Well! I'm the clever one of the family!" Jamesy declared, and in the laughter that greeted this sally, there was an easing of constraint.

"Will you still be my teacher?" Emma asked.

"Only till Easter," Betony said. "Then, when your daddy and I are married, I shall be your stepmother instead."

"Will you be coming to live with us?"

"Of course she will, silly!" Jamesy said. "What did you think?"

Emma fell silent, and while her sister and two brothers vied with each other for Betony's attention, she wandered out to the garden alone. At tea-time, when Betony took her place at the table, there was a marigold on her plate, and Emma, slipping into the chair opposite, was watching her with steady eyes.

"My favourite flower," Betony said. She took it and held it to her nose. "How did you know it was my favourite flower?"

Emma merely looked away, almost as though she hadn't heard. She reached for a piece of bread and butter and was scolded for it by aunt Doe.

"Visitors first, Emma. *You* know that."

Chris offered the plate to Betony, and Jamesy passed her a dish of jam. Stephen, in his place at the head of the table, watched with relief and some amusement as his children put themselves out to please. Once he met Betony's glance, and a smile passed between them, out of their eyes. "My God! I do love her most damnably!" he thought, and looked away hastily for fear of betraying his feelings too much, under the watchful eyes of his children.

Joanna was talking about the wedding. She was already picturing it, at the church, with herself and Emma as bridesmaids.

"It's a long time to wait, until Easter, isn't it?"

"The time will soon pass," said aunt Doe.

Chapter 13

They were married on Easter Monday and spent their honeymoon in Wales. When they returned to Holland Farm aunt Doe, true to her word, took herself off bag and baggage to the cottage she had bought in Holland Lane.

"We shall be better friends this way," she said to Betony. "The children are your responsibility now. You don't want a watcher in the house."

But always, during the busy times on the farm, or when some domestic crisis occurred, she would come without fail, rattling into the yard on her old ramshackle bicycle, scattering the poultry in all directions and shouting at them in Hindustani.

"Here comes aunt Doe!" Chris would say. "Trying to see how many chickens she can run over before she gets to the back door!"

At shearing-time she would be there, helping to prepare the shearing-feast; at harvest-time she would be there, working tirelessly in the fields; and always, on any family occasion, she would come to lunch or tea and join in the family celebration. When Chris won first prize in a ploughing-match; when Joanna was made head girl of her school; when Jamesy's design for a village hall was accepted by the Huntlip parish council, earning him the sum of twenty guineas; when Emma had a poem called "Autumn Leaves" published in *The Chepsworth Gazette:* these were landmarks in their lives, and the celebration was not complete until aunt Doe was in the house, to add her word of encouragement and praise. Christmas, birthdays, anniversaries, brought her to them laden with gifts, bought as always at church bazaars and rummage sales.

She enjoyed having a home of her own. She called her cottage "Ranjiloor". It stood next to that of her old enemy,

238

the retired schoolmaster, Mr Quelch, and she delighted in vexing him. Her garden was full of docks and nettles, tall purple thistles and willow-herb, and the seeds, floating into his well-kept plot, would bring him storming to the hedge.

"I will *not* get rid of my nettles! – The butterflies like them!" aunt Doe said. "As for the thistles and willow-herb, did you ever see anything so beautiful?"

"Wretched woman!" the old man would say. "You only came to live here to be a plague to me!"

Although her garden was a wilderness – she had sown the willow-herb there herself – she was able to grow all sorts of things merely by clearing a small space and sticking a cutting in the ground.

"You'll never get a clematis to grow like that, not in a month of Sundays!" Mr Quelch said scornfully, but the clematis flourished and so did everything else she grew.

Often she broke off bits of his shrubs, where they overhung his wall in the lane, and these in due course became small bushes, flowering among the nettles and docks.

"I've no idea what it's called," she would say, when her visitors admired some unusual shrub. "You'd better ask Mr Quelch next door. He knows the name of everything."

She could grow better carrots and onions than he did and to add insult to injury would leave great bunches outside his door. He never got the better of her, but he sometimes took her by surprise. One evening she played her violin and the next morning, over the hedge, asked if the noise had disturbed him.

"Yes, it did!" he said to her. "You need to tune up on your middle G!"

"I can't tune it up. The peg's got loose."

"Let me have it," the old man said, "and I'll see what I can do for you."

Aunt Doe gave him the violin and he fashioned a new peg for her. He cut short her thanks with a wave of his hand.

"I couldn't stand that faulty G! But now you can do your worst!" he said.

* * * * *

Emma's poem, "Autumn Leaves", came as a surprise to everyone but Betony. It was she who had prompted the child to write it, and it was she who had suggested sending it to the children's page of *The Chepsworth Gazette*. It had all begun during a walk, when Emma, treading the dead leaves, suddenly said to Betony: "I love the autumn, don't you?"

"Why do you love it particularly?"

"I don't know. I just do."

Betony waited patiently. The child sometimes talked when they were alone, but she needed time.

"It's because of the smell," Emma said. "And because of the berries everywhere. All that colour on the trees!" Then, having glanced behind her as though afraid of being overheard, she said: "I've got a poem in my head."

"Say it to me," Betony said.

"Oh, no, I couldn't do that. I haven't thought of the words yet. Only the feeling, that's all."

"Well, write it down when you get home."

"I expect it will have gone by then."

But that night at bed-time, when Betony went in to say goodnight, Emma produced the poem, neatly written on ruled paper, from under her pillow.

Joanna was just a little put out by Emma's success with this poem of hers. After all, she had once made a serious study of the subject of writing, and she could have given Emma some very valuable advice, if only Emma had bothered to ask.

"I didn't want your advice," Emma said.

"No, that's just it. You always think you know best, my girl."

"The writing of a poem," Betony said, "is rather a private affair, I think."

But Joanna knew all about such things.

"I thought of being a writer myself once, only I grew out of that some time ago." She wrinkled her nose at Betony. "Well, everyone does, don't they?" she said.

"Not quite everyone," Betony said, "otherwise we should have no books."

"With Emma, though, it's just a phase."

"Hark who's talking!" Jamesy said.

Joanna was very grown up these days. She knew there were more important things in life than writing novels and poetry. She had earnest discussions with Betony on the subject of God and religious vocation.

All the children called her Betony, though Emma, in the early days, sometimes called her "Miss Izzard" by mistake, and once made the family laugh by putting up her hand, as in the classroom, when she wanted to gain Betony's attention. The village school had a man in charge now. He was thin and pale and sandy-haired and his name was Mr Toogood.

"Toogood for what?" Chris asked.

"Toogood to be true!" Jamesy said.

"Toogood for this world!" Joanna capped.

The headmaster's name was a huge joke to them. Emma could never mention school without their laughter breaking over her. Once she suddenly burst into tears, struck at Jamesy with her fists, and ran from the room.

"Whatever's the matter with our little Emma, getting into a paddy like that?" asked Chris.

"You tease her too much," Betony said. "You should try listening to her for a change, instead of jeering at everything she says."

"She ought to be used to us by now. She ought to know we mean no harm."

Betony saw, as aunt Doe had seen, that Emma was being held back.

"You should give her a chance to grow up."

But she knew all too well that she wasted her breath. Emma was the baby of the family. She always would be, all her life, and everything she said would always be met with teasing laughter.

Betony got on with all the children. They saw that her interest in them was genuine, and they brought all their troubles to her, as well as their joys. Chris liked to argue with her about politics; the state of the world in general and of agriculture in particular; and the running of the farm.

"If we were to invest in a single tractor –"

"It would mean a man thrown out of work."

"I might have known you'd side with dad!"

"Of course," said Stephen, joining in. "It's a wife's duty to side with her husband. Isn't it in the marriage vows?" And, alone with Betony, he said once: "Am I an old stick-in-the-mud?"

"Sometimes you are," Betony said.

"When?" he asked, somewhat piqued.

"Over this business of the wireless, for instance."

"Let's not have *that* all over again!"

"Well, you did ask me," Betony said.

"I should have known better," he said with a smile.

He was against the wireless. "Noisy spluttering things!" he said. "Why should we want to hear signals from the North Pole?" Yet when the wireless came into the house at last, he would stand transfixed, listening to it, and make himself late feeding the cows.

"You may as well sit down to it, dad."

"No, no, I'm just off," he would say, and would still be there ten minutes later.

The news coming over the wireless was not too good at that time. Everywhere there was grave unrest. The General Strike was in the offing. There was even fear of civil war.

"I'm not surprised!" Betony said. "What does the government expect?"

"It seems as though they expect the worst, judging by the preparations that are going forward."

"Then I hope they get it, that's all."

"You don't mean you hope for civil war?"

"I hope for something that will make the powers-that-be see sense."

"The solutions to our problems don't grow on trees, I'm afraid."

"No, I know," Betony said. "But the government – and, as Bob Tupper says, there's not much to choose between one and another – is not looking for solutions in the right place. They are not *trying* hard enough. That's why there is so little trust among the working-people of our country."

And when the General Strike was over, broken by government strategy, she felt that hope and trust among the working-people would not be revived for many a long

242

and bitter day.

* * * * *

One Sunday in May, 1926, aunt Doe fell off her bicycle, on her way home from church. Mr Quelch found her lying in the road and she was taken to hospital.

"The fuss that man makes, you'd never believe! No doubt he hopes I shall be laid up. But there's nothing whatever the matter with me. Not so much as a scratch anywhere."

But there *was* something wrong with aunt Doe. She had thrombosis in both legs. The doctors advised amputation.

Sitting up in her hospital bed, she told Betony how she had overheard the two specialists talking, only a couple of paces away.

" 'That right leg will have to come off,' I heard one of the so-and-so's say. 'Probably the other as well.' So I drew my curtain and said to him: 'That's *my* leg you're talking about, young man, and *I'll* say whether it's to come off or not!' "

Betony was deeply moved by the old lady's fortitude. It was a moment before she could speak and even then she could not match aunt Doe's composure.

"Will you take their advice?"

"I haven't decided yet. I'm keeping the blighters in suspense!"

In the end, a few days later, she decided against the amputation.

"I think I prefer to take my chance."

While she was still in hospital, she received a visit from Mr Quelch. He sat on the edge of the visitors' chair and tried to make her change her mind.

"A wheelchair wouldn't be so bad. I could easily wheel you about."

"Up and down that steep hill? Don't be ridiculous, Mr Quelch!"

"You'll die if you don't let them amputate."

"I shall die anyway," aunt Doe said. "The only difference between you and me is that I have an inkling of when I shall go. But dead or alive, I'm keeping my legs!"

So she went home to her little cottage and lived a

perfectly normal life. She rode her bicycle to church; dug her garden and mowed her grass; and sowed her rows of wallflower seeds, for filling her borders the following year. Then one day she collapsed and died. Mr Quelch went in, and she lay on the floor. He fetched Stephen immediately.

"Stubborn to the last, that cousin of yours! Why couldn't she listen to good advice? I'd have looked after her, silly old trout!"

There were tears in the old man's eyes, and after the funeral, when the grave had been filled in, he planted a few "slips" from her favourite rose. It was the wrong time of year of course.

"But I daresay they'll grow – for her," he said.

That was the middle of July. Soon the oats were ripening palely in the Freelands at Holland Farm and the men were heard sharpening their scythes. They missed aunt Doe at harvest-time, leading the way out to the field, with her long mannish stride and her heavy shoes and her dark blue straw hat tied over her head. They missed her at every family gathering, and remembered her always, at every turn, even when her name was not actually mentioned. If anyone left a morsel of food on a plate, someone else was sure to say: "The people in Calcutta would be glad of that!" and if anyone expressed too nice a fastidiousness, someone else was sure to say: "I've seen worse that that in Ranjiloor!"

Among the treasures aunt Doe left, there was a dressing-box, which went to Emma, a Ghurka's knife, which went to Chris, and a piece of ivory scrimshaw, which went to Jamesy. She left Joanna her violin. And each of the children received a hundred and fifty pounds.

Joanna was almost seventeen. She would soon be leaving school, but had not yet decided on a career. Having flirted in the past with music, writing, medicine, and religious work, she had now discarded them all and so far nothing had taken their place. She talked about it to the family.

"I want to do something – Oh I don't know –" And, in despair at expressing herself, Joanna flung her arms out wide. "Something *different*!" she exclaimed.

"You could be a lady balloonist," said Chris.

"Or go as a missionary to the Isle of Wight," said Jamesy.

"What about charming snakes in the market-place at Chepsworth?"

"Or deep-sea diving for pearls at Land's End?"

The boys were full of frivolous suggestions. They came up with something new every day. But when Joanna knew about aunt Doe's legacy, she decided to spend it in travelling through Europe for three months with her school-friend, Elaine. Elaine was going with her parents and they had invited Joanna to join them.

"You don't mind if I spend aunt Doe's money like that?"

"Of course I don't," Stephen said. "You can spend it as you please."

"When I come back," Joanna said, "I shall know what work I want to do."

The older children were growing up. Only Emma remained a child. She was doing well at the village school and would probably win a scholarship to the girls' grammar school in Chepsworth in due course.

"You'll be going to Lock's," Betony said. "I went there, after leaving Huntlip. You'll like it, I'm sure."

"What shall I do afterwards?"

"What do you think you want to do?"

"Wanting's no use," Emma said. "That doesn't get you anywhere."

Emma wanted a great many things. She wanted passionately to be able to draw, like Jamesy; to play the piano, like Joanna; to have fair hair like Betony's; to save Mr Toogood from a terrible fire. Often she wished she were somebody else: Flora Macdonald or Edith Cavell; St Teresa or Joan of Arc; Maggie Tulliver or Becky Sharp. She would practise being cold and impassive, denying herself her favourite foods. Then she would switch to the opposite, saying clever, wounding things and snatching the best cake from the dish. She would change her character every few days, almost as often as she changed her frock. She would try something new and cast it aside.

"Emma, my child, just be yourself!" Stephen said once, in exasperation.

But Betony knew that for some children, and Emma was one, it was difficult to know what that "self" was. She had to find it. She had to explore.

"I wonder," she said to Betony once: "I wonder what it's like to be really wicked."

"I hope you're not going to try it out."

"No, I'm putting it into a poem instead."

* * * * *

Sometimes the whole family spent a Sunday at Cobbs. The two boys enjoyed the carpenter's shop. Sometimes Betony went alone, on a week-day, perhaps; but however frequently she went, her father's greeting was always the same.

"Hello, my blossom. You're quite a stranger nowadays."

She had always been his favourite child, and although he was happy to see her married, he missed her sorely at every turn.

"I seen Jack Mercybright last week. He was driving some sheep along the road, out not far from Capleton Wick."

"Where are they living? Did he say?"

"Somewhere near Oakshott, seemingly."

"Nothing more precise than that?"

"I *did* ask him where, but you know what he is. Strikes me he don't never want us to know."

Betony felt that this was true. She had tried often to track them down, but always, by the time she had word of them, they had moved to another place. She worried about Linn and the little boy. She thought of her dead foster brother, Tom Maddox, whose child Robert was, and she felt that she had let him down.

"But what can we do," her father said, "when they make it so plain that they don't want no help from none of us?"

"We can go on trying," Betony said.

The recession was worsening with each year that passed, and the signs of it were everywhere. A great many men, tramping the roads, travelling from one "spike" to the next, called at the farm in search of work. Betony always gave them food and a shilling, perhaps, to set them on their way, just as aunt Doe had always done, and she listened to what they had to say. Once Stephen came into the house just as a man was walking away.

246

"That man went right through the war," she said. "He's a skilled toolmaker out of a job. He hasn't worked for nearly three years. A land fit for heroes? It makes me ashamed!"

The children of the village itself: sometimes she saw them in the fields, pulling a few turnip-tops or a few leaves of kale, on their way home from school: ragged, ill-shod, all skin and bone, especially those whose fathers had no work. She was on good terms with Mr Toogood, the headmaster, and sometimes she called on him and his wife.

"Some of these children come to school without any breakfast but a cup of tea. They have a slice of bread and margarine at dinner-time and they go home to God-knows-what in the way of supper."

"Yes, I know," Betony said.

She still sent baskets of apples to the school every autumn, and whenever the weather was hard in wintertime, she sent a copper can full of hot baked potatoes every day till the weather improved. Mr Toogood gave them out the moment they arrived, and the children devoured them, skins and all. But one angry mother stormed into the school and railed at him for giving her Ernie "charity".

"What did you say to her?" Betony asked.

"I said this was one decision Ernie was entitled to make for himself."

One evening in the spring of 1928, Betony and Stephen walked in the fields above the farmhouse. From the top of the holl, as they looked down over their own land and that of their neighbours round about: on bright green corn and darker pasture; cattle and pigs and flocks of sheep; with plum orchards in blossom here and there: England looked a land of plenty.

"And so it should be," Betony said, "if only things were properly run."

"I don't see much change in the offing yet. Not for a year or two anyway. Perhaps the thirties will be better."

"Perhaps we need to do something to try and *make* them better."

"What can we do?"

"I don't know. I wish I did."

Stephen gave a little laugh. He drew her arm into his.

"You want to take the whole world and turn it upside down," he said.

"I want to turn it the right way up."

The evening was fine. The air smelt of greenness and freshness and life. There was a gentleness in the wind. They walked together, arm in arm, enjoying the softness of the evening. In the home pasture, next to the house, the mare, Thisbe, was showing off with her new foal. In the meadow known as Long Gains, the shepherd was going the round of his flocks, for lambing time was close at hand. Life at Holland Farm was fair. Of the world beyond – what of that? It would be easy, Betony felt, to shut it out and forget about it.

"There ought to be *something* we can do."

* * * * *

One Saturday morning in May, Challoner called in his motor car, on his way in to town. He returned a shotgun he had borrowed. He and Stephen stood in the yard, and all the time as Challoner talked his gaze was following Betony as she went to and fro, feeding the hens. When she went indoors, he spoke of her.

"You did a good thing when you married that girl. It's given her something to do with herself, instead of poking her nose into men's affairs and stirring things up, as she used to do. A woman's place is in the home."

As Challoner drove away, a boy on a bicycle rode into the yard, bringing the morning's newspaper. Stephen, on his way into the house, glanced inside it, at the back page. There was an advertisement for a debate to be held in the Shire Hall in Chepsworth on Friday, May the twenty-first. Among the speakers would be Mrs Betony Wayman of Holland Farm, Huntlip, who would open the debate with this question: "Unemployment in our land: Is the government doing enough?"

Stephen Wayman smiled to himself. He went indoors in search of his wife.

SEEDTIME AND
HARVEST

Chapter 1

Five roads met at Herrick Cross and Clew Wilson's garage, standing on a strategic corner, commanded a view of all five. Above the repair-shop, somewhat shabby but clear enough, was a large sign in green and white: "Herrick Cross Garage; proprietor C.L.E. Wilson; repairs to all makes of motors; agricultural repairs a speciality."

The front wall of the garage was a popular place for advertising local events and a large poster, hand-printed, had recently been pasted over the rest. Clew's assistant, Charlie Truscott, wiping his hands on a piece of rag, stood reading the poster for the third or fourth time. "On Saturday, September 13th., at 8 o/c in the Village Hall at Herrick St John, Dancing to the music of Mr Gray's gramophone. Everyone welcome. Tickets 1/6." Now and then, as Charlie stood, constantly wiping his hands on the rag, he would glance along the empty main road, shimmering in the afternoon heat.

Clew came to the garage door and stood smoking a cigarette. He nodded towards a Fordson tractor, standing nearby, newly repaired.

"Is that old man Lawn's?"

"Ah. That's it."

"When're you taking it down to him?"

"In a minute," Charlie said. "I'm just reading about the dance."

"Decided whether you're going yet?"

"No, not yet. What about you?"

"Oh, I shall go, I daresay. Bloody Norah will see to that."

Bloody Norah was Clew's wife. They were devoted, he and she, but always called each other names. Charlie, who lodged with them, knew it was nothing more than a joke.

"There'll be plenty of girls there," Clew remarked. "That

1

should suit you, shouldn't it?"

"Whatever they say about me," Charlie said, "it's mostly lies."

"It's high time you settled down. Found yourself a decent wife. We'll need your room when the nipper comes."

Charlie Truscott was thirty-five. At nineteen he had gone to the war. He had fought in Gallipoli; then in France; and when he got home in 1919, his girl had married another man. No more commitments after that. "Love them all – but not too much!"; that had been his motto since then; and so far no one had changed his mind.

"What're you watching for?" Clew asked, as Charlie kept glancing towards the main road.

"I'm not watching for anything. What's there to see at this time of day?"

"You'll know that poster by heart pretty soon. You've read it often enough, by God!"

Clew went back to work in the repair-shop, tinkering with his own little van. There were two lorries in for repair, but Charlie had said he would deal with them. For all his easy, unhurried manner, Charlie did most of the work in the garage, and Clew himself was the first to admit it.

"Charlie's a glutton for work," he would say. "But it's no good trying to hurry him. He's got to do it in his own time."

Along the main road from the Lincton direction, a group of boys were coming home from the school at Ryerley. At Herrick Cross they separated, two of them going towards Herrick Granville and three towards Herrick St John. One boy, alone, swinging his satchel by a broken strap, turned down Horse Lane towards Herrick Green, and when he had vanished round the bend, Charlie threw down his oily-rag and went to the door to call to Clew.

"I'm taking that tractor to Bellhouse now."

"About bloody time!" Clew called back.

* * * * *

Charlie, on the tractor, soon caught up with the boy in Horse Lane. He stopped and offered him a lift, and the boy rode on the step behind him, looking out over the fields

2

where rooks were feeding on the stubble and where, here and there, ploughing had started, filling the air with the smell of moist earth. The boy's name was Robert Mercybright. He was almost eleven years old. Charlie turned and glanced at him.

"Harvest's nearly over at Bellhouse, I hear?"

"There's only the barley to be got in. Granddad said they were carting today."

"How is your granddad nowadays?"

"Pretty fit, considering."

"Not too much trouble with his leg?"

"I reckon it hurts him sometimes, but he never says so. You know what he is."

"It doesn't stop him working, I know that. I saw him a week ago, harvesting, up in that field above the brook. He can still show the young chaps a thing or two, bad leg or no."

Charlie, rounding a bend in the road, slowed down and came to a halt. A cock-pheasant was crossing in front of them, and they watched it squeeze through a gap in the hedge, to join its mate in the stubble-field. Then Charlie drove on again, down through Hurley's watersplash, and up the steep hill on the other side.

"How's your mother nowadays?"

"Oh, she's fine."

"How'd she enjoy her holiday? Did she go away somewhere?"

"No, she was busy making jam."

"I suppose she'll be back at work this evening? Up at the Fox and Cubs, I mean, pulling pints for thirsty chaps? I'll maybe pop in. I'm thirsty enough. It's been pretty warm again today."

Chatting to the boy, Charlie drove on, round the last of the snaky bends to where the road ran straight for a change. Here, the fields on either side belonged to Bellhouse Farm, and the men and women working in them paused to wave to the man and the boy churring along the narrow road.

"Is your granddad among that lot?"

"No, he'll be up in the barley-field."

"Where d'you think I'll find Mr Lawn?"

"Same place, most likely," Robert said.

Soon they came to a small cottage, set back a little from the road. Charlie stopped to let the boy down, glancing all the time towards the cottage, but seeing no sign of movement inside. He spoke above the noise of the tractor and Robert, one hand on the garden-gate, turned back again to hear what he said.

* * * * *

Linn Mercybright, in the kitchen, saw her son arrive on the tractor and busied herself preparing his tea. She swirled hot water round in the pot, emptied it into the ashes in the hearth, and took the tea-caddy down from the shelf. The tractor still churred at the garden-gate and whenever she glanced out of the window, taking care not to be seen, she smiled to herself, secretly, wondering what the man and the boy could find to talk about all this time.

At last the tractor drove away. She turned to the table, busily, and when Robert came into the house, the first thing she saw was his school-satchel, dangling from its broken strap.

"There! You've broken that strap again! I do wish you'd take more care of it. These things cost money. They don't grow on trees."

"I can soon mend it," Robert said.

"I've boiled you a nice fresh egg for your tea, so don't be too long about washing your hands."

"Can I take it out to the fields?"

"No, you must sit and eat properly."

She cut two pieces of bread and butter and laid them on the boy's plate. He came and sat down and she poured out his tea.

"Who was that who gave you a lift?"

But she knew well enough who it was. There was no mistaking Charlie Truscott, clad in his dark blue overalls, with his cap well down on one side of his head. Charlie was known for miles around; she had often seen him driving about the Herrick lanes; and sometimes at the Fox and Cubs she had served him with drinks and cigarettes.

"It was Charlie Truscott," Robert said. "He was bringing

4

Mr Lawn's tractor back."

"He seemed to have plenty to say to you, throbbing away outside the gate."

"He wanted to know if you could dance."

"Dance?" Linn repeated. She gave a quick laugh. "And what business is it of his, whether I can dance or not? Whatever made him ask such a thing?"

But she knew quite well why Charlie had asked. She had seen the posters everywhere and knew all about the Saturday dance that was being held at Herrick St John. It was to be a great event. Everyone was talking about it.

Holding her teacup between her hands, she blew into the hot tea. There was a certain warmth in her face, and her son, as he ate his soft-boiled egg, looked at her in some surprise. He was as dark as she was fair. He favoured his dead father in looks; the father he had never known; and his brown eyes, looking at her, were Tom's eyes all over again: deep and dark, with a serious gaze that could be quite disturbing to her at times.

"*Can* you dance, mother?" he asked. It was a thing unheard of to him. His mother rarely went anywhere. She would never have worked at The Fox and Cubs if it hadn't been that money was short and it was the only work to be had. "*Can* you dance?" he asked again.

"Never you mind!" Linn exclaimed. "Just get on and eat your tea. But don't bolt it down or you'll make yourself ill."

Robert certainly ate very fast. He wanted to get out to the harvest-field. The last of the egg went into his mouth and the empty eggshell was turned upside down.

"Have you got any homework to do?"

"Only a bit. I can do it in bed."

"Oh, very well, off you go. You can take your granddad's fourses to him."

When Robert had left the house, Linn cleared the tea-things and washed them up. By then it was five o' clock and she went upstairs to change her dress, ready for her evening at the Fox and Cubs.

* * * * *

She took the short cut across the fields. The pub was deserted when she went in but Fred Oakes could be heard in the cellar and three crates of bottled beer were already stacked on the bar. She hung up her coat and hat and busied herself, unloading the bottles, placing them on the shelves below. Fred came up the cellar steps and dropped another two crates on the floor.

"Did you have a good holiday?"

"Yes, thanks. It made a nice change."

"People were asking where you were. One or two in particular."

"That was kind of them, I'm sure." Linn did not ask who the people were. "It's always nice to be missed," she said.

"Seen the poster about the dance?"

"Goodness, yes, they're everywhere!"

One of the posters hung in the bar.

"I suppose you'll be wanting the evening off next Saturday, eh?"

"Oh, *I* shan't be going to the dance."

"You'll be the only one who's not, then! There hasn't been so much excitement in the place since that airship went over last March."

Soon the first customers came in: two labourers from Daylong Farm; and Linn drew two pints of old-and-mild.

"You're back from your holidays, then, I see? Blackpool, was it, or Ilfracombe?"

"Neither," she said, "I stayed at home."

"Best place, too. Where else can you spit?"

"Bill, he's in a spitting mood," Abel, his mate, explained to Linn. "We'll both be laid off this back-end. We've just heard the bloody news."

"Oh, I am sorry!" Linn exclaimed, but although her concern was real enough, it had its roots in her own affairs, for the same thing would happen at Bellhouse Farm and she knew that her father, aged seventy-two, might well be among the unlucky ones. "Oh, I am sorry, I really am!"

"Ah," said Bill Reed, wiping his mouth, "nobody wants us labouring chaps, once we're over forty, like."

"Hark at him!" Abel scoffed. "He'll never see sixty-six again!"

6

"Well, that's over forty, ent it?" Bill said.

By seven there was a crowd in the bar, mostly men from the nearby farms. Then Clew Wilson came strolling in, with Charlie Truscott close behind, both of them straight from their work at the garage and still wearing their overalls, though Charlie, she noticed, had scrubbed his hands. Fred Oakes served them with their drinks and they stood a little way away, chatting together as they drank and smoked. Once Charlie Truscott met Linn's eye and raised his glass, saluting her. Clew said something, quietly, and Charlie reddened to the ears.

When they had both finished their drinks, Clew came to the bar again and put the two glasses in front of Linn.

"Same again. Two of the best. The first one only lays the dust."

Watching her as she handled the beer-pump, he noticed the fairness of her skin and the play of light on her red-gold hair. Charlie was nobody's fool, he thought. The girl had a special quality.

"Charlie wants to know if you'll go to the dance with him on Saturday night."

Linn did not answer immediately. Clew had taken her by surprise. She put his brimming glass on the bar and looked at him with a steady gaze. Charlie, she knew, was listening.

"Why doesn't he ask me himself?"

"I dunno. I suppose he's shy."

"Oh no I'm not!" Charlie said, He came forward and stood at the bar. "Clew's just having his little joke. I can manage my own affairs."

"I'll leave you to it, then," Clew said, and, taking his drink, he walked away to join a few men at the skittle-board.

Linn put Charlie's glass on the bar and he stared for a while at its head of froth. Then at last he looked at her, and in spite of his reputation as a ladies' man, she saw that he was unsure of himself.

"Well? What about it? Will you come?"

"I'm too old to go dancing," she said, "but thank you for asking me, all the same."

"You and I are much of an age. If you're too old, why, so am I."

7

"How do you know what age I am?"

"Something young Robert told me once."

"Oh, that wretched boy of mine! Giving my secrets away like that!"

Her laugh and the way she looked at him gave him back his confidence.

"Well, what about this dance?" he said. "Are you coming with me or not?"

His eyes, very blue beneath their fair brows, looked at her searchingly, with a bright gleam, and his usual smile, absent till now, began spreading slowly over his face.

"If you don't come, I shan't go at all, and you will have done me out of a treat."

"All right! I'll come!" She nodded and smiled. Suddenly she felt very young. "If I can get the time off − "

"Don't worry, I'll soon fix Fred. He relies on me to look after his motor. He knows he'd better keep in with me."

Charlie put a florin on the bar and she gave him his change. He pocketed it and picked up his drink.

"I'll call for you just before eight. It'll only take ten minutes or so, walking from your place to Herrick St John."

"That means coming out of your way. Couldn't I meet you at the hall?"

"No," he said firmly. "Certainly not. I'm calling for you in the proper way."

Linn moved away to serve someone else and Charlie, leaning against the bar, watched her over the rim of his glass. After a moment Clew came back.

"Did you fix it up with her?"

"Yes, she's coming," Charlie said.

"They never say no to you, I suppose?"

"I wouldn't say that."

"Well, we'd better get home to our supper, my lad, or we'll have Bloody Norah on our tail."

"Right," Charlie said, and finished his beer.

He put his empty glass on the bar and followed Clew out of the pub, giving Linn a wave as he went. After supper, he told himself, he would go back to the garage and tackle the work that was waiting for him. It would probably take until midnight, but that was no hardship to him. He often

8

worked late at night, and with the Saturday dance in mind, he had plenty to think about.

* * * * *

When Linn got home at eleven o'clock that night, her father was getting ready for bed. He was lighting his candle at the lamp and Linn, in a sudden fit of mischief, bent over it and blew out the flame, laughing at him like a naughty child.

"How's Robert? Is he in bed?"

"Of course he's in bed. He has been for hours."

Jack, as he lit his candle again, glanced at her in a questioning way, sensing the mood of excitement in her. She answered the glance by reaching up and planting a kiss on his bearded face. Then she went to hang up her coat.

"You know Charlie Truscott, don't you, dad?"

"Everyone knows him. Why, what's he done?"

"He's asked me to go to the dance with him. Have I been foolish? – I said yes!"

"Go by all means. Why shouldn't you go? Going to a dance is no great to-do."

"You don't think, at my age, I'm cheapening myself?"

"Be prepared for gossip, that's all. Charlie's a good enough chap in his way, but he's got a bit of a name where women are concerned, and *you've* got to take more care than most, if you mind what people say about you."

"Yes. I know. And I *do* mind."

Her son was illegitimate. She had made no secret of the fact since coming to live at Herrick Green, and she took it for granted that Charlie Truscott, like everyone else, knew the truth about her and her boy. She had borne the sly glances for nearly twelve years, in the many places where she had lived, and a certain hardness had grown in her. She had not looked at another man since Robert's father, blind and in pain, had died on the day of his baby's birth. But now, Charlie Truscott. – What about him? She felt a pang of anxiety.

"Maybe I shouldn't have said I'd go. What do you think? I do wish you'd say."

"Go and be damned to it," Jack said. Limping, he walked

9

towards the stairs. "You've had little fun in your life all these years. Go and enjoy yourself while you can."

Yes. And why not? Where was the harm? It was only a dance, after all, and she had given Charlie her word. Her earlier mood began to return and she stood for a while in a happy trance, listening to her father's step on the stairs and the little quiet sounds above as he entered the bedroom he shared with her son. Then the clock on the mantelpiece chimed, reminding her that it was late. She lit her candle and turned out the lamp; made sure the door was properly bolted; and went up to bed.

* * * * *

Saturday night was fine and warm. The village hall at Herrick St John was already crowded to the doors when Charlie and Linn arrived there, and a few young men stood about outside. They all knew Charlie and spoke to him and Linn was aware, as she mounted the steps, that they were looking her up and down.

"Not much room for dancing, Charlie, if that's what you've come for," one of them said, "but the moon is shining round the back!"

Charlie ignored them. He might have been deaf. His hand rested lightly on her arm as he guided her into the crowded hall. Inside, where a gramophone played an old waltz, more than forty dancing couples moved with difficulty about the floor, hot and perspiring under the lamps. People had come from everywhere and many were gathered at the trestle table where three or four shiny-faced women were kept busy selling drinks.

"It's a bit of a squeeze," Charlie said. He took her coat and hung it up, jostling to reach the row of pegs. Together they edged on to the floor and he smiled at her, drawing her into his arms. "Take your partners for the sardine shuffle . . . "

"I haven't danced for years," Linn said. "Not since the war, when I was a nurse, and they held a dance at the hospital, to celebrate Armistice Night. I'm out of practice, I'm afraid."

"You'll soon get the hang of it again."

10

"I'm old-fashioned, too. If they play a foxtrot I shall be lost."

"I'll soon teach you," Charlie said.

Charlie was very neatly dressed in a dark blue suit and striped blue tie. His shirt was spotless, his white collar crisp and his light brown hair, bleached fair at the temples, was smoothed down with a lick of grease.

"I bet I know what you're thinking," he said. "You're thinking I'm tidily dressed for a change."

"My thoughts were not so rude as that."

"What *were* your thoughts?"

"I'm not sure that I ought to say."

"Go on, I'm tough, I can take it," he said.

"Well, I was thinking," Linn said, "that you look more yourself in your overalls."

Charlie gave a little grimace. There was disappointment in his eyes. He had taken great care in dressing that night.

"Overalls!" he echoed wryly. "Maybe I should've come in *them*!"

"You're not hurt by my saying that?"

"Get away! I told you — I'm tough."

"I'm not so sure about that. And I only meant — "

"Yes, what did you mean?"

The dance ended. They stood and clapped.

" — That I liked you *best* in your working-clothes."

"So long as you like me, that's all right. It'll do to be going on with, anyway."

Charlie was a man who believed in making the best of things. He was a born optimist and it showed in the upward curve of his mouth and the laughter-lines about his eyes. He had a smile that spread and spread, until his whole face was creased with it, and when he laughed his listeners, whether they shared the joke or not, found themselves laughing with him.

"Ladies and gentlemen!" said the voice of the Master of Ceremonies. "The next dance, by special request, is that old favourite, *The Evergreen Waltz!*"

The new record was put on and the gramophone gave a sad sigh. There was applause from the audience. Mike Gray had forgotten to wind it up. The omission was soon

11

rectified and the strains of *Evergreen* filled the hall. The dancing was not so restricted now because some of the couples had gone to sit out.

"That's better," Charlie said. "Now perhaps we can really dance." And as they glided together he said: "You're not so out of practice after all."

"It all comes back when you hear the tunes."

"Like riding a bicycle, as they say."

"I've never ridden one in my life."

"Never ridden a bicycle? I don't believe it!" Charlie said.

"Is it such a terrible thing?"

"It's a calamity!" Charlie said.

"What nonsense we're talking!" Linn exclaimed. "How can I dance properly when you keep making me laugh all the time?"

But she was happy, laughing with him, and he, whenever he looked at her, was filled with a sense of discovery. She was never like this at the Fox and Cubs. There she had always been rather reserved and he had been attracted by that, but tonight she was gay and full of fun, and this was unexpected bonus indeed.

"Why don't you dance with some of the other women here?"

"Are there any others?" Charlie said.

He could not take his eyes off her.

* * * * *

A little while later, having found a seat for her, he went to the table to buy drinks. While he stood waiting his turn, a man named Easton spoke to him, shoving an elbow in his ribs. Charlie knew him well by sight. He was the Herrick chimney-sweep.

"You're enjoying yourself all right!" Easton jerked his thumb towards Linn, who sat by the window, fanning herself. "You know how to pick 'em. I will say that."

"Thanks," Charlie said. The man was drunk.

"Jack Mercybright's daughter, ent she? Works at the Fox and Cubs at night? You shouldn't have too much trouble there. You know what they say about barmaids." Easton leant forward, smelling of drink, and put his mouth to Charlie's ear. "*And* she's got a kid at home ... One on account, as the saying is ... One whose dad never paid the bill ... "

"Look," Charlie said, in a quiet voice, aware of the people standing nearby, "supposing you just shut your mouth?"

Easton looked at him in surprise.

"I just thought I'd let you know."

"You needn't bother," Charlie said. "I already know what I need to know."

"Is that a fact? I might've guessed!" Easton grinned from ear to ear. "You never was one for wasting time."

"Get out of my way," Charlie said.

When he returned to Linn with the drinks, his face was still brightly flushed and his eyes still glittered angrily.

"What's the matter? Why are you cross?"

"Something somebody said to me."

"Was it Bert Easton?"

"Yes, that's right."

"What did he say?"

"Oh, never mind."

But Linn could guess what Easton had said. She had lived with such sneers for one third of her life. They followed her wherever she went and she had become inured to them. Drinking her glass of lemonade, she looked at Charlie, drinking his beer.

"You know Robert is illegitimate?"

"Yes. I know. It's nothing to me."

He looked at her: a long, straight look, letting her see how little he cared; and Linn looked back, without reserve, letting him see that she trusted him. They were cut off from the crowd in the hall; its noise seemed distant, dreamlike, unreal. The dancers shuffled about the floor; records were changed on the gramophone; the MC gave out the name of the tune. Linn drank the last of her lemonade and set aside the empty glass. She waited while Charlie drank his beer, then she got up and touched his arm.

"Come and teach me to foxtrot," she said.

* * * * *

13

At a quarter to ten Clew Wilson arrived with his wife Norah.

"Don't tell me I'm late. I know we are. It took *her* an hour to find my studs." Clew had his hand on Charlie's arm and was looking towards the refreshment table. "Never mind the dancing. I'm dying of thirst. Come on, I'll let you buy me a drink."

But Charlie and Linn were about to leave and Charlie was trying to find her coat.

"Leaving?" Clew said. "Don't talk so daft! The evening hasn't hardly begun."

"It *is* rather early, I know," Linn said, "but really I think I've danced enough."

"Me too," Charlie said. "I could do with a breath of fresh air."

He had found Linn's coat at last and was holding it for her to put on. Clew was watching him like an owl.

"Well, if you must, you must, I suppose! But don't stop too long at Hedley Sharp's stile."

Norah gave Clew a kick on the ankle and he turned to her in injured surprise.

"All I meant was, there's a heavy dew falling tonight. I wouldn't want them to catch a chill."

"We know what you meant," Norah said.

"I'll say goodnight to you, then," Charlie said.

"I'll say the same," Clew said with a wink.

Outside, as they left the lights of the hall behind, Charlie took hold of Linn's arm, guiding her first few halting steps into the darkness of the lane. But after a while, when he knew she could see, he dropped his hand to his side again.

"You don't want to take too much notice of Clew. He's all right. He's a good friend to me."

"You lodge with them, I believe?"

"Not for much longer," Charlie said. "They've got a baby on the way. When that arrives – next April some time – I shall have to find somewhere else."

"Where will you go?"

"Oh, I don't know. There's always rooms to be got somewhere. Or I might get a place of my own, who knows? A lot can happen between now and next April."

The night was very warm and still, and as they walked

14

along the lane they could hear the ripping and tearing sound of cattle grazing in the field, just the other side of the hedge.

"There's a lot of good beef in that field. I wouldn't mind a ha'penny for every pound Hedley Sharp makes when he sells them at the Fatstock Show."

Charlie, although he could not see the cattle in question, knew exactly what they were. Visiting all the farms as he did, doing repairs on farm vehicles, he saw a great deal of what went on in the fields and, being himself a farmer's son, he remembered everything he saw.

"Tell me about yourself," Linn said, "and about your life on your father's farm."

"What is there to tell?" he said.

And, the way he told it, it was little enough. His father had farmed at Hardingley, on the other side of Worcestershire. During the war things had been good and his father, keeping abreast of the times, had spent his money on modern improvements.

"When I came home after the war, he'd got tractors and balers and I-don't-know-what, so I went on an engineering course to learn about maintenance and repairs. By the time I'd finished that the slump had begun and farming was going downhill. My father went bankrupt in '24 and the shock of it made him pretty ill. Farming was finished for me after that so I answered an advert for a motor-mechanic and that's how I come to be working for Clew."

Charlie gave a self-conscious laugh.

"Not much of a story, is it? There's hundreds like me, who could tell that same tale."

"That doesn't make it any less sad."

"It was sad for my father, certainly. He never got over losing his farm and he died in the winter of '26."

"Haven't you any family at all?"

"Two married sisters in Canada and a cousin farming in New South Wales. Otherwise I'm all alone."

"You've never thought of working on a farm again?"

"What, as a labourer? No, not me! You won't catch me on a farm again, not in a hundred thousand years!"

And yet, as Linn knew, Charlie could not keep away from

15

the land. Driving about on garage affairs, if he saw a man at work in a field, he had to stop and talk to him and often it led to his giving a hand. Once, when her father had been grubbing up an old hedge, Charlie had stopped for over an hour and had helped to uproot six damson trees. "The earth fairly flew!" her father said. "You could see *he's* no stranger to mattock and spade!"

"No, farm-work is over for me," Charlie said. "I like to have a few bob to spend." He jingled the coins in his trousers pocket. "Mechanics get pretty good pay. At least I can put a bit by every week, which is more than many poor devils can do these days."

Now and again he glanced at Linn's face. Did she think him boastful, he wondered, talking about the money he earned? Did she think he was out to impress? It was difficult to tell: he could see her but dimly by the light of the stars; and although she listened attentively, she said very little in reply.

"Nearly there," he said with regret, as they took the fork into Bellhouse Lane, and then, when they came within sight of the cottage: "I see there's a light in your window still. I suppose your dad's waiting up for you?"

"Oh, yes, he's sure to be. He never goes to bed until I get home. Will you come in for a cup of tea?"

"You sure it's no trouble at this time of night?"

"I shall be having one, anyway."

* * * * *

While Linn made the tea, Charlie and her father sat and talked, one on either side of the hearth, her father smoking his old briar pipe, Charlie smoking a cigarette. They talked of the changes taking place on all the farms in the neighbourhood: how Mr Lawn of Bellhouse was putting more land down to grass and developing his dairy herd, and how Mr Pointer of Daylong was going over to poultry and geese. Farmers now would do anything, just to keep the privilege of starving to death on their own bit of land.

"That chap at Raisewood is stocking his land with pheasants and such and letting the shoot to a syndicate. It's the

16

only way he can make it pay."

"You can't call it farming, though, can you, by God?"

"Better than having the bailiffs in . . . "

"Ah, better than hanging hisself in his barn . . . "

Linn, having given them their tea, sat at the table drinking her own. She had no part in this talk of theirs and, listening to them, she smiled to herself, amused at the way they left her out. She might not have been in the room for all the notice they took of her. They were intent on their own talk and never even glanced her way.

But Charlie was aware of her all the same. He never for an instant forgot she was there. Somehow he even divined her thoughts, sensing that she was well pleased by the way he gossiped with the old man, and that she was happy to be ignored.

He was aware of the kitchen, too: its cheerfulness and homeliness: everything in it lovingly cared for; clean as a pin and shining bright, in spite of the poverty obvious there. The kitchen told him a lot about Linn. It was like an open book and in it he read her character.

The clock on the mantelpiece struck eleven.

"Glory be! Is that the time? I'm keeping you people out of your beds."

He picked up his mug and drank his tea. Linn offered him more but he shook his head.

"No, thanks, it's time I was gone. But that was the best tea I've had in years. Norah's no good at making tea. She never bothers to warm the pot."

"Now you know where to come," Linn said, "whenever you want a decent cup."

There was no archness in her tone. The smile she gave him was friendly, not coy.

"Supposing I take you up on that?" Charlie said on his way to the door.

"You must try and make it a Sunday," she said. "I'm always free on Sunday nights."

"Sunday. Right. We'll make it a date."

"Thank you for taking me to the dance. I really enjoyed it. It made such a change."

"I'm glad you were able to come," Charlie said. "Good-

17

night to you both. Be seeing you!"

A smile and a wave and he was gone. Linn closed the door and bolted it. Jack got up stiffly and knocked out his pipe.

"I'll say this for Charlie Truscott. — When he says he's going he damn well goes. He don't stand on the step for hours, too frightened to take the plunge."

"I wonder if he *will* come again . . . "

"I daresay he will. He said he would."

"You don't mind him popping in?"

"It's all-as-one if I mind or not. It won't be *me* he'll be coming to see."

Chapter 2

But sometimes, to give him his due, as Linn said, Charlie would call when she was not there and would spend an hour or two talking to Jack, leaving before she returned from her work. Or he would call on a Sunday morning and take young Robert out for a jaunt, sometimes in some ramshackle car, sometimes on the back of a motor-cycle that he was "trying out" for a friend.

"I hope you don't drive too fast," Linn said, "especially on that new main road."

"No harm will come to Rob through me. I give you my solemn word on that."

He and Robert were good friends. Charlie took care that it should be so. But his liking for the boy was genuine – Linn was perfectly sure of that – and as far as Robert himself was concerned, Charlie Truscott could do no wrong.

"Mother."

"Yes?"

"Can I talk to you?"

"Goodness! Whatever's coming?" she said. "Is it something to do with school?"

"No," he said, with a fierce scowl. "That's the last thing I want to talk about."

"I'm sorry to hear it," Linn replied.

She hoped that Robert, the following spring, would agree to sit the scholarship exam and try for a place at the Grammar School, but the boy himself loathed the idea. All he wanted was to leave school as soon as he could and go to work on one of the farms, preferably Bellhouse, with his grandfather.

"Well, if it isn't school," she said, "what is it you want to talk about?"

"It's about Charlie Truscott," Robert said.

19

"What about him?"

"If Charlie asks you to marry him . . . "

"Oh, it's *that* sort of talk! I might've known!"

"Mustn't I ask you questions, then?"

"No. You mustn't. It isn't polite."

Linn was making an apple pie. She placed a piece of dough on the board and rolled it out with her rolling-pin. A well-greased dish stood close at hand and she placed the pastry over it, trimming the edge with the back of a knife. Robert watched, his dark eyes intent, admiring the skill and speed of her hand as the knife went round the edge of the dish and the ribbon of pastry fell to the board. Linn's glance flickered over his face.

"If by any chance I *was* to marry Charlie . . . "

"Yes, what?"

"Only supposing, you understand."

"Yes, all right."

"It means he would be your stepfather. Have you ever thought of that?"

"He'd still be my friend, though, wouldn't he?"

There was a wistful look in his eyes and a message of trust that went straight to her heart. He had known few friends in his young life, for her father, in his search for work, had moved many times in recent years, and they had rarely been settled anywhere for more than six months, until coming to Herrick Green.

"Yes," she said gently, touching his face. "Charlie would always be your friend, I'm sure of that."

"Are you going to marry him, then?"

"Don't be in such a hurry," she said. "People need time to think of these things."

Briskly, she turned to her pie again, piling the slicèd apples into the dish and sprinkling sugar over them. She took the remaining dough from the bowl and began rolling it out on the board.

"Don't you think I'm rather old to think of getting married?" she said.

"I don't think you're old at all. You haven't gone grey or anything."

"No, not yet!" she said with a laugh. "But it won't be long

now, I don't suppose."

"Why won't it?"

"Oh, just because!"

She was always laughing these days and the boy could not get over it. He had seen her unhappy so much of his life, trudging about from place to place, always unsettled, always so poor, always beset by anxieties. But they had been fifteen months at Herrick Green and his mother had grown to like the place. Luck had been with them during that time and now she was full of little jokes.

"You look like a girl," he said to her, "especially when you laugh like that."

"Goodness! You *are* buttering me up today!" She took a piece of apple from the pie and popped it, sugary, into his mouth. "There!" she said gaily, laughing again. "That's what you get for flattering me!"

* * * * *

What her young son had said was true: a glance in the mirror told her that; she was indeed like a girl again and felt as she had done at nineteen, before things had happened to change her life.

She had been full of laughter then; her childhood and girlhood had been full of joys; but the war had come and put paid to that. War, and its aftermath of waste, had made her old before her time. But those bad years were behind her now; she was grasping at happiness while she could. There were plenty of things to make her content: she and her father were both in work; they had a good cottage, tied but rent-free; and they had been settled for over a year. All this to Linn was purest balm, after the years of worry and want. And, of course, there was Charlie Truscott.

She saw him almost every day and by now they knew each other other well. She knew of his four years' soldiering; of the girl who had jilted him while he was away; of his careless career with women since then. Charlie, like herself and so many others, had lost four years of his life in the war. He never talked about it directly, but once in the bar at the Fox and Cubs, when somebody mentioned Kemal Pasha, he

21

suddenly said with bitterness: "Don't talk to *me* about the Turks! I had a bellyful of them when I was out in Gallipoli!"; and his face, in that moment, was terribly harsh.

But Charlie was resilient; always the happy optimist; and whatever had happened to him in the war, he had retained his youthfulness. At thirty-five he was still a boy; full of energy, full of zest; and in his company Linn recaptured something of her own lost youth. The sight of him driving some old sputtering tractor along the mazy Herrick lanes, standing up to it, scorning the seat, eagerly looking over the hedges to see what was happening in the fields, always brought a smile to her lips and caused a disturbance in her heart. Charlie drove with a certain panache, "standing up in the stirrups" as Robert said; he wore his cap at a jaunty angle, always had a spanner stuck in his belt, and carried a packet of cigarettes tucked in the bib of his overalls.

"What a lot you must smoke in a day!" she said once.

"Don't you approve of it?" Charlie asked.

"Oh, it's not that. Good gracious no! My father smokes and I'm used to it. I was only thinking what it must cost."

"Cigarettes are cheap enough, but I'd give it up if you wanted me to."

"Would you really?" she asked, surprised.

"Yes, if it really mattered to you."

Linn was impressed. She looked at him. But after a while she shook her head.

"I shan't ask you to give it up. What sort of woman would I be if I asked you to do such a thing for me?"

Charlie's face relaxed in a smile.

"Golly! That's a relief!" he said. "For a moment I thought you were going to say yes!"

"Why, you're nothing but a sprucer, after all! You never *meant* to give it up."

"Didn't I? Well, I don't know!" There was mischief in his eyes. "All I can say is this," he said, "I'm glad you never put me to the test!"

* * * * *

Friday was Linn's shopping-day, when she went to Bennett's at Herrick St John and stocked up with groceries for the week. One wet Friday in October she was surprised, on getting home, to find her father already there.

"I've been laid off," he said, grim-faced. "The rain has put paid to ploughing for the time being – what tiddly bit there is – and Mr Lawn has sent me home."

"Oh, dear, so it's come at last!" She hoisted her baskets on to the table and leant over them, wearily easing the stiffness in her arms. "How long for? Did Mr Lawn say?"

"He'll send for me when he needs me again. God only knows when that'll be!"

"At least he won't be turning us out of this cottage."

"No, he'll be charging us rent instead."

"How much will it be?"

"Two shillings a week."

"Oh, well, that's not too bad." She went to hang up her coat and hat. "We can manage that all right."

"Yes, well, maybe we can. – *If* we stop here!" her father said.

"What do you mean by that?" Linn said. Facing him, she was suddenly still. "Why shouldn't we stop here?"

"Because we'd be better moving on, going some place where I can get work."

"Are you serious?" Linn exclaimed. "Are we to go through that again, traipsing about from place to place, living like gipsies, the three of us?" Standing before him, her hands on her hips, she unleashed the full fury of her wrath. "Have you any idea how many times we've upped sticks and moved in the past six years? It's happened no less than thirteen times! Yes, you may stare, but that's the truth! Thirteen times we've shifted about, pillar to post, Robert and me, and if you think I'm going to start again – "

"It's no fault of mine we've had to move. I have to go where the work is."

"There *isn't* any work on the land these days! It's time you woke up and accepted that fact! You're entitled to a pension now. It's high time you swallowed your stupid pride and put in a claim like anyone else."

"God Almighty! Ten bob a week! What good is that, I'd like to know?"

"So long as I'm working, we can manage all right. Plenty of men are retiring these days, once they're drawing their pension, and you've earnt your rest more than most, what with your bad leg and all."

"I can still work, bad leg or no, and there's jobs to be had if you look for them."

"Then why not leave them for the younger men? Those with wives and young children to keep? You're not obliged to work any more and it's up to you to stand aside."

"Are you saying I'm past it?"

"All I'm saying is that I am not willing to leave this place and go traipsing about again the way we have done in the past!"

There was silence in the room. Jack sat, stony-faced, the smoke from his pipe swirling about him, clinging in wisps to his beard and moustache. Linn, still trembling after her outburst, turned to the baskets on the table and began unloading her groceries. Tea; sugar; matches; lard; she checked them against her shopping-list; and, glancing at her father's face, she tried to speak normally.

"I'm glad I made all that damson jam. It's gone up a ha'penny at the shop. Here are the laces you asked me for. Leather ones, I hope that's right? I told Mrs Bennett they had to be strong. Oh, yes, I nearly forgot! – I asked about the corduroys and she's got some your size at twelve-and-six. I asked her to put them aside for me."

Jack took the pipe out of his mouth and pressed the tobacco down in the bowl.

"Is it because of Charlie Truscott that you don't want to move from here?"

"I just want to be settled, that's all. That's a good enough reason, I should have thought."

"Are you going to marry him?"

"Why, you're as bad as Robert!" she said, doing her best to answer lightly. "You're both very free in quizzing me." She leant again over her basket and took out candles, sultanas, and rice. "Charlie hasn't asked me yet," she said in a carefully guarded tone.

"And what'll your answer be when he does?"

"I'll think about that when the time comes. *If* it ever

24

comes at all."

Jack got up and limped to the door. He snatched down his cap and put it on.

"Are you going out?" she said. "I was thinking of making some tea."

"You needn't bother on my account!" And he went out into the drizzling rain.

He had not gone far along the road when Charlie drew up in Clew Wilson's van.

"I was just on my way to your place."

"Not to see me, though, I'll be bound." Jack jerked his thumb towards the cottage. "Linn's just got back from doing the shopping. I daresay you know the way by now."

"Anything up?" Charlie asked.

"Yes!" Jack said. "The price of jam!"

* * * * *

"I just met your dad outside. It seemed he was in a bit of a mood."

"He's been laid off, that's why."

"Ah, of course, I ought to have guessed." Charlie watched her making the tea. "Jack's not the only one," he said. "It's much the same everywhere, this time of year."

"I know that. So does he. And yet he talks of moving on!" Linn brought the teapot to the table and sat down opposite Charlie. "We've just had words about it," she said. "I told him I wouldn't move again." She poured tea into two mugs and pushed Charlie's across to him. "We've just got nicely settled here. It's too much to ask, it really is."

Charlie could see that she was upset. He had come at the right time, he thought.

"I've just been down to Herrick Green. There's a cottage to let there. It's a nice little place, right by the ponds, just this side of the Ryerley turn. It only needs a lick of paint and a bit of new wallpaper here and there. Apart from that it's in pretty good shape."

Pausing a moment, he studied her, waiting for her to meet his gaze.

"It's just about the right size for us . . . You and me, your

25

father and Rob ... So what do you say to moving there? That's not too far away for you? Not too much of an upheaval, like?"

The tears, so close, now filled her eyes, and her voice when she tried to answer him was held back painfully in her throat.

"You know how it is with me?" Charlie said. "You know what I'm trying to say to you?"

Linn, having found her handkerchief, was trying to wipe away her tears.

"Do I?" she said, in a small voice.

"It's nearly twelve years since my girl let me down and married another man," he said. "Twelve years is a long time and I've never thought of marriage since then." Suddenly, as he looked at her, there was uncertainty in his eyes, and after a while, when he spoke again, it was with a husky, self-conscious laugh, as though he was making fun of himself. "Now *you've* come along and changed all that! Now I think of it all the time!"

Reaching across the table to her, he spread his hands in mute appeal, and when she responded by putting her own hands into his, he held them in a warm hard grasp, as though he would never let them go.

"I'd do anything in the world for you. Do you believe me when I say that?"

Clinging to him, she gave a nod, and now when the tears overflowed in her eyes she was helpless to brush them away, and they fell in little splashing drops, trembling and glistening on her cheeks before splashing down to the front of her dress.

"You don't ask what I might do for you."

"So long as you marry me," Charlie said, "I don't ask any more than that." He gave a sudden worried frown. "I don't know what your dad will say – "

"Dad will just have to settle down," she said with a certain decisiveness. "And he *will* settle down, I'm sure of that, when he knows how much it means to me."

Gently withdrawing her hands from his, she fumbled again for her handkerchief, which had fallen down into her lap. She wiped the tears from her cheeks and eyes and looked at him through her wet lashes.

"Tell me about the cottage," she said, "that we're going to live in at Herrick Common."

* * * * *

By the time they were married, in November, the new rented cottage was standing empty and it was arranged that Jack and Robert should move in while the couple were away on their honeymoon. A great many new things had been bought, including a brand-new double bed, and Jack, having plenty of time on his hands, was to make a start on the decorating.

At Fred Oakes's insistence, the wedding-breakfast was held at the Fox and Cubs, and from there Charlie and Linn set out on their honeymoon. Clew had lent them his motor-van and they started at noon from Herrick Cross without knowing where they were going. They had made no plans of any kind; they just took to the road and drove westwards; and soon those green hills, which normally formed their distant horizon, were rising close beside the road.

There was a great sense of adventure in setting out on the road like this and yet a feeling of safety, too, because now they were bound together in every way and the unknown held no fears for them. Sitting side by side in the warmth and closeness of the van, their intimacy grew with every mile of road they covered, so that the promises made in church that morning were already being affirmed, deep in their physical consciousness. Affirmed in flesh and blood and bone; acknowledged in every fleeting touch; confessed in the glances they exchanged and in every word they spoke to each other.

Familiar hills were left behind. Strange hills and mountains took their place, rising steeply on either side and closing behind them, fold upon fold. Wet weeping clouds hung on their tops and rolled along their grey-green flanks, and at three o' clock the rain came down, blowing aslant on the gusty wind. There was no traffic on these roads and often the only life they saw was the sheep and curly-coated

27

cattle grazing along the mountainsides. Linn and Charlie had the world to themselves and they travelled through it, mile after mile, shut in together, close and warm, with the rain coming down, blanching the landscape, and the sweet smell of mountain turf coming in at the half-open window.

"Just fancy!" Charlie said. "Not a single soul knows where we are!"

"No," she said, "not even us!"

"Are you getting worried?" he asked.

"Well, I *am* just beginning to wonder where we shall get a bed for the night." Peering out through the misty windows, she could see nothing but rain and hills, and, in front, the wet winding road. "It's ages since we passed through a village, let alone a town," she said. "If you ask me, we're thoroughly lost."

"I know where we are all right."

"Where are we, then?"

"We're somewhere in Wales!"

Laughing, they drove on through the rain, and Linn, with a shiver, tucked her rug more closely about her, wrapping it round her knees and thighs.

"We shall very likely end up by having to sleep in the van!"

But she was not really nervous at all. Even her shiver was only pretence. Nobody else in the world, she thought, had ever had a honeymoon like this, and the uncertainty of where they would sleep was all part of the great adventure. Snug, with the rug wrapped warmly round her, she looked out at the bleak landscape, and even the rain was beautiful. Would the world always look like this now that she was married to Charlie and the rest of her life was in his hands? Sitting beside her, driving the van, he was the master of her fate and she was content that it should be so. As to the future, what of that? It, like their destination today, was unknown and mysterious and no one could guess what it might hold.

She took hold of his arm and gave it a squeeze and he turned his head to look at her.

"Happy?" he said.

"Yes. And you?"

"Surely you don't have to ask me that?"

* * * * *

They were driving through open country now and the mountains were being left behind. The Vale of the Tywi; Carmarthen; St Clears: all were blotted out by rain; and because it rained they kept pressing on, southwards now, towards the coast, where there was just a teasing hint of lightness and brightness in the sky.

"Here are your villages," Charlie said, "and here are your towns."

And, as the day was drawing in, he began looking out for somewhere to stay.

"Not a hotel?" Linn exclaimed. "I've never stayed in one in my life!"

"Come to that, neither have I!"

But Charlie always knew what to do. New experiences did not frighten him, or, if they did, he hid it well. And when, in the little hotel at Llanmell, he wrote their names in the register, he did it quietly, without any fuss, in a way she admired.

The holiday season was over and they were the only guests. A fire was lit in the sitting-room and their supper was laid on a small table close by the hearth: green pea soup with croutons in it, followed by haddock in parsley sauce, with boiled potatoes and buttered beans; then, for pudding, junket and prunes. Mr Hughes, the proprietor, waited on them and cleared away, while his wife in the background nodded and smiled, never speaking to them directly but enquiring through her husband whether there was anything they wanted.

"No, thanks, we're fine as we are."

If there was anything, would they ring?

"Yes," Charlie said. "Thanks. We will."

Perhaps a hot water bottle in their bed?

"Well," Charlie said. He glanced at Linn.

"No, thank you, I'm sure we shall be quite warm enough."

There was confusion in her face but if Mr Hughes saw it he gave no sign. Quietly he withdrew and the sitting-room door was closed on them. Charlie got up and switched out the light.

"Nice old couple."

"Yes, they are."

"D'you think they guess we're on our honeymoon?"

"I don't know."

Charlie came and sat on the couch. He put his hand over hers.

"Tired?" he said.

"Yes, just a bit. I shan't be sorry to see my bed."

Confusion again. Linn looked away. But after a moment she began to smile.

"What's the joke?" Charlie asked.

"Oh, I don't know! Everything! Us . . . This place . . . Our being here . . . " She let her head drop on his shoulder and he looked at her in the firelight. "I wonder what Dad and Robert are doing now."

"We can send them a post-card tomorrow," he said. "We can put on it 'Wish you were here'!"

"I'm not putting that! It wouldn't be true." She leant against him, closer still, and felt his lips touching her hair. "This is just us. Our special time." She put up her face to receive his kiss.

Their bedroom was at the top of the house. Rain lashed the window continuously and wind moaned in the narrow chimney. Sometimes bits of soot fell down and ratttled among the paper flowers that decorated the fire-place.

On the wall above the bed there hung a text in a criss-cross frame, bearing the words "Thou God Seest Me", and illumined with an enormous blue eye. Linn stood at the foot of the bed, undoing the buttons at the front of her dress.

"I don't like that eye looking down at me."

"That's soon remedied," Charlie said. He turned the text towards the wall.

He came to her and touched her throat. His hand moved slowly and tenderly, inside the opening of her dress, his fingers exploring the soft smooth skin between her shoulder and her neck.

"You don't mind *me* looking at you, I hope?"

With his hand on her throat, he could feel the quickening

of her breath and the little hurried throb of her pulse beating underneath the skin. Her eyes were suddenly very dark, full of the feeling she had for him, and she answered him in a tremulous whisper.

"I shall have to get used to that, shan't I?"

Her arms went up to clasp his neck.

* * * * *

By morning the rain had stopped and they walked along the sands at Pendine, all the way to Saundersfoot. There was a lightening of the sky, and whenever the sun struggled through, it was with a gentle surge of warmth.

Once they took off their shoes and stockings and went to the very edge of the sea, Linn with her skirts wrapped round her thighs, Charlie with his trousers rolled to the knees. They stood where the tide came sidling in: a sidelong swirl, surrounding them, licking their feet and then covering them; cold, very cold, numbing their flesh. Linn had never paddled before. Her flesh seemed to shrink upon her bones.

"Oh, it's so cold! So cold!" she said.

"Don't you like it?" Charlie asked.

"Oh, yes, it's lovely! It's grand!" she said.

The noise of the sea filled her ears; its great sweeping waves came mounting the beach, running, white-edged, up the pale golden sand with a sly, deceitful, slow-seeming swiftness; coldly, silkily licking her feet and lapping the cringing flesh on her shins.

Then, as the wave receded again, how the sand slipped and dwindled under her feet! She felt the whole world was yielding beneath her, slipping and sliding away with the tide. The earth seemed to tilt most dangerously and she flung out her arms in a gesture of panic, feeling that the sea would bear her away. But Charlie was there and she clung to him. His strong arms went round her, holding her tight, and his confident body was braced against hers, steadying her and supporting her.

"It's all right," he said, "you're perfectly safe."

"Yes, I know! I know!" she cried.

Frightened, exultant, she clung to him, her cold-tingling feet gripping the sand, her toes curled into its quick-shifting wetness, until it became quite still again.

"I thought I was going to be swept away!"

"Not while I've got hold of you!"

Laughing above the noise of the sea, they clung to each other, warm and close, watching and waiting for the next sweeping wave.

* * * * *

At Saundersfoot they had some lunch. Then they walked back by the sands again.

"Shall we move on tomorrow, d'you think?"

"Oh, no, let's stay! I like it here."

So they stayed a full week at the Llanmell hotel, waited upon by Mr Hughes and with Mrs Hughes smiling and nodding in the background.

"What's the betting it's green pea soup?" Charlie whispered at dinner one night.

"With some kind of fish for the main course . . . "

"Followed by junket, you mark my words."

But they had no serious fault to find with the food, or indeed with anything else. Every day they walked by the sea, sometimes buffeted by the wind, quite often soaked by a shower of rain. They grew accustomed to sand in their shoes; to the tingle of wind-burn in their cheeks; to the taste of salt on their lips and hands.

"Oh, I wish this week would last and last! I wish we could take the sea home with us!"

"We *could* stay longer, if you like."

"Don't be silly. Think of the cost."

"I've still got a bit of money left."

"That doesn't mean you must spend it, though."

The weather was fine for their last day. They sat on the sand and gazed at the sea.

"You looking forward to going home?"

"Yes," she said simply, squeezing his arm. She thought of the cottage he had rented, overlooking the Herrick ponds; of her father and Robert, already there; of the new double

32

bed and the chest-of-drawers and the lino patterned in blue and gold. "For almost the first time in my life I shall live in a cottage that isn't tied."

When they left the next morning it was raining again, a steady downpour that lasted all day.

"Maybe one day we'll go back to Llanmell . . . "

"Yes, in the summer, when it's fine."

"A second honeymoon," Charlie said.

"Staying with Mr and Mrs Hughes . . . "

"Green pea soup for supper every night . . . "

"That awful text on the bedroom wall . . . " Linn's hand flew to her mouth. "Heavens!" she said, looking at him. "Did you turn it the right way round?"

"No," he said, "I never did."

Linn's guilty laughter mingled with his.

* * * * *

The cottage, when they had seen it last, had been a dingy shade of brown, for its roughcast walls had never known the touch of a whitewash brush. But Jack had been busy during their absence and now, when they came home to it, it was transformed, a dazzling white, and the woodwork was painted black and cream. The shrubs in the garden had been pruned and the grass leading down the edge of the pond had been mown till it looked like a bowling-green.

Jack and Robert came out to them and helped to carry their luggage in.

"I can't get over it!" Charlie said. "I thought we'd come to the wrong house!"

"Did you really?" Robert said. There was excitement in his eyes. "Granddad did most of it. I only gave him a hand, that's all."

"Oh, it's beautiful!" Linn exclaimed.

Inside the cottage as well as out amazing changes had taken place. The kitchen walls, newly distempered, were now a pale primrose yellow, and the parlour walls were shell-pink. But the best and most beautiful room of all was Linn and Charlie's bedroom, overlooking the garden and ponds. The wallpaper, bought at Bennett's shop, had been chosen specially for this room and Linn, surveying it from the doorway, thought she had never seen anything quite so pretty as its pattern of blue-grey trellis-work with full-blown yellow roses on it, rioting among their leaves. Her mouth opened in a neat round o and she let out her breath in a little gasp.

"I never dreamt it would look like this!"

"I can't get over it!" Charlie said. "The work that's been done in one short week!"

Jack, with his pipe in his mouth, unlit, stood with his hands in his trousers pockets, and Robert, taking his cue from him, lounged beside him as though unconcerned, while the newly-weds walked about the room, exclaiming at everything they saw.

"This paper's been hung by a master hand! I can't hardly see the joins at all, the pattern's been matched up so perfectly."

"I do think that frieze is beautiful!"

"Just look at this lino, how it's been cut, fitting all round the doorway here."

"Dad was always good with his hands."

"Somebody's even lined the drawers."

"*And* made the bed for us!" Linn exclaimed. "They've worked so hard, the pair of them!"

Jack removed his pipe from his mouth and looked at Robert.

"Seems your mother's quite pleased," he said.

"Are you, mother? Are you pleased?" The boy was almost beside himself. His unconcern had been costing him dear. "Do you like what we've done in the house?"

"Oh!" Linn said. She was overcome. "How can you ask me such a thing?"

"Well," said Jack, with a little grunt, "You'd better come down and have some tea."

* * * * *

"So you ended by spending your honeymoon in Wales? We had your post-card from Pendine."

"Oh, it was lovely there!" Linn said. "I wish you could see

it, so beautiful . . . "

"What sort of weather did you have? Rain, I suppose, the same as here?"

"No, it wasn't the same at all! The rain is quite different in Wales!" she said.

"Wetter, for one thing," Charlie said.

"Is it really?" Robert asked.

"Charlie's just teasing you," Linn said. "He's a terrible tease, this husband of mine."

Sitting upright in her chair, flushed and brimming with happiness, she kept glancing from Robert to Jack.

"Well, did you miss me, both of you?"

"We missed your cooking," Robert said. "Granddad's not much good at it. He burnt the sausages yesterday."

"Is that all I am to you, then, just a cook?"

"I'll tell you what, young Rob," Charlie said. "If you were to ask your mother nicely, you might get a special treat for dinner tomorrow."

"What special treat?"

"Green pea soup!"

There was plenty of laughter at teatime that day as they told Jack and Robert about the hotel, and Charlie made such a tale of it that when he was done the room was quite dark and Linn had to rise and light the lamp.

Robert, seeing how dark it was, suddenly made a face of disgust. He had wanted to take Charlie out and show him the waterfowl on the ponds. Now darkness had come and it was too late.

"Never mind. You can show me tomorrow."

"It's not only ducks. There are dabchicks as well. One day I even saw a coot."

"There's plenty to see out there, then, it seems?" Charlie looked at the boy's eager face. "D'you think you'll like living here in this house?"

Robert gave a shy nod.

"Not too lonely?" Charlie asked. "We haven't got many neighbours here."

"We've got Mrs Ransome," Robert said.

"Is that in the cottage opposite? Have you seen her?"

"Seen her?" said Jack. "I should think we have! She was in

and out of her door like a jack-in-the-box the day we moved in, and as for that little dog of hers, he's a handful and no mistake!"

"What's she like?" Charlie asked.

"Oh, a good enough neighbour, I should think."

Linn, as she cleared away the tea-things, listened to her menfolk talking together and felt a glow of thankfulness. Her son's joy in his new home was plain to see: he was full of the hundred and one sights he wanted to show Charlie next day; and her father, it seemed, had accepted the change and was settling down to it, for her sake.

"How long do honeymoons last?" Robert asked.

"That all depends," Charlie said. "For your mother and me, tomorrow will be the last day, I suppose. Then it's back to work for us and settling down to plain married life."

"Well," said Jack, lighting his pipe, "it seems to suit you well enough."

Charlie exchanged a glance with Linn.

"I've got no complaints so far," he said.

Chapter 3

The three ponds, strung out beside the road, were a never-failing source of delight to Robert, and he would sit for hours on the bank, watching the mallards and pintails as they dived and fed in the cool clear water.

"Will they go away when the bad weather comes?"

"If you were to put out food for them, they might well stay, bad weather or no."

Winter that year was mild on the whole but in January there were severe frosts. Robert put out crusts for the birds and watched from a distance while they ate. To his great joy, the mallards remained all winter, often coming into the garden itself to sit in the sun on the grassy bank. They grew quite used to the sight of the boy watching them, so silent, so still, and sometimes if he was patient enough they would even take food out of his hands.

The frosts, when they came, lasted three weeks and every morning before school Robert went out with a heavy hammer to break as much of the ice as he could, so that the ducks could still swim. In the third week of January the ice was so hard it could not be broken and then on Saturday afternoon children from the villages around came to skate or slide on the ponds.

Robert hated them there at first because they kept the ducks away, but the lure of the ice was too strong and soon he was out sliding with the other children. A few of the luckier ones had skates and he would stand watching enviously as they skimmed the length of the three ponds which, in winter, became as one. He longed to be able to skate with them, but skates in the shop at Overbridge cost twenty-five shillings, and such a sum was out of his reach, at least this winter, anyway. Next winter? Well, perhaps! But he knew he would have to save very hard to raise such a sum even by then.

Soon the ice was gone from the ponds and there was a hint of spring in the air. The mallards and pintails swam in the ponds and in April nested among the reeds. There was plenty to watch as they played and displayed in the act of courtship and to Robert, lying along a willow branch that stretched out over the water, winter with its ice and ice-skates soon seemed nothing but a dream.

"You will be careful, won't you?" Linn said. It brought her heart into her mouth to see the slender willow branch bending under him as he climbed. "If you should slip and fall into that pond – "

"For pity's sake don't fuss the boy, he knows what he's doing," her father said.

"I shouldn't worry if he could swim – "

"If he falls in, he'll soon learn to swim! That's how I learnt when I was a boy." And before Linn could protest at this: "I'll keep an eye on him, don't you worry. I've got little else to do with my time."

Time had hung heavily on Jack's hands all through that winter and early spring. He hated having nothing to do and although he tried hard to accept his position he felt his dependence like a sore. When he drew his pension each week, he insisted on giving Linn half, and nothing she or Charlie said would ever dissuade him.

"I always like to pay my way, such as it is," he used to say.

Out of the five shillings he had left he paid for his own tobacco and drinks, making two ounces of twist last a week and, when he went to the Fox and Cubs, making a pint last an hour.

"Gentleman of leisure now, eh, Jack?" Fred Oakes said to him.

"Ah, that's me," Jack agreed. "I've left my carriage and pair outside."

One evening when he was at the bar, drinking his beer and talking to Linn, Fred came in from the back of the house and put his arm around her shoulders.

"You been drawing your dad a free pint? Well, that's all right, I don't mind. – Just so long as it's only one!"

Jack, his face like a thundercloud, drank the last of his old-and-mild and set the empty glass on the bar.

"I always pay for the drinks I have. I always have done, all my life. When I can't pay, I go without."

He turned on his heel and walked out and Fred gave a little awkward laugh.

"Laws, he's a funny chap, your dad, taking me up so sharp," he said. "I only meant it in fun, you know."

"Did you?" Linn said. She moved away from his circling arm. "Dad won't see it like that, I'm afraid. I doubt if he'll come in here again."

"Can't the old fellow take a joke?"

"No, nor insults, either," she said.

The incident rankled with her all the evening and at closing-time, when Fred locked the door, she told him that she wanted to leave.

"Just cos of what I said to your dad?"

"Partly that, I must admit. But there is another reason as well."

"What other reason, for God's sake?"

"A personal one," she said, with reserve.

Fred regarded her narrowly, enlightenment dawning in his face.

"Have you told old Charlie?" he asked with a grin.

"Yes, of course, " she said primly.

"You surely don't need to worry yet? It can't be soon, by the look of you."

"I'd like to leave next week all the same."

"Oh, very well, if you insist."

"Yes," she said, "I've made up my mind."

She had never liked working at the Fox and Cubs and when, at the end of the following week, she left the place for the last time, it was without a trace of regret, except for the money she would lose.

"Never mind that," Charlie said. "I'm earning good wages, aren't I? I can surely afford the odd baby now and then!"

"It's only going to be one, I hope."

"Well, one at a time, anyway."

Ever since her pregnancy had been confirmed, Charlie had been in a state of excitement, unable to think of anything else. One day he went into Overbridge and came back with a beautiful cot, bought at Johnson's furniture store. It was a delicate shade of blue, with pink and white daisies painted on the panels, and with one side that slid up and down. He had also bought the bedding for it: a soft-padded mattress, pink and white; a tiny pink pillow, edged with lace; two blankets, two sheets, and a pink satin quilt.

Linn was upset when she heard how much these things had cost. She scolded him for his extravagance.

"Damn it all!" Charlie said. "I don't have a baby every day and I reckon it deserves the best."

"Yes, but this is ridiculous! All your savings gone in a flash!"

"I'll soon make it up when I get my rise."

"And when will that be, I'd like to know? Clew's been promising it to you for months but there's not much sign of it as yet."

"Well, he's got his kiddy to think about now."

"Clew takes advantage of you," Linn said. "He always has done. He's that sort."

"I wouldn't say that. Clew's always been a good friend to me – "

"All the hours you put in for him, so he should be a good friend to you! That garage would never pay so well if it wasn't for all the work you do there."

Linn placed the bedding in the cot, arranging the pillow, the blankets, the quilt. Although worried about the expense, she couldn't resist their prettiness, and Charlie said teasingly:

"Am I to take them back to the shop and say I don't want them after all?"

"You!" she exclaimed, rounding on him. "Hopeless spendthrift that you are!" She leant away from him, held by his arms, and beat at his chest with both her hands. "Our baby will think we're millionaires!"

But when he left her to go back to work, she was stooping over the cot again, raising and lowering the side panel to see how the lock and ratchet worked.

* * * * *

Linn had known so much poverty, especially in the past few years, that the fear of it was with her still, and now that there was a baby coming, the future caused her anxiety.

"Have you got that rise yet?" she would ask Charlie week after week.

"No, not yet. Next month, Clew says."

"If you were to work in a garage in town, you could earn more than you do at Clew's."

"And spend it on bus fares, to and fro? I don't see much sense in doing that."

"You'd still be better off, even so. Haven't you any ambition at all?"

"No," Charlie said, "I don't think I have."

"Not even for my sake, and the sake of our baby when it comes?"

"It's no good wheedling me like that. We've had this out a dozen times." Charlie would do a great many things to please her, but in this he remained adamant. "I'm quite happy where I am. The wages I get are not too bad. And I shouldn't *care* to work in the town."

Clew's garage suited him fine. He could come and go pretty well as he pleased and arrange his hours to suit himself.

"So long as the work gets done," Clew would say, "that's all I ever worry about."

And the work always *was* done; Clew knew that; Charlie never let him down. "Agricultural repairs a speciality," Clew's signboard announced boastfully and Charlie, of course, was the specialist. He was rather possessive about it. Any work that came in from the farms always had to be left for him.

"That Sammy Cooper's elevator? I'll see to that!" he would say.

"Ah, but when?" Clew would ask. "You're up to your eyebrows as it is."

"Some time tonight. You leave it to me."

The garage light would burn until all hours; sometimes until after midnight; but although it was Charlie who worked so late, it was Clew who yawned throughout the day.

41

"Teething! Wind! We're getting it all. You'll know what it's like yourself pretty soon."

"Bloody Norah" had now been joined by "the blinking nuisance": a baby weighing, according to Clew, ten and a half pounds at birth.

"What are you calling him?" Charlie asked.

"We're calling him Oby," Clew replied, and as Charlie stared, nonplussed, he explained: "Oby-quiet-you-little-sod!"

Babies' names were on Charlie's mind. He talked about them constantly.

"What do you favour?" he asked Linn. "Surely you must have *some* ideas?"

But Linn was always busy these days and on this particular Sunday afternoon she had a skirt spread out on the table and was busy removing the waist-band so that she could let out the pleats.

"Don't talk to me now, I'm busy," she said. Nail-scissors poised between her fingers, she looked at him with a little frown. "Haven't you got anything to do?"

"Oh, yes, there's plenty to do."

"Then why not do it, for goodness' sake, instead of hanging about round me?"

Robert, coming into the room at that moment, overheard these sharp words. He crept behind his mother's chair and took his boots out of the hearth.

"Must you jog my arm like that?" Linn demanded pettishly. "Look how you've made me cut the cloth!"

Robert had scarcely touched her at all. He stared at her with indignant eyes.

"Come on, young Rob," Charlie said. "This is no place for us men. You can come and give me a hand outside."

He and the boy went out together and spent the rest of the afternoon creosoting the garden fence.

"You mustn't mind if your mother snaps. It's a difficult time for women, you know, when there's a baby on the way."

"Will she be like that all the time, right up until the baby comes?"

"I don't suppose so," Charlie said. "I was going on at her

about the baby's name, you see, and it got on her nerves."

"What names do *you* favour?" Robert asked.

"Well, now you ask me," Charlie said, "I think Sally's a pretty name . . . So's Priscilla . . . So is Jane . . . " He paused and dipped his brush in the pail. "But only if it's a girl, of course."

Robert turned from painting the fence and laughter bubbled up in him. He and Charlie enjoyed many a quiet joke together. Charlie could always make fun of himself and the boy felt drawn to him by this.

"You want it to be a girl, don't you? You've set your heart on it?" he said.

"How did you guess?" Charlie said.

* * * * *

Towards the end of April, Jack was taken on again at Bellhouse Farm.

"There, what did I tell you?" Linn exclaimed. "I said Mr Lawn would take you back as soon as spring came round again."

She was overjoyed for him. His life had its proper purpose again. And it was a truly remarkable thing to see the upright way he walked now that he had a job to go to and money he felt he could call his own. But there was one thing that angered her: he immediately stopped drawing his pension.

"You're not earning such a lot that you can afford to throw ten shillings down the drain! It's *your* pension. You're entitled to it."

"If it's mine," Jack said, "I can do what I like with it, and what I like is to leave it alone."

Nothing she said would change his mind. He was immovable, like a rock.

"They'd probably stop it, anyway, once they knew I was earning again."

There was another thing that caused her vexation at this time. Robert was now eleven and a half and she wanted him to sit the exam that might mean a place at the Grammar School. His headmaster at Ryerley thought he stood a good chance of passing, if only he put his mind to it, but Robert himself would have none of it. All he wanted was to go on a farm. The Grammar School was nothing to him.

"Wouldn't you like to get on in the world? Education is a very fine thing and if you do well at the Grammar School all sorts of careers might be open to you."

"God Almighty!" her father muttered. "When shall we hear the last of that?"

It was late one Sunday evening. Jack and Charlie were playing cards. Robert had been on his way to bed, but Linn had detained him for over an hour, doing her best to win him round. She leant forward, out of her chair, and laid a coaxing hand on his arm.

"Won't you do it, to please me? It would mean such a lot if you said yes."

The boy was unhappy. He hung his head. He hated to deny her anything, especially when she looked like that, in that soft, beseeching way she had, with a hint of sadness in her eyes.

"I'd never pass, anyway, even if I did sit the exam."

"Mr Maitland thinks you would."

"He's off his hinges," Robert said.

"Well, why not try and see for yourself? Then, if you fail, that's an end to it. There's surely no harm in just sitting the exam?"

"I ent so tarnal sure of that! I shouldn't care to sit and fail."

"Then how would you feel if you sat and passed?" Linn's eyes were alight with triumph. She felt she had him within her grasp. "How would you feel? You tell me that!"

"I'd feel a bit proud of myself, I suppose."

"Of course you would! And so should I!"

"But I don't *want* to go to the Grammar School! It means I'd be stuck there for years and years."

"No, it wouldn't, not necessarily. You needn't go if you feel like that. Just sit the exam and see what happens."

"What, win a place and not take it up?"

"At least we'll have seen what you can do. That's all I ask, just to see, that's all."

Robert was silent, hesitating. He looked at her in a searching way.

44

"I dunno," he said at last. "If I pass and get a place, you'll start on me to take it up."

"No, I shan't. I give you my word. Honour bright and cross my heart."

There was silence in the room. Jack and Charlie were listening, and their game of cribbage had come to a halt. The boy, in his stillness, stood like a post, until Linn, with a gentle tug at his arm, brought him to himself again.

"Won't you, Robert, just to please me?"

"Well," he said, wavering.

"It's surely not too much to ask, just to sit an exam?" she said. "Just to show me what you can do?"

Suddenly her father spoke, harshly and impatiently.

"For God's sake leave the boy alone, instead of nagging him all the time! He's told you what he wants to do. Leave him alone, let him choose for hisself."

"And be a labourer all his life?"

"*I've* been a labourer all my life. I dunno that it's done me much harm."

"It certainly hasn't done you much good!"

Linn's tone was suddenly tart and Robert, disliking it, moved away. He had been about to yield to her but her words to his granddad had altered that. Linn saw it plainly in his face. She knew she had lost her hold on him.

"Goodnight, mother. I'm going to bed."

"Is that all you have to say to me?"

"I don't care to be tricked," he said, "and that's what you'd got in the back of your mind."

"Won't you even hear me out?"

"No," he said, and she let him go.

Afterwards she turned on her father.

"Did you have to butt in like that? I'd very nearly persuaded him – "

"You're too fond of persuading people. You should let them alone for a change."

"Jack's in the right of it," Charlie said. "It's no good trying to cajole young Rob. He'd hold it against you later on."

"I thought you at least would be on my side. You went to a good school. You know what a great advantage it is."

"What did it do for me?" he said. "I'm a mechanic, that's all."

45

"But you know so much about so many things! You can talk to anyone, anywhere, about anything under the sun!" she said.

"Young Rob'll make his way all right. He knows his own mind and it's clear as a bell. I doubt if the Grammar School would do much for him."

"We'll never know, shall we?" she said. "He will have thrown the chance away."

Later that year, in July, the scholarship winners were named in the local newspaper. There were two boys from the Herricks among them and later still, when the winter term started, they could be seen at Herrick Cross, smart in their dark green blazers and caps, waiting for the bus into Overbridge.

"You could have been one of them," Linn said to her son. She had yearned for it with all her heart. "I'm sure you're as clever as that Barton boy."

* * * * *

But although she reproached him from time to time, there was no real discord between him and her: they were much too close for that; and she was content to take pride in him for what he was, putting out of her mind what he might have been. He was her darling, and a good son to her. He considered her in every way.

At holiday times he worked on the farms, to earn a few shillings for himself, but he never spent his money on ice-cream or sweets; instead he bought toothpaste and soap and socks; things that he knew would help her out. He rarely spent money on childish things but that year, as the autumn passed, and he thought of the winter coming again, he began to long for the ice-skates seen in the shop in Overbridge, price twenty-five shillings.

So every evening after school and all day on Saturdays he worked spreading muck at Brooky Farm. The farmer, Hedley Sharp, had promised him the sum of sixpence an hour but the money would only be paid, he said, when the whole twenty acres had been spread. It was heavy work for a young boy; the muck-heaps, in rows up and down the field, seemed to have set like heaps of cement; his arms ached, lifting the stuff, and his hands were soon covered in blisters.

"That Hedley Sharp!" Linn complained. "He's got no right to work you so hard! You're not to go down to Brooky again. I simply won't have it, do you hear?"

"I ent stopping now," Robert said. "I've got money owing to me and I mean to have it, every groat. I'm saving up to buy my skates."

"I could give you those skates for your birthday next month. I've got a bit of money put by."

But Robert would not hear of it.

"That money's put by for the baby," he said, "to buy the extra things you'll need." He was stubborn and would not be moved. "Besides," he said, with a jut of his jaw, "I *want* to buy them for myself."

In time the last of the muck was spread and Sharp pronounced himself satisfied. He paid Robert for twenty hours' work and gave him a bonus of eighteen pence.

"You're a sticker. I will say that. Are you willing to come again and do some jobs around my yard?"

Robert nodded. He was quite game. He needed another thirteen-and-six.

* * * * *

Linn in these months was suffering. The burden she carried was crippling her, giving her dreadful pain in her back, and although there were only two months to go, it seemed the time would never pass.

"Isn't there anything to be done?" Charlie asked.

"No, there's nothing. I asked the nurse. Just to rest every day, she said."

He could not bear to see her in pain and to know that he was responsible. The knowledge filled him with terrible guilt and sometimes at night when she groaned and cried out he suffered with her to such a degree that the perspiration poured from his face.

"Surely there's *something* I can do?"

"Yes, you can put your hand on my back."

"Here?" he said.

"No, here, lower down."

The touch of his hand brought some relief, even if only for a while. He closed his eyes in agony, trying to draw the hot throbbing pain out of her body, into his hands. God! The trouble men brought to their wives! Was it love that brought this about? No, he thought, hating himself, love was the name men gave to lust, to explain themselves and absolve them of blame. Love was something altogether different. Love was what he felt for her now, when he would have given half his life to undo the harm he had wrought in her.

And yet, along with the agony, as she drew his hand away from her back and placed it over their unborn child, there was a fierce exultation too. *His* baby, moving in her! *His* own body, renewed in hers! And he lowered his frantic, exultant face until he was lying against her breast, while his arms enfolded her, tenderly, asking forgiveness for her suffering yet guilty, even now, of desiring her.

"It's all right," she whispered. "Don't tremble so."

"I shouldn't have done this to you," he said.

"Don't be silly. It's the nature of things." And then, with a smile in her voice, she said: "The trouble is, I'm a bit old to be having a baby, I suppose."

"At thirty-six? Get away!" he said.

But her words struck new fear into his heart and afterwards, in the weeks that followed, whenever he saw that she was in pain, the fear rose up again, choking him. He watched over her constantly; went home early from work every night; and did his utmost to make her rest.

* * * * *

The autumn was passing rapidly. Soon there came a nip in the air and a whiteness on the distant hills. Robert was impatient to buy his skates and on Saturday mornings, at first light, he was in the yard at Brooky Farm, working the old-fashioned chaff-cutter or pulping swedes to feed the stock.

One Saturday morning when he was there, Hedley Sharp's housekeeper, Mrs James, came out of the house and called to the stockman, Bert Johnson, to fetch a cockerel and kill it for her. Bert brought the cockerel into the yard and carried it to the chopping-block, where the wood-axe lay handy, its blade in the block.

Robert turned to the barrowload of swedes and began loading them into the pulper. He did not want to see the cockerel killed. He tried to close his ears to its squawks and the dull thud of the axe descending. But the cockerel, beheaded, still writhed and kicked, and such was the strength in its vibrant nerves that it kicked itself out of Bert's hands and flopped to the ground. Robert saw it; it was close by his feet; its wings still flapping furiously, its bloody neckbone protruding and wriggling, out of the collar of severed flesh.

"Would you believe it?" Bert exclaimed. He gave a startled, disgusted laugh and lunged towards the flapping bird. "Die, you beggar, die!" he said.

Robert felt sick and turned blindly away. He felt he had to escape from the yard. And because he scarcely knew what he was doing, he failed to see the heavy lorry swinging in at the farmyard gate. There was a loud screeching of brakes and a man's voice shouting at him. He threw up his arms to protect himself.

The lorry, before it lurched to a stop, caught him a glancing blow with its mudguard and somehow he was flung on his back, jarring his spine on the rough cobbles. The white-flashing pain of it made him cry out and yet no sound escaped his lips: the shrieking was in his spine and his brain. The dark silent world seemed to topple about him, lit by flashes of splitting white light, but after a while he could see again, and by then he was closely surrounded by people: Bert Johnson and Hedley Sharp; the lorry driver and Mrs James.

"You all right, boy? Can you get up?"

"What the hell's going on?"

"He stepped right in my way. I was just turning in – "

"Poor little boy! He's as white as a sheet!"

"Here, young fellow, let me give you a hand."

Bert and the driver helped him up. He stood, still in dimness, supported by them, on legs that seemed nailed to the base of his spine. But slowly, gradually, the pain grew less sharp. The dimness dispersed and he stared at his feet.

"You all right, boy? You ent badly hurt?"

Robert nodded. He couldn't yet speak.

"You've just about knocked yourself for six. What did you think you was doing, my lad, walking slap in the path of a lorry like that? You sure you're all right? Can you stand by yourself?"

"Yes," Robert said, "I think I can."

"Well," said Bert, "you'd better be sure!"

The two men let go and he stood by himself, staring helplessly at his feet. He walked a few steps and the pain was like fire, but he tried not to let it show in his face. Hedley Sharp stood over him.

"Seems to me you'd better go home."

"I'm all right. Honestly."

"How much have you earnt this morning so far?"

"I don't know." He tried to think. "I got here at seven or thereabouts – "

"Well, never mind. I'll give you three bob." Sharp pressed the coins into his hand and folded his fingers over them. "Now get off home and don't come back. It's nothing but a nuisance, employing you boys. There's always some bother comes of it."

"Oughtn't he to come in and sit down?" Mrs James asked indignantly. "Just look at him! He looks like death!"

"Why, if he wants to, he can," Sharp said.

But Robert had no wish to linger there, if he wasn't to be allowed to work. His only idea was to get away and hide himself somewhere, away from all eyes, while he fought off the sickness and the pain.

* * * * *

On his way home he went into the woods and stretched himself out on a grassy bank. He lay there so still, among the dead leaves, that a rabbit, emerging from a nearby burrow, began cropping the grass near his feet. He could see the sunlight through its pink ears, and could hear the noise of its busy teeth as it nibbled a single sappy stalk, held between its two front paws.

Watching the rabbit, he came back to life. The feeling of sickness passed away and with it the worst of the bone-splitting pain. When the rabbit had gone away he rose gingerly to his feet. It was only half a mile's walk to his home and by the time he arrived there, he was quite himself again, except for some stiffness in his limbs and a sort of cramp at the base of his spine.

His mother was out when he got in. She was with Mrs Ransome, across the road. When she returned at ten o'clock she asked him to fetch some coal for her and, seeing the pallor in his face as he carried the heavy scuttle in, she looked at him in sudden concern.

"Have you been overworking again, down at Brooky Farm?" she asked.

"I had a bit of a fall," he said. He gave her a reassuring grin. "I'm a bit stiff, but it's nothing much."

"I wish you wouldn't go to that place. That Mr Sharp takes advantage of you."

"No, well, as a matter of fact, I shan't be going there again."

"Oh, and why's that?"

"I've got enough money for my skates now."

* * * * *

That afternoon, Charlie went with him into town, and the skates were bought. Robert carried them home in their box and took them out for his mother to see: splendid silver-shining things with upturned blades, each engraved with the word, *Mercury*.

"There!" Linn said. "So you've got them at last! Now perhaps we shall have some peace!"

Robert sat down in a chair by the fire. The walk back from town had tired him. He sat and examined the skates in his lap.

"Why does it say *Mercury* on them?"

"It's the name for quicksilver," Charlie said. "It's also the name of a Roman god – the one who had little wings on his heels – and that's how you'll feel when you're out on the ice,

51

speeding along on those skates of yours. You'll be like a god, with wings on your heels, quick as quicksilver and twice as bright!"

Robert looked at him with a smile. The thought of it made him impatient to start. He rose and went to look out at the pond, where the willow trees were turning yellow and the leaves were fluttering into the water.

"All I need now is the ice!" he said.

He turned to walk to the table again, to lay the skates in their brown cardboard box. His mother watched him with a frown.

"Why are you walking like that?" she asked.

"Oh, I'm a bit stiff, that's all. Got a bone in my leg, as granddad would say."

"Didn't you tell me you had a fall?"

"Yes, that's right, so I did." Carefully he avoided her eye. "I fell in the yard at Brooky this morning but it's nothing to worry about," he said.

That was October the thirty-first. On the following Monday morning, playing football at school, Robert collapsed on the playing-field and was unable to get up. He was taken to hospital in Overbridge and Linn and Charlie were sent for at once. The fall in the yard at Brooky Farm had damaged his spine. Both his legs were paralysed. There was a strong possibility that he might never walk again.

So, by the time winter came and the three ponds were covered in ice, Robert sat in a wheelchair and the ice-skates, so splendid and silver-bright, lay in their box at the bottom of the cupboard in his bedroom.

Chapter 4

Robert remained in hospital for three months, encased in plaster, unable to move. The X-rays had shown that he had a fracture in his spine and the surgeon, Mr Tate, breaking the news to Linn and Charlie, had said it would take three months to heal.

"If only he'd told us straight away!" Linn kept saying, again and again. "Instead of making so light of it, as though it was just an ordinary fall!"

For many nights she was unable to sleep. She was haunted by the sight of Robert's face, white and fine-drawn with suffering, as he lay so still in his hospital bed. She reproached herself for her carelessness.

"I should have seen for myself," she said. "When he said he'd fallen at Brooky, I should have taken more notice, instead of letting it pass like that. For God's sake, what sort of mother am I? I should've *known* there was something wrong!"

"How could you know?" Charlie said. "He hid it from all of us, not only you."

"If only he'd been less foolishly brave – "

"According to what the surgeon said, it wouldn't have made much difference, even if we had known sooner."

"I can't believe that!" Linn said. "If he'd gone to hospital straight away he wouldn't be in such agony now. And who knows what he's done to himself, struggling on for two days and then taking part in a football match?"

She sat in her chair beside the hearth. Charlie and Jack sat opposite. She looked at them with stricken eyes.

"We don't even know if he'll walk again!"

"Why torture yourself with thinking that?"

"You're forgetting I've been a nurse. D'you think I don't know the danger he's in?"

"They say the fracture will heal in time."

"He could still be paralysed even then."

"The surgeon didn't tell us that."

"They never tell anyone anything! Not until they can't help themselves. But I know what spinal damage can do. I saw it often during the war."

Charlie and Jack looked at each other. They were both helpless and sick at heart. There was nothing they could do to allay her fears.

"Well," Charlie said, with an effort, at last. "Whatever we might fear for him, we must keep it to ourselves. If Rob himself should fear such a thing – "

"Do you think I'd tell him?"

"No, I know you wouldn't do that, but you're not very good at hiding things and I'm scared he'll see it in your face."

"I know! I know! I shall have to take care!"

Sometimes she came close to breaking down. That such a thing should happen to Robert, a boy who had so much good in him! Was there no end to the cruel tricks that fate could deal out so casually? She knew she would need all her courage and strength to get through the months of uncertainty and give him the hope and faith he would need.

"Robert won't see anything, except what I mean him to see," she said, and that was a promise made in her heart.

But her visits to the hospital were an ordeal for her and she was always glad when Charlie or Jack accompanied her. They could always find plenty to say. Her father would talk of his work on the farm; how this or that field had come under the plough; how the threshing-machine had broken down and how they had found a dead rat in the works. And Charlie, with his quiet jokes, could even bring a smile to the boy's worn face.

"What're the nurses like in here? Do they look after you properly?"

"They're all right," Robert said. "Nurse O'Brien especially. She's the one with the dark hair."

Charlie, discreetly turning his head, eyed the nurse at the end of the ward.

"I like the look of her myself. If it weren't for your

54

mother sitting there, I'd be making up to your Nurse O'Brien." And then, after a pause, he said: "What do you do with yourself all day?"

"Mostly I watch what's going on."

"Do the other kids come and talk to you?"

"Only for a few minutes, that's all. The nurses are very strict about that. I have to keep still all the time, you see."

Linn reached out and touched his arm.

"Well, you were always good at that. Even as a little boy you could always keep as still as a mouse . . . "

Robert made a wry face.

"I reckon I've had enough of it now. When I get this plaster off – "

"Ah," said Charlie, with a little laugh, "we shan't see you for dust, then, eh?"

"It won't be for ages and ages yet."

"Oh, I don't know," Charlie said. "You've had three weeks of it, haven't you? Another three weeks and then three more – "

"Then another three after that – "

"There!" Charlie said. He slapped his knee. "We've soon made the time go, haven't we, eh?"

"I wish it *would* go as fast as that."

"So do we," Charlie said. "The house is not the same without you and as for those ducks of yours, out on the ponds, I'm sure they miss you watching them."

"You'll feed them, won't you, if the weather turns bad?"

"You'll be home to feed them yourself by then.

* * * * *

Autumn that year was beautiful. The berries were thick on the hedgerow trees and the leaves, changing colour, were like sullen fire. But Robert, in hospital, saw none of this. The earth and its marvels were hidden from him. All he could see was a patch of pale sky framed by the window close to his bed.

"Is there ice on the ponds yet?"

"No, the weather's as mild as mild."

"I wouldn't have been able to try my skates, then, even if I wasn't laid up like this?"

"No, that's right, but it's early days yet. We could still get a cold snap before we're through."

Linn, on the other side of the bed, looked at Charlie with a frown.

"There'll be no skating for Robert yet. Not this winter at any rate."

"Well, we shall see," Charlie said. "When he comes out of that plaster-cast – "

"Ah, when!" Robert said. He pulled a wry face and patted the cast. "Duddy old thing! I could smash it to bits!"

At regular intervals, during this time, the surgeon came to check Robert's legs, to see if there was any sign that sensation might be returning to them.

"Has Mr Tate been to see you today?"

"Yes, he was round this morning at ten."

"What about those legs of yours?"

"They're just the same," Robert said. "I've still got no felth in either one." His eyes were very dark and deep, looking out from his thin, tired face. "I've got to have patience, I suppose."

"You've always had plenty of that," Linn said. "A more patient boy couldn't be found if we searched from here to the end of the world."

During these visits she was cheerful and bright; she knew she had to be, for his sake; but between times she came close to despair.

"If Robert is not going to walk again . . . "

"You mustn't think like that," Charlie said. "Whatever happens, you've got to have faith."

"Faith!" she repeated bitterly. "It's easy enough to talk about faith but *I* know how slim his chances are!"

In her condition, heavy with child, she found the hospital visits a strain, and as she drew closer to her time, Charlie begged her to stay at home.

"Robert won't mind. He'll understand. He's a sensible chap and he knows how it is, with the baby due at the end of the month."

Linn, however, would not be persuaded.

"I'm his mother and he needs me!" she said. "I'm cer-

tainly not going to let him down! He bears it all so patiently
. . . Surely I can bear it too?"

Her own sufferings were nothing, she felt, compared
with what Robert had to bear. The worse of it was the
uncertainty. She feared for the future and what it held.

"I could bear almost anything if only I knew he was going
to get well."

The baby was due at the end of November and Linn
continued to visit the hospital every day right up to the last.
Charlie, to spare her as much as he could, always took her in
Clew's van, but he still felt the strain was too much for her,
and on November the twenty-sixth he tried yet again to
dissuade her from going.

"I'm not taking you in today, I think it's nothing but
madness," he said.

"If you don't take me I'll go by bus. Dad'll go with me,
won't you, dad?"

"You take notice of Charlie," Jack said. "You'd be better
stopping at home."

But Linn set her face against them both.

"If you won't go with me I shall go by myself."

"Think of the baby," Charlie said. "I won't have you
taking risks like this. You know what Dr Graham said – "

"I don't care about the baby! I only care about my son!"

"You don't mean that," Charlie said. "Why, you've
wanted this baby with all your heart, just as much as I want it
myself."

"Not any more I don't!" she cried. The truth of what she
felt broke out. She could not keep it secret any more. The
thought of the baby was hateful to her: coming now, just at
this time, when her son lay helpless in hospital and she
could not think of anything else. "I wish it had never been
conceived! I wish it was dead!" she said with a sob.

Charlie, white-faced, turned away, and Jack followed
him outside.

"You mustn't take too much notice of her, she don't
rightly know what she's saying, just now. It'll all be quite
different once the baby's come."

"I hope you're right," Charlie said. "What sort of chance
will the poor mite have if its own mother turns against it?"

That afternoon, as usual, he came to the door in Clew's van to drive Linn into Overbridge. She got in beside him without a word and he gave her only the briefest glance. On the journey they had a puncture and he had to stop and change the wheel. It took him only ten minutes or so but when he got into the van again, Linn was sitting hunched in her seat, with her arms folded across her stomach. She turned to him with wide-staring eyes and her voice, when she spoke, was no more than a whisper.

"Charlie, we'll have to go back!" she said. "My pains have started. I feel – rather ill."

* * * * *

Linn was in labour for only six hours but the birth itself was a difficult one. The doctor had to use instruments and the baby, a girl, was stillborn. Charlie, when he saw the tiny bundle carried out of the house by the nurse, broke down and wept. He felt he would never get over it. But Linn herself felt no grief whatever. All she felt was a sense of guilt because she had wished the baby dead and the wish had been granted by a cruel God.

"Charlie, do you hate me?"

"No, of course not," he said. "It wasn't your fault the baby died."

"Wasn't it? I'm not so sure. Maybe if I'd taken more care –"

"You mustn't think like that," he said. "You must just think about getting well."

Later she spoke about the cot. She wanted him to take it away.

"It'll have to be sold . . . And the bedding too . . . You must put a notice in Bennett's shop . . . We shall need every penny we can get to pay Robert's hospital bills . . . "

"Yes, all right, I'll see to it."

The next day Charlie went to see Robert and broke the news to him.

"Your mother's all right. Or she will be quite soon. But your baby sister was born dead."

Robert lay perfectly still, looking at Charlie with hurt,

hopeless eyes. He knew what the baby had meant to him.

"Was it all because of me?"

"How do you mean?"

"Mother worrying. Getting upset. Is that what made the baby die?"

"No," Charlie said. He was very firm. "That's got nothing to do with it. It was what they call a breech-birth. It means the baby was the wrong way round. Dr Graham did all he could but . . . " Charlie gave a tired shrug. "These things happen. You know that. It was certainly nothing to do with you."

"How is mother taking it?"

"Well," Charlie said. He looked away. "She doesn't say much. She keeps her feelings to herself."

He drew a sheaf of comics from his pocket and laid them on the bed.

"I brought you something to read," he said.

"Thanks," Robert said. He glanced at them. "When will mother be able to come?"

"Not for a week or two, I'm afraid."

"She *is* all right, isn't she?"

"Yes, she's all right, I give you my word. She's got to take it easy, that's all, until she gets her strength back again, but she'll be in as soon as she can."

Charlie sat in silence a while. Then, abruptly, he slapped his knee.

"Damn it all! I nearly forgot! Your mother's going to make you a cake, as soon as she's on her feet again, and she wants to know what sort you'd like."

"Any sort," Robert said.

"You'll have to say. You know what she is."

"One with cherries in it, then."

"Ah, cherries. I knew you'd say that."

Charlie, as he sat with the boy, did his best to talk cheerfully, but he had no heart for it, not today, and he knew that Robert understood. The boy lay and looked at him helplessly. In some ways he was old for his age.

"I'm sorry about the baby," he said.

"Yes, well," Charlie said, and his voice caught huskily in his throat. For once he was at a loss for words. He looked at his watch and rose from his chair. "I shall have to leave you now. I'm all behind at the garage these days. But I'll be in to see you every day and as soon as your mother's well enough I shall bring her along in Clew's van."

He waved to Robert from the door.

* * * * *

Linn, as she slowly recovered her strength, never talked about the lost baby. To her it was as though it had never been. She had banished all thought of it from her mind and even the first feeling of guilt had soon been buried in forgetfulness. The dead baby girl was nothing to her. All her thoughts were of her son.

One day, however, lured out by the mild weather and feeling almost herself again, she walked as far as Herrick St John to get a few messages from the shop. There was a notice in the window: *Cot for sale, never used*; and at sight of it her eyes filled with tears. She turned away and went home again. It was dinner-time and Charlie was there.

"What's the matter? You're crying!" he said.

"I'm crying for our dead baby," she said. "You wanted her so, and I let you down."

Charlie took her into his arms.

* * * * *

Robert spent Christmas in hospital. The new year came in and was still very mild and whenever they went to visit him they would find him lying on his back, staring up at the patch of sky framed by the window above his bed. He had another month to go before the plaster would be removed and the days were dragging with terrible slowness.

Confinement was beginning to tell on him, draining the strength from his muscles and bones. He seemed to shrink and become very small; his shoulders and arms were painfully thin, and his face, which had been a clear healthy brown, was now pinched and sallow and too finely drawn; the skin stretched tight over the cheekbones, stressing the hollows underneath.

But although the time dragged so dreadfully, and although he suffered from bed-sores and the constant itching of his skin as it shrank inside the plaster-cast, the boy remained patient to the end.

"What do you think about," Charlie asked, "lying there so still all day?"

"I pretend I'm out in the fields with Granddad, walking behind the plough," he said. "I plough right up to the headland, maybe, and in my mind I'm calling out, 'Come by! Come by! Come by!' to the team. Then I plough down the next stretch and I'm looking out for partridges . . . The rooks are down on the stubble behind and I can hear them squabbling . . ." Robert broke off and gave a shy smile. "I've ploughed up acres and acres," he said, "while I've been lying here in bed."

"What about those legs of yours? Any feeling in them yet?"

"No," Robert said. He made a face. "The nurse comes and tickles my feet sometimes but they're both as dead as brushes still."

"Oh, well," Charlie said, "only another week or so – "

"Eleven days," Robert said, and his jaw had a resolute tilt to it. "Just let me get this plaster off and *I'll* soon get my legs to move!"

"Ah, the nurses had better watch out for themselves if they come and tickle you after that!"

But secretly Charlie and Linn were afraid, and the day before the plaster was to be removed they spoke to the specialist, Mr Tate.

"What are the chances at this stage?"

"That's difficult to answer. There ought to be every chance for him but there's still no sensation in his legs and I have to admit that worries me."

"Yes, it's been worrying us as well."

"Tomorrow, when the plaster has been removed, we shall X-ray his spine to see if the fracture has healed."

"What if it hasn't?" Charlie asked.

"He'll have to go back into plaster again. But if the fracture has properly healed, I'm hoping the boy will be able to move and will gradually make a recovery."

"When shall we know?"

"Come in at three o' clock tomorrow afternoon. Ask to see me. We should know by then."

* * * * *

Although they were there promptly at three, they were kept waiting until half-past-four. Linn by that time was beside herself and when at last Mr Tate appeared, and they were ushered into his room, his expression confirmed the worst of her fears. He sat down behind his desk, his hands folded on its edge, and they sat opposite, erect in their chairs.

"The news is a mixture of good and bad. The X-rays show that the fracture has healed and on that score we are very well pleased. But both legs are still paralysed and I am forced to conclude that the nerves from the spine may have suffered some damage."

Linn's face became very white.

"What sort of damage?" she asked numbly.

"That we can't say. We have no means of assessing it. But there are two possibilities." The surgeon paused, looking at her. He spoke slowly and deliberately. "If the nerves from the spine have been severed," he said, "then I have to tell you that your son will never walk again." Another pause and then he went on: "If, on the other hand, the nerves have only suffered bruising, there is a chance that he will recover. But I cannot say how long it will take or whether the recovery will be complete."

Although he spoke so slowly and clearly, his words at first had no meaning for her. She had to go over them in her mind.

"And out of those two possibilities . . . you can't say which is most likely?"

"No, Mrs Truscott, I'm afraid I can't. Only time will tell us that."

"What about Robert?" Charlie asked. "Does he know he might not walk again?"

"Certainly not," the surgeon said. "It would be most unwise to tell him of that possibility."

"So," Charlie said, carefully, "assuming that the nerves

are only bruised, how would you rate his chances then?"

"Robert's a strong and healthy lad. I would say he had every possible chance. As soon as he's back in his own home and begins to pick up the strength he's lost – "

"Can he come home today?" Linn asked.

"No, he should stay here another three days. It will take him at least that long to get used to sitting up again. It will also give you time to make arrangements for having him home." The surgeon turned to Charlie again. "Ideally, the boy should have a wheelchair. Is such a thing within your means?"

"Yes," Charlie said, "I'll see to it."

"Tomorrow we shall start the boy on certain exercises, to keep the leg-muscles flexible. It is essential that these should be continued at home and I will arrange for you to come in and be shown how to do it yourselves."

"Can we see him?"

"Yes, of course." There was a slight hesitation. "I'm afraid you'll find him rather downcast. He expected to walk immediately and he's going to need all your support in facing up to another long wait."

"This long wait," Charlie said, "before he gets properly better, have you any idea how long it will be?"

"I'm afraid not."

"Weeks? Months?" Charlie persisted.

"It could be as much as six months. Perhaps even longer. I just can't say."

The surgeon rose and came round to them. He motioned them to stay where they were.

"Before you see your boy, Mrs Truscott, I'll get the nurse to bring you some tea. It will give you time to collect yourself."

As soon as the door had closed on him, Linn crumpled and began to cry, silently, bowing her head. Charlie leant forward and took her hands.

"Poor old Rob," he said quietly. "It seems he's not out of the wood yet."

"Will he ever be?" she said.

"I know it's asking a lot of you, but you've got to be brave for *his* sake."

"You don't have to tell me that!" she said.

A nurse came in with two cups of tea.

* * * * *

When they went to see Robert, he lay in the same bed as usual, propped this time on a mound of pillows.

"Well, and how does it feel," Charlie asked, "now you're out of your chrysalis?"

Robert gave a tired shrug. The day's events had exhausted him. There were deep lines about his mouth.

"I still can't move my stupid legs."

"No, we know," Linn said. "We've just come from seeing Mr Tate."

"We expected too much too soon," Charlie said. "But the fracture has healed, one hundred per cent, and that's good news, isn't it, eh?"

The boy lay looking up at them His face was bleak with disappointment and his voice, when he answered, was tremulous as he fought against weakness and hopelessness.

"I thought I was going to walk!" he said, and angrily turned his face to the pillow, to hide the brightness in his eyes.

"So you are!" Charlie said. He reached out and took the boy's hand and held it in a warm hard grip. "So you are going to walk!" he said. "But it's going to be a longer job than any of us bargained for."

Robert turned on the pillow again.

"How long a job? Did Mr Tate say?"

"He says it might be as much as six months, so we've got a long haul in front of us. But you'll be coming home soon and now you're out of that plaster-cast you'll be picking up strength in no time at all. Then we shall see to those legs of yours. They've got to be taught how to move again and we shall see to it, your mother and me, once we've got you home with us."

Pausing, Charlie looked at him, giving his hand another squeeze.

"You're going to have to be patient again, and bite on the bullet, as they say. Do you think you can manage that?"

Robert's face was expressionless. His glance flickered towards Linn and she leant forward, across the bed, reaching out to him silently.

"I've got no choice, have I?" he said.

Chapter 5

While the weather remained mild, he sat in his wheelchair out in the garden, watching the waterfowl on the ponds. Sometimes the ducks would come on to the bank, to sit preening themselves in the sun or to eat the food he put down for them. He sat so still that they trusted him and one mallard duck in particular would even perch on the step of his chair and take the bread from between his feet.

On wet days he sat by the kitchen window. Charlie had fixed a large mirror up on the wall of the window-recess and, by moving it on its hinge, the boy could still see the garden and ponds. He sat there as long as the daylight lasted. He could forget himself, watching the ducks.

"Are you all right?" Linn would ask.

"Yes, I'm fine," Robert would say; but his schoolwork lay beside him, untouched.

"Anything you'd like me to bring from the shop?"

"No, nothing, thanks," he said.

Once he asked, unexpectedly, if she would ever have another baby, and she said no.

"Why not?" he asked.

"I'm getting too old."

"That's not the real reason," he said. "It's because you've got to look after me."

"Why, *you're* no trouble, sitting there! And it's only until you can walk again."

Robert looked away from her. His spirits, just now, were at a low ebb.

In February there was ice on the ponds and children came there to skate again. Charlie wheeled Robert out to the garden and he sat wrapped in a warm woollen rug. He asked Charlie to fetch his skates and when they were brought out to him he gave them to Mrs Ransome's grand-

66

son and watched him go skating over the ice.

"Jimmy can keep them if he likes, I shan't be needing them," he said.

But Charlie, at the end of the afternoon, saw that the skates were returned to him.

"You may not skate this winter, it's true, but next winter, well, we shall see!"

"Why pretend?" Robert said. "I know I'm not going to walk again."

"Oh yes you are!" Charlie said. "I'm going to see that you do, my lad!"

Every morning before going to work and every evening when he got home Charlie would go to Robert's room and put him through his exercises. He had taken it on himself; "I'm stronger than you," he said to Linn; and she, because the sight of her son's twisted legs always caused her such distress, was only too willing to leave it to him.

He would wrap hot towels round Robert's legs and try to rub some warmth into them. Then he would lift each leg in the air, until the hip-joint was forced to work, and would bend the leg over at the knee, slowly but firmly, doubling it back, until the boy's heel was touching his haunch. He did this over and over again; so many times for each leg; and then he would work on the ankles and toes. And always at the end of it he would go to the bottom of the bed and, placing his palms against Robert's feet, would push against them with all his strength, trying to get the boy to push back.

"Are you pushing? See if you can. Put your hands on your knees and help them a bit. Can you feel me pushing your feet? I'm waiting to feel you pushing back."

But there was no life in the boy's legs; he had no power over them; nor could he feel Charlie's hands on his feet.

"I can't! I can't! It's no use!" he cried.

"I'll tell you what!" Charlie said once. "It seems to me you're not trying enough. You're leaving me to do all the work and I don't know that I care for that."

"You needn't bother!" Robert said. "It's a waste of time, anyway."

"You in one of your moods today? Feeling sorry for yourself?"

"Wouldn't *you*," Robert flashed, "if *you* was lying here like this?"

"Yes, well, maybe I would. But it's no good giving in to it. You ought to try and make up your mind to enjoy those things you *can* still do."

"What things?"

"Well," Charlie said, and there was a pause.

"When you've thought of them, let me know!" Robert said with great bitterness.

"There's your schoolwork for a start. Mr Maitland takes the trouble to send it out and you never even give it a thought."

"Have you seen it?" Robert demanded. He reached out to the bedside table and snatched up the papers lying there. He riffled through them impatiently. "Fractions and percentages! Exports from the Argentine! Arkwright and his spinning-machines!" He threw the papers down again. "What do I care about such things?"

"You should try and make yourself care. At least it would occupy your mind." Charlie got up from the bed and drew the bedclothes over the boy's inert body. "What about when you walk again and have to go back to school?" he said. "Think how behind-hand you're going to be if you don't keep up with your lessons now."

But his words made no impression on Robert. The boy lay with his face averted and when Charlie said goodnight his response was barely audible.

Downstairs Charlie spoke to Linn.

"That boy is beginning to brood. Something will have to be done about it."

"What can be done?"

"I wish I knew!"

* * * * *

That winter Jack was laid off work again. It meant he had plenty of time on his hands, and every fine afternoon he would push Robert out in his wheelchair, all round the mazy Herrick lanes.

One afternoon they were caught in a storm and hurried

home at a spanking pace with thunder crackling overhead and lightning flashing white in the clouds and a shower of hailstones stinging their faces. By the time they were safe indoors, Robert was in a state of excitement, his face glowing from the sting of the hail and his eyes alight with exhilaration.

He sat in his usual place at the window and watched while the thunderstorm spent itself; the hail bouncing against the glass; blanching across the purple sky; and pimpling the surface of the pond. He was quite disappointed when the hail stopped and the thunder died away in the distance.

"How do we get thunderstorms?" he asked when Charlie came in from work that evening.

"It's the electricity in the clouds."

"Yes, but how does it get there? What makes the hail? What makes the wind?"

Charlie made a wry face. He had to admit he didn't know. He looked at the boy for a little while and then, suddenly, slapped the table.

"I'll tell you what, young Rob!" he said. "We'll go into town and look it up!"

"Look it up where?"

"In the library, of course."

"Aren't you working tomorrow?" Linn asked.

"Any old time will do for work!"

The following morning, first thing, Charlie borrowed Clew's van and took the boy into Overbridge. They went to the Public Library and returned with three books and all through that day Robert was deeply absorbed in them.

"Do they tell you what you wanted to know?"

"Yes, they tell you *everything*."

"I see you've been drawing diagrams."

"I'm making an anemometer – when I can get the bits and bobs."

"What do you need?" Charlie asked. "I'll have a look round the garage scrap-heap and see what I can get for you."

Before long, with Charlie's help, Robert had his own little weather-station out in the garden. The anemometer whirled in the wind; the rain-gauge stood on a wooden box out in the middle of the lawn; the barometer hung on the woodshed wall.

"Shall I be able to dry my clothes?" Linn would ask when she did the washing, and Jack, on the watch for night-frosts, would ask: "What about my lettuces? Had I better cover them up?"

On clear nights Robert studied the stars. He sat in his bedroom, in the dark, gazing eagerly out of the window and finding his way among the constellations until they became as familiar to him as landmarks were in the daytime on earth. He could put a name to each of the groups that dominated the western sky – strange, magical names, most of them, that had come to England out of the east – and could plot their courses throughout the year.

Some nights he counted as many as thirty falling stars and was fascinated by their plight. Where did they go to, those swift specks, that slid across the sky and fizzled out, like dying sparks from a blacksmith's anvil? Would the earth, itself a star, also fizzle out in time and be lost in the everlasting dark? Robert felt himself very small, under the teeming sky at night, yet the feeling brought him no distress. Instead there was a kind of comfort in it. He could forget himself, watching the stars.

* * * * *

Linn didn't like it when the boy sat alone in his room at night. She worried about him constantly.

"I'm sure it gives him strange ideas, staring at the stars so long," she said. "Don't you think we should fetch him down?"

"Why do you fuss so much?" Jack said. "He's happy up there. Just leave him be."

Robert certainly had plenty to occupy his mind now and Mr Maitland, calling at the cottage once a fortnight, was much impressed by the change in him. The boy had chosen his own field of study and the schoolmaster now brought him work that covered his new range of interests. Robert could not have enough of it. There was always some "project" in front of him. And in the essays he wrote at this time

70

there were little touches of boyish humour: "Copernicus, Pole Star of Astronomy, left the University of Cracow . . . "

Whereas before he had rarely if ever read a book, now, Linn felt, he was reading too much. Often Charlie bought them for him and soon the boy had quite a collection: books on wildfowl, the weather, the stars; on physics, mathematics, chemistry: he devoured them all eagerly. There was always a book in the seat of his wheelchair; always one beside his bed.

"You'll ruin your eyes with reading so much," Linn said, scolding him, and at night when she blew out his candle she would take the matches away with her. "No more reading for you tonight. It's time you settled down to sleep."

But the boy smuggled matches upstairs and relit the candle when she had gone. He read and read until all hours. It was easy enough, at the first sound, to blow the candle out again.

One night, suspicious, Linn went up and looked in on him. The boy lay quite still, as though asleep, and when she went closer to the bed, with her own candle in her hand, he stirred and pretended to blink at the light. Linn, however, was not deceived.

"You've been reading, haven't you?"

"How do you know?"

"I can tell by the smell of the candle," she said. "You've only this instant blown it out."

"I wanted to finish a chapter, that's all."

"I won't have you reading by candlelight. It's bad for your eyes. How many times have I told you that?"

"Hundreds of times," Robert muttered.

Charlie, having followed Linn upstairs, lounged in the doorway, listening. He moved towards Robert's bed and spoke in a conspiratorial whisper.

"What you should do is this," he said, and, after licking his finger and thumb, he pretended to pinch out a candle flame. "That way it won't smell so much and then your mother will never know."

It was a joke between him and the boy, delivered with many a wink and a nod, but Linn became furiously angry and rounded on him with blazing eyes.

"Why do you tell him things like that? He never used to disobey me. Now he does it all the time. And it's all your fault for encouraging him!"

"Laws, where's the harm?" Charlie said. "If he's got a chapter he wants to finish — "

"I know these chapters!" Linn exclaimed. "He's been reading for over two hours!" She set her candle down on the table and thrust her hand under Robert's pillow. She drew out his book and opened it, showing Charlie the printed page. "Look at that print, how small it is! Do you want him to be *blind* as well as a cripple all his life?"

Charlie was silent, staring at her, and she was suddenly overcome. She stood for a moment, struggling with herself, then turned and hurried down the stairs. Charlie sat on Robert's bed and the boy spoke to him bitterly.

"So there's the truth of it, out at last! I shall be a cripple all my life!"

"No," Charlie said. "It's not the truth. We're damn well not going to *let* it be!"

"Mother thinks it, anyway, and she was a nurse so she ought to know."

"She didn't mean to say what she did. It just slipped out, the ways things do, because she hates to see you like this, laid up helpless as you are."

"Does she? I ent so sure of that! I reckon it suits her to have me like this. It means she can keep me under her thumb!"

"Here!" Charlie said. He was shocked and grieved. "That's no way to talk, young Rob!"

"Maybe not but it's what I feel!"

"Then you've got it all wrong," Charlie said. "All she wants is for you to get well. If you knew how she prays for you every night — "

"Prays!" Robert said, with bitter scorn. "What good does *that* do I'd like to know?"

"Well," Charlie said, helplessly, "not much so far, I must admit." He put up a hand and rubbed his jaw, which was bristly and harsh for want of a shave. "I reckon we'll have to try something else."

Under Charlie's bright blue gaze, Robert's bitterness

slowly melted. A reluctant smile tugged at his lips. Charlie, with his quiet jokes, could still unpick him even now, and soon he was giving a wry, sheepish grin, although the hurt still remained in him and was seen as a shadow in his eyes.

"I was getting in one of my moods again."

"You were," Charlie said, "and not without cause."

"Feeling sorry for myself . . . "

"You're bound to get those moods sometimes. You wouldn't be human otherwise."

"D'you really think I shall walk again?"

"I *know* you will," Charlie said.

"You're just saying that to buck me up."

"So what if I am? That's the start of it, being bucked up. If the doctors can't do any more for you – and they've said they can't – then it's going to be your own private battle and it starts up there in that mind of yours."

Charlie got up and went to the cupboard. He took Robert's ice-skates out of their box and hung them up by their leather straps from a hook in a rafter in the ceiling.

"Whenever you feel down in the dumps, you just take a look at those skates. Next winter you'll be putting them on. You'll go skating like mad on the ice on the ponds. Can't you imagine the feel of them, the ice underneath you, like green glass, and the trees flashing past all white with frost?"

Robert looked at him doubtfully. It was easy enough to imagine such a thing but the reality seemed a long way off.

"Will it really happen like that?"

"I'm as sure about it as if I was God. But it's up to you to be sure as well. You've got to feel it in your guts. And if anyone tells you you're not going to walk – you just tell them to go to hell!"

"Even my mother?"

"Yes, even her."

When Charlie had gone downstairs Robert, with his hands behind his head, lay looking up at the dangling skates which, swinging gently from their hook, caught a faint gleam of candle-light.

"I *will* walk again. I *will*! I *will*!"

Charlie, in the kitchen, spoke to Linn.

"You shouldn't have said that in front of Rob, about his

73

being a cripple," he said.

"I know! I know!" She was full of remorse. "I say these things! I could kill myself!" She looked at him with anguished eyes. "Is he very upset?" she asked.

"Of course he's upset! What d'you expect?" And then in a gentler tone he said: "You'd better go up and put things right."

* * * * *

Every Friday morning an ambulance called at the cottage and took Robert into hospital. He remained there all day, undergoing treatment.

"What do they do to you?" Charlie asked.

"They put me on a special bed and hang weights on my feet. The idea is to stretch my spine."

"Is it doing any good?"

"I dunno. It's hard to say. I still can't feel anything they do."

Regularly, once a month, he was examined by Mr Tate, and at the end of the third month, Linn and Charlie asked to see him.

"It's six months since his accident. Isn't there anything more to be done for him?"

"Mrs Truscott," the surgeon said, "I believe you were once a hospital nurse?"

"Yes, I was. It was during the war."

"Then you must know, better than most, the limitations of medical knowledge in cases of spinal injury."

"But that was fourteen years ago. Surely there's been some progress since then?"

"We are doing all we can."

"God knows, it's little enough!" Linn exclaimed harshly.

"You are keeping on with the exercises?"

"Yes, yes. Every morning and night. For all the good it ever does!"

"He's certainly very fit and strong, all things considered," the surgeon said.

"But there's still no improvement," Charlie said. "Still no feeling in his legs."

"I did warn you that it might take some time."

"You mean there's still hope, then?" Charlie said. "Even now, after six months?"

The surgeon's smile was inscrutable.

"There's always hope, Mr Truscott," he said.

He excused himself and went away and after a while Robert was wheeled out to them by a nurse. They went home with him in the ambulance.

After these days at the hospital, Robert was always quiet and subdued. Linn said the treatment exhausted him but once, when he was alone with Charlie, he confessed that the hospital made him afraid.

"It's the other kids I see there. One boy – he's about my own age – has been in a wheelchair for eighteen months. He thinks he's going to walk again but I don't think he is."

"Why not?" Charlie asked.

"His legs have gone a funny shape. *He's* growing and they're not." Robert gave a lopsided smile. "I reckon *I* shall get like that if I'm stuck in this chair for another year."

"You feeling down in the dumps again?"

"Well, yes, just a bit, I suppose."

"I'll soon shake you out of that!" It was time for Robert's exercises. Charlie pulled the bedclothes back and took a firm hold of the boy's left foot. "I'm going to give you what-for tonight!"

He began to bend the boy's leg at the knee.

* * * * *

As the spring weather improved, Robert sat out of doors again, often with a sketchbook in his lap. He had an aptitude for drawing, especially for capturing the life in things. He drew Linn on a windy day, wrestling with the washing on the line; he drew his grandfather working the pump; and he drew Charlie, all arms and legs, chasing Mrs Ransome's dog, who had run away with the copper-stick. He was helpless, trapped in his chair, but his drawings were full of energy and the swift bright movement denied to him.

Early in May, Jack was taken on again at Bellhouse Farm, and at this same time Linn had the offer of a job, cleaning at the vicarage in Herrick St John. It meant she would be away all the morning and she was worried by the thought of leaving Robert so much alone.

"That's no problem," Charlie said. "I'll take him up to the garage with me."

So every morning when he went to work, Charlie pushed Robert in his wheelchair up to the garage, and the boy sat outside in the sun, with his schoolwork or his sketchbook to hand. There was plenty to watch on the five roads and plenty of things for him to draw.

One day a motorist drew up for petrol and oil and to have his tyres checked. While Charlie was dealing with it, the driver got out to stretch his legs. He was a man of fifty odd, bald save for a ring of grey hair that hung in crisp curls over his collar, and with a pair of piercing dark eyes. He saw Robert in his wheelchair, just outside the repair-shop door, and went to exchange a few words with him. He came back to the car again and stood over Charlie as he pumped up the tyres.

"That your boy in the wheelchair there?"

"He's my stepson," Charlie said.

"What is it that's wrong with him?"

"Both his legs are paralysed. He fell on his back and fractured his spine. The fracture healed but he still can't walk."

Charlie moved from one wheel to the next and the motorist followed him round.

"How long is it since he had the fall?"

"It's about six months."

"What do the doctors say about him? I suppose there's some damage to the nerves?"

"Yes, that's right," Charlie said. He straightened up and faced the man. "You a doctor yourself?" he asked.

"Not exactly. I'm a homoeopath."

"Ah," Charlie said, somewhat blankly.

"Many people would call me a quack."

"That's honest, anyway." Charlie glanced across at Robert. The boy was well out of earshot. "What the doctor says is this – if the nerves have been cut, there's no hope for him, but if it's a question of bruising, then there's a chance he'll walk again."

"What treatment is he having?"

"Exercises at home every day. Traction at the hospital once a week. None of it's done any good so far."

"You should take him swimming," the man said. "As often as you like. Every day if you can. I've had some experience in this field and I can vouch for its benefits."

"Are you serious?" Charlie said. "How can he swim if he's paralysed?"

"He'll soon learn if you give him a hand. You'll be surprised what he can do. I suppose there's a swimming-bath in your town?"

"We've got a pond right next to our house. Will that do?"

"Oh, yes, as long as it's clean."

"Ought I to check with the specialist first?"

"Check by all means. Certainly. But it won't do any harm, I assure you, and it may do some good."

"Yes," Charlie said. "Thanks a lot. I'll give it a try, anyway."

The man paid for his petrol and oil, got into his car, and drove away. Charlie stood for a moment in thought. Then he went into Clew's bungalow.

"Can I use your telephone? I want to ring the hospital."

Help yourself," Norah said.

* * * * *

Charlie and Jack built a wooden platform, jutting out from the bank of the pond, with three shallow steps going down from it into the water. Under the water, to cover the mud at the foot of the steps, they laid three big slabs of stone. On the platform itself they erected a sturdy wooden rail, forming three sides of a square, so that Robert, on coming out of the water, could stand supporting himself on his hands while Charlie rubbed him dry with a towel.

"Is the platform safe?" Linn asked.

"Safe as houses," Charlie said.

"I've never swum in my life," Robert said. "How can I swim if I can't move my legs?'

"The chap at the garage said you could and I'm going to

77

teach you," Charlie said. "You're not frightened, are you, Rob?"

The boy gave a grin.

"When are we going to start?" he asked.

"We'll start tomorrow if the weather's still fine. I'll come home in my dinner-hour and we'll get you down into the pond for your first lesson. We're going to show those ducks a thing or two, you and me, in the water out there. We're going to make them sit up and stare!"

Here Jack put in a word.

"It ent only the ducks that'll stare if you go swimming in that pond without a stitch of clothes on," he said. "Mrs Ransome'll have a fit."

"Tell Mrs Ransome to stay indoors!"

"Don't be silly," Linn said. "You can't go swimming in the nude."

So the first lesson had to wait until she had been into Overbridge and had bought two costumes for them to wear. It was a joke to the man and the boy. They pretended to get their costumes mixed and there was a lot of laughter between them before they were ready for their first bathe.

But underneath all the laughter, when Charlie carried the boy to the pond and stepped with him into the water, there was a certain stillness of thought; a stillness and silence in their hearts as though hope, having secretly gathered there, was lying low, afraid to be heard. And that was the way of it, every day, while Charlie bathed with the boy in the pond: a great many jokes and much merriment; sometimes even a great deal of noise; but underneath it a stillness and silence; a gathering of unspoken thoughts.

The summer was fine and dry that year. It was 1932. There were weeks of sunshine, without any rain, and the long days of June were very hot. And every day, without fail, Charlie would bathe with the boy in the pond, either in his dinner-hour, or in the evening after work.

Robert had no fear of the water, even at the very beginning; he put himself into Charlie's hand and trusted him absolutely; and within three days he knew how to swim. It mattered not a jot that his legs were useless, floating behind him like two sticks; his arms were strong and they did it all;

and whenever Linn came out to watch, he always had some new trick to show her. He would disappear under the water and come up again some distance away or would swim into a bed of reeds and bring her an iris in his mouth.

"Isn't the water cold?" she asked.

"No, it's as warm as warm!" he said.

"Well, do take care, won't you?" she said. "Don't stay under too long at a time."

But Charlie was always close at hand, watching over the boy as he swam. He never left anything to chance and would haul him out afterwards, up onto the wooden platform, where a clean dry towel hung on the rail.

"Come on, you porpoise, out of that! You've had enough for one day, my lad, and I've got work to get back to, mind!"

The boy would hold on to the wooden rail, his hands upon it and his elbows stiff, supporting himself by the strength of his arms. Charlie would pull his wet costume down, until it hung about his waist, and would rub him hard with the rough towel. Then he would wrap him round in it and carry him indoors to get dressed.

Once when they were alone together, sitting on the bank in the warm sun, each drying his hair, Charlie said casually:

"Is it doing you any good? D'you feel any difference in your legs?"

"I dunno," Robert said, and there was a frown between his eyes. The question had brought a stab of fear and he shied away from it, inwardly, wishing Charlie had never asked. "I dunno," he said again. "I suppose it's too soon to expect much change."

"Ah, that's right, it's early days yet. How long've you been swimming now? Five weeks? Six weeks? That's no time at all!"

"I'll tell you this much!" Robert said, and gave a quick laugh, trying to drive the fear away. "I'll tell you this much – I'm enjoying it!"

"You don't need to tell me that, my lad. You'd stay in that water all day long if I didn't drag you out of it. Now you hurry up and dry that hair or you'll have your mother after you."

* * * * *

All through that summer, people who passed along the road grew used to seeing Robert and Charlie splashing about in the pond, throwing a big rubber ball to each other or swinging from the ropes that Charlie had hung from the willow trees. Sometimes Mrs Ransome would stand at her garden gate and watch, and her little white terrier dog, excited at seeing the ball tossed about, would run to and fro along the road, yapping shrilly; frantic to join them in their games but too nervous to take to the water.

"That boy of yours! He swims like an eel!" Mrs Ransome said to Linn. "The things he gets up to in the water there, you'd never dream he was paralysed." And once she said hesitantly: "Is it doing him any good?"

"I don't know. I wish I did."

Charlie himself had no doubts at all.

"Of course it's doing him good," he said. "He's enjoying it and it's making him strong. Why, you've only got to look at him to see how strong and healthy he is."

"But he still can't walk," Linn said.

"No, well, these things take time."

"How long do you mean to go on?"

"As long as it takes," Charlie said.

"What about when the summer's over? It'll be too cold for swimming then."

"I'll take him to the baths in Overbridge." Charlie, turning to glance at her, caught the ghost of a smile in her face. "What're you smiling at?" he asked.

"You," she said simply. "You never give up. You do so much for that boy of mine . . . You give up so much of your time to him . . . "

"I'd give up a whole lot more than that to see our Robert walking again."

"Yes, I know you would," she said.

Charlie never seemed to lose faith that he would get Robert to walk again. If he ever had any doubts, he kept them carefully to himself. "I'll get you out of that wheelchair even if it kills me!" he said, and every day, swimming with Robert in the pond or exercising his legs indoors, he watched for signs of change in him.

One day when they swam in the pond the sky was somewhat overcast and a sly wind blew from the east. Charlie, hauling the boy on to the platform and putting him to lean on the rail, saw that he was shivering.

"Are you cold?"

"Well, just a bit."

"I'll soon fix that!" Charlie said.

He snatched the towel from the rail and began rubbing the boy's body, peeling his bathing-suit down to the waist to get at his shoulders, his back, his chest.

"I'll give you gooseflesh!" he exclaimed, and, stooping, he towelled the boy's thin legs, rubbing at them with all his strength till the white skin turned red on the calves and thighs.

He put so much energy into the rubbing that he made himself breathless and red in the face, and Robert, supporting himself on the rail, had to grip harder with his hands, bracing himself, his arms stiff and straight, as Charlie's vigorous work with the towel threatened to rock him off his feet. His head was thrown back; his shoulders were hunched; he gave a sudden laughing shout.

"That's enough! I'll have no legs left!"

"Why, can you feel it?" Charlie said.

He stopped rubbing and stood erect, the towel hanging between his hands. The boy turned his head to look at him. Their eyes met in a still, steady stare.

"Could you feel me rubbing you?"

"I dunno. Maybe I could."

"You made enough fuss," Charlie said.

"Yes, well," Robert said. "I'm only flesh and blood, you know."

"You must've felt something, shouting like that."

"I dunno. I'm trying to think." The boy looked down at his legs and feet. He gave a little shaky laugh. "You was going at me so hard . . . I thought you was going to have me over . . . "

"Look, I'm telling you," Charlie said. "You felt something, I'm sure of that."

"Did I?"

"Yes, of course you did. You hollered at me to stop rubbing you. You've never hollered about it before."

"You've never rubbed so hard before."

"Here!" Charlie said. "Let's get you indoors."

He wrapped the towel round the boy and lifted him into his arms. He ran with him into the house. Linn had just come in from work. She was putting a match to the fire in the range. When Charlie ran in with the boy in his arms she looked at them in some alarm because they were both unusually quiet.

"Is anything wrong?"

"No, far from it," Charlie said. He sat the boy in an upright chair. "Rob's got some feeling back in his legs."

Linn's face became very pale. She could not believe what she had heard. She turned from Charlie towards her son and dropped on her knees in front of him. He sat wrapped in the big white towel and Linn, taking hold of it with both hands, drew it tightly across his chest, feeling its wetness, absently. She looked at him with hungry eyes.

"Is it true what Charlie said? The feeling is coming back at last?" Her hands moved over his legs, touching his thighs, his knees, his feet. "Can you feel me touching you?"

"No," Robert said. He shook his head. "I can't feel anything in them now. It was just something . . . Out there on the platform . . . I'm not sure if I felt it or not . . . "

"I was rubbing his legs," Charlie said, "and he suddenly shouted to me to stop."

"It's supposed to begin in the hips," Linn said. "That's what they said at the hospital." She looked at Robert slumped in his chair. "Was that where you felt it? In your hip?"

"Yes, I think so. The right one, I think."

"What was it like, this feeling you had?"

"Oh . . ." Robert said. He tried to think. "It was a sort of buzzing," he said. "Like when you hit your funny-bone . . . But I can't be sure if I felt it or not. It could've been just my fancy, that's all."

"No," Charlie said, "you felt it, I'm sure."

"Then why can't I feel it now?"

"Those legs of yours have been dead for ten months. It's bound to take a bit of time for them to get back to normal again. But at least it's started, that's the main thing. At least we know there's life in them."

"Yes," Linn said, "at least we know that."

She rose from her knees and took a dry towel from the string above the hearth. She draped it over Robert's head.

"It's time we got you properly dried. You'll catch a chill if we don't watch out." Briskly she turned towards Charlie who stood dripping water onto the mat. "You, too," she said to him. "For goodness' sake get dried and dressed."

There was some sharpness in her voice and later, when Charlie had eaten his lunch and was going back to work again, she followed him as far as the gate.

"Did he really feel you rubbing him or did *you* put the notion into his head?"

"The boy felt something. I'll swear to that."

"Robert himself is not so sure."

"No, and neither are you, it seems."

"I think it's wrong to build up false hopes. You can see how worried he is by it all. It's all very well to talk about faith but don't you *ever* have any doubts?"

"I never *let* myself have any doubts – and neither should you."

"Knowing how slim his chances are, how can I help it?" Linn exclaimed.

"At least you can keep them from Rob," he said.

* * * * *

The following morning, as usual, he took Robert to the garage with him. Then, at twelve, he brought him home and they swam together in the pond. It was Friday September the tenth. The day was fairly sunny and warm. Robert lay on his back in the water, letting it lap softly over him.

"I'm making the most of it while I can. The summer will be over soon. It'll be too cold to swim here then."

"There's always the swimming-baths in the town."

"It'll take too long, going all that way. You already give up a lot of your time. Then you have to work late at night."

"We'll fix something up. You leave it to me."

"Is it worth it?"

"Of course it is! What about that buzzing in your leg?"

"I ent felt it since yesterday. *If* I ever felt it at all."

"Give it time, boy. Give it time."

Together they floated in the water. Then Charlie did a roll.

"Come on, young Rob, it's time we were out. I reckon you've had your whack for today."

They swam back to the platform and Charlie scrambled up the steps. He lifted Robert out of the water and set him to lean on the wooden rail. And then Mrs Ransome's little dog, always alert for a chance of mischief, ran eagerly onto the platform and pulled the towel from the rail.

"Hi!" Charlie shouted. "Come back, you tyke!"

But the dog was already running away, trailing the towel over the grass, uttering little deep-throated growls, and Charlie had to go after him. He chased the dog along the bank and out into the road itself. There the rough gravel cut his bare feet, slowing him down, but he caught up with the dog at last and, with Mrs Ransome's help, managed to wrest the towel from him.

He was on his way back round the edge of the pond when Robert gave a sudden cry and he saw that the boy, although leaning forward against the rail, was no longer holding on to it. Instead he stood with his elbows bent and his hands spread out in front of him.

"Charlie! Look! I can stand by myself!"

Charlie, for an instant, stood transfixed. Then he began to run again and was just in time to catch the boy as his brief strength gave out and he clutched at the rail. Flinging the towel over him, Charlie caught him up in his arms, and the boy gave a little gasping sob, half laughing, half crying, against Charlie's neck.

"Charlie, I stood! Did you see me stand?"

"I saw it all right! You bet I saw!" Charlie held him close-wrapped in his arms. "You damn nearly gave me a heart-attack, standing like that when my back was turned! You just about gave me the fright of my life!"

"My legs are all right – "

"Of course they are!"

"I'm going to walk! I know I am!"

84

"Well!" Charlie said, in a gruff voice. "Haven't I said so all along?"

And Mrs Ransome, having seen and heard everything, ran along the road in her carpet slippers, her little dog yapping at her heels, going towards Herrick St John to meet Linn coming home from work and carry the miraculous news to her.

Chapter 6

By the end of September, Robert was walking: carefully at first, with the aid of crutches; but then, as his strength and confidence grew, the crutches were discarded and he walked by himself.

The wheelchair, no longer needed, was presented to the hospital and towards the end of October, Robert was told that he need not attend for treatment again: he had made a full recovery. Mr Tate and the nurses shook hands with him and he walked out with Charlie and Linn.

It was a fine autumn day and together they walked home across the fields. When they had to cross the brook, Robert leapt it from bank to bank, turning to watch as they crossed by the bridge.

"You can go on if you like," Charlie said. "You don't have to stick with us old folk."

"Oh, it's all right," Robert said.

But gradually, as they walked along, his stride lengthened and he left them behind. His youthful energy knew no bounds, now it had been released again, and whenever he came to a gate or a stile, he would vault over it in one bound, just for the joy of using his legs.

"I wish I could meet that chap again," Charlie said, watching him. "The one who told me to teach Rob to swim. If he could see that boy today! *He's* the one I'd like to thank."

Linn made no answer. Her heart was too full. And Charlie, seeing her overcome, drew her arm into his. They walked slowly along the path, enjoying the warmth of the autumn sun, and Robert strode ahead of them, covering the ground with his long, loping stride.

"There's no holding him now," Charlie said. "He'll be home before we're even half way."

* * * * *

Robert was always on the move these days. He meant to make up for the year he had lost. He was attending school again now and whatever the weather he always walked. To sit at a desk was galling to him but at least there was football twice a week. He had always been a keen player but now he played with such passion and verve that he was almost unbeatable. No one could take the ball from him once he had it at his feet.

Movement was all he cared about and he wanted to do everything. If he saw his grandfather splitting logs, he itched to take the axe from him. If he saw that his mother was washing clothes, he would hurry to turn the mangle for her. And out in the fields, whenever he saw a man at work, ploughing the stubble or drilling corn, he longed to be in that man's shoes. But in this he had to contain himself: he would not leave school for another year.

Autumn was very wet that year; the three ponds overflowed their banks and remained flooded for weeks on end; so that when winter came and brought hard frosts, the water was one great stretch of ice. And this time, when children came to skate there, Robert was among them, leading the way, skimming along in a zig-zag course, between the straggling beds of reeds, while Mrs Ransome's little dog slithered behind him on the ice, snapping and snarling at his heels.

Leaning forward, swinging his arms, in a rhythm that matched the thrust of his legs, he would go faster and faster still, his skate-blades cutting along the ice and making a loud hissing noise. The trees that divided one pond from the next would loom up tall in front of him and he would go weaving between their trunks, leaping over the up-jutting roots, and so out to the next open stretch.

He felt he could never have enough of it, this marvellous movement over the ice, with the ghostly trees going silently past, and the ice-spray flying up from his skates, stinging and tingling in his face. He would skate back to the wooden platform where Charlie and Jack stood watching him and would circle in front of them like a young god.

"Charlie, you was right!" he said. "It's exactly how you said it'd be! – Wings on my heels, like Mercury!"

He would go skimming off again, faster and faster, in figures of eight, while the other skaters, circling nearby, watched him display his easy skill.

"You're an awful show-off, Mercybright!" one of his school-mates said to him, but Robert merely gave a laugh.

Once such a charge would have made him squirm, but now it was nothing, it left him untouched. He would never take movement for granted again; he knew all too well how precious it was; and somehow the knowledge set him apart; gave him a special quality; something that was bringing him swiftly to manhood, even though he was only thirteen.

Charlie and Jack perceived the change and because they were men they understood it. The boy had a certain look in his eyes, as though he could see to the ends of the earth, and whatever he saw held no fears for him.

"I wouldn't mind being Robert's age, with my life in front of me," Jack remarked; but then after a while he said: "Though the times won't be any more easy for him than they have been for the likes of me."

* * * * *

Jack had been laid off again that winter and Mr Lawn had made it clear that this time, when spring came around, he would not be taken back. Jack was now seventy-five. He had to accept that his working-life was over and done. Younger men needed the jobs and there were not enough to go round. But it was a bitter pill for him to swallow and Linn, as the winter months went by, saw him growing more morose.

"Why can't you accept it?" she said. "All the hard work you've done in your life, it seems to me you've earned your rest."

"Rest!" he exclaimed contemptuously. "I'll get plenty of rest when I'm in my grave!"

"Yes, and that'll be sooner than you think, if you hang about the fields in this bitter weather! Why can't you stay at home in the warm?"

And yet, when he did sit in the kitchen, his presence there was irksome to her.

"Must you drop your ash like that? Those cushion-covers

have just been washed."

"What's a little bit of ash? It'll help to keep the moths away."

"Can you move your chair for a moment? I want to sweep in the corner there."

"Yes, I'll move!" He rose from his chair. "I'll take myself off, out of the way, while you make clean cleaner, like all your kind!"

"You're not going out in this east wind?"

"The east wind is nothing to me. It's the weather indoors I can't abide."

When springtime came and the weather improved he was more restless than ever because now there was work going on in the fields and he was not a part of it.

"If only we had a bigger garden or could get an allotment for him," Linn said, talking to Charlie at bedtime one night. "I hate to see him moping like this, mooching about, getting so sour. He's never been idle in his life."

"No, I know, but what can we do?"

* * * * *

One afternoon in early summer when Charlie, at the garage, had his head under the bonnet of Clew's van, a smart motor-car drew up and a man got out to speak to him.

"Mr Truscott?"

"Yes, that's right."

"I'm looking for some people called Mercybright. The girl at the Post Office sent me to you."

"You've certainly come to the right man. Jack Mercybright is my father-in-law."

"Then you must be married to his daughter, Linn."

Charlie nodded.

"Is anything wrong?"

"No, nothing's wrong. Quite the reverse. I'm a solicitor. My name is Todds. I have some business with your wife and I've come from Hotcham on purpose to find her."

"What sort of business?" Charlie asked.

"I don't think I should tell you that until I've had a word with her. Can you direct me to your home?"

"I've got a better idea than that. I'll come with you and show you the way."

Charlie went to the garage door and called out to Clew.

"I'm just popping home for a while. I shan't be gone long."

"Famous last words!" Clew called back.

Charlie returned to the smart car and got into the passenger-seat. Mr Todds was sitting at the wheel.

"Take this first turning left," Charlie said, "and I'll tell you the rest as we go along." He glanced at the stranger curiously. "Hotcham you've come from, did you say? My wife was born not far from there. A place called Niddup, I think it was."

"Yes, that's right. At Brown Elms Farm."

"Is your business connected with that?"

"Yes, Mr Truscott. It is indeed. A family matter, as you might say."

"Can't you give me a hint what it is? I'm just about bursting to know!" Charlie said.

The solicitor gave him a brief smile.

"All in good time, Mr Truscott," he said.

"Turn left here," Charlie said, "then it's the second lane on the right."

* * * * *

Robert, coming home from school and finding a motor-car at the gate, stared at it in astonishment. He walked round it, admiringly, and Mrs Ransome, on the watch, came to her hedge and called to him.

"Seems you've got a visitor."

"Who?" Robert asked. "Do you know?"

"Gent with a brief-case. Stranger to me. Charlie came with him in the car. He's been in there for two hours and the door's been shut the whole time. Don't ask *me* what it's all about. You'll only find out by going in."

Robert walked slowly up the path. Sure enough, the front door was closed, an unusual thing in summertime, and it caused him some uneasiness. But when he opened the door and went in, and the four faces were turned towards him, he saw that whatever had brought the stranger there, it was nothing to cause anxiety. He sensed some excitement in the room; something unique in the atmosphere; the best Minton teaset was out, for a start, and some papers lay spread among the teacups and plates; and his mother, rising as he went in, had a warm pink colour in her cheeks.

"This is my son, Robert," she said. "Robert, this is Mr Todds."

The stranger got up and shook Robert's hand. He said "How d'you do" and sat down again. His manner was formal and somewhat stiff but he had a humorous look in his eyes.

"Mr Todds has brought us some news. He's come all the way from Hotcham to see us."

"It's your mother he's come to see," Charlie said.

"What sort of news?" Robert asked. Among the papers on the table he saw his mother's birth-certificate. "Good news or bad?"

"My auntie Philippa's died," Linn said. "She's left me some money in her will. Mr Todds has been trying to find us for months. He put an advert in the papers, but we never saw it, I can't think why." She turned towards the solicitor. "Such a worry you must have had, following us all over Worcestershire. The times we've moved, my father and me, you'd think we were gipsies, until we came here."

Mr Todds smiled. He began gathering up the papers, sliding them into his brief-case. He pushed the birth-certificate towards her.

"Well, at last I *have* found you, that's the main thing. And now I really must be getting along." He closed his brief-case and rose from his chair. "I'll leave you to talk over the good news with your family."

"Won't you have another cup of tea?"

"Thank you, but no. I've already lingered long enough, enjoying your hospitality, and it's quite a long way back to Hotcham, you know." He leant forward and shook Linn's hand. "You'll be hearing from me again quite soon and Miss Guff's legacy will be coming to you in due course. It isn't a very large sum so there shouldn't be any undue delays."

"You've really been very kind, Mr Todds."

"I'm only doing my job, that's all."

Charlie and Jack stood up and the kitchen suddenly seemed crowded. There was some jostling at the door as Mr Todds said goodbye to them, and then he was gone down the garden path, turning to wave to them from the gate. When they had seen him drive away, they came in from the step and Linn closed the door. She stood with a bemused smile on her lips, regarding her father, her husband, her son; and they stared back, in a moment of silence, the same smile lurking in each of them, because of this incredible thing that had come like an arrow out of the blue.

"I can't get over it," Charlie said.

"It takes some believing," Jack agreed.

"How much is it?" Robert asked.

"Try and guess!" his mother said.

"I dunno. How can I guess? The man said it was no large amount — "

"Your mother's been left five hundred pounds!" Charlie gave the boy a shove. "What do you think of that, young Rob? That's made you open your eyes, by gosh!"

"It's made us all open our eyes, myself included," Linn said.

"I never even knew you had an auntie Philippa," Robert said. "You never mentioned her before."

"It's all such a long time ago, that's why. My auntie Philippa owned Brown Elms Farm and your granddad acted as bailiff for her. But she and your granddad fell out, you see, and we've never had any contact with her, not since coming away from there. I was only five years old. I don't remember her very well."

"Seems she remembered *you*," Charlie said.

Robert looked at his grandfather. He knew nothing of the old man's life in those far-off days at Brown Elms Farm.

"What was auntie Philippa like, that you should've fell out with her?"

Jack removed his pipe from his mouth and pressed the tobacco down in the bowl. He scratched his bearded cheek with the stem.

"Miss Philippa liked to run folk around. I didn't care to be run around so I upped sticks and came away. And that's about all there is to it."

"What's happened to the farm?"

"Seems she left everything to the church, except for two or three legacies, like the one your mother's to get."

"I can't get over it!" Charlie said. "To think I married a wealthy wife! Any chance of a bit of a loan?"

"I haven't got it yet," Linn said.

"Well, just put me down for a couple of quid!"

"Isn't it time you got back to work?"

"Yes, you're right, just look at that clock! Clew will have something to say to me!" Charlie put his cap on, pulling it down at the side of his head. "*I* haven't come into money," he said. "*I've* still got my living to earn!"

When he reached the door he paused, looking back at Linn's bright face.

"Five hundred pounds! Just think of that! What are you going to do with it?"

"Goodness, what a thing to ask! I haven't had time to think yet!"

* * * * *

But in fact she knew what she meant to do. The idea had come to her almost at once, within a few minutes of hearing the news, and in the two hours that had passed since then, a definite plan had grown in her mind.

Robert was sitting talking to Jack, asking questions about Brown Elms Farm, and Linn, as she prepared his tea, listened to them talking together and now and then put in a word. But all the time, at the back of her mind, her great plan was taking shape.

"Robert, are you going out?"

"Yes, I was going down to the farm."

"Well, some time I want to talk to you, but later will do, when you get back."

"Is it about the legacy?" He looked at her with a teasing smile. "Had I better stop at home?"

"No, there's no hurry," Linn said. "I want to talk to your granddad first."

When Robert had left the house, Linn made her father sit

down with her, with pencil and pad on the table before them, and a local newspaper, some days old, open at the columns of "Land for Sale."

"I'm thinking of buying a little farm."

"Glory be! So that's the idea? I knew you'd got something in your mind."

"What do you think of it?" she asked.

"I reckon I'd better light my pipe."

"Old tobacco-face, puffing away! I suppose you can't think without all that smoke?"

"Tell me about this farm of yours."

"What I've got in mind is a smallholding, twenty or thirty acres, perhaps. Something we can work by ourselves. I thought we'd go in for poultry. There's money in that, don't you agree?"

"So long as you don't expect to get rich by it . . . "

"If we can make a living from it, that's all I ask. It would be worth it, wouldn't it, to have a bit of land of our own?"

"It'd certainly give me something to do." He looked at her from under his brows. "That's the idea, ent it?" he said. "That's why you want to buy a farm, so's I'll have something to do with myself?"

"Well, and what's wrong with that?" she asked.

"Nothing, so far as it goes," he said. "I'm just thinking of Charlie, that's all. That money you've got coming to you could set him up in his own garage. Maybe you should consider that."

Linn frowned. She gave it some thought. But after a moment she shook her head.

"Charlie can get work easily. He's still a young man and a skilled mechanic. Mechanics earn good pay and he could do better if he had more push."

"Will he mind moving from here?"

"I don't think he will. It might even do him good if he has to shake himself out of his rut."

Jack gave a grunt.

"Seems we shall all be shook out of our rut, now you've come into money," he said. "And what about Rob? Have you thought about him? He's set his heart on getting a job at Bellhouse next year."

"Now he won't have to, will he? He'll have his own farm to work on instead."

"Raising poultry? He won't care for that."

"Why ever not, for goodness' sake? My little farm will be his one day. Surely that's better than working for someone else all his life?"

"I dunno. I ent so sure. I reckon you'd better talk to him."

"Yes, well," Linn said. "I don't think I'll mention it to him yet. The first thing is to find our farm."

"Farms are easy enough to find. They're going begging everywhere. But whether they're worth having or not is another matter altogether."

"At least land is cheap just now."

"Oh, ah, it's cheap as dirt. I've heard of land going for sale for as little as five pounds an acre in recent times. That was over at Riddington. But a place of the size you've got in mind, twenty or thirty acres, well, there's nothing like that in this neighbourhood. You'll have to look further afield."

"What about Spatesbridge or Etherington?" Linn, with the newspaper in her hand, was reading through the advertisements, marking the possibles with a cross. "Twenty-five acres at Gudgington . . . That won't do, there isn't a house . . . Smallholding at Newton Kings . . . Sixty acres, that's too big . . . "

Jack, puffing away at his pipe, looked at her through the rising smoke.

"Shouldn't you speak to Charlie and Rob before going any further?" he said.

"There's no harm in seeing what's for sale."

* * * * *

Charlie and Robert, when they heard of her plan, stared at her in astonishment. Charlie's blue eyes opened wide.

"Buying a farm? Are you serious? Why, no one can make it pay these days!"

But gradually, as Linn explained, he began to come round to the idea. A smallholding. Yes, of course. Poultry and eggs, there was profit in that. They could keep a couple of cows, perhaps, and any surplus milk they had could go to fatten a pig or two. So long as the farm was small enough, they could manage the work themselves. It would mean security, in a small way, and they would have a house of their own.

"I reckon maybe you've got something there. What does Jack think of it?"

"Oh, I go along with the tide," Jack said.

"Dad and me have talked it out. He's in favour. Of course he is."

"It didn't take you long," Charlie said, "to decide how to spend your legacy." He was full of admiration and looked at her with wondering eyes. Then he turned towards Robert. "Your mother's a woman of enterprise. She knows how to make up her mind about things. She's given us something to think about, eh?"

Robert smiled and gave a nod. He, too, was looking at Linn.

"I'm just trying to imagine it . . . Mother as farmer, milking the cows . . ."

"Is it so strange?" Linn demanded. "I've seen enough cows in my life, heaven knows!"

"You've never milked them, though, I bet."

"I can soon learn, can't I?" She went to and fro about the kitchen, setting their supper in front of them. "Anyway!" she exclaimed. "I've got three men to do things like that!"

"There!" Charlie said, winking at Robert. "It's started already. I knew it would. The grand lady farmer, flouncing about, telling us what we've got to do. She's beginning to play the part and it just about suits her down to the ground. See how she puts her nose in the air? That's what money does for folk!"

Linn sat down at the table with them. Charlie spoke more seriously.

"There are no smallholdings hereabouts."

"No, it'll mean going further afield."

"What about Charlie's job?" Robert asked.

"Oh, that's nothing to worry about." Charlie brushed the problem aside. "There's plenty of work for mechanics and such." Linn's plan had taken hold of him. He was warming to it more and more. "When are you going to start looking round?"

"I thought I'd wait till the money came."

"Much better start straight away. It'll save time when the money does come."

"Well, I *have* marked two places in the paper . . . "

Linn's eagerness overflowed. She went to fetch the paper at once and Charlie, as he ate his supper, read the advertisements she had marked.

"The one at Etherington's nearest. You can get there by bus from Overbridge. Or, if you wait until Saturday, I can take you in Clew's van."

"Oh, I can't wait until then!" Linn said. "We shall go tomorrow, dad and me."

"You won't settle anything, though, not till I've seen it, will you?"

"Don't be silly. Of course we won't." Linn sent him a sidelong glance. "I know what's wrong with *you*!" she said. "You don't like to be left out of things!"

"No, well," Charlie said. He had finished his cottage pie and was looking down at his empty plate. "Any chance of a second helping or are you busy to think of such things?"

"You!" she said, springing up at once. "I'll box your ears if you don't watch out!"

She herself had no appetite. She was too full of plans and ideas. She could think only about her farm which she pictured, green and neat and trim, somewhere out near Etherington. Her eagerness was shared by them all and they sat up late, the four of them, talking about the legacy and the great plan resulting from it.

"I can't believe it," Robert said. "It all seems too good to be true, somehow."

"It does, that's a fact," Charlie said. "I can hardly believe it myself. But your mother's soon got used to it. Just look at the way she's sitting there, with us three men gaping at her, hanging on every word she says. There's money written all over her and it's already giving her some sort of style."

"What nonsense you talk!" Linn said, but she was enjoying it all the same. Her face was flushed with excitement. She could hardly wait for tomorrow to come.

Lying in bed, late that night, her head in the crook of Charlie's shoulder, she told him what her father had said

97

about using the money to buy a garage.

"Did he say that? That was good of him. But the little farm is a better idea. I shan't have trouble getting work, not so long as there's cars on the road, and the pay is good, considering."

"That's what I told him," Linn said. "A farm was the first thing I thought about. I set my heart on it straight away. And it *is* my money, after all."

Stirring, she turned her body to his, and they fell asleep in each other's arms.

* * * * *

The farm at Etherington was a disappointment; so was the one at Spatesbridge; the first was eight miles from the nearest good road, the second was close to the River Ail and was apt to be flooded in wintertime; so Linn and Jack went to Overbridge and called on the three land-agents there, collecting lists of farms for sale.

They travelled a good many miles in the next few weeks, but of the twelve small farms they viewed, none was suitable to their needs. On this the house was much too big; on that the house was tumbling down; on this the water supply was condemned; on that the fields were terribly steep, the farm being perched on the side of a hill. In fact, as Linn said to Charlie one night, the farm she had pictured in her mind, neat and trim and clean and good, was nothing so far but a will o' the wisp.

Early in June the money came. Linn opened a banking account and was given a cheque-book in return. She took it home and locked it away.

"Five hundred pounds in the bank!" Charlie said. "How does it feel to be so rich?"

"The money won't be there for long. It'll have to come out when we find our farm."

"Ah, when!" Charlie said. "You seem a long way from finding it. Maybe I'd better come round with you."

"What difference would that make?"

"I might see points that you and Jack miss."

"I don't think dad misses much."

"Two heads are better than one, and I was brought up on a farm, remember. My father always said there was no such thing as a bad farm — only bad farmers, he used to say."

Linn was tired and rather cross. The disappointments were wearing her down. She answered Charlie irritably.

"Your father went bankrupt, didn't he?"

"Not through bad farming," Charlie said. "And what's that got to do with it?"

"Oh, never mind!" Linn said. "I'm just a bit grumpy, that's all. All that way to Woollerton and just for nothing yet again!"

"Ah, well," Charlie said, "you'll find a place in time, I suppose."

But all through June and early July her journeys with Jack were equally fruitless.

"Any luck yet?" Robert would ask, coming home from school, and Charlie, coming home from work, would ask the same thing in a different way: "Found your little Utopia yet?"

One Friday evening, surprisingly, Charlie came home at six o' clock.

"I reckon I've found your farm," he said.

Linn stood and faced him, her hands on her hips, and Jack looked up from his newspaper.

"It's a place over near Mingleton, fifty acres, mostly grass. It's already been a poultry farm but the people have gone so of course there's no stock. But there's hen-coops there, twelve of them, and there's a few huts that'd do for pigs. There's a bit of an orchard behind the house — apples and pears and a few plums — and the house itself is in good shape although it's been empty quite a while."

"You seem to know a lot about it."

"So I should. I've been over there."

"Why didn't you tell us first?"

"I had the chance of a lift with Pete Hale. It was him that told me about the farm. He had business in Mingleton and offered to take me in his car."

"Haven't you been to work at all?"

"Of course I've been to work!" Charlie said. "I took a few hours off, that's all. But I've certainly got some catching-up

99

to do. I must go back when I've had my tea."

Linn, as she drew up the fire in the stove and placed three kippers in the pan, listened while Charlie described Stant Farm. Now and then she put in a word and Jack, too, had questions to ask. Charlie was able to answer them all.

"I thought we'd go over tomorrow afternoon, all four of us, as it's Saturday. We have to get the key from the neighbouring farm and I said we'd be there at half-past-two. Clew says we can borrow the van."

"It seems you've got it all arranged."

"There's no point in wasting time."

"Fifty acres is too big."

"Not if it's going cheap, it's not."

"How cheap?" Linn asked.

"They're asking six-pound-ten the acre but I reckon they'll come down on that."

"Why should they come down on it?"

"Because it's stood empty for nearly a year and the land has got a bit run down."

"The usual story," Linn said. She turned the kippers in the pan. "We've seen quite a few places like that, in the past two months, dad and me."

"You wait till you see Stant Farm! It's just what you're looking for, no doubt of that, and a nice little neighbourhood round about. I talked quite a bit with the Triggs next door – they're the ones that've got the key – and I said you'd be sure to be interested."

"Did you indeed?" Linn said.

"You don't sound any too thrilled about it."

"I don't like being rushed into things."

"Laws!" Charlie said. He glanced at Jack. "If that's what you call being rushed no wonder you haven't found a place!" He sat down at the table and began cutting slices of bread. "You'll like Stant Farm. I know you will. And if we play our cards right I reckon we'll get it for a song."

"What do you mean by 'we'?" Linn asked. She forked a kipper onto a plate and put it on the table in front of him. "I thought *I* was the one who was buying the farm."

"Why, yes, certainly. You're the one that's got the money."

"Just for a moment," Linn said, "it seemed to me you'd forgotten that."

Charlie's smile died from his lips.

"Look," he said. He was suddenly hurt. "You don't have to go and look at the place if you don't want to. It seemed a pretty good buy, I thought, but it's no odds to me one way or the other." He picked up his knife and fork and cut the head and the tail from his kipper. "You go ahead and find your own farm. It's no odds to me where we go. It's only the place I shall live in, that's all!"

"Don't be silly," Linn said. She placed the other two plates on the table and hung her oven-cloth up on its nail. "It's just that you *are* rather inclined to run things – "

"Not any more!" Charlie said. "I shall keep out of it from now on!"

"How can you keep out of it if you're driving us over to Mingleton?"

"Oh, I'm driving you over, then? I'm allowed to do *that* much in the Great War?"

"Don't be silly," she said again.

Her father came to sit at the table and she glanced at him with a little smile.

"Charlie's in a mood," she said. "See if you can put things right."

"You must put things right your own selves. You're both fully grown, the pair of you, though to hear the way you've been going on you might be two children of ten years old."

"Both of us or is it just me?"

"I'm taking no sides," Jack said. "I've got more sense than taking sides when a man and his wife are having words."

But Linn knew by his straight look that he held her to be in the wrong and, taking her place at the table, she did her best to make amends.

"I've never been to Mingleton. What sort of place is it?" she asked.

Charlie was silent, ignoring her. Jack had to answer her instead.

"It's a good enough place in its way. It's got a market and plenty of shops and a railway station and all that."

"How far is it from here?"

"I'd say thirty miles. Perhaps thirty-five. Charlie can tell you better than me."

"Charlie's still in a mood," she said.

"Oh no I'm not!" Charlie said.

"Then why aren't you talking to us?"

"Because I've got nothing to say, that's why. I'm keeping mum, for safety's sake."

But Charlie was not one to sulk for long. His sense of humour prevented it. He removed a fishbone from his mouth and looked at her with a sidelong glance.

"Anyway, you should know by now! — I never could eat a damned kipper *and* talk at the same time!"

The atmosphere was eased between them. He was soon himself again. And when he left to go back to work he said:

"You'll like Stant Farm. I know you will. It's exactly what we're looking for."

"Yes, well, we shall see," Linn said.

* * * * *

The house at Stant Farm was very small; no more than a cottage, as Linn remarked, with two rooms down and two up and a lean-to scullery at the back; but it was a solid, forthright place, built of the local Flaunton stone and, with its roses climbing the walls and its scented jasmine over the porch, it had a beguiling prettiness. Of the two windows in the kitchen, one looked out on the steep farm track and down to the lush green valley below, where, hidden among the trees, the little loop-line railway ran, close beside the River Mew.

Although the farm stood on a rise, its six fields were level enough, and were sheltered from the prevailing wind by an ash copse and a belt of young pines. Above the pines lay another small farm, Slipfields, and above that again was the open common locally known as Flaunton Heath. Below Slipfields and Stant, surrounding them, were the bigger farms with their great open fields, and Charlie, walking about with Robert, pointed them out to him by name.

"That's Piggotts, just below, and over there is Innings," he said. "Beyond Innings is a farm called World's End and down the side of the valley, there, is a farm called Flag Marsh."

Robert was interested in the big farms. He stood for some time looking out over Piggotts, where the haymakers laboured in the sun, and then strolled down as far as Innings to see what breed of sheep they had there. In fact, as Charlie laughingly said, Robert paid more attention to the surrounding farms than he did to Stant itself.

"*This* is the place we've come to see! Aren't you interested in it?" he said.

"You bet I am!" Robert said. He looked at Charlie with shining eyes. "And to think that mother can buy it outright! A house and fifty acres of land! I still can't believe it, even now."

To him Stant Farm was a perfect place. He hoped his mother would feel the same. But down there, on the bigger farms, was where he would go looking for work when the time came for him to leave school.

He and Charlie, exploring Stant, poked into the hedges and ditches and tried to discover how the land-drains ran. The hedges were badly overgrown and the ditches needed digging out and in the lowest field of all, where the land-drains had long fallen in, the pasture was sour and choked with reeds. All the field-gates were in ruins, and the track leading down from the farm to the road was deeply rutted, in need of repair. But the land, for the most part, was in good heart, and in five of the six fields the grass was still sweet and green, for the "keep" had been sold to a neighbouring farmer and his cattle were grazing even now in the two fields next to the house.

"Come on, young Rob," Charlie said, "let's see what your mother and granddad think."

The four of them came together again in the little garden in front of the house. The sun shone fully upon them there and even the wind, which came from the east, breathed on them with a hot dry breath, bringing with it the smell of the hay that was being turned in the fields at Piggotts.

"Well?" Charlie said. "What do you think?" His face was screwed up against the sun and his blue eyes were narrowed into slits, looking keenly out at Linn from under their jutting, light-coloured brows. "I see you've been round pretty thoroughly."

"I don't know," Linn said. "I would've liked a bigger house." Looking at it, she shielded her eyes, putting one hand to the brim of her hat and bending it down in a shadowing curve. "I would have liked three bedrooms," she said, "so that Dad and Robert needn't share."

"It don't worry me, sharing," Jack said.

"No, nor me," Robert said.

"It's much more land than we really need. More than half will be going to waste."

"Not if we run things right," Charlie said. "With fifty acres to play with, we can even grow corn to feed our stock."

"It's all so badly neglected, too. Just look at those hedges, all overgrown. As for the outbuildings at the back, there's scarcely a roof on one of them!"

"That's all to the good, in a way. It means we can beat them down on the price."

"Yes, but what a lot of work!"

"We'll get it done in time," Charlie said. "At least the house is in pretty good shape, considering it's been empty a while."

"Why did the other people go?"

"The old man got sick. Then he died. His wife's gone to live with her son in Wales." Charlie pointed up towards Slipfields. "I heard about it from the Triggs when I called to pick up the key," he said. "You'll like the Triggs. They're a nice old pair. They'll be good neighbours, I'm sure of that."

Down in the valley a train clacked past. They saw its smoke above the trees.

"I don't like the railway being so close."

"Why, it's only a single-line track, that's all. There's only five or six trains a day. And that'll be an advantage, too, if we want to send stuff away on the train. The Triggs send eggs to Baxtry from here. The milk-train stops at Scampton Halt."

"You've gone into it all very thoroughly."

"I reckon I've covered the essentials all right." Charlie, with a grin, looked at Jack. "It's about a mile to Scampton from here and about the same to Flaunton," he said, "and it seems there's good pubs in both of them!"

"What about the shops?" Linn asked.

"The grocer at Scampton delivers out here, and he sells just about everything. There's a school for Robert in Mingleton — that's only two miles across the fields — and Sam Trigg says there's a garage just outside Scampton that's been advertising for a mechanic. I thought of calling on the way home to see if the job is still open."

Charlie reached up to the climbing rose and broke off one of its crimson blooms. He held it under Linn's nose and she sniffed at it in an absent way. He put in into his buttonhole.

"But it all depends if you like the place. You're the one who's buying it."

"I don't know," she said again. "It takes a lot of thinking about." She stared away, over the fields, trying to see them as her own. The decision was suddenly frightening to her and she turned to her father in search of guidance. "Dad?" she said. "What do you think?"

"I reckon you could do worse," Jack said.

"But could I do better, that's the point?"

"You might if you go on looking, perhaps, but the farms we've seen so far ent been a patch on this one."

"I'll tell you what!" Charlie said. "Rob and me will stroll up to Slipfields and take the key back to the Triggs. You and Jack have another look round. It'll give you a chance to talk things out."

"Yes, all right. You go on up."

Linn and her father were left alone. She watched him as he filled his pipe.

"What do you really think of it?"

"I've already told you what I think."

"Robert likes it. There's no doubt of that. But he is just a bit inclined to agree with everything Charlie says. '

"There's no harm in that," Jack said, "so long as Charlie's in the right."

"*If* he is. I wish I knew."

"You beginning to have second thoughts about spending your money on a farm?"

"Oh, no, it isn't that."

Jack struck a match and lit his pipe. In the brilliant sunlight, the flame was almost invisible. He threw down the match and trod on it.

"Maybe you'd like the place better," he said, "if you'd been the one that found it."

Linn gave a little startled laugh.

"Am I such a wretch as that?"

"Don't ask *me*. Ask yourself."

"I'm just being cautious," she said. "I'm weighing all the pros and cons. It's a bigger place than I had in mind so a lot depends on how much it costs. If they're willing to climb down a bit – "

"You should let Charlie handle that. He's had experience in the past."

"So have you," Linn said.

"Not on the business side, I ent. But Charlie knows what he's about. He's got his head screwed on all right, and he *is* a farmer's son, after all."

"As though I could ever forget it!" Laughing, she took her father's arm. "Let's go round the place again. I want another look at the barn and sheds."

By the time Charlie and Robert returned, she had decided to buy the place. She went to meet them and tell them the news and Jack, looking over the farmyard wall, saw them join hands and dance in a ring, watched by a group of astonished bullocks.

"I knew she'd come round to it!" Charlie said. "I knew it was just the place for us!" And as they drove down the steep bumpy track, he kept glancing back at the little farm. "My wife a landowner! What a lark!"

On the way into Mingleton to see the agent and make an offer, Charlie stopped at the garage in Scampton and got out to speak to a sandy-haired man who was tinkering with a break-down truck.

"Frank Fleming?"

"Yes, that's me."

"I heard you were wanting a skilled mechanic."

"You've left it a bit late, chum. The job's been filled a month or more."

"Oh!" Charlie said. "Just my luck!"

He turned and walked back to the van and Frank Fleming followed him. The man's eyes seemed never still, but roved about over the van; over the people sitting inside; over Charlie himself, his clothes, his walk.

"As a matter of fact, my new chap is not much good. I doubt if he'll be stopping long."

"Oh?" Charlie said. "What then?"

"How much experience have you had?"

"Nine years in a garage at Herrick Cross. My boss there will give me a reference."

"What about wages?" Fleming said.

"At the moment I'm getting three-pound-fifteen."

"That's more than I pay the chap I've got."

"But he's not much of a mucher, you said."

"No, that's right, he's n.b.g. . That's why he won't be stopping long."

"Sounds like you are offering me his job?"

"You bring your reference with you next time. Then we'll talk about it again."

"Yes, well," Charlie said, "I'll think about it, anyway."

He got into the van and drove on towards Mingleton.

"What a shabby old garage," Linn remarked.

"Aren't they all these days?" he said.

Chapter 7

They moved to Stant Farm on October the seventh and two days later Jack began ploughing the eight acre field on the other side of the track from the house. The weather was open and work went ahead at such a pace that the field was ploughed, harrowed, and sown with oats, all within the space of a fortnight; and by the first week in November there was a green haze on the ground as the tender blades came pushing up.

They were all proud of this first field of corn. Charlie had helped with the harrowing and Robert had helped with drilling the seed, so when they looked out on the gentle greenness, the triumph was shared by all three. But Jack, of course, had done most of the work, for Robert was at school all day and Charlie was working at the garage in Scampton.

"You're our full-time man," Charlie said. "Rob and me, we're just casuals."

Jack worked with horses and tackle borrowed from Slipfields, the farm next door, and the oatseed had been bought from there. Sam and Jane Trigg were glad to see Stant occupied again and they wanted to help in every way.

"You may as well use our horses. They're not overworked up here with us. The missus and me, we're getting on. We don't do more work than we can help."

The Triggs sold them their first stock: two Redpoll cows, each yielding two gallons a day, and two Redpoll heifers "guaranteed" to be in calf.

"Guaranteed?" Charlie asked with a grin.

"Well," said Sam, "they've been to the bull."

"There's no guarantee till the calf starts to kick."

"My missus is the best guarantee. She says she can tell by the look in their eyes."

"Get away, you old scoundrel, you!"

But both heifers were indeed in calf and one of them even came into milk fully two months before she calved; and when in due course the calves were born and both turned out to be heifers, it seemed that fortune was smiling on them.

As soon as the pig-sties had been repaired, they bought two young sows, and these also came from Slipfields. Linn at first had her doubts about buying stock from the Triggs. She wanted to look round the market first.

"Sam breeds good stock," Charlie said. "Why waste time looking elsewhere?"

"We get it no cheaper, buying from him."

"No, of course not," Charlie said. "He's got to live, the same as us. But we do save a bit on transport costs."

"Yes, I hadn't thought of that."

So Linn, always anxious to save money, bought her first pigs from Sam Trigg. Stocking the farm was a costly business and she was dismayed, over the months, to see her bank-balance dwindling so small. Whenever she went to the poultry sales, she would be drawn to the cheaper birds, but her father insisted she should buy the best.

"Cheap always comes dearer in the end."

"Those brown pullets look all right to me."

"D'you *want* to throw money down the drain?"

"Don't be silly. Of course I don't."

"Then buy good stock. It's the golden rule."

Always, after some argument, she allowed herself to be guided by him. He was experienced; he must surely know best; and she knew she had a lot to learn.

"So many things to buy!" she said. "I do nothing but pay out all the time!"

But she was proud of the little farm coming to life before her eyes; of the poultry and geese in the orchard-field; of the sows with their piglets in the paddock; of the four beautiful Redpolls who would hang their faces over the wall and watch while she worked in the garden. The barn was packed with feeding-stuffs stored away in shiny new bins; there was plenty of hay and some bought straw; and, in the sheds, all manner of tools.

"So many tools!" she would say. "Yet there's always something we haven't got!"

"You don't need to buy a pruning-saw. Sam says we can borrow his."

Sometimes in the evenings Sam would saunter down to Stant to see how things were progressing there and always, on a Friday night, he would go with them to the pub in Scampton.

"How're you getting on at the garage? Is Fleming treating you pretty fair?"

"Oh, all right," Charlie said.

"He's a bit of a cadger, from what I've heard. You want to watch out for him on that score."

"Thanks for the warning," Charlie said.

* * * * *

He had not been keen to work at Frank Fleming's garage, since it meant taking another man's job, but Linn had swept his scruples aside.

"You've got to put yourself first. You'll never get anywhere if you don't."

"I don't know about that," Charlie said.

But when he had called at the garage again, Fleming had persuaded him.

"I'm sacking this chap, anyway, as soon as I find a better man, so it might as well be you as any other."

Certainly the garage was convenient for Charlie: by taking the path across Piggotts Farm, he could be there in ten minutes or so; and when Linn began supplying eggs to the grocer in Scampton, Charlie was able to deliver them on his way to work in the morning.

The garage was a busy one; busier than Clew's at Herrick Cross; for Scampton was a large village and straddled the main road from Baxtry to Kitchinghampton.

Fleming employed two other men besides Charlie: Jerry Jackson, a young apprentice, and George Cressy, in his late twenties, who did odd jobs about the place. George, as Charlie soon discovered, was not quite right in the head. He told everyone that he was a Red Indian. Strangely enough he looked like one, for he had a coarse ruddy complexion and a hawklike face with prominent cheekbones, and wore his hair cropped very short, revealing a large strong bumpy skull.

"Don't stand any nonsense from him," Fleming said, on Charlie's first day. "He's here to work, like anyone else, whether he's touched in the head or not."

Cressy was within earshot when this was said. He was busy sweeping the garage floor and when Fleming had gone out the apprentice, Jerry, spoke to him.

"Did you hear what the boss said about you?"

"Yes, I heard. I'll get him one day."

"What'll you do? Scalp him, I suppose?"

"Yes, and you!" Cressy said.

Jerry looked at Charlie and grinned but Charlie turned away from him. He took a packet of cigarettes from his pocket and offered one to George Cressy. George looked at him in surprise.

"Gold Flake, is it? Thanks a lot. You're a pal and no mistake." George handled his cigarette as though it might have been gold itself. "I won't smoke it now, I'll keep it," he said. He tucked it away behind his ears.

As he moved on, sweeping the floor, Jerry Jackson met Charlie's eye.

"George doesn't smoke. He never has. He'll give it back to you one of these days."

George was supposed to work in the mornings only: that was all Fleming paid him for; but in fact he hung about the garage until it closed in the evening.

"I've got nothing else to do and it keeps me out of mischief," he said. He had once been in trouble with the police, after a fight with a man in a pub, and had seen the inside of Gloucester gaol. "I shan't make *that* mistake again. I'm keeping out of trouble now."

* * * * *

Robert loved the little farm. Somehow the place had got hold of him. The grey stone house and the way it stood, looking out over the valley; the smooth soft greenness of the fields, especially in the morning light; the warm sweet

111

smells when he entered the barn, of hay and straw and barley-meal and apples sweating in the loft: All these things somehow worked on him and sometimes he would stand transfixed, trying to fathom what it was that made Stant Farm a place apart.

"I suppose it's because it's our own," he said, talking to Charlie one day. "There's something about it . . . Oh, I dunno . . . It's as though I've lived here all my life."

He went to school in Mingleton now. It seemed a terrible waste of time, having to go to a new school just for one term, but the months were passing quickly enough and at Christmastime he would be free to take his place in the grown-up world.

As the longed-for day drew nearer, however, it brought a problem to vex his mind, for his mother by now had made it clear that she expected him to work at Stant. She talked about it all the time. The subject was very dear to her heart.

"Your own farm to work on, just think of that! You'll be your own master, here at Stant, and you'll never be laid off in bad weather as you would if you worked for someone else."

But although he loved Stant Farm, he had no wish to work there. He looked towards the bigger farms, Piggotts or Innings or World's End, where he could learn to do everything and be the kind of all-round man his grand-father had been in his prime. He knew he should tell his mother this but it was a difficult thing to do and the longer he shirked telling her the more difficult it became. Instead he talked to Charlie and Jack one Sunday morning when they were out mending a gap in the paddock fence.

"You'll have to tell her straight," Jack said. "It's your own life and you'll soon be a man. You should start as you mean to go on."

"But what on earth is she going to say?"

"She won't like it. There'll be a great fuss. But you mustn't be ruled by your womenfolk or you won't have a soul to call your own."

Robert felt the truth of this. He knew he ought to strike out for himself. But the prospect of spoiling his mother's bright dream caused a sinking in his heart and Charlie, reading it all in his face, came to his rescue with a suggestion.

"Have you tried for a job yet?"

"No, not yet."

"Then why not leave it for a while? You're only fourteen and there's bags of time. Why not do as your mother wants and work here at Stant for a little while? Give it a year, say, just to please her?"

"A year!" Robert said. It seemed like an age.

"A year's not long," Charlie said. "It's only twelve months, after all." Putting a pointed stake in a hole, he held it while Jack hammered it in. "Your mother's so bucked about getting this place, it'd be a pity to spoil it for her, but she'll have got on her feet by then and it won't be such a blow to her when you tell her you want to work somewhere else."

Robert stared into the distance. Suddenly he made up his mind.

"All right! I'll give it a year! It seems only fair, till the farm's on its feet."

It was a great relief to him that the problem had been resolved like this. How very simple it all was, with Charlie on hand to point the way! Smiling, he turned to Jack again.

"Charlie's got all the answers!" he said. "I should've come to him before."

"So long as you're satisfied," Jack said.

"Well," Robert said, sheepishly. "It's like Charlie says – a year's not long."

And so it happened that when he left school and began working at Stant Farm his mother had no reason to suspect that his joy in it was less than her own.

* * * * *

In fact he was happy enough for a time, for his first job as a working-man was helping Jack to cut and lay the overgrown hedges, and this was work that he enjoyed.

The boy did his best to follow his grandfather's skilled example, cutting so far through the stem of each thorn, bending it over into the hedge, and, with a quick sharp upward stroke of his billhook, severing the spike that stuck up from the base. Then the split stakes, at intervals, hammered well into the ground, and lastly the tight-woven hazel-rods, the "etherings" as his grandfather called them, twisted all along the tops to prevent the newly bended stems from springing upright again in the hedge.

Mitten, billhook, rubbing-stone: Robert enjoyed the use of these things; but would he ever have his grandfather's knack of turning the billhook after a cut so that, in a single up-and-down movement, two stems were cut instead of one? Would his wrists ever harden and grow strong instead of aching, burning-hot, as they did now at the end of each day? Yes, the skill and the strength would come: he was determined that they should; and he worked on, diligently, trying to match the good clean strokes that his grandfather managed so easily.

There was much useful timber cut from the hedges; pea-sticks, bean-sticks, hedging-stakes; and enough kindling to light their fires for twelve or eighteen months to come. At the end of it all the rubbish was burnt and they watched the great heaps crackling up, the red sparks flying in the dusk of the day, and the smoke with its acrid breath-catching smell drifting across the darkening fields.

The winter days were cold and dry: just the right weather for hedging and ditching; and by late March it was almost all done. How neat and tidy the hedgerows were now, and how much more light was let into the fields, now the tall timber had been removed. Charlie, whenever he walked round the farm, was full of praise for Jack and Robert, because of the work they were doing there. Every day there was something new: a ditch cleaned out or a gate repaired; mole-hills rolled out in the pastures; fences painted with creosote: there were improvements everywhere.

"Aren't you proud," he said to Linn, "at owning such a place as this?"

"Oh!" she said. She could not find the words. "Sometimes it all seems too good to be true!"

Linn's pride in her ownership was equalled only by her pleasure and pride in seeing her father and her son working together in the fields. *She* had provided them with that work and it was like a miracle. On Friday evenings, after supper, she paid them their wages for the week. Account-book and cashbox were brought to the table; money was carefully counted out; and the figures were entered into the book.

She kept her accounts most beautifully. Charlie had shown her how it was done and she had proved an apt pupil. The farm was a serious thing to her; she meant to see that it paid its way; and she watched every penny that came and went in every single business transaction. Her husband, her father, and her son looked on in some astonishment as this shrewd and capable woman-of-business developed so swiftly under their eyes.

"Where do you get it from?" Charlie asked. "How come you know how to handle it all when you've only been in it five minutes or so?"

"I've got good teachers in you and dad. I would never have had the nerve to start if it wasn't for you two backing me up."

And of course it was true. She was the repository of all their wisdom and experience. Jack could tell her "within three grains" how much corn the poultry should have and Charlie, after a visit to Mingleton, could tell her which corn-merchant she would do best to trade with. In all these things she learned quickly. Backed by her grasp of facts and figures, she could drive a hard bargain with any salesman who called at the farm, and she had a flair, when selling her produce, for scenting out buyers everywhere.

That was on the business side: no man could beat her there, Charlie said; but on the farm itself, it was a different story, and sometimes her quickness led her astray.

One day in spring, when she looked out of the kitchen window, she saw that Sam Trigg's cattle had got into the field where the oats were coming on so handsomely. The cattle were spread all over the field, eating the corn and trampling it down, and Robert, talking to Sam nearby, seemed not to see what was happening.

Linn went running out of the house and up the steep track, shouting to them and waving her arms. They turned to her in some surprise.

"Have you no eyes?" she said to them. "Just look at those

cattle in that field! Can't you see they're eating our corn?"

"That's what they're there for," Robert said. "Granddad asked Sam to put them in. The corn is coming on too fast. It wants eating down, granddad says, to make it tiller out a bit."

"Oh!" Linn said. She stood abashed. She felt she had made a fool of herself and a brief glace at Sam Trigg's face showed her that he was highly amused. "That's all right, then. I needn't have fussed."

"No," Robert said. He looked away. "Everything is under control."

The boy was trying not to smile and Linn, perceiving it, was suddenly piqued.

"I suppose it was rather funny to you, to see me come rushing up like that?"

"Well, yes, just a bit, I suppose." He glanced at her and the smile was there, flickering about his lips. "I thought the house was on fire," he said.

Sam Trigg reached out and patted her shoulder.

"Don't worry, Mrs Truscott. I'll see that my cattle behave themselves."

Linn turned and went back home. The incident had nettled her. And yet she was filled with an angry shame that she, who had lived all her life on the land, should be so ignorant of its ways.

* * * * *

Charlie teased her endlessly. It was still a joke to him that she was now a "woman of means" and sometimes he called her "Lady Stant." At the same time he admired her, because of her business acumen, and because her ownership of the farm was giving her new confidence. It showed in the brightness of her eyes and a certain challenging look she had, as though to say, "I know my worth." She had always been a beautiful woman and now, although in her thirty-ninth year, an age when most women lost their looks, her beauty had somehow been enhanced.

They had been married for more than three years and in that time he had never grown tired of looking at her. But now, because of this challenging look in her eyes, he was falling in love with her all over again. He would stand watching her, secretly, while she was busy about the farm, or he would leave what he was doing and go in search of her in the sheds. And Linn, by the way she looked at him, showed that she knew and understood; showed that she shared this heightened awareness that had sprung from the change taking place in their lives.

"I'm seeing a lot of you today."

"Yes, well," Charlie said, "now that I've got a rich wife, I mean to keep an eye on her."

"Rich indeed! What a lie! My little legacy's nearly all gone."

"It's tied up in the farm and the stock, where you can see it every day. That's a lot better, to my mind, than a heap of pound notes in the bank."

"But we've got to have money all the same. We can't do without it, in this world."

"You're doing all right with your butter and eggs? And Jack did all right with those weaners last week? Why, the money's coming in hand over fist! I can tell by the way you smile to yourself whenever you're doing your accounts."

"And how do I look when I'm paying the bills?"

"Like this," he said, and gave a great scowl.

"You!" she said. "You're a lying toad! Why do you come pestering me? I get on better by myself." She turned again to sorting her eggs. "Now look what you've made me do! I've put three Grade A's in with Grade B!"

"Your Grade B customers won't mind."

"*I'm* the one that'll mind," she said. "There's a difference of twopence a dozen between those two grades."

"Twopence a dozen! Fancy that! You won't be able to sleep tonight, thinking what a close shave you had, nearly losing that halfpenny!"

It was true that she watched her pennies carefully; she had been obliged to most of her life, during the years of poverty; and the profits to be made at Stant Farm were too small and too hard-won for her to abandon her carefulness.

There was a covered market in Mingleton and every Wednesday morning Linn would travel in on the bus, carrying two baskets of eggs, with a few surplus pounds of butter, perhaps, and anything else that came to hand. Sometimes it might be watercress, picked from beside the spring at Stant; sometimes it might be sprigs of sage or posies of snowdrops and violets: these things looked well on her little stall and whatever she took was always sold. Home-made jam and apple jelly; chutney and brawn and white cottage cheese: her customers soon looked out for these things and she could have sold twice as much if only she had had it to sell.

One Wednesday afternoon, when most of the market folk had gone, and Linn was bent over her takings, counting the coins in their cardboard box, a man's voice suddenly spoke, startling her by its loudness and gruffness.

"Are these eggs really fresh, missus?"

Linn sat up indignantly, a sharp rejoinder on her lips, but the words were bitten off in a laugh, for it was Charlie standing there.

"What are you doing here in town?"

"I've been to the depot to fetch some tyres. I can give you a lift home if you like, if you don't mind the dirt of the garage van."

"What about these last few eggs?"

"Never mind them! You can chuck 'em away!"

"I've got some shopping to do, before going home."

"Right, I'll come with you and give you a hand."

Linn had a good many calls to make; she always shopped on market days; and with Charlie to carry her baskets for her, she did not mind how much she bought. A bolt of grey flannel for making shirts; oil-cloth to cover the kitchen table; a new pair of rubber boots for Robert; and two new galvanized iron pails: all these things she bought today because Charlie was there to carry them and they would be going home in the van.

"What about a bag of coal while you're at it?" he said.

"Am I loading you up too much?"

"Get away! It was just a joke!"

"At least let me take one basket," she said.

But Charlie wouldn't hear of it; the burden was nothing to his strong arms; and they walked through the streets of the town together, stopping to look in every shop window and even lingering on the bridge to watch the barges pass underneath. It was a rare thing indeed for them to be out in the town like this, just the two of them, shopping together, strolling along and taking their time.

"We ought to get out like this more often."

"There's always too much to do on the farm."

"Your father and Robert could manage all right."

"Perhaps we could come one Saturday, then."

"And go to the pictures, what about that? It's Fred Astaire at The Plaza next week."

"Then have tea at the Copper Kettle . . . "

"Right, it's a date," Charlie said. "I'll write it in my diary."

It was only their nonsense, talking like this, but the day for them was an unusual one and the freedom of it had made them gay. They were like young lovers, a boy and a girl, who had stolen a meeting unlawfully; but they knew it would never happen again: too many things would get in the way.

* * * * *

Charlie drove her all the way home and carried her shopping into the house. Then he went back to work at the garage, where Fleming was looking out for him.

"You took your time! You've been gone two hours!"

"The old van packed up, climbing Glib Hill. It took me an hour to sort it out."

"Funny it always happens to *you*."

"I was always unlucky," Charlie said.

Whereas with Clew at Herrick Cross Charlie would have answered truthfully, with his new employer he was devious. Fleming had grumbled more than once because Charlie had been a few minutes late arriving for work in the mornings and there had sometimes been arguments.

"You should've been here at eight o' clock."

"Why, what happened?" Charlie asked.

"Never mind the smart remarks. Your hours are from eight to six. I expect you to remember that."

"You never complain," Charlie said, "when I stop on late to finish a job."

"I haven't noticed you stopping on."

"Haven't you? You will next time! I'll put in a claim for overtime."

"I'm not paying overtime. It's quite as much as I can do to pay your wages as it is without any bloody overtime."

"Talking of money," Charlie said, "you owe me for those eggs I brought."

"I thought I paid you."

"No, not yet. You owe me two bob."

"Two bob for two dozen eggs? Is that what you call cost price?"

"You'd pay three-and-sixpence at the shop."

"Can you change me half-a-crown?"

"I can change you a five-pound-note if you like."

"Can you, by God?" Fleming said. "And you farmers say farming doesn't pay!"

Charlie had only been making a joke; trying to lighten the atmosphere; but always, where money was concerned, Fleming had a jealous eye.

"I wonder you bother to work for me when you could be living like a lord on that farm of yours."

"Nobody lives like a lord on the land. Not these days at any rate. And the farm belongs to my wife, not me."

"I suppose she wears the trousers, then?"

"I wouldn't say that," Charlie said.

"She's the one with the money, though, and you know what they say? – Money talks!"

The fact that Charlie lived at Stant Farm seemed to fascinate Frank Fleming. He was always asking questions about it: whether it had a mortgage on it; whether the profits were worthwhile.

"I nearly bought it once," he said, "when it was empty all that time."

"Why didn't you?" Charlie asked.

"I couldn't raise the wind, that's why. Not all of us have got rich wives."

"I didn't know you were interested in farming."

"No, well, I'm not. But they say it's a healthy life, don't they, especially for growing kids?"

Charlie began to understand. He knew the Flemings had

a sickly child.

"How is Timothy these days?"

"He needs building up a bit," Fleming said. "Plenty of milk and eggs and that. He'll soon pick up when summer comes and he can get out to play in the sun."

The boy Timothy, aged seven, had been ill with diphtheria the year before and Fleming's wife, talking to Charlie, said he had nearly died from it. He was still too delicate to go to school and all through the winter he stayed indoors.

As the spring advanced, however, Fleming would sometimes bring him out, dressed in a warm coat and cap, and would walk round with him, holding his hand, showing him the cars in for repair and letting him watch the men at work. The little boy was deathly pale, with dark blue rings under his eyes, and bones as delicate as a bird's.

"This is your uncle Charlie Truscott. He's the one that brings you the eggs. Aren't you going to say how d'you do?"

The little boy put out his hand. It was cold and limp in Charlie's grasp.

"Hello, young fella," Charlie said. "Want to see me working the jack?"

The little boy gave a nod.

"Right you are, then! Here we go!"

"Your uncle Charlie lives at Stant. Maybe he'll let you go up some time and see the animals on the farm. You'd like to do that, wouldn't you, Tim?"

"Ah, that's right, you come," Charlie said. "We'll have a new calf in a week or two. I'll let you know when it's arrived and your dad can bring you up to see it."

He was not keen to have Frank Fleming at the farm, but how could he deny this child, whose face was that of a small ghost and who looked at him with such wide, wistful eyes?

In fact, when the new calf was born and Charlie mentioned it at the garage, Frank Fleming shook his head.

"Tim's not really up to it. He's still a bit weak. Maybe I'll bring him later on."

Fleming watched over the little boy and protected him at every turn. He would bring him out on fine days and let him talk to Charlie and Jerry; but George Cressy, the odd-jobman, was not allowed to talk to him.

"Cressy only frightens him. It's all this Red Indian stuff of his. He was at the house once, cleaning the windows for my wife, and Timothy got talking to him. Cressy cut his thumb with a knife and wanted to do the same to Tim, to make them blood-brothers and all that rot. Tim's had nightmares over that and if I see Cressy pestering him he's out on his ear straightaway."

"George doesn't mean any harm. He's fond of kids. He's one himself."

"I'm taking no chances, anyway. I don't trust him no more than an inch."

"Why have him here if you feel like that?"

"I couldn't get a *normal* man to do what he does for a pound a week."

"Is that all you pay him?" Charlie said.

"I've got to watch my money, you know, the same as anyone else these days. I don't see *you* giving much away."

Fleming was a cadger, as Sam Trigg had said, and every week without fail, when Charlie brought him his two dozen eggs, Fleming would try to avoid paying; and whenever Charlie reminded him, he always made the same remark.

"A shilling a dozen and you call that cost price? You want to get rich quick, don't you, mate?"

Fleming was the sort of man who was always out of cigarettes. He would make a great show of patting his pockets in search of them and then, on finding the packet empty, would fling it across the repair-shop.

"You ent got a fag, I suppose, Jerry?"

"Sorry, Frank, I've just smoked my last."

"Me, too," Charlie would say. "I'm thinking of trying to give it up."

Once, when Fleming was cadging like this, George Cressy came to him and held out an old sweet-tin containing four or five cigarettes.

"Here you are, Frank, you can have one of these."

"Thanks, George, you're a pal," Fleming said. But when he had lit his cigarette and had drawn on it a couple of times, he made a face of deep disgust. "Bloody hell! They're as stale as old boots! How long've you had them, for God's sake?"

"Not all that long," Cressy said.

"I suppose they're a Red Indian brand?" Fleming said. "Blackfoot, are they, or Cherokee?"

"That's a du Maurier," Cressy said. "Mr Wrennam gave it to me when he was in a while back."

"Tastes like old cowpats!" Fleming said.

"I shan't give you my fags again. I'll keep them for my mates at the pub."

"Yes, you do that," Fleming said. "It'll save me from an early grave!" And as Cressy walked away he said: "Heap big load of old stinking rope! That's how it tastes, this fag of yours!"

"Why do you bait him?" Charlie said. "He'd be all right if you left him alone."

Fleming merely blew smoke at him.

Chapter 8

Robert was suddenly growing tall. He was shooting up amazingly. Half way through his fifteenth year he was almost as tall as his grandfather, and this spurt of growth had taken place in the eight months since coming to Stant. "It must be something in the air," Charlie said, teasing him, but Linn watched over him anxiously, afraid that he was outgrowing his strength. She would fill his plate at mealtimes and try to force second helpings on him and was always bringing him milk to drink.

"Why don't you leave the boy alone instead of making a fool of him?" her father said in exasperation.

"He's so terribly thin, I can't help worrying," Linn said.

"That boy is as strong as a horse. If he's thin, and I daresay he is, it's because you're always nagging him."

Sometimes it was Robert himself who rounded on her impatiently.

"Mother, how many more times? — I don't *want* a glass of milk!"

"Very well. I only asked. There's no need to snap my head off. You're very touchy nowadays."

"I don't blame him," her father said. "The way you go on, you'd think growing up was some sort of disease, instead of the natural thing it is."

Sometimes Linn would laugh at herself. She perceived the truth of her father's remark and did her best to look at her son as though he were just someone else's boy, seen to be growing and shooting up. But this was a feat beyond her powers and every time she came upon him, busy about his work on the farm, it was always with a sense of shock.

"How you are growing!" she would say. "You're really becoming quite a man!"

But although she said it so many times, she found it a

difficult thing to believe. It really was too absurd that this boy of hers should be suddenly towering over her; that his legs were so long and could take such strides; that his voice had deepened so ridiculously and that he had the shadow of a moustache that had to be shaved off every morning.

Where had the years fled to, that her baby, her child, her little boy, should have vanished into the past like that? And sometimes, even while she laughed, she would be seized with a spasm of pain because this only child of her flesh was suddenly a stranger to her: a creature of moods she could not understand; shrugging, perhaps, when she spoke to him, or answering with a careless word; eyeing her sometimes in such a way that she found herself wondering at his thoughts.

Yet her pride in his manhood knew no bounds. Seeing him at work on the farm; his skill in tending the animals, and the way they followed him everywhere; his strong, clever, sensitive hands, able to do so many things; his quiet voice and his confidence: all these drew her closer to him, even though his manner to her was sometimes brusque and hurtful. And although she breathed not a word of it she thought him rather a handsome boy, for Robert, with his straight black hair, his deep dark eyes and smooth brown skin, his easy bearing and his height, stood out easily in a crowd; and Linn, whenever he went with her to the livestock market, noticed the glances that came his way.

Robert himself was quite unaware of attracting attention like this. His eyes would be on the stock for sale and his mind would be on the business in hand, and when that business had been completed, he expected to go straight home. He had no taste for trailing around, looking at stock they did not mean to buy, and would draw Linn's attention to the market clock.

"Yes, just a minute," she would say. "I want your opinion on these geese. I'm thinking we might increase our stock."

Or it might be the guinea fowl, or some new patent feeding-trough, that Robert had to go and see.

"Mother makes such a meal of it," he complained once to his grandfather. "I could've been home by half-past-ten if it wasn't for all this trailing about."

125

"You went and made a mistake, boy, when you tied yourself to her apron-strings. You'll never do a proper man's work while your mother's got hold of you, running you round."

"No, well," Robert said, "it's only until the end of the year, then I shall get a proper job."

"*If* you can tear yourself free," Jack said.

* * * * *

Linn had recently bought three goats, a billy goat and two nannies. The idea was that they should graze the "bit of rough": the ten acre field of tussocky grass, up by the copse at the top of the farm, where they would eat the brambles and briars that infested this neglected ground.

The goats, however, had other ideas, and they were always breaking out. It was the billy that caused the trouble. He, with his long, powerful horns, could push his way through any hedge, and where he went the nannies followed. "Old Moses," Charlie called him, "leading his tribe to the promised land." Once they got into the garden and did a lot of damage to the currant-bushes before they were discovered there. They would have to be tethered, Linn said, and she asked Robert to see to it.

Jack and Robert detested the goats. They were more trouble than they were worth. The nannies would never stand still to be milked and every day, morning and evening, Linn called upon Jack or Robert to come and hold them still for her.

One night the billy got out of "the rough" and was discovered in the morning nibbling the turnip-tops in the Corner Field. Robert was sent to fetch him out.

"And perhaps this time," Linn said crossly, "you'll see that you tether him properly."

"Don't blame *me*!" Robert said. "The brute has eaten through his rope!"

"What you should do," Charlie said, "is to dip the rope in creosote."

"Damn the goats!" Robert said. "I don't know why we have them!"

"It's surely not too much trouble," Linn said, "just to look after three goats for me?"

But it was not only the goats. His mother was always on at him. She would call him away from his proper work to hunt down a rat she had seen in the barn or to oil the hinge on the dairy door or to remove a dead bird that had drowned itself in the drinking-trough. Whenever two cockerels got into a fight she would call upon Robert to separate them and she was always asking him to watch out for hens that were laying away.

On Wednesdays, when she went into town, Robert fed the poultry for her. Sometimes there was a mash to be mixed and Linn's directions were precise. Everything had to be done just so. Even when scattering corn for them, there were certain rules to be observed.

"You know that speckly hen with two toes? And the three whites that are moulting just now? I want you to stay and watch over them and see that they get their proper share.

But this was not a man's way and Robert forgot these niceties. He scattered the grain and that was that. But it so happened, one Wednesday morning, that Linn returned to the house for her purse and saw how little attention he paid to these precise directions of hers.

"Didn't you hear what I said to you about those hens that need special care?"

Robert gave a careless shrug.

"I reckon they get their share all right."

"I don't understand you lately," she said. "You used to take pains in pleasing me but now you don't seem to care at all. You don't even listen to what I say."

Robert merely turned away, muttering something under his breath, and Linn had to hurry to catch her bus.

* * * * *

Robert's moods seemed to get worse and her patience was sorely tried at times. Often the boy avoided her. She would call for him and he would not come. Once, on going into the barn, she heard him slip out by the other door, and when she followed he was not to be seen.

"Didn't you hear me calling you?" she asked him, later, at dinner-time. "This morning, early, in the barn?"

"You're *always* calling me," he said.

One day she sent him down to the village, to deliver some cards at the houses there, advertising produce for sale.

"But that'll take me hours!" he said, and his face was like a thundercloud.

"Don't you want the farm to do well?"

"What I want is a chance to get on with some proper work!" Angrily he went to the door and yanked his jacket down from its peg. "I'm supposed to help with running the farm but what have I done these past few weeks? – Nothing but fiddle and waste my time!; I don't do a stroke of proper work. Granddad has to do it all."

"Your granddad can manage well enough."

"That's just it!" Robert said. "I ent needed here at all! I'm nothing but an errand-boy!"

He snatched the cards from the kitchen table and thrust them into his jacket pocket.

"Don't get them dog-eared, please," Linn said. "I took such trouble writing them out."

Robert was gone the whole afternoon. Milking-time came and he still wasn't back. Linn, when she went to bring in the cows, called to her father across the yard.

"Have you seen Robert anywhere?"

"Why, has he slipped his leash?" Jack said.

It was well after six when Robert appeared. The cows were back in the pasture by then and Jack was working the pump in the yard while Linn sluiced her milking-pails out in the trough. Robert came strolling in at the gate and stood before them, silent and still, his hands thrust deep in his trousers pockets. They both stopped work to look at him.

"Where have you been all this time?"

"I've been to Piggotts to see Mr Madge."

"Piggotts?" she said. "Whatever for?"

"To ask for a job on the farm." Defiantly he met her gaze. "I'm to start next Monday morning," he said. "Mr Madge will want my cards."

"I don't understand you," Linn said. Her voice was quiet and icy cold. "Why should you want to do such a thing?"

128

"It's what I've *always* wanted to do. You've heard me say so often enough. A proper job, on a proper farm, learning all-round farming work."

"Isn't this a proper farm?"

"You know what I mean," Robert muttered.

"Isn't a smallholding good enough? Even when it's your very own?"

"No. I'd sooner work elsewhere."

"In that case," she said, controlling herself, "it seems you've done the only right thing."

"Yes, I reckon I have," Robert said.

"It's your own life. You must do as you please."

"Yes, I aim to," Robert said.

Linn bent over the trough and turned her pail in the brimming water, sluicing it round and round with her cloth. Jack, his face expressionless, was occupied in lighting his pipe. He took a step backwards, out of range, as the water slopped on to the flags.

"You'll drown us all in a minute," he said, "splashing about in a temper like that."

Linn let go of the pail again and stood up straight. She looked at her father with blazing eyes.

"I don't understand this son of mine! Turning his back on his own farm and going to work for someone else! Where's the sense in doing that?"

"I told you from the start," Jack said, "he'd never be happy raising hens."

Linn, with an effort, faced her son.

"What's the matter with raising hens? There's a living in it, isn't there?"

"There's nothing wrong with it," Robert said. "It's just that I want to do other things. I don't want to spend my life walking about with a pail in my hand, mixing bran-mash and collecting eggs. That's not my idea of a man's proper work. I want to do something more than that."

" 'A man's proper work'!" Linn exclaimed. "You say that with your granddad there? Do you count yourself more of a man than him?"

"Don't point at *me*!" Jack said. "I'm an old man, I've had my day. This little farm is about my mark. But Rob's got his

129

life in front of him. Of course he wants to do something more – so did I when I was his age – and you've got no right to stand in his way."

Linn's glance faltered and fell. She stared at the water in the trough and her hands moved about in it, absently, groping for her cloth. She found it at last and wrung it out.

"I shan't stand in his way," she said. "If he's really made up his mind, there's nothing more to be said on the subject. We'll leave it alone, finished and done with, and no more words on either side!"

"Amen to that!" Jack said.

"I'm just disappointed, that's all, that he takes no interest in his own farm. I thought when I bought this little place – "

"You just said there'd be no more words!"

"Yes! Very well! I'll say no more!"

She rattled her pail on to the flags.

* * * * *

When Charlie came home and heard the news he looked at Robert reproachfully.

"I thought you were going to give it a year, at least till your mother was on her feet."

Robert shrugged.

"Mother don't really need me here. She and granddad can manage all right."

"It's all the same if we can or not!" Linn was bending over the range, cutting up a hot meat pie and dishing it out onto four plates. "We had no say in it, did we?"

"It's a good farm, Piggotts," Jack remarked, as Robert came to sit at the table. "You'll be well-teached there, sure enough."

"It's the best farm in the neighbourhood, that's why I chose it," Robert said. "I was lucky to get taken on."

"Only the best will do for our Rob!" Charlie said in a hearty voice, and glanced anxiously up at Linn. "He must've made a good impression, to get taken on straight away like that."

Linn said nothing in answer to this but went to and fro, busily, till all four plates of food were set out.

"Your mother's upset," Charlie said. "You caught her a bit of a winger, you know, suddenly going off like that."

"I'm not upset!" Linn said. "I've had time to get over it now!" She drew out her chair and sat down. "Not that Robert seems to care whether I'm upset or not!"

Robert sat staring at his plate. His mother's anger weighed on him. It was like a darkness over his mind.

"I'm sorry if you're upset," he said, "but I reckon I'm entitled to work where I please."

"It was the way you went about it more than anything else," she said. "Sneaking off to Mr Madge, without a word to anyone! Getting into a temper like that because I asked you to deliver those cards!"

"It's not only that."

"What is it, then?"

"It's all sorts of things," Robert said.

"I should like to know what they are."

"Hell and damnation!" Jack said. "The boy has told you plain enough so for God's sake leave it and let's have some peace!"

Linn, surprised by her father's outburst, lapsed into silence, folding her lips. Charlie passed his cup to be filled. Robert picked up his knife and fork.

After supper the boy rose and looked at his mother uncertainly.

"Shall I go and shut up the hens?"

"You must please yourself," she said, "but it's surely not a man's proper work!"

Robert went out to the chicken-ground and after a while Charlie followed him. Together they shut up the hens for the night and then stood leaning over the gate. Down in the valley a train went by and Charlie looked at his luminous watch.

"That's the last train out to Baxtry," he said.

"I wish I was on it!" Robert exclaimed.

"Come, now, you don't mean that."

"No, well, maybe not, but with Mother making all this fuss – "

"It *was* a bit on the sudden side. Why didn't you tell her first?"

"She'd have talked me out of it. She'd have played on my feelings and wheedled me round."

Charlie had to admit it was true. He had seen it often in the past. But now the boy was growing up; becoming harder; asserting himself.

"Mother runs me around all the time. Granddad knows. He sees it all. He said I ought to strike out for myself and today I decided he was right."

"You'll find you're run around just the same when you go to work for Mr Madge."

"That's different," Robert said. "It's more like — oh, I dunno! — it's more like the proper order of things."

"Your mother's desperate fond of you."

"I know that," Robert said, and shifted a little, uncomfortably. "But mother'd have me tied in knots if she got too much of a hold on me. It's better for me to break loose now before the knots get too hard to untie."

"Ah, well," Charlie said. "It's not as though you're leaving home. Your mother'll get over it, given time."

* * * * *

Sometimes, working in the fields at Piggots, Robert would stop and exchange a salute with his grandfather up in the fields at Stant. At first he experienced a feeling of guilt, seeing the old man there all alone, but the guilty feeling did not last long because he felt he had done the right thing and knew that his grandfather understood.

Soon he belonged heart and soul to those big open fields where he worked by day and where, during that fine summer, the whole of the sky seemed to rest on his shoulders. Every morning, when he set off, it was with a tingling sense of excitement, for the farmyard was a busy place between five and six o' clock and he enjoyed the bustle there. It was a source of pride to him to be part of such an establishment; to help feed the horses and harness them and to watch the carters, responsible men, leading the teams out to the fields; and he looked ahead to future days when *he* would have charge of such a team and would lead it out to work in the fields.

At present, however, being a newcomer and only a boy, he was given more humble tasks, and day after day he bent his back, working with his hoe in the turnip field. The older, more experienced men would pause now and then to ease their backs, and perhaps even chat for a minute or two; but Robert could never afford to do that if he was to keep pace with them. He had to keep at it, ceaselessly, and never dared take his eyes off the work for fear that he would miss his stroke and cut out the tender turnip-plant as well as the choking growth of weeds.

Often, after such days as these, his back felt as though it would break. The muscles in his arms would be all a-tremble and when he got home in the evenings he had scarcely enough strength left to wash himself under the pump in the yard.

"You've got what's known as a hoer's back," Charlie remarked cheerfully.

"Don't I know it!" Robert said. "I shouldn't mind overmuch if I never saw another turnip again!"

"Yet that is what you prefer," Linn said, "to working here on your own farm!"

She made these bitter remarks sometimes. Her feelings would keep breaking out. But she had to admit that Robert seemed a lot happier now. He no longer spoke to her carelessly; never slipped away, avoiding her; and was always willing to lend a hand with whatever needed doing at Stant. So things were back to normal with them. There was closeness between them, as of old, and although her disappointment remained, she tried to keep it to herself. And she could not help a feeling of pride when, on meeting Mr Madge, he spoke so warmly about her son.

"He's a good boy, that Robert of yours. There aren't many boys nowadays who will do what they're told and a bit more besides. He's as keen as mustard and got a good brain. I wish I had a few more like him."

"Yes," Linn said, somewhat primly. "Robert could have done all sorts of things, if he hadn't chosen to go on the land."

* * * * *

Linn's little farm was doing well. It was beginning to pay its way. And in August there came a stroke of luck, for the Triggs at Slipfields, who were feeling their age, decided to sell most of their poultry and offered it to her at bargain prices. It followed that they would no longer be supplying eggs to the dealer in Baxtry and this again was lucky for Linn.

"The contract's yours if you want it," Sam said. "They asked me to recommend someone else so just say the word and I'll give them your name. Do you think you can manage it?"

"The problem is transport," Linn said. "Getting the eggs to Scampton Halt."

"Jim Smith allus took 'em for us. He'd do it for you if you asked him to."

"I've got a better idea," Charlie said. "I think we should have a motor-van."

"Don't be ridiculous!" Linn said. "Dad'll never drive a van!"

"Oh? Why not?" her father said.

"Well," she said, "you never have."

"And you think I'm too old to learn, I suppose?"

"Besides, where's the money coming from?"

"You can afford it," Charlie said. "It would be an investment, buying a van. Think of all the time it'd save when you've got dressed fowls to take here and there. You could even learn to drive yourself."

"Oh dear me no!" Linn said. "I should be frightened out of my wits."

That was going too far. She would not consider such a thing. But the idea of the motor-van was worth considering, certainly; she could see its advantages clearly enough; and if her father was willing to learn to drive – "

"Of course I'm willing! Why not?" Jack said.

Within a week the van was bought: a second-hand Ford, costing eighty pounds; and in no time at all, it seemed to Linn, Charlie had taught her father to drive. Jack's left knee, injured in his youth, gave him a lot of trouble at first, but Charlie did something to the clutch-pedal and after that the problem was eased.

So Sam Trigg's poultry came to Stant and Linn took over Sam's contract, supplying a hundred dozen eggs every week to the dealer in Baxtry. Jack took the eggs to Scampton Halt every Monday morning and promptly at the end of each month Linn received the dealer's cheque.

"You'll soon be a millionaire," Charlie teased, "if you go on the way you're going now."

"With my corn-merchant's bills as high as they are? – That's not likely!" Linn said.

But still, all in all, she was pleased with herself. The farm was successful, in its small way; her father was happy, having plenty to do; and fortune seemed to be on their side.

* * * * *

"I see you've got yourselves a van," Fleming, at the garage, remarked to Charlie. "How much did you pay for it?"

"We paid as much as it was worth."

"If only you'd come to me first, I could have fixed you up with a van through a cousin of mine out Froham way."

"The way I see it," Charlie said, "it's better not to shop on your own doorstep."

"Is that why you don't get your petrol here?"

"Jack fills her up in Mingleton when he takes my wife to the market there."

"That farm of yours must be doing well if you can afford to run a van."

"It's not doing badly," Charlie said.

* * * * *

Summer was dry and warm that year and before long they were cutting their oats, using Sam Trigg's horses and mowing-machine. Robert, of course, was too busy with the harvest at Piggotts to do much at home, but Charlie, in every spare moment he had, was out in the eight-acre field with Jack, fussing over the two horses or tinkering with the old rusty mower. Although the harvest was a tiny one, the excitement of it got into him and he could think of nothing else.

"It takes me back to the old days, working on my father's farm. Funny the way it gets hold of you. I suppose you could say it's in the blood."

The field of oats was a magnet to him. He would hurry out after breakfast, "just to set up a shock or two", and would make himself late going to work. Linn was always scolding him. She would follow him out to the field and take the cornsheaves from his hands.

"You know what Fleming is about time. Why provoke him and make matters worse? You only make trouble for yourself."

And sure enough, at the garage, Fleming would be waiting at the door.

"That's the third time you've been late this week."

"So long as the work gets done just the same, what does it matter?" Charlie said, quoting Clew at Herrick Cross.

But Frank Fleming was not like Clew. It annoyed him that Charlie came in late.

"You think you can do as you damn well please, just cos you've got a farm of your own. You think it makes you cock of the walk."

"*You* waste more time grumbling at me than *I* ever waste by coming in late."

And Charlie would walk past him, into the garage repair-shop, where Jerry Jackson stood listening.

"It properly gets up Fleming's nose, that little farm of yours, doesn't it? He just can't seem to leave it alone."

"He's glad enough," Charlie said, "to get his eggs and butter cheap."

The weather continued fine and warm and on the third Sunday in September the oats were carted from the field and stacked at one end of the barn, where the roof was soundest and they would be dry. Charlie and Robert helped with the carting and it was finished by mid-afternoon. Jack, Charlie noticed, was rather quiet: quieter even than usual; and when the last load had been got in, he went and sat on the bench in the yard.

"You feeling all right?" Charlie asked.

"I'm in a bit of a swither, that's all."

"Seems you've been overdoing things."

136

"I'm feeling the heat," Jack said. "I'm just going to sit and cool off and maybe smoke a quiet pipe."

But although he took his pipe from his pocket and sat with it in his hands for a while, he made no attempt to fill it and light it and seemed, Charlie thought, watching him, to have gone into a kind of trance, staring fixedly at the ground as though trying to remember something.

"You sure you're all right?" Charlie said.

"I've already told you, I'm right as rain." Jack looked up at him irritably. "You taking that horse and cart back to Trigg?"

Charlie and Robert exchanged a glance. Charlie gave a little nod and Robert climbed into the cart. Charlie opened the gate for him and closed it when the boy had passed through. He turned and walked back across the yard. Jack was still sitting on the bench, but now he was leaning against the wall, with one hand pressed against his chest. Sweat was pouring from his face and neck, and the front of his shirt was wet with it. He was breathing heavily through his nose. Charlie hurried across to the pump and filled a dipper from the trough. He took it and held it for Jack to drink, and when the old man had recovered himself, he helped him to sit up straight again.

"How many turns have you had like this?"

"One or two. It's the heat, that's all."

"The heat wouldn't give you a pain in your chest."

"Who said anything about a pain?"

"I'm not simple," Charlie said.

"That's just a touch of wind," Jack said. He rubbed at his chest with his knucklebones. "It's passing off again now."

Certainly he was looking better. The colour was coming back to his face and he was breathing more normally. Charlie picked up his pipe from the ground and gave it to him.

"You should see the doctor," he said.

"Just cos I've got a touch of wind? A dose of bicarb'll soon fix that." Jack began filling his pipe. Soon he was puffing away at it. "You don't have to stand guard over me. I'm as fit as a flea now."

"I'm just taking a rest," Charlie said. He sat down and lit a cigarette.

"I suppose you'll go blabbing to Linn in a minute."

"It's only right she should know."

"She fusses enough as it is. A fine how-d'you-do we shall have if she gets it into her head I'm sick."

"It's no good expecting me to keep quiet about it."

"That's the trouble with husbands. They can never keep nothing from their wives."

Linn came out of the house and found them sitting smoking together. With her hands on her hips, she stood laughing at them.

"Is this how the work gets done?" she asked.

"Your dad's not feeling too good," Charlie said. "He's had a bit of a funny turn."

Linn's laughter gave way to a frown.

"What sort of funny turn?"

"I came over twiddly," Jack said. "It's a warm day for the time of year."

"He had a pain in his chest," Charlie said. "He says it's happened a few times before."

"Father?" she said anxiously. "What've you been keeping from me?"

"Here we go! We're in for it now! I told you how it'd be!" Jack said.

"Can't I get any sense out of you?"

"I'll tell you this much! – I ent dying yet!"

"If you've got a pain in your chest, you should go and see the doctor."

"There's nothing much wrong with me, except that I'm getting on in years, and the doctors can't do nothing for that."

"You should see him all the same."

"Yes, well, maybe I will. – When I've got nothing else to do!" Jack got up and knocked out his pipe. "Right now I'm going to milk the cows."

"I'll go and fetch them," Charlie said.

Jack went off into the byre. Charlie went to bring in the cows and Linn went with him as far as the gate.

"Is it his heart, do you think?"

"He says it was just a touch of wind."

"Do you believe that?" Linn asked.

138

"Well," Charlie said, and gave a shrug. He did not want her to be too much alarmed.

At that moment Robert returned.

"How's granddad? Is he all right?"

"Right as rain, or so he says. But your mother's worried it may be his heart."

"Shouldn't he see a doctor, then?"

"We're working on it," Charlie said.

Jack appeared at the cowshed door and called across the yard to them.

"I thought you was bringing in the cows?"

"Just coming!" Charlie replied. He looked at Linn and Robert and grinned. "Plenty of life in him yet!" he said.

* * * * *

The next morning, after much prodding from Linn, Jack went to see the doctor in Scampton, and that evening, at supper-time, Charlie and Robert heard the result.

"Seems it's my heart, the doctor says. The pump's not working as well as it should."

"I reckon you knew that," Charlie said.

"Maybe I did. It ent a very surprising thing in a man who's passed his three-score-and-ten."

"Not too much exertion, then?"

"Nor too little, neither," Jack said.

"Did he say you could still drive the van?"

"He said I could do what I damn well please – "

"I'm sure he never said that!" Linn said.

" – But not too much of it at one time."

"He said you should rest every afternoon."

"He said to me, being a poor old man, that I warnt to be nagged by my womenfolk."

"Oh, what a fibber you are!" Linn said.

"He also said – and these was the doctor's very words – that I warnt to be kept waiting for my fittles."

"Lies! All lies!" Linn exclaimed. Now that her father had been to the doctor and the verdict had been reassuring, relief had done much to lighten her spirits and she was full of teasing laughter. "You're nothing but an old humbug!"

she said. "I can see there's nothing much wrong with *you*!"

But although her fears had been allayed, she still worried about the old man, and spoke to Charlie about him that night.

"I do hope Dad will be sensible. I'm afraid of his overdoing things."

"Jack's no fool," Charlie said. "He'll look after himself all right and I can help out with the heavy jobs."

"You've got your own work to think about."

"I can easily fit things in."

There was not much Jack could not do. He took his afternoon rest every day, if only to keep the peace with Linn, but in almost every other respect he carried on with his work as before.

"I ent an invalid," he would say. "I've just had a bit of a warning, to remind me that I'm getting old." And once, looking at Charlie, he said: "There's no need for you to creep about, doing my jobs behind my back. I'll soon ask when I need your help."

But Charlie never waited to be asked. He was always up at five o' clock, out in the yard, feeding the stock, and he always made sure that any heavy lifting work was done before he left the farm. Robert, too, helped as much as he could, before going off to his work at Piggotts.

"How bad is Granddad, do you think? Mother's been dropping hints to me that I ought to come back and work at home."

"There's no need for that, I'm sure," Charlie said.

"You don't think the farm is too much for him?"

"Dr Reeves doesn't think it is. I spoke to him the other day when he called at the garage for petrol and he said there's no reason why your granddad shouldn't keep on working for years."

"That's all right, then," Robert said. "Mother had me worried at first."

"He's got to take it easy, that's all, and it's up to us to see that he does."

Chapter 9

That winter was very wet. Rain fell for weeks on end and the steep farm track ran like a stream. Early in the new year gales ripped half the tiles from the barn roof and one of the old sheds collapsed.

"There'll be no lack of jobs for me to do when the weather lets up," Charlie said.

At the garage in Scampton, rain got into the oil-sump, so that oil and water overflowed, flooding the whole of the garage yard and running into the roadway. Charlie and the other men were kept busy all day with brooms, trying to prevent the oil and water from flooding into the repair-shop, and Frank Fleming ran to and fro, almost beside himself with rage. Because of the bad state of the yard, motorists were keeping away and he was losing petrol sales, and then, to complete his misery, the village policeman called on him, threatening him with a summons for fouling the road and causing danger to passing traffic.

Fleming's bad temper lasted for days. Even when the yard had been cleared and work was back to normal again he still found fault with everything and one of his chief grievances was the repair-shop stove.

"If you was to do some work for a change, you wouldn't have time to feel cold!" he would say, and he grudged every can of coke that was burnt. "If you had to buy that coke yourselves, you wouldn't be so free with it!"

One day George Cressy, arriving at the garage soaked to the skin, stood by the stove drying himself. Fleming came in and saw him there.

"I thought you Red Indians was supposed to be tough! But you're as much of a molly-coddle as them two palefaces there!"

George Cressy looked at him, his face impassive, his eyes like grey ice.

"You don't believe I'm an Indian?"

"Do I hell!" Fleming said.

"One of these days I'll prove it to you."

"You needn't bother!" Fleming said.

The next morning George arrived with terrible burn-marks on his face: two horizontal lines on his forehead and two on each cheek: deeply scored, an ugly red, stretching and puckering the skin.

"Good God!" Jerry exclaimed. "Whatever have you done to yourself?"

"I burnt myself with a hot poker, that's what I done," George said, and looked around, pleased with himself, as the three other men stared at him. "In front of the mirror, at home last night, after my mum and dad was in bed."

"Christ!" Charlie said, wincing, appalled. "What made you do a thing like that?"

"I wanted to test myself," George said. "There ent many men around here who could burn themselves on the face like that and never once cry out with the pain."

Fleming eyed him in contempt.

"Only an Indian, I suppose?"

"*You* couldn't do it. I'm damned sure of that."

"Too bloody right, I couldn't, by God! *I'm* not tenpence short, my lad!" Fleming flung away from him and began to slide back the big garage door. "You get a broom and sweep this floor and not so much of your stupid chat! And don't go near my wife and boy with that bloody horrible face of yours or I promise you I'll break your neck!"

A little while later, sweeping the floor, George picked up some old nuts and bolts and put them into his trousers pocket. Fleming happened to see him do it. He made George turn them out again.

"I won't have you thieving things from here. You can put them nuts and bolts in the box. Either that or pay for them."

"How much'll you charge him," Charlie asked, "just for a few old nuts and bolts?"

"There's too many things disappearing from here and I aim to stop it," Fleming said.

"What sort of things?" Charlie asked.

"There's a couple of spanners gone for a start. *And* a

couple of cans of oil. Somebody's had 'em. They can't have walked."

"I hope you don't mean me," Charlie said.

"You do your own repairs, don't you, on that little old van of yours? You certainly never bring it in here. You must need a few odds and ends in the way of tools and oil and that."

"What things I need I can buy for myself."

"You always seem pretty flush, I must say, and that's another funny thing."

"What do you mean?"

"I'm often skint myself," Fleming said, "but you never seem to have trouble that way."

"It must be the good wages I get."

"Ah, and the rest!" Fleming said. "I know how it is with all you chaps when you take the money for petrol out there. 'A bob for me and a bob for the boss!' That's your motto, isn't it?"

"You seem to know a lot about it. Is that how it was with you yourself when you worked for Sutton's in Mingleton? Is that how you managed to raise the wind to set up in business on your own?"

"You want to watch out!" Fleming said, red in the face. "I could have you under the clock for saying things like that to me!"

"You started it, not me."

"Supposing you get on with your work?"

"That's all I ask," Charlie said.

* * * * *

That afternoon he was sent out to a car that had broken down on Glib Hill. When he got back at three o' clock, Jerry was alone in the repair-shop, sitting by the stove, drinking his tea. He pointed to something on the floor and Charlie saw that it was a pound note, dirty and much blackened with grease.

"One of Fleming's little tricks?"

"Yes, and he's marked it with a cross, just to make sure we're properly copped, if we should happen to pocket it."

143

"He must be crackers," Charlie said, "if he thinks we'd pinch his rotten pound."

Jerry shrugged.

"He tried it on the last chap we had. *He* was daft and fell for it."

Charlie stooped and picked up the note. He looked at it for a moment or two, then folded it into a narrow spill. Dirty and blackened as it was, it was now unrecognizable, and he laid it down in front of the stove.'

"If he can play tricks, so can I."

A little while later, when they were both working together, George Cressy came in with his broom and shovel.

"All right if I sweep in here?"

"What, again? That's the third time today. All right, if you insist."

At half-past four Fleming came back from his tea-break. The lights were on in the repair-shop and outside it was almost dark. He stood inside the door for a while, feeling in his pockets for cigarettes, and then came forward into the light. In another moment he was at the stove and was lighting his cigarette with the spill. He dashed out the flame on the toe of his boot and dropped the spill on the floor again. Warming himself at the stove, he watched George Cressy sweeping the floor.

"You just swept in front of here?"

"Yes, this minute. Why, ent it clean?"

"Then you must've found something on the floor."

"What sort of something? Nuts and bolts?"

"You'd know what it was if you'd picked it up."

"I've picked up nothing," Cressy said.

"Ah, I wonder!" Fleming said. He drew on his cigarette again and let the smoke curl out of his nose. He called across to Charlie and Jerry. "I want a word with you two!"

"Sounds ominous," Charlie said. He turned, wiping his hands on a rag. "What's it about?"

"There was a quid on the floor here just now. I'd like to know where it's bloody well gone."

"As a matter of fact," Charlie said, "you've just lit your fag with it."

Fleming's face became brick-red. He picked up the spill

and undid its folds. The pound note was two thirds burnt. He turned to Charlie with a snarl.

"You've gone too far with me this time! You're getting your cards, you cheeky sod!"

"Wait a minute!" Jerry exclaimed. "You can't sack Charlie just like that! Dammit, Frank, can't you take a joke?"

"It's all right, Jerry," Charlie said. "I'm not worried. I've had enough."

"Oh, *you're* not worried, not *you*!" Fleming said. "There's always the farm, isn't there?" He came close to where Charlie stood and thrust out his jaw aggressively. "That's been your trouble all along! You think cos you've got that farm of yours you can damn well do as you like with me! But you're mistaken, I'll soon show you that!"

"You've already shown me," Charlie said. "You've given me notice. Isn't that enough?"

"Who said anything about notice? You can take your cards and leave right now!"

Charlie, though angry, managed a shrug.

"So long as you pay me for this week's work – "

"I'll pay you all right!" Fleming said, "I'll pay you off and give you your cards and then you can bloody well sling your hook!"

In his rage, as he turned away, he collided with George Cressy.

"Look here," said George, blocking the way, "if you're sacking Charlie, you'll have to sack me!"

"Right! It's a bargain!" Fleming said. "You can leave together! Two birds with one stone!"

"George didn't mean that," Charlie said. "You've no call to take it out on him."

"I *do* mean it, Charlie," George said. He pushed his broom into Fleming's hands. "There you are! It's all yours! You can sweep your own floors from now on!"

"Get out of my way!" Fleming said. He flung the broom to one side.

He walked across the repair-shop and went into the glass cubicle that served him as office. The three men stood in a group together, watching him rummaging though his desk.

"God, what a turn-up!" Jerry said. "How're you two going

to get jobs? There's over a thousand unemployed, just in Mingleton alone, and it's getting worse all the time."

"Thanks a lot," Charlie said. "I suppose you're trying to cheer us up?"

Fleming now came out of his office and thrust Charlie's employment card into his hand. Charlie made sure that it was stamped and counted the money he found inside.

"Two-pound-fifteen? What's the idea?"

"I've docked you a pound for the one that got burnt." Fleming's revenge was sweet to him and his pale, bright gaze was still for once, dwelling on Charlie's angry face. "You don't get the better of *me*, old son! You should've known better than try it on!"

He turned towards George Cressy and thrust a pound note into his hand. Charlie again put in a word.

"Won't you change your mind about George?"

"Just to please you? Will I hell! You can get out, the pair of you, and never mind the fond farewells!"

Charlie reached for his jacket and cap and put them on. He slung his dinner-bag over his shoulder and moved to the door. George Cressy followed him and Jerry went with them to see them off.

"So long, Jerry. Watch out for yourself. There's always the odd thunderbolt, even in the wintertime."

"Ah, I know, and when it falls — "

"Yes, what then?"

" — I'll see you in the dole-queue!"

Outside, in the rain, Charlie drew up his jacket collar. He looked at George Cressy's red-scarred face.

"You shouldn't have left because of me. It's like Jerry said, jobs are scarce."

"You don't catch me stopping on in a place where a mate of mine gets sacked like that."

"Well, it's too late for the Labour Exchange and too early for opening time, so I reckon we may as well go home. If I hear of a job that'd suit you, I'll look you up at the Hit and Miss."

"I'll do the same for you," George said.

* * * * *

When Charlie got home, just after five, Linn and Jack were in the kitchen.

"You're home early for a change."

"I've lost my job, that's why," he said. He watched the smile fade from Linn's face. "Fleming and me, we had a row. It's been in the air for quite a time. Anyway, he's paid me off. Me and George Cressy, the two of us." Charlie put his money on the table, as he always did on Friday nights. "I'm afraid it's a bit short this week." He told her about the burnt pound note.

"Why did you play that trick on him? You should've known he'd hate you for that."

"Yes," Charlie said, "I should've known." He went to hang up his jacket and cap. "I suppose you'll say I asked for it."

"You do seem to go out of your way to ask for trouble sometimes."

"It was bound to happen in the end. Fleming's had it in for me. I've felt it coming these two months or more."

"Then you should have had more sense than to go provoking him like that. How will it be when you go for a job and they ask for a reference from Frank Fleming?"

"I admit I hadn't thought of that."

"There are queues every day at the Labour Exchange. I see them whenever I go into town."

"They're not skilled mechanics, I don't suppose."

"So you think you'll get a job all right?"

"I don't know until I've tried. I shall have to hope for the best."

But although he spoke cheerfully, Charlie in fact was sick at heart. He too had seen the queues outside the door of the Labour Exchange; the men and young lads in the Mingleton streets, idling away their empty days; the others who tramped the country roads, begging coppers wherever they could, as they went from one workhouse to the next. It seemed he had made a mess of things; he had joined the ranks of the unemployed; the shabby loiterers; those without hope. And yet, in spite of everything, when he thought of Frank Fleming and the garage, he had no regrets: only a sense of deliverance, as though he had put down a heavy burden and was now free to do as he pleased.

He wished he could talk to Linn about this and make her understand how he felt, but he could see by her worried frown and the way she avoided looking at him that she would be out of sympathy with anything he had to say.

With Jack, however, it was different. He looked at it from a man's point of view. He understood and sympathised.

"You can't work for a man like Fleming, who's always out to trip you up. I reckon you're better out of it."

"At least he could've stayed," Linn said, "until he'd got another job."

"How could I stay when I'd got the sack?"

"That was something you brought on yourself."

When Robert came in and heard the news, he had a crumb of comfort to offer.

"If Fleming won't give you a reference, there's one man who will and that's Mr Madge. He's always saying what a first-class mechanic you are. He'd give you a reference like a shot."

"What good will that do?" Linn demanded. "*He* was never Charlie's boss."

"It cheers me up all the same," Charlie said, "to know there's *someone* who thinks well of me."

"It seems to me you're cheerful enough," Linn said in a dry tone. "No one would think, to look at you, that you'd just been thrown out of work."

"Well, there's no point in moping, is there? I daresay something will come along."

No, he could not explain to Linn that his work at the garage, under Fleming, had been a kind of enslavement to him and that now he felt he had been released. He lay beside her in bed that night and knew she would never understand.

"Is the Labour Exchange open on Saturday?"

"Yes, until twelve o' clock, I think."

"You'll be able to go first thing, then," she said.

"Ah, that's right, first thing," he agreed.

* * * * *

At ten o' clock the next morning, however, Charlie had still not left the farm. Linn looked out of the kitchen window and saw him in the three acre strip, cutting a barrowload of kale for the pigs. She went out and spoke to him.

"It's after ten, did you know?"

"Yes, I heard the church clock strike."

"You said you were going into town."

"I reckon maybe I've changed my mind."

The sharp blade of the fagging-hook went cutting through the frosty kale and Charlie stood upright, straightening his back. He dropped the cut kale into the barrow and wiped his wet hand on his overalls.

"I've been doing some thinking," he said, "and I reckon it's better to wait a bit." He laid his fagging-hook in the barrow and stood lighting a cigarette. "There's no end of jobs to be done on the farm and it seems to me a good idea if I get a few of them done now before I go looking for work elsewhere."

He pointed towards the end of the barn, where the lean-to shed had collapsed in the gales.

"I could rebuild that shed for a start. I could see about mending the barn roof and laying that concrete in the byre. Then there's the pig-huts in need of repair and the benches you need putting up in your dairy – "

"I know what needs doing," Linn said, "but how long is it all going to take?"

"Two or three weeks. A month. It depends."

"Think of the wages you'll lose in that time."

"Think of the money I shall save by getting everything ship-shape here."

"Have you talked about it to Dad?"

"No, I thought I'd speak to you first."

"Why, will you take notice of what I say?"

"Well," Charlie said. He smiled at her. "I should like to know what you think."

"I think you should go and look for a job."

"So I shall! No question of that! But there's so many things wanting doing here that it seems to me only common sense – "

"If you hang about for two or three weeks, you might

miss all sorts of jobs elsewhere. I certainly see no sense in that."

"Oh, I shall find a job all right. You've got to have faith in my good luck."

"I knew you wouldn't listen to me. You'll please yourself. You men always do."

"I hoped I was going to please you too."

Once again he essayed a smile, but Linn's glance was satirical, and after a moment she turned away. When she got to the gate, however, she paused and stood looking back at him.

"Seeing you're so keen to please – "

"Yes? What?"

" – Perhaps you'd milk the goats for me."

Charlie threw back his head and laughed.

"I'd milk the billy if you were to ask!"

He took hold of the wheelbarrow and began wheeling it up the field. He walked with just a hint of a swing and, going round to the pig-pen, even hummed a tune to himself. The feeling of freedom was growing on him. He felt immense, like a man reborn.

* * * * *

He lost no time in carrying out his plans, and soon a lorry came to the farm, delivering timber and galvanized iron, bricks and tiles and sand and cement. First he repaired the barn roof and then he began rebuilding the shed.

One morning when Linn, on her way to the dairy, stopped to watch him laying bricks, he spoke to her about George Cressy.

"I wondered if you could give him some work. There are plenty of jobs he could do around here."

"No," Linn said, "he's dangerous."

"There's no harm in George if he's treated right."

"Didn't he burn his face?" she said. "Didn't he get in a fight once and hit a man with a beer-bottle?"

"George wouldn't do half those things if only people would leave him alone."

"That's what I mean to do – leave him alone. I'm certainly

not having him here."

"He lost his job through me," Charlie said, but, seeing that Linn remained unmoved: "No, well, maybe you're right. It was just a passing idea."

The following Friday, after work, Charlie went down to the Hit and Miss to buy a packet of cigarettes. George Cressy was at the bar and was buying drinks for all his friends.

"I've got a job on the railway," he said. "I'm a ganger, I work on the line. It's a full-time job and I get good pay — nearly four pounds with overtime. Better than sweeping the garage, eh?"

"Seems you've done pretty well for yourself."

"The only thing is, I don't like my boss. I'll take a hammer one of these days and lay him out in front of a train."

"You don't mean that," Charlie said.

George merely grinned at him.

"Come and have a drink," he said.

Charlie, however, shook his head. He had no money to spend on drinks. His last few coppers had just gone on a packet of twenty cigarettes.

"No, thanks, George. Not tonight."

"Some other time, then?"

"Ah, that's right."

* * * * *

The shed was rebuilt and the pig-huts repaired; a new concrete floor was laid in the byre; and twenty loads of hardcore, fetched from the Council rubbish-heap, were tipped on to the farm-track to fill up the ruts and pot-holes. But this was only a beginning; there were many more things he wanted to do; and one of his most cherished ambitions was to drain the miry ten acre field, so badly choked with reeds and rushes, and bring it into cultivation.

"But surely that would take years?"

"All the more reason for starting now."

"We've managed without that field so far. I think we're wiser to leave it alone. Cleaning the spring is more urgent than that."

"Yes, you're right," Charlie said, "and getting the water piped down to your dairy."

He was never at a loss for things to do. He kept himself busy from dawn to dusk. And the marvellous part of it all was that he could come and go as he pleased. He had not known such freedom for twenty years; not since his youth on his father's farm; and every single day that dawned was like a splendid holiday, even though he worked so hard.

* * * * *

"I see you've got Charlie milking your goats," Jack remarked to Linn one day. "Seems that chap'll do anything to please you."

"Only so long as he's pleasing himself."

"What do you mean?"

"I never asked him to stop at home and do all these jobs about the farm."

"You'll benefit from it all the same."

"Yes, I daresay," Linn said.

Jack looked at her with a frown.

"It ent all fun and games for him, working without any wages, you know. He never comes to the pub these nights, nor he ent smoked for a day or two. He won't let me treat him. Oh, no, not him! He's earning no money so he goes without."

"And whose fault is that? Not mine!" Linn said. "Charlie's doing what he wants to do."

"That don't make it any less worthwhile."

On the following Friday evening Linn, as usual, paid her father his weekly wage and he prepared to go to the pub. He looked at Charlie, who sat by the fire, hidden behind the Daily Express.

"What about coming down with me? I can afford to stand you a pint."

"Not tonight," Charlie said. "I've got a few jobs to do."

"All right, please yourself, you're an obstinate beggar," Jack said.

The door closed and he was gone. Linn and Charlie were left alone. Charlie got up out of his chair and put his paper under the cushion.

"I reckon I'll get that washtub in that you said needed seeing to."

"Never mind the washtub," Linn said. "You've done quite enough for one day."

She took a pound note from her cashbox and pushed it across the table to him. Charlie looked at her in surprise.

"What's the idea?" he said with a laugh. "I don't want paying for what I've done."

"Why not? You work hard enough. It's only fair that you should be paid."

"Yes, but look here! It's hardly right. I chose to stop and work at home. You were against it. You said so straight."

"It's only for a little while, until you get a proper job."

"Even so," Charlie said. He eyed the money uncertainly.

"Go on, take it, it's yours," she said. "You've got to have something in your pocket to go for a drink on a Friday night. Go after dad and catch him up. You know he likes your company."

"Was it Jack who put you up to this?"

"I don't know why you should think that. I do have some ideas of my own."

"Right, if you're sure, I'll take it, then." He picked up the note and pocketed it. He went to the door for his jacket and cap. "I suppose, now I think about it, the farm can stand it well enough? It won't go broke, anyway, just for the sake of a pound, eh?"

Linn made no answer to this, but looked at him over her spectacles.

"I'll tell you what!" Charlie said. "As soon as I'm in a proper job I'll pay you back what you've given me!"

"Now you're just being silly," she said.

Charlie grinned and went out after Jack.

* * * * *

He had never been a great drinking man, but he liked his pint of beer now and then, and he liked the company at the pub. He and Jack would sit with Sam Trigg in the snuggery at the Hit and Miss and their pints would probably last them an hour.

153

"Your sort'll never make me rich," the landlord, Billy Graves, would say. "All you do is polish my chairs!"

Always, when Charlie went to the pub these days, George Cressy was bound to be there. The burns on his face had healed now but the terrible ugly scars remained and he would carry them all his life. George was proud of these scars of his; he regarded them as emblems of honour; proof of his courage and endurance.

"There's not many chaps who would have the guts to burn theirselves like that," he would say, and his mates in the pub were quick to agree.

"I couldn't do it."

"No, nor me."

"It takes a special sort of man to do a thing like that, George. I reckon you must have nerves like steel."

But Charlie, as he said to Jack, had his doubts about these "mates." George had more money to spend these days; often he ordered drinks all round; and one or two of the younger sprigs had taught him a new accomplishment: to drink a pint of beer at one go and follow it down with a "chaser" of rum.

"Why do you let him drink so much?" Charlie said to Billy Graves. "It'll lead to trouble in the end."

"It's his own money, after all. He can spend it as he likes."

"So long as it ends up in your till?"

"We've all got to live," Billy said. "I'll never get rich on what *you* spend here."

* * * * *

Charlie had been at home for a month and yet there remained a host of things still waiting to be done on the farm. He was busy at this time, fencing the new chicken-ground and moving the hen-coops on to it, and soon, if the weather held good, he would tackle what ploughing had to be done. It was now early March. The ground was beginning to dry out and there was a sweetness in the air. And at Piggotts Farm, Robert reported, the first of the season's lambs had been born.

"I should like a few sheep, myself," Charlie said. "With so

much land lying idle, we could manage a few quite easily – "

"And who would look after them," Linn asked, "when you're back in work again?"

"I daresay I could fit it in."

"When are you going to start looking round?"

"I want to plough the old chicken-ground first and get it sown with turnips and kale."

"Dad did the ploughing last year. Why don't you leave it to him?"

"That was before his heart trouble. I don't think he should do it now. It would be too much for him."

Linn had to admit it was true. Her father was beginning to feel his age, and although he had suffered no more attacks, he became tired more easily.

"It's the spring weather," he would say. "It makes me lapsadaisical."

And Charlie, when he harrowed the chicken-ground, noticed that Jack, at the end of the field, burning the weeds and couch-grass, often paused to lean on his fork.

"Are you feeling all right?" he asked, stopping the horse at the headland.

"Just a bit out of sorts, that's all."

"What did the doctor say to you when you saw him last time?"

"He said I'd probably last for years – so long as I take it easy."

"Then mind and be sure to take his advice."

"That's what I *am* doing," Jack said. "That's why I'm leaning on this fork, instead of walking behind that horse."

There was no bitterness in his tone; only a stolid acceptance of things; and that was the surest sign, Charlie thought, that the old man was feeling his age. But Jack had a quick-seeing eye even now. Nothing much escaped him. He took his pipe out of his mouth and pointed with it at the horse's hooves.

"Simon's got a shoe loose. You'll lose it if you don't watch out. I'll go and get the toolbox."

* * * * *

One Sunday evening Sam Trigg strolled down to see Charlie and Jack and the three of them went to the Hit and Miss. George Cressy was at the bar, already the worse for drink.

"How are things on the line?" Charlie asked.

"Don't mention the line to me! The railway's given me the push! I had a row with Jim Taylor and cracked his rotten skull for him so they gave me my cards and paid me off."

"I'm sorry to hear it," Charlie said.

"You needn't be sorry on my account! The railway ent heard the last of me! I'll get even, you see if I don't!"

"You go easy," Charlie said. "You'll get into trouble, talking like that."

He and Jack and Sam Trigg took their drinks to the snuggery. George Cressy remained at the bar. A few of his usual friends were there and he was plying them with drinks while he told them over and over again of the fight he had with his boss on the line.

"He's pretty far gone," Jack remarked. "Is he speaking the truth, d'you think, about putting that chap in hospital?"

"You never quite know with George," Charlie said.

"He ought to be locked away," said Sam.

The evening passed quietly enough but there came a moment when George found he had spent all his money. He turned his empty glass upside down and looked round at his circle of friends.

"I've treated you lot often enough. It's high time you treated me back."

There were five men in the group at the bar but none was willing to buy him a drink.

"I'm as broke as you are, George. You know how it is with us married men."

"Me, too. I'm just about skint. I only came in for a box of matches."

"Billy will give you a drink on tick if you ask him nicely and don't crack his skull."

"You could always stop and wash out the glasses."

"Or you could pawn your tomahawk."

George Cressy looked at them. His coarse-skinned face was darkly flushed and the scars stood out on his cheeks and forehead.

"It's a very funny thing," he said, "but mates are only mates to me when I've got money to spend on them."

Charlie and Jack and Sam Trigg were on their way towards the door.

"Charlie?" George said. "What about you? Are you going to stand me a drink?"

"Strikes me you've had enough. It's time you thought about going home."

"I don't want to go home!"

"Come outside for a minute, then. I want a private word with you."

George followed them out of the pub and they stood on the narrow pavement. Charlie took two half-crowns from his pocket and held them up for George to see.

"If I give you that, will you go straight home?"

"All right. Whatever you say."

Charlie gave him the five shillings and George put it into his pocket.

"I'm just popping back for one last drink."

"Dammit, George, where's your sense?"

"One drink's all right. There's no harm in that." George was already turning away. "So long, Charlie. Thanks for the sub. I'll do the same for you one day."

Charlie was left with Jack and Sam.

"That warnt very clever of you," Sam said.

"No, I could kick myself," Charlie said.

They walked home together through the gathering dusk.

George, at the bar of the Hit and Miss, had five pints of brown ale lined up, together with five tots of rum. He looked at the group of men nearby.

"I suppose you think I'm treating you, but you can bloody well think again!"

"You're never going to drink that lot yourself?"

"Aren't I, by God? You just watch!"

They watched him drink the first glass of beer and follow it down with a tot of rum. Billy Graves grinned from behind the bar. George wiped his mouth with the back of his hand, reached for his second glass of beer, and raised it slowly to his lips. His audience watched him, cynically, as the beer went gurgling down his throat.

157

"Mad bugger!" one of them said.

* * * * *

At Stant Farm, just before ten, Charlie and Jack were out in the yard, seeing that all the shed-doors were closed. The wind was blowing from the north east and with it came the sound of a goods train rumbling along the valley below.

"There goes the last train for the night." Charlie glanced up at the sky. "It should mean the dry weather will hold, when we can hear them as plain as that."

He and Jack went indoors to bed. Darkness descended on the house. The little farm was at rest for the night.

Down in the winding valley bottom the goods train rumbled on its way, its engine glowing in the darkness, sending sparks into the trees and casting an angry torrid flush on the smoke uncurling from its chimney. Up on the bridge in Ratter's Lane, where the road went over the railway line, a figure stood poised on the parapet, with knees bent and arms outspread, in a position ready to spring.

As the engine passed under the bridge, George Cressy screwed up his face, closing his eyes and holding his breath while the hot smoke swept over him. When the engine had travelled on and the smoke was blowing away on the wind, he opened his eyes cautiously and peered down into the darkness, watching the trucks as they passed below. Nostrils dilated, he took a deep breath, and, uttering a loud blood-curdling cry, leapt from the edge of the parapet, into an open truck full of coal.

Facing towards the rear of the train, he made his way swiftly along it, leaping from one truck to the next and throwing things over the sides as he went. Pit-props and concrete blocks, crates of spring cabbage and boxes of fruit, were thrown on to the sides of the track; and then he came to the iron girders, loaded into the last three trucks: great heavy things, twenty feet long, twelve inches by ten inches; those on top lashed down with ropes. He picked his way over them until he was in the last truck of all and there he loosened the ropes on their cleats.

The train was now passing Scampton Halt. George lifted

one of the girders on to the rear edge of the truck; tilted it from the other end; and sent it screeching over the edge, on to the railway line itself. The train travelled away from it and he saw it glinting in the moonlight. He heaved another girder up and sent it slithering after the first. Sweat started out on his forehead and his breath came noisily from his throat, bursting from nostrils and mouth together, as he heaved the girders on to the ledge and shouldered them over on to the line.

Suddenly the whistle blew. The train was approaching Glib Hill Tunnel. George stepped on to the edge of the truck and dropped lightly on to the line. He scrambled up the steep bank and the trees received him into their shade. The train ran clacking into the tunnel.

* * * * *

Just after six the following morning, Charlie loaded four crates of eggs into the van, and Jack took them down to Scampton Halt. Fred Mitchell, the Halt attendant, should have been there at six o' clock, but more often than not he was late and to save himself trouble he always left the gate unlocked. Jack unloaded the crates of eggs and carried them down on to the platform.

He was not the first to have come to the Halt that morning: two local farmers had been and gone, probably while it was still dark; and four churns of milk from Flag Marsh and two from World's End already stood on the platform's edge, waiting to go on the milk-train from Chantersfield to Kitchinghampton.

Jack set down the crates of eggs and looked at his watch. It was now twenty-past six. He strolled along the little platform and stood at the end of it, lighting his pipe, patiently waiting for Fred Mitchell to come. The sun was up in the sky now, shining along the narrow track and glinting along its pair of rails. A jackdaw was pecking about on the line.

Jack turned and began to stroll back but something, somehow, was troubling him. Something he had seen and yet not seen. He paused and looked up and down the line, shielding his eyes against the sun. Up the line, all seemed

159

well, but down the line something was wrong. Something was gleaming, out of place, and his first quick heart-stopping thought was that one of the rails had been dislodged and was sticking upwards from the track. Then, as his eyes focussed better, he saw that it was an iron girder lying, one end between two sleepers, the other tilted over the rail.

He got down on to the line and ran towards it. He stooped and took hold of its uptilted end and dragged it, screeching, across the rail to send it toppling clear of the track, into the grass at the foot of the embankment. When he stood up there was sweat on his brow and he wiped it away with his jacket sleeve. He put his pipe into his pocket and stood for a moment to recover his breath and then, staring along the line, he saw, a hundred yards further down, another girder lying there.

"God!" he muttered. "How many more?"

He took out his watch and looked at it. It was now six-twenty-six. In twelve minutes' time, at six-thirty-eight, the first train of the day would be passing Scampton Halt, travelling towards Mingleton, and he knew it would be a passenger train. A glance back at the Halt platform told him that Fred Mitchell had not yet arrived. There was no one on hand to help him, and he knew that the nearest signal-box was two miles away, at Upper Royne. So he set off again, down the tracks, boots sometimes pounding the wooden sleepers, sometimes crunching the granite chips; and in his mind one agonized question: how many girders lay on the line?

As he ran along the track he thought he heard the train coming; thought he heard its whistle blow; but it was only his imagination: the noise of the train was in his head. He ran on at a steady pace, heaved the second girder clear, and saw at once that there was a third. With scarcely a pause he carried on. Sweat dripped into his eyes and he blinked it away, shaking his head. His breathing was painfully difficult; he gulped in air through his open mouth but there was no room for it in his chest; his lungs were squeezed against his ribs. His feet and legs had become leaden and three or four time he almost fell, catching his foot against a sleeper and stumbling forward, arms outstretched. But each time he recovered himself and ran on at the same steady pace, telling himself to lift his feet.

Ten girders he removed from the line, heaving each one clear of the track, safe at the foot of the steep embankment. Now he was close to Glib Hill Tunnel. He stood and stared at its round black mouth. Were there more girders inside? If there were, he had done the wrong thing, for a crash in the tunnel would be far worse than any crash out in the open. He went a little way into the darkness, peering along the vanishing track, and then stood still, listening.

This time it was not his imagination. This time he really could hear the train and could feel its vibration in the rails. He returned to the open line again, wondering if he could stop it, but he knew that, rounding the gradual bend, travelling at perhaps sixty miles an hour, the driver would never see him in time. So he stood to one side, in a place of safety, a little way up the grassy track.

He thought the train seemed terribly slow as the engine first hove into sight, coming like fate round the broad bend. He had the strange fancy that it was going to grind to a stop. Then, abruptly, its whistle shrieked; the engine came booming along the track and even in his place of safety Jack felt he was going to be swept away. Its stench in his nostrils. Its din in his ears. Then the engine had gone past him, into the dark mouth of the tunnel, which pressed down on the coil of smoke, sending it rolling and billowing sideways, choking him with its heat and fumes.

There were five carriages in all. He thought he saw faces staring at him. The last carriage passed and he was alone. He listened fearfully, dreading a crash, but the train was running normally and soon he heard the change of sound that meant it had emerged at the end of the tunnel. He listened again, head bent; heard the train running into the distance; and knew that the rest of the line was clear.

When he stepped down from the bank again, his body felt as though it was melting. There was a weakness in his bones, and in his stomach a terrible sickness. With trembling hands he took off his cap and used it to wipe his face and forehead. He stood with it pressed against his eyelids, fighting the darkness that rose like a fog, closing in from the sides of his brain. Suddenly he opened his eyes. His cap had fallen from his hands and now lay on the ground at his feet. He stared down at it, helplessly, knowing he could never pick it up.

Pain had come some minutes before, but he had not acknowledged it. Now it impaled him, spearing his chest, and as it spread outwards, wave upon wave, his left arm became maimed with it, seized, immovable, in its grip. The surging of the pain was stopping his breath. He waited, quite still, for it to pass, but instead it moved in quickening waves, outwards from his overtaxed heart and up to his throat, choking him.

His mouth was open, but he could not breathe. He felt himself splintering, flying to bits. The pain, if it increased any more, would send him spinning from the face of the earth. He took a few paces along the track and felt he was hurtling through empty space. His arms flew up and his hands went out, seeking to ward off the unseen dangers, but what they were he never knew, and the cry that started from his lips was cut off suddenly in a gasp. He fell forward on to his face and lay quite still beside the track, and not very long afterwards the milk-train, emerging from the tunnel, ran slowly past his body. The driver saw him lying there. He reported it when he got to the Halt.

Chapter 10

The funeral expenses were paid by the railway company. An official called on Linn at the farm to offer his condolences and to make the necessary arrangements. It was the least they could do, he said, for the man who, by his selfless action, had prevented a tragic accident.

"If there's anything more we can do, I hope you will let us know, Mrs Truscott."

"No, there's nothing more," Linn said.

The company also sent a wreath: an expensive thing of hot-house lilies, the scent of which was over-sweet and hung heavily on the air in the church. The wreath should have been a solace to her, but the sight of it lying on the coffin made her feel uncomfortable, and Robert put her thought into words when he talked about it, later, at home.

"That wreath seemed all wrong for Granddad, somehow. He was never much of a one for show."

Linn could not get over the manner of her father's death. The thought of it haunted her constantly.

"If only he hadn't been so *alone*!"

"Yes, if only," Charlie said.

"Other people send goods from the Halt. Why couldn't it have been one of them who saw the girders on the line? And if Fred Mitchell hadn't been late – "

"Try not to dwell on it too much, you'll only upset yourself," Charlie said.

At first it was thought that the girders had fallen from the train by accident, but after a while, as gossip spread, it became common knowledge that George Cressy had been responsible. Charlie reproached himself bitterly.

"If I hadn't given him that money to spend, he wouldn't have got so crazy-drunk, and the whole thing might never have happened," he said.

163

"You weren't to know," Linn said. "You did your best to send him home."

Later they read in the newspaper that George had been sent to Gloucester gaol and later still Charlie heard that George, on coming out of gaol, had made his way to Liverpool and "gone as a stoker on the ships." Nothing much was heard of him after that and it was to be five years before he was seen in Scampton again.

* * * * *

Charlie was still working at home. He no longer thought of getting a job. From the day of Jack's death, he had stepped into the old man's shoes, and took it for granted that this state of affairs would now continue indefinitely. It seemed the obvious, most logical course, and sensible in every way. In fact it seemed so obvious that he never thought to discuss it with Linn and when the subject did come up he spoke of it as a settled thing.

"Sometimes I think it must've been fate, my losing my job at the garage like that, as though I was meant to be on hand to take over when your dad died."

It was a wet day in April and he and Linn were in the dairy. Linn was washing the day's eggs and Charlie was sorting them into grades.

"As a matter of fact," Linn said, "I've been meaning to talk to you about that."

"Talk away, then. I'm all ears."

"When you first stopped at home, it was only supposed to be for a while, and then you were going to look for a job."

"But that's all changed now Jack's gone. You can't run the farm by yourself."

"If Robert gave up working at Piggotts, he could help me run the farm."

"That didn't work when you tried it before. Robert didn't care for it."

"He might have changed his mind by now."

"Then why hasn't he mentioned it?"

"He wouldn't like to, while you're at home."

"You mean I'm standing in his way?"

For a moment Charlie remained quite still, frowning at the crock full of eggs. Then his hands resumed their work, grading the eggs into their trays.

"Seems we'd better talk to Rob and get it sorted out with him."

"Yes, I'll ask him," Linn said.

But when she mentioned the matter to Robert he stared at her in astonishment.

"Leave Piggotts? Whatever for? I thought Charlie was running things here?"

"Don't you want to come back and take over running your own farm?"

"Well, I dunno, it all depends." He looked at Charlie uncertainly. "If Charlie's wanting to get a job – "

"That's just your mother's idea," Charlie said. "I'm quite happy as I am."

"Then I don't see what all the fuss is about."

"Is it fussing," Linn said, "to expect my one and only son to take an interest in his own farm?"

"Mother, we've been through this before!" Robert said impatiently. "If I was really needed here, I'd come like a shot, you know I would. But if Charlie's willing to stop as he is – "

"Oh, Charlie's willing enough!" Linn said. "Charlie's already dug in his heels!"

Charlie and Robert looked at each other. The boy was indignant on Charlie's behalf and an angry retort rose to his lips, but Charlie, with a shake of his head, warned him to let the matter drop. He himself spoke in a quiet voice.

"So long as I know where we stand, you and me, I reckon that's all that counts," he said. "Your mother seemed to think I was in the way of your coming back here to work but now I know that isn't true, well, it seems we've sorted it out all right."

"Yes," Robert said, "I reckon we have."

But later, out in the yard with Charlie, the boy mentioned the matter again.

"What's up with Mother suddenly? Why is she making such a to-do?"

"She's still upset," Charlie said. "Your Granddad's death

has hit her hard. She's not too keen on me stepping into his shoes like this, but she'll get over it, given time."

* * * * *

The farm by now was Charlie's whole life and he was full of plans and ideas. He wanted to bring every inch of land under proper cultivation and eventually, when that was done, the farm would be able to carry more stock.

"And where is the money coming from to carry out these schemes of yours?"

"Money ploughed back into the farm is money invested," Charlie said. "Every farmer will tell you that." And then, as Linn remained silent, he said: "Don't you care for my ideas?"

"I don't care for risking my money."

"No, well, that's up to you. You know if the farm can stand it or not."

"While we're on the subject of money, I've been doing some thinking lately, about your getting a job again."

"I thought we'd already settled that."

"*You* may have settled it. *I* have not."

Linn, with her egg-book in front of her, had been totting up the figures in it. Now she paused and looked at him.

"If I got a man to help me here, it would cost me thirty-two shillings a week. *You* could earn more than twice that as a skilled mechanic in a garage somewhere."

"Yes, I suppose that's true," Charlie said, "but money isn't everything."

"Oh, that sounds very fine, I'm sure, but you like spending it well enough!"

"Are you trying to tell me that I'm not really earning my keep by what I do in the way of work?"

"Now you're just putting words in my mouth."

"A man wouldn't do the hours I do, not for thirty-two shillings," he said.

"So long as he did what I asked him to do, I should be quite satisfied."

Charlie got up out of his chair and stood lighting a cigarette, looking down at Linn's bent head as she turned the pages of her egg-book.

"It seems you'd sooner have just about anybody working here, so long as it's not me," he said. "Is it on account of your dad? Because I took over after him?"

"It's because you take over *everything*!" Again she looked up and met his gaze. "First you decide to stop at home and now you're full of big ideas for making changes everywhere! Lately I've begun to feel that it isn't really my farm at all!"

"I made some suggestions, that's all. You soon let me know if they don't suit. You're the gaffer around here. *You're* the one who says what's what."

"And who takes notice of what I say? I want Robert to work the farm but I haven't got my way over that!"

"Robert's made it perfectly plain that it doesn't suit him to work at home."

"But it does suit you?"

"It suits me fine."

"When I first met you, years ago, you said you'd never go back to working on the land again."

"Aren't I allowed to change my mind? I'm going back to my old roots. It's what I was born to, after all."

"What I don't understand is that you should be content to stay at home and draw your wages from your wife."

"What difference does it make? Your dad drew his wages from you and so did Rob while he was here — "

"The difference is this — that *you* are my husband!" Linn exclaimed. "Is it so hard to understand?"

Charlie was silent, looking at her. Then, with a sigh, he turned away and threw his cigarette-end into the stove. After a while he spoke again.

"So long as *I* don't mind," he said, "I don't see why it should worry *you*."

He took out his watch and looked at it. It was time for him to go on his rounds. He went to the door and there he paused.

"It seems to me only common sense that I should work the farm for you, but if you're really against it and the money means as much as all that, well, just say the word and I'll get a job."

But Linn had already said the word and Charlie, she felt,

had chosen to ignore it. She had made her feelings plain enough and he had merely shrugged them aside. Whatever he said about pleasing her, he went his own way and that was that.

* * * * *

Although in time Linn came to accept the situation, her feelings about it remained the same, and she tried to explain them to herself. Charlie, the skilled motor-mechanic, going to his own work every day, had been a man of independence and she had been able to look up to him; but Charlie, working at Stant Farm, relying on her for his living, had forfeited something of her respect; and it was a great disappointment to her that, instead of forging his own way in the world, he had chosen the easier path, content to be her hired man.

Once she tried to explain it to him but he had a knack, somehow, of always putting her in the wrong.

"You mean you thought more highly of me, just because of the money I earnt?"

But he understood well enough what it was she was trying to say. Secretly, in his heart of hearts, he felt the loss of his dignity, but he was building it up again by working extra hard on the farm; by keeping everything spick and span; by making improvements all the time and increasing productivity.

There was good ground lying idle at Stant. They could easily raise a handful of sheep, if only Linn would agree to it, and if he could drain the ten acre field and clear the reeds and rushes there, they would be able to grow more corn. But first money had to be spent. That of course was inevitable.

"I'm not spending money yet," Linn said. "Not till I'm sure I've got it to spend. Perhaps in another year or two, well, then I might consider it."

Charlie's schemes would have to wait. She would have *some* say in the farm's affairs.

* * * * *

As it happened, however, Charlie did not have to wait long for the first of his schemes to bear fruit because in the autumn of that year the Triggs retired from Slipfields and went to live in Scampton and Charlie, who had so often borrowed Sam's horses, was given the chance of buying them.

"He says we can have them for thirty pounds. That's too good a chance for us to miss. They're past their prime, it's true, but they'll be good for a few years yet, to do what horse-work we have here."

Linn, after some thought, agreed, and then Charlie said casually:

"Seems to me a good idea if we buy those few sheep of Sam's as well. He's got twelve ewes and they've been with the ram. That's just the right number to suit us here."

Once again Linn agreed. Plainly the chance was too good to miss. Soon the two horses, Simon and Smutch, were grazing the orchard field at Stant and the twelve ewes, all in lamb, were grazing "the rough" up by the woods.

"So Charlie's got his sheep at last?" Robert said to Linn when they came.

"Haven't you noticed that Charlie always gets what he wants?"

"Born lucky, that's me," Charlie said.

He was proud of his little flock and prouder still when, the following spring, he had fifteen lively lambs in the fold. Only five of these were tups and they were sold in the summer sales. Charlie kept the ewe-lambs and his flock now numbered twenty-two.

"Shall we be able to graze so many?" Linn asked doubtfully.

But it seemed there was no problem there, for Slipfields as yet remained unsold, and Sam had given Charlie permission to let the sheep graze over his land.

"What happens when Slipfields *is* sold?"

"That new ley will be ready by then. There's the orchard, too, to give them a bite. We've plenty of keep, be sure of that, and plenty of kale to help out in winter."

Slipfields stood empty for a whole year. Nobody wanted land these days. Farming had become a dirty word. But

169

then suddenly the place was sold, to a Major Alec Shaw and his wife who came, it was said, from somewhere near London.

Major Shaw was a tall, handsome man in his middle forties who was seen strolling over his fields with a walking-stick and binoculars, pausing every now and then to make notes on a scrap of paper. Mrs Shaw was slight and fair-haired and not too keen on visitors. When Charlie called on them and spoke to the major in the yard, Mrs Shaw kept out of the way, doing something in the barn, and then slipped quietly into the house when she thought Charlie wasn't looking. But Shaw himself was friendly enough.

"I've never farmed in my life before so I shall be keeping an eye on you and picking your brains when I get the chance."

He intended to specialize in poultry, he said, and was starting off in a small way with a few bantams and guinea-fowl. Later he would go in for pigs and of course he would keep a cow or two.

"I may be only a plain soldier, but I've read all the books on the subject, you know, so I daresay I shall muddle along."

"Well, you know where to come," Charlie said, "if you should ever need help."

When he got home afterwards and Linn asked him about Alec Shaw, Charlie could find little to say.

"He seems a nice enough sort of chap. Easy to talk to, anyway. I don't know about his wife. She was busy and kept out of the way."

"Will they be good neighbours, d'you think?"

"He won't be anything like Sam Trigg."

"Surely you must have guessed that when you heard that he was an Army man."

"Yes, well," Charlie said.

"What does that mean?"

"Oh, I don't know . . . There was something about the chap that didn't seem to ring quite true."

Soon it became common talk in the district that "Major" Shaw was a bit of a sham. His rank had been borrowed for show, people said, and some even doubted whether he had been in the Army at all. Charlie's suspicions had been right, it seemed, and whenever he met Shaw afterwards every meeting confirmed them anew.

"He's a chancer and no mistake! The stories he tells would fill a book! He says he was chosen to escort the King and the Prince of Wales when they were out at the Front that time and once, according to what he says, he helped General Robertson to choose a horse!"

Shaw told Charlie he had fought at Mons and been reccommended for the Military Cross. "Only for doing my duty, you know!" But the Military Cross, as Charlie knew, had not been struck until 1915 and that was only one of the slips by which Shaw was revealed as a fraud.

"Still," as Charlie said at home, "so long as he farms his land all right and does something about his thistles, that's all we need worry about Major Shaw."

* * * * *

Thistles flourished at Slipfields and all through that autumn and winter the seed drifted down over Charlie's neat clean fallow lands so that when, in spring, he sowed his turnips and mangolds, the thistles sprang up as thick as thick and hoeing the rows was doubly hard. Once he complained about it to Shaw and the man was full of apologies.

"I suppose I must seem slow to you, but I've drawn up a list of things that need doing, and I'm going through it systematically. The thing is, I need more stock — I'm looking out for a few pigs — but you know how it is nowadays, stretching out your capital."

"We can help you there," Charlie said. "We've got some weaners due to be sold in a week or two. You can buy a couple direct from us."

"Splendid! Splendid! Just the thing!"

Payment for the weaners was slow in coming. The whole of the summer passed by before Major Shaw remembered the debt and then only half of it was paid.

"I'll let you have the remainder," he said, "as soon as I get my bacon-money."

The rest of the debt was never paid and Charlie perceived he had made a mistake. He never fell out with Shaw about it but any help he gave after that was merely in the form of advice.

"What I need," Shaw said, "is a good strong man to give me a hand."

"That's easy," Charlie said. "There are plenty of 'em wanting work."

But here again, when Shaw had a man to do a week's work, he paid only half his wages and promised the rest "at the end of the month."

"That's the sort of man he is," Charlie said to Robert and Linn. "He owes money everywhere and no one will give him credit now. As for running the farm, well, it'd break Sam's heart if he saw it now."

"I see Mrs Shaw on the bus sometimes, going in to the market," Linn said. "She never speaks to anyone and the other women say she's stuck-up. But I don't know. I think she's ashamed. She never has anything much to sell. I don't know how they manage to live."

Charlie had met Mrs Shaw only once, and that was at the Hit and Miss, soon after she had come to Slipfields.

"Shaw got her to play the piano. She was very good at it. She played every tune anyone asked for and we had a regular sing-song. Then Shaw got up and passed round his cap. He did it as though it was just as a joke but he scooped up the money right enough. His wife's never been to the pub again. Like you say, I expect she's ashamed."

* * * * *

Charlie was as busy as ever these days. He had started draining the ten acre field and every spare moment he had was spent in digging new ditches, draining the water from the sour reedy land, into the winding brook below.

Linn was not interested in his schemes. She told him he was wasting his time. But he could not bear to see good land neglected, and all that year he persevered, inspired by the thought of the crops he would grow once the field was sweet and clean.

It was hard work ploughing these ten acres, for the turf

was rough and tussocky and had lain undisturbed for many years, but it was all done eventually and the acid-green of the old grass gave way to the darkness of newly turned soil. Before the field could be sown, however, it needed a heavy dressing of lime, and Linn refused to co-operate.

"It was *your* idea to plough up that land but its *my* money that has to be spent, buying the lime and the seed," she said, "and when it's done where's the point of it all?"

"We could carry more stock for a start."

"The farm is well-stocked enough as it is."

"If I can't get the lime," Charlie said, "all my work will have gone for nothing."

"You should've thought of that before. *I* never asked you to plough up that field."

And of course it was true. There was no denying it. But Robert, seeking his mother out in the dairy, took the matter up with her.

"Why d'you always set your face against everything Charlie wants to do?"

"We don't need that extra ground."

"Why not let Charlie decide that? He's the one that does the work. He's slaved like a black these two or three years, pulling this little farm together, and what thanks does he get from you? – Nothing but jeers and sneers all the time!"

"I don't know why you should take Charlie's side against me."

"I don't want to take sides at all, but I reckon I have to speak my mind. Charlie's been a good friend to me. When I hurt my back that time it was Charlie who got me walking again and that's something I don't forget."

"I know what Charlie did for you. I don't forget it, either."

"Don't you? I ent so sure!" And then, in a gentler tone, he said: "I reckon I've been pretty lucky in the step-father you chose for me and I don't much care for the sharp way you speak to him sometimes nowadays."

"It seems to me a very strange thing that a son should take it upon himself to scold his mother in this way!"

Abruptly she turned to face him, and he looked at her with his deep dark gaze, distressed by the hint of tears in her eyes. But he showed no sign of giving way. It was Linn whose feelings had to yield.

"I suppose you're in the right of it and I'm in the wrong as usual. It always does seem to work out like that." Briskly she resumed her task of cleaning out the separator. "Charlie shall have his way," she said. "Sooner or later he always does."

* * * * *

In October 1937 Robert had his eighteenth birthday and was old enough to go to the pub.

"You know my stepson?" Charlie said to Billy Graves. "He's eighteen today. I've brought him in to celebrate."

"Teaching him the way he should go?"

"Yes, that's right, just a half at a time."

"He won't go far wrong in your company."

"I'll buy you a drink for saying that!"

The pub was busy for a Monday night, because Saturday had been Mingleton Fair Day and now the fair-people, moving on, were encamped for the night on Scampton Green. Many of them were in the bar and Charlie, somewhat carried away, lost a lot of his pocket-money to a man performing the three card trick.

Because of the merry company, and because it was a special occasion, he and Robert remained there until closing-time. By then he had only a shilling left and stopped in front of an old man who had a bunch of coloured balloons, painted with jokes and comical faces, fastened together by their strings.

"I'll give you a bob for the lot," he said.

"Right, they're yours," the old man agreed.

Charlie, rather pleased with himself, carried the balloons triumphantly home, a journey not without its dangers, especially when climbing stiles, but with Robert always close behind, only too ready to lend a hand and make matters more complicated. They had even more difficulty getting the tangled bunch of balloons through the low doorway into the cottage and there was a good deal of laughter between them before, with a final fumbling flourish, Charlie presented them to Linn.

"There you are! Balloons!" he said.

"You're terribly late," Linn said.

"Well, look what I had to carry home!"

"I was getting quite anxious about you both."

"I was getting quite anxious about myself!"

Charlie and Robert exchanged a glance and again the laughter spluttered up.

"Robert's no good, he's drunk," Charlie said.

"And you're quite sober, I suppose?"

"Me? I'm as jober as a sudge!"

"Oh, yes, I can see that!"

"Here, take your balloons," Charlie said.

"I don't want your silly balloons!"

"But I just spent my last bob on them!"

"More fool you, then!" Linn exclaimed.

"Look at this one," Charlie said. He pointed to a round smiling face painted in white on a red balloon. "Don't you think it's like Sam Trigg?"

But Linn refused to look at the balloon. She pushed it aside impatiently.

"Wasting your money on rubbish!" she said. "Keeping Robert out so late, drinking and smoking until all hours!"

"He's got to learn some time, hasn't he? He's eighteen today, that makes him a man. And Billy Graves said to me – "

"I don't want to hear what he said!"

"H'mm," Charlie said, frowning at Robert. "The wind's in the east here and no mistake!" He gave the bunch of balloons a shake and they bobbed about on their strings. "What the hell shall I do with these?"

"Take 'em to bed with you!" Robert said.

"I'll have to put them in the wash-house."

"Shall I come with you and give you a hand?"

"I've got too many hands as it is!"

Charlie bundled his way through the kitchen and out into the wash-house beyond. He removed the wooden lid from the copper and dropped the balloons into it. He did his best to press them down but they only kept bobbing up again, so he put the lid on top of them, leaving it perched at a rakish angle. When he returned to the kitchen, Robert stood on the hearth alone, hands deep in his jacket pockets.

"Mother's gone up to bed," he said.

"Best place for her," Charlie growled.

"I don't think she's too well pleased with us."

"Me, not you," Charlie said. "She thinks I'm leading you astray." He looked at Robert sheepishly. "We didn't have all that much to drink."

"We had what we wanted. There's no harm in that. It's not every day a chap is eighteen."

"I wish I was eighteen again," Charlie said. "A bachelor chap. No cares in the world." He turned to the door and bolted it. "I reckon I'd better go up to bed and put matters right while I've got the chance."

"Goodnight, Charlie."

"Goodnight, young Rob. Don't forget to turn out the lamp."

Linn was already in bed, lying with her face to the wall, when Charlie went quietly into the bedroom. He got no response when he spoke to her so he blew out the candle and undressed in the dark. Groping his way into bed, he sensed that she was still awake, and at first he lay flat on his back, teased by a stirring in his flesh as his shoulder and arm and part of his thigh met and just touched her warm soft body. After a moment he turned on his side and they lay back to back in utter stillness, a little cold space between them where the air ran down under the bedclothes. Was she pretending? He never knew. His eyes closed and he slid into sleep.

* * * * *

In the morning, at breakfast, he defended himself. Robert had already gone to work. He and Linn were alone at the table.

"We were nowhere near drunk, neither of us. We were just a bit merry, that's all. You must've seen *that* often enough, living with Jack all those years."

"There's no need to bring my dad into this."

"At least *he'd* have seen the funny side."

176

"You must have had more than a pint or two if your money's all gone as you say it has."

"That's another tale altogether. I lost a good bit to a fair-chap who was doing the three card trick."

"Does it make it any better that you spent it on gambling and not on drink?"

"No, nor worse, if it comes to that. My money's all gone and that's all-about-it."

"And what'll you do for the rest of the week?"

"I shall grin and bear it," Charlie said.

Money was not that important to him. He would certainly not ask his wife for more. When his last cigarette was gone he would just go without, and as for having a drink now and then, he could take it or leave it, there was no problem there. It was easy enough, he told himself, to get through the week without any money.

On the following Friday, however, when Linn had gone down to the village, the vicar's wife called at Stant, selling poppies for Armistice Day. Charlie had to go indoors and take some money from Linn's cashbox. He wrote a note on a scrap of paper: IOU 2/-; and put it inside with the three poppies.

Linn, coming home from the village, tired, was cross at finding the note in the box.

"Since when has an IOU been needed between a husband and wife?"

"I just wanted to have things straight. It's your money. I owe it to you. You can stop it out of my wages tonight."

But Linn, that evening, paid him full, and he looked at her enquiringly.

"Have you forgotten the sub I've had?"

"Yes," she said, "I've forgotten it."

"Seems I've been forgiven, then, for coming home merry on Monday night?" Lounging back in his chair, he put his money into his wallet, looking at her with his slow-spreading smile. "That's good news. I'm relieved about that. I was wondering what I had to do to get back into favour again."

Linn, with her account-book in front of her, was making an entry on the page. But she was well aware of his gaze and she sent him a bright glimmering glance with just a hint of mockery in it.

"I'll tell you what you can do," she said. "You can get rid of those silly balloons that are bouncing about in my scullery."

Charlie tilted his head and laughed. Her glance had kindled new warmth in him, and his coolness of the past few days, which had shielded him from her disapproval, melted away like snow in the sun. He rose lazily to his feet and, passing close behind her chair, put out a hand to touch her, letting his fingers lightly rest on the smooth soft skin at the nape of her neck.

"There is just one other thing," she said.

"Oh, and what's that?"

"I'd rather you didn't go to my cashbox when I happen to be out of the house."

There was a hard silence between them. Charlie stood looking down at her. Then, at last, he found his voice.

"I wouldn't have gone to it today if it hadn't been that I had no choice."

"No, I know. I realize that. I just thought I'd mention it, that's all."

She was bent over her accounts again and was dipping her pen into the ink. Charlie went out to the scullery and soon there came a series of bangs as, one by one, he burst the balloons. She did not look up when he came back but spoke to him over her shoulder.

"I suppose you feel better, doing that?"

"I'm going down to the Hit and Miss."

"It's getting to be a habit," she said. "Is your money burning a hole in your pocket?"

Charlie went out without answering her.

Chapter 11

1939. A year of world-wide anxiety. The people of England learnt a lot about Europe during the spring and summer that year. Places they had not heard of before now became familiar names and simple maps in the newspapers illustrated their significance.

"Exactly where is Albania?" Linn asked.

"It's between Yugoslavia and Greece," Charlie said. "See, it shows you on the map."

"And what is this big arrow for?"

"It's to show how Italy invaded her."

"Italy? Not Germany?"

"It seems they're both as bad as each other. They're carving Europe up between them and helping themselves to what they want."

"And one of these days," Robert said, "*we* shall be on their chopping-block."

Linn turned from the small map in the newspaper to the large map in the atlas which Charlie had opened on the table before her. Albania, she saw, was a tiny place and quite a long way from Great Britain. She closed the atlas and set it aside and reached for her basket of needlework. She had learned enough geography for one day.

Out in the yard, later that night, Charlie and Robert stood talking together.

"Mother thinks the war won't come. She's not facing up to reality."

"I can hardly believe it myself. I thought we'd dealt with all that but it seems we've got it to do again."

"It'll be my turn this time."

And Charlie, looking at him, was grieved. Robert was now nineteen. Just the age Charlie had been when he had fought in Gallipoli and seen so many comrades die. Was

179

another generation of young men to be swept away like grass into the furnace? Was the whole world to erupt again?

"I went into town today and put my name down on the Army Reserve."

"Shouldn't you tell your mother that?"

"Not till I have to," Robert said.

* * * * *

At the Hit and Miss these nights there was a great deal of war-talk and the chief pundit was Major Shaw.

"Hitler ought to be stopped now before he gets any further," he said. "It's no good throwing the mastiff a bone when he's got his eye on your game birds."

"You going to tackle him yourself, Major?" Billy Graves asked, with a wink all round.

"I should certainly hope to play my part," Shaw replied affably.

"It's easy enough saying Hitler ought to be stopped," said a labourer from Flag Marsh Farm, "but just how is it going to be done?"

"A well-aimed turnip in the right place, that should fix him," somebody said.

"Tie him up to Berenger's bull."

"Get my missus on to him!"

But as that summer passed away, and the newspaper headlines became more stark, and the little maps with their sinister arrows appeared with greater frequency, the general talk began to change; and although there were still plenty of jokes, they now had an underlying grimness, as though they had reached the bedrock of truth. And on Sunday the third of September, the jokes, the rumours, the fears, the ideas, the theories and the prophecies, were overtaken by reality. England and Germany were at war.

* * * * *

Robert was called up immediately. He had to report at the Drill Hall in Baxtry and from there he would go into training at an Army camp in the north of England.

180

"But you don't *have* to go!" Linn said. "If Mr Madge was to speak for you, you could get exemption, I'm sure you could!"

"There are plenty of older men there who can do my job until I come back."

"Won't you even ask Mr Madge? Not even for my sake?"

"Mother, you don't seem to understand – "

"It's you that doesn't understand! *I* was a nurse in the last war, out in France, in the thick of it! I know better than you what it's like!"

"And why did you go as a nurse?" he asked. "You felt you had to, didn't you? Well, that's what I feel about going to fight, and nothing you say will change my mind."

In no time at all he was gone. Linn and Charlie were left alone and her bitterness overflowed on him.

"If you were in a proper job, Robert would still be here," she said. "He'd have had to stay to run the farm."

"I guessed you were thinking that," Charlie said.

"Of course you guessed! It's true, that's why!"

"Rob would have gone just the same, whether I was here or not."

"What makes you so sure?"

"I know our Rob."

"And I don't? My own son?"

"Seems like that by the way you talk."

Linn's gaze fell before his. She knew he was only speaking the truth. Nothing would have kept Robert at home.

"I'm sorry I said those things to you."

"That's all right," Charlie said. "I know you don't mean them half the time."

* * * * *

Linn became resigned in time and when Robert came home on leave, she welcomed him with a smiling face, betraying only a mother's pride at seeing him in his uniform.

"How handsome you look! And how smart!" she said. "And how lucky you managed to get your leave just in time for your birthday!"

Robert was twenty that October but looked a lot older

than his years. She felt a little shy with him until he changed into old corduroys and gave her a hand in the dairy, and then he was just her son after all, teasing her in his quiet way and looking down at her from his great height.

He still played his boy's tricks on her: hanging her skimmer up out of reach and putting potatoes into her shoes; but he would never really be a boy to her again. He was now a soldier and she looked at him with new eyes. In his hands, and in the hands of others like him, lay England's defence against the enemy and, God willing, her deliverance.

"What do you do in the Signals?"

"I'm learning to operate radio. Setting up field communication systems and that sort of thing."

"Over there, in France," she said, "in the trenches, eventually?"

Robert and Charlie exchanged a smile.

"There'll be no trench-fighting this time, mother. Everything's mechanized nowadays. Tanks. Aeroplanes. Long-range guns. It'll all be quite different this time."

"But there'll still be danger, won't there?"

"Not in the Signals," Robert said. "It's a cushy number, as they say."

Linn did not believe him, but she asked no further questions. Instead she talked about the farm and when his forty-eight hours were up she sent him away with butter and eggs and pots of home-made damson jam.

* * * * *

During the first months of the war, rumours abounded in Scampton and the district around, but all were without foundation. No hordes of enemy aeroplanes had come to bomb the towns and cities. No enemy troops had been dropped by parachute out of the sky. Nor had any spies been caught trying to blow up the Mingleton Power Station. The war as yet, in those early days, was being fought a long way off, and only its terrible tragic echoes were heard in quiet English homes when people read their newspapers or listened to their wireless sets.

Still, the war brought changes, nevertheless, and these

could be noted everywhere. Sign-posts had been rooted up and place-names removed from railway stations, and many goods trains nowadays carried mysterious humped-up loads covered over with camouflage sheeting. More barges were seen on the river; land-girls arrived to work on the farms; and an aerodrome was being being built somewhere outside Chantersfield. Windows were blacked-out everywhere and the nights were lit only by the moon and the stars.

Winter that year was very severe. There were heavy falls of snow, followed by prolonged frosts, and Charlie had his work cut out, protecting the poultry from the cold and the danger of marauding foxes. Animal-food was in short supply and when the last of the kale was gone there was nothing left for the pigs to eat. He had to watch them in their pens, noisily sucking pebbles and stones and spitting them out, as though in reproach, into the empty feeding-troughs. And as soon as the worst weather was over, making the roads passable, there was only one course open to him: he had to call the butcher in.

"The government keeps asking us to step up production but how are we to do that when we can't get the food to fatten our pigs?"

"Don't ask *me*!" the butcher said.

*　*　*　*　*

During the spring, at lambing-time, Charlie was out at all hours, with his ewes in the lambing-fold. Some nights he never slept at all for he had joined the Civil Defence and was on duty two nights a week patrolling up on Flaunton Heath. Every Saturday afternoon he drilled with the other volunteers on Scampton Green. He had a steel helmet and an arm-band but no uniform as yet and he drilled with a broomstick on his shoulder because there were not enough rifles to go round.

"Drilling again!" he said to Linn. "That takes me back a tidy few years! I can almost smell the barrack-square!"

Among the Civil Defence Volunteers there was a familiar scarred face. George Cressy was back from his travels. He greeted Charlie as an old friend and appeared to have sobered down a little.

"I don't get into fights any more. I'm saving it up for when the Jerries come. I'll soon show *them* a thing or two!"

Charlie mentioned George to Linn.

"It seems to have done him a bit of good, knocking about the world like that. It's knocked a few of the corners off."

"Don't speak to me about that man."

Linn at this time was unhappy and Charlie knew why. Robert had been due home on leave, but at the last minute he had written to say that he was spending it with a friend, climbing the hills in Cumberland.

"That's disappointing for us," Charlie said, "but I'm glad our Rob is making friends and enjoying himself while he's got the chance."

"Before he's sent abroad, you mean?"

"No, I wasn't thinking of that. Just getting about and seeing new places, that's all I meant."

"But he will be sent out, eventually?"

"Try not to worry too much about that. You only get yourself upset."

"How can I help worrying? It's easy enough for you to talk. You're so wrapped up in your work on the farm, you never think of anything else!"

Charlie turned away with a sigh. He could not come close to her at this time. Her disappointment was too intense.

"Talking about the farm," he said, "the man from the War Ag is coming today so I'd better get on about my jobs so that I'm finished when he comes."

* * * * *

Many farmers in the district resented the War Agricultural Executive Committee, which told them how much stock they must keep and exactly what crops they must grow in their fields. They called it the War Aggravation Committee and one farmer at Upper Royne had ordered its representative off his land with a loaded shotgun.

But Charlie, when the War Ag official called at Stant, welcomed him with open arms. He conducted the man all over the farm; watched him testing samples of soil; and gave him all the help he could. When at last it was all over and the man had written out his directives, Charlie shook him by the hand, watched him drive away down the track, and went indoors to talk to Linn.

"We've got to plough forty acres!" he said. "Just think of that! Four fifths of our land! Potatoes! Corn! Sugar-beet! All sorts of things we've got to grow and I've got to get my skates on if I'm to get it all done this spring!"

Charlie was in a state of excitement. He riffled through his official "forms" and spread them out on the kitchen table, jabbing his finger at this one and that, and showing Linn his "authorities" for obtaining fertilizers and seed and the loan of a War Ag tractor and plough.

"He seemed a decent, sensible chap. And he knows what he's doing, I will say that, not like the chap they had at World's End."

Linn put on her spectacles and bent over the printed forms.

"I wonder he didn't ask to see me. It does just happen to be my farm."

"Why didn't you come out? You knew he was coming at two o' clock."

"You should have brought him in," she said.

"Yes, well, maybe I should, but I didn't think you were interested."

"Not interested?" she exclaimed. "When the whole farm is going to be changed and pulled about around my ears?"

"It won't be changed that much. The sheep will have to go, of course, but we shall still keep the poultry and maybe get a few pigs again. It's just that we've got to expand a bit and cultivate every inch of ground. I've always wanted to plough up more land – "

"And now you're happy! You're getting your way!"

"Look," Charlie said in a quiet voice. "The War Ag decides what we shall grow and we've got no choice but to do as they say. I don't deny it pleases me. I'm about as pleased as Punch – or I was until a moment ago when you started pitching into me – but all that is beside the point. There happens to be a war on and we've got to do what we're damned well told!"

He began to gather up the papers, drawing them into a neat pile, but Linn reached out to take them from him.

"I haven't read them yet," she said, "and they do concern me, after all."

"Read them by all means," Charlie said. He bundled the papers into her hands. "And the next time the War Ag man comes round you can damned well deal with him yourself and pass his orders on to me. Then when it's been through the proper channels – Home Office, War Office, House of Lords, – maybe you'll be satisfied and *I* can get on with doing the work!"

He snatched up his cap and went to the door and there he paused looking back at her.

"I know what's started you off like this. It's because young Rob is not coming home. Well, I don't blame him, not one jot! He knows how it is with you and me – how we're at odds so much of the time – and I tell you straight I'm not surprised if he chooses to spend his leave elsewhere!"

He went back to his work in the fields and his anger stayed with him, hour by hour, the taste of it lingering on his tongue, its bitterness like a purge in his blood. But after a time his mood changed and he was filled with self-disgust. Why, in hitting out at her, had he chosen the cruellest of weapons? Why had he mentioned Rob at all? It would be difficult to face her now. He shrank from it and hated himself. Yet face her he must, without delay, or the quarrel would only harden between them and misunderstandings would only grow worse.

* * * * *

"I'm sorry I brought Rob into it. I shouldn't have done, I realize that. I've come in to try and put things right."

"You can't rub it out, like words on a slate. My memory's not so convenient as that."

"At least you could try to understand. If you hadn't pitched into me about the man from the War Ag – "

"Where's the point in saying you're sorry when all the time you think I'm to blame?"

"I reckon maybe we're both to blame. The things we say to each other sometimes . . . And it's nothing new, either, is it? We've been at odds like this for years."

"Have we?"

"You know we have."

Charlie, with his hands in his trousers pockets, stood watching her lighting the fire. He tried to think of the right thing to say.

"I made a mistake, didn't I, stopping at home to run the farm? I should've done what you wanted me to do and got a job as mechanic somewhere."

"It's a bit late to be saying that now."

"I did what I thought seemed best at the time."

"You did what you wanted to do," Linn said.

"That doesn't necessarily mean it was wrong."

"Anyway, it's all in the past."

"No, it isn't, it's always there. It comes between us all the time. I remember what you said to me, years ago, when we talked once before. You said you had more respect for me in the days when I went out to work and earnt good money of my own. That's still the trouble, even now. The respect has gone, hasn't it? I thought, by working hard on the farm, I could maybe win it back again, but it seems as though I made a mistake."

"Where's the point in talking like this?"

"I hoped it might help to clear the air. – Put things right before it's too late."

"Too late? What do you mean? Are you making some kind of threat?"

"All I'm trying to say is, the way things are between us now, that'll go from bad to worse if we don't do something to put it right."

Linn put more coal into the stove and pulled the kettle onto the hob.

"I suppose you want me to pat you on the head and say it was my fault all the time and not to worry any more about it?"

"Is that how you see me? As a small boy?"

"How do you see yourself, I wonder?"

"I see myself as your husband," he said. "I see us

187

together, man and wife, working together and running the farm. But it isn't often like that now. We don't pull together. We're always at odds."

"And whose fault is that? When that man called here today you didn't even bother to fetch me out."

"I've already said I'm sorry for that."

"You're always leaving me out of things. You seem to forget the farm is mine."

"Not much chance of forgetting that when you're always throwing it up to me!"

The words slipped out against his will. His good intentions were going astray and anger was rising in him again. He made an effort to fight it down.

"You say I keep you out of things but what about you? When you first bought the farm I used to help you with the accounts but now you keep it all to yourself."

He looked at her sadly, appealing to her, but she was busy about the range, opening the damper to heat the oven ready for cooking the evening meal.

"You shut me out all the time," he said. "You make me feel – oh I don't know! – as though I'm nothing to you any more. Nothing much more than a hired hand."

"Now you're just being silly," she said.

Turning away from the range, she glanced through the window, into the yard, where the two horses, Simon and Smutch, were eating the ivy on the wall.

"You've left the horses out," she said. "Hadn't you better see to them?"

He went without another word.

*　*　*　*　*

At least there was always plenty of work to keep him occupied at this time. No sooner had the War Ag tractor arrived than he was sitting up in its seat, ploughing the slopes of the Spring Field. Day after day, while the weather held, he was out breaking new ground, pausing only to snatch a quick meal and then rushing back to work again.

Sometimes he even worked at night; ploughing, harrowing, drilling corn; and Linn, lying alone in bed, was unable to sleep for the noise of the tractor churring out in the fields in the dark.

"Do you have to work at night?"

"Yes, if I'm to get done in time."

"Well, if you want to kill yourself – "

"I'm not so easily killed as that."

He could not rest, all through that spring, but was on the move like a man possessed, filled with a passion to get things done.

"It suits you, this war, doesn't it?"

"You'll be saying I started it next," he said.

As soon as the corn was safely sown, he was busy planting potatoes, and to help him he had three men from the village. Linn looked out and saw them at work in the field on the far side of the track. She heard their voices, distantly, and sometimes the sound of merriment.

"Who are those men you've got working with you?"

"Does it matter who they are?"

"The one with his hair cropped short," she said. "It's George Cressy, isn't it?" And when Charlie failed to answer: "That man caused my father's death. Why do you bring him to work on my farm?"

"I've got to take what men I can get."

It was perfectly true. Labour was difficult nowadays. But to Linn it seemed as though Charlie went out of his way to do those things she hated most and she could scarcely speak to him until George Cressy, with his brutish, scarred face, had finished his work and gone from the farm.

* * * * *

Charlie, calling at the Hit and Miss for the first time in weeks, caught up on the local news.

"I suppose you've heard Major Shaw is gone?"

"Gone? Where to?"

"Gone to win the war for us!"

"Good God!" Charlie said.

"I hear he's left a few bills unpaid so he's not too popular round about."

"What about his wife?"

"She's still up at the farm," Billy said. "I thought you'd have known, being neighbours of theirs."

"No, I've been busy," Charlie said.

At home he talked about it to Linn.

"I don't know how she's managing, stuck up at Slipfields by herself. The Major must be off his head, going and leaving her like that."

"Maybe you ought to call on her and see if she needs any help."

"Yes," Charlie said, "maybe I should."

When he went up to Slipfields, however, he found he was not welcome there. Mrs Shaw was in the yard, carrying pails of mash for the hens, but she set them down when she saw him coming and stood with her hands on her hips, easing the stiffness in her back. Her fair-skinned face was pinched and worn and there were dark rings under her eyes. She stood without speaking as Charlie came up.

"I heard your husband had gone," he said. "Is it true?"

"Oh, yes, it's perfectly true." She looked at him with hostile eyes. "I suppose you've come like all the rest to say he owes you money?" she said.

"Why, no," Charlie said. He was taken aback. "I came to see if you needed help."

"No, thanks, I can manage," she said.

"I'm not so sure about that." Charlie looked round at the mess in the yard: pig-muck heaped against a wall; doors hanging askew on the sheds; scraggy chickens pecking about, even in the house itself; and the carcasses of two dead piglets lying on an ash-heap near the door. "It looks as though things had got on top of you here."

"If they have, that's my affair."

"It might be mine later on." He pointed towards the nearest field, where thistles and docks and charlock were already growing three feet high. "That'll mean extra work for me when those weeds of yours sow themselves over my land."

"So you've really come to lodge a complaint?"

"I've just come as a neighbour, that's all, to give a hand if you needed it."

"I've managed without my neighbours' help so far and I

shall continue to do so," she said. "Please go away and leave me alone."

"Right!" Charlie said. "Whatever you say!" He had not expected such treatment as this. "I'm sorry I troubled you, Mrs Shaw. I'll bid you good day."

He carried his indignation home.

"I made a mistake going there. She'll just have to get on with it. But she'll find herself in the soup pretty soon when the War Ag man sees the state of that place."

"Did you warn her of that?"

"I didn't get the chance," he said. "All I got was a flea in my ear."

"She's probably upset at her husband going off like that. Perhaps if I went up myself . . . "

"Try it by all means," Charlie said. "At least you know what to expect."

But when Linn went up to Slipfields, she found the door closed against her, and received no answer to her knock.

"I have a feeling she was there and just didn't want to see me."

"Well, no one can say we haven't tried. If she wants to shut herself up like that – "

"She's certainly a very strange woman."

"What did I tell you?" Charlie said. "If you'd heard the way she spoke to me! I might've been something the cat had brought in by the way she looked down her nose at me!"

"She had no right to treat you like that when you were only trying to help."

"No, well," Charlie said. "She'll have to manage as best she can."

It was a long time since he and Linn had talked like this. They were drawn together, in agreement for once, by the strange behaviour of Mrs Shaw, and Linn even gave a little shocked laugh when Charlie said in a cynical way that perhaps the Major had had good cause for going off and leaving her.

"I shouldn't care to live up there, with chickens in and out of the house, pecking about on the kitchen table."

"Now you're just making it up!"

"Oh no I'm not. It's true, every word. The door was open

and I saw it myself."

"I suppose she just can't cope with it all. Perhaps if you were to go up again, now she's had time to think about it, she might be a bit more sensible."

"What, go up there a second time, just to get my head bitten off? No, not likely! That's asking too much."

But after a while, as Linn persisted, Charlie gave in and agreed to go. He felt he could do anything when he and Linn were at one like this; talking together so comfortably; looking at things in the same way and finding something to laugh about. He felt a new surge of confidence that their old understanding would be restored and that all the niggling grievances that had somehow grown up in the past few years would now be put away at last.

"All right, I'll go. But only because you ask me, mind! If the decision had been mine I'd have left her to stew in her own juice!"

* * * * *

This time, when he called on Mrs Shaw, she was trying to work the pump in the yard. He could hear it as he walked up the fields and he knew straight away that something was wrong. The woman was merely exhausting herself. She thought by working the handle hard she could bring the pump to life for her but Charlie could tell that the valve had gone.

At sight of him she stood quite still. Her face was shiny with perspiration and she was too breathless to speak at first. She looked at him with tired acceptance, pushing at the strands of straight fair hair that clung about her forehead and eyes.

"You seem to be having trouble," he said.

"I think the well has run dry."

"No, there's plenty of water there, but you need a new foot-valve."

"How do you know?"

"I can tell by the sound."

"It means getting a plumber, then?"

"No, I can do it," Charlie said. "I've got a spare valve at

home. I'll nip back and get it. It won't take long."

When he returned with the spare valve, the woman was no longer in the yard, but was out in the paddock, feeding the hens. He removed the stone slab that covered the well and lowered himself into it until he was standing on the wooden beam set in the stonework at either side. Ten or twelve feet below the water reflected a fragment of sky. He took a spanner from his belt and began loosening the joints on the pipe and while he was busy doing this Mrs Shaw returned to the yard and stood leaning over the well.

"It's terribly deep down there."

"Plenty of water, though, like I said."

"Supposing you were to fall in?"

"I reckon I'd very likely drown."

"Why, can't you swim?" she asked, alarmed.

Charlie, as he worked with his spanner, cocked an eye at the water below.

"I don't think I should get very far. There's not much room to strike out down there."

"I wish you'd answer me seriously. If you should slip and fall in, I want to know what I ought to do."

"You should send for the Fire Brigade straight away. There's nothing like a dead man for ruining your water supply."

"I see you're determined to have your joke."

"May as well – while I've still got the chance!"

"Can I do anything to help?"

"Yes, you can take hold of this," he said.

He passed the pipe up to her and swung himself up out of the well. She watched while he replaced the valve and when he was in the well again she lowered the pipe down to him, staying to watch while he fastened the joints. Ten minutes later, having first primed the pump, Charlie was working the squeaky handle and water was gushing from the spout, filling the bucket underneath and overflowing into the trough.

Watching Helen Shaw's face as the water came gushing out of the spout Charlie could see that, in trying to work the pump, she had spent the last of her strength and courage. At sight of the water she was almost in tears, and although she quickly recovered herself, glancing away and blinking her eyes, she could not hide what it meant to her to see the water flowing again.

"How long had you been struggling with it?"

"Oh, I don't know! Hours!" she said. She gave a little breathless laugh. "I tried yesterday and today. I kept on trying – . It was silly of me."

"You should have come and asked for help."

"After what I said last time?"

"I reckon we'll forget about that."

"You're being more kind than I deserve."

"Got any more buckets to fill?"

"I think I can manage now," she said.

"I may as well do it, while I'm here."

He worked at the pump for twenty minutes. He carried water to the boiler-house, where she was mixing swill for the pigs, and he filled every drinking-trough he could find. He then went to work on the muck in the yard, forking it into a wheelbarrow and wheeling it into the nearest field, and as he passed to and fro, he noted the things that needed doing. The sow in her pen had ten piglets and he saw that four of them were boars: they would have to be castrated soon. There was a sickly cow in calf in one of the old ruined sheds and it looked as though she would soon be calving. As for the poor scraggy fowls that roamed about all the over place, something would have to be done about them if they were to earn their keep, he thought.

But there was little stock on the farm and Mrs Shaw, showing him round afterwards, explained why.

"I had to sell a lot of things. There were certain bills to be paid. But perhaps it's just as well, after all, now that feed is hard to get."

"Well, so long as you can keep going all right . . ." Charlie looked at the tumbledown fields. "But you'll have the War Ag up here soon. I'm afraid they won't like what they see."

"They've already been twice," she said. "I saw them coming and stayed in the house. They pushed some papers under the door but I haven't dared to look at them."

"They're bound to catch up with you in the end. Then what are you going to do?"

"I don't know." She gave a shrug. "I'll cross that bridge when I come to it."

The future, he saw, was too much for her. She lived her life one day at a time. And whatever despair she felt when alone, with him she was putting up a show, giving a smile as though to say, "What does it matter, anyhow?" He wanted to ask about her husband but he felt that this would be tactless, so he merely took his leave of her and said in a casual, off-hand way:

"I'll come up again when I've got the time and give you a hand with this and that. But if you need me in a hurry, you've only got to come and ask."

"Yes. Thank you. You're very kind." She took a purse from her apron-pocket and undid the clasp. "I haven't paid you for the valve."

"I don't remember how much it cost."

"Please. Do try. I'd rather pay."

"Call it a couple of shillings, then."

She paid him and he went off home.

* * * * *

Linn had gone into town that morning. She came back at twelve o' clock.

"Did you go and see Mrs Shaw?"

"Yes, and a lucky thing I did." He told her about the faulty pump. "She was about done in with it all. It's like you said, she really can't cope. I reckon she'd have killed herself if she'd gone on trying to work that pump."

"What a good thing you went," Linn said.

"What a good thing you sent me!" he said.

He was often at Slipfields after that. He went once or twice a week and did those things he had seen needed doing. He dealt with the boar piglets; helped the sickly cow to calve; and mended the doors on the sheds. Often he mucked out the pigs for her and once he cleaned the kitchen chimney, which was so terribly choked with soot that she had not lit a fire for six weeks. During that time she had had no hot food. She had lived on bread and cheese and milk.

"I don't think you eat well enough."

"Oh yes I do. I eat what I need."

"At least you'll be able to cook something now, even if it's only eggs."

"Yes, if the chickens lay for me."

"Ah, we must see about *them*!" Charlie said. "Get them to buck up their ideas a bit. Don't they know there's a war on?"

Once she said to him, rather shyly, that since she could not afford to pay him for the work he did, she would like him to take two or three piglets, once they were of an age to be weaned.

"I don't want paying for what I do. An hour or two's work! What is there in that?"

"But you've got so much to do on your own farm and then to come up here as well – "

"Poof!" he said, dismissing it. "It's nothing to a man like me!"

He was never shy with her. He already felt that he had her measure; knew how to deal with her independence and how to turn her objections aside; and he found he could always make her laugh. Once he took his scythe with him, to cut the thistles in the fields; she saw him coming, a long way off, and when he arrived at the yard gate, she was there to open it, laughing at him as he passed through.

"What's the big joke?" he asked.

"You with that scythe!"

"Old Father Time, that's me," he said. "The end is in sight for those thistles of yours!"

Laughter transformed her pale thin face and sometimes he caught a fleeting glimpse of the beautiful girl she must have been before marriage and anxiety had brought her to her present state.

"Do you ever hear from your husband?" he asked, when he felt he knew her well enough.

"Yes, I've had two letters," she said. "He's staying in London, with some friends. He says he's working for the Ministry. Intelligence work. Very hush-hush. He can't tell me more than that, he says."

"Ah," Charlie said. "Yes. I see."

Helen Shaw looked at him. Her eyes were a very clear blue.

"It's all a story, of course," she said. "I daresay you know what Alec is like. He lives in a world of make-believe."

"What's he really doing, d'you think?"

"Barman in a pub or club somewhere. That's his usual stand-by."

"I suppose he'll turn up here again one day?"

"If I'm still here, I suppose he will."

"Why, are you planning to move?" Charlie asked.

She gave a little hopeless shrug.

"When the War Ag people catch up with me, I shall have no choice about it. I can't farm this place as it ought to be farmed and they'll turn me out neck and crop."

"It might not be as bad as that."

But Charlie knew what she said was true. The W.A.E.C. had the power to requisition neglected land and evict the farmer at a month's notice and it was only a question of time before Slipfields came under their scrutiny.

"What'll you do? Where will you go? Have you got any family?"

"I've got an aunt in Hertfordshire. She might have me, for the rest of the war, and I would have to get a job."

"But you mean to stay, till they turn you out?"

"I don't know. I shall have to see." Again she shrugged

and gave a smile. "I've lost the will to make plans," she said.

* * * * *

Sometimes as he worked, cutting the thistles, she would come and watch him. She would stand looking over the gate and he, as he moved from one clump to the next, would glance up and see her standing there. Then perhaps when he looked again she would have gone; he would hear the clatter of pails in the yard and the grunting and squealing of the pigs as she tipped their food into the trough; or he would hear the squawk of the hens as she chivvied them from their nests in the barn.

She, as she went about her chores, would hear him sharpening the blade of his scythe. The sound of it travelled down from the fields, *wheep-whaup, wheep-whaup, wheep-whaup*, echoing all around the yard and following her wherever she went. Charlie knew she could hear him; he would give the scythe an extra rub; and when at last he had made her glance up, he would wave to her and go on with his work.

By now he felt he knew her well and his feeling for her was one of pity. He was struck by the loneliness of the life she lived, stuck away up here on this farm, where she never really seemed to belong. And when he had finished his stint for the day he would stop and talk to her.

"Have you heard from your husband lately?"

"Yes, I had a post-card. He hopes I'm managing the farm all right."

"He should be here to see to it."

"Alec has always been like that. Always full of wonderful schemes for setting himself up in business – usually with someone else's money. Once it was a newspaper shop. Then it was a private hotel. Another time it was breeding dogs. But none of his schemes ever worked. We've cleared out of a dozen places, up and down the country, and we've left a trail of unpaid debts. Then he decided he wanted to farm . . . He pictured himself as a country squire . . . "

"Where did he get the money from?"

"He said he won it on a horse."

"Wasn't it true?"

"I don't know. I haven't known what to believe since I married him fifteen years ago."

"What about his Army career?"

"He *was* in the Army, for ten months. A second-lieutenant, in 1919. But there was some unpleasantness . . . Something to do with the mess funds . . . That was before I knew him and I only heard of it afterwards, from someone else. He told me, when I met him, that he had served all through the war and he's kept up the story ever since."

"He's not very good at it," Charlie said.

"No, I know," she said with a smile, and then, looking at him, she said: "I suppose I'm being disloyal, talking about Alec like this?"

"Sometimes it helps to talk," Charlie said.

They had been leaning on the gate. Now he moved and took up his scythe, placing it carefully over his shoulder, the blade pointing safely down behind.

"Here I go! Old Father Time! Anno Domini, that's me!"

He always tried to leave her with a smile on her lips. He hoped that his nonsense and his jokes, and the brief spell of companionship, would tide her over till he came again. She saw nobody but him. He was her only link with the world.

Sometimes he talked about her to Linn.

"Couldn't you go up and see her? That'd make a change for her, having a woman to talk to sometimes."

"Yes, of course," Linn said, "if you think I'll be welcome there."

But she never went. There was never time.

"I've got my hands full nowadays, filling in all these forms," she said.

But Charlie felt it was just an excuse.

"You could make time if you really tried." One day when he went up to Slipfields Mrs Shaw had received a letter from the W.A.E.C. .

"They say they're sending a man to see me at nine o'clock on Tuesday morning and if I'm not here to speak to him they are going to summons me."

"I've been thinking about that."

"And I've been avoiding thinking about it!"

"What if I was to be here when he comes, as a neighbour, to give my advice?"

"Do you think it would do any good?"

"I don't know. We'd have to see. We might be able to work something out, if you still want to stay here, that is." Charlie looked at her searchingly. "*Do* you want to stay?" he asked.

"Well!" She gave a little laugh. "It *is* a roof over my head!"

"Right, I'll come along, then," he said.

* * * * *

When he was setting out for Slipfields, just before nine on Tuesday morning, Linn came and asked him to move the separator and butter-churns out of the dairy because she was going to whitewash the walls.

"I can't do it now," Charlie said. "I'm just off to Slipfields to see Mrs Shaw. The War Ag man is coming this morning and I said I'd be there to see fair play."

"But it won't take you more than ten minutes."

"Ten minutes will make me late. I said I'd be there on the dot at nine."

"Oh, very well, never mind."

"I promised, you see."

"Yes, I see."

"I shan't be gone long. I'll move those things when I come back."

"Yes, all right."

Linn, however, was impatient to start. She had already cleared the dairy out, removing everything she could carry, and had even mixed the bucket of whitewash. She looked at the separator and the churns, which stood in her way close to the wall, and made up her mind to move them herself.

Charlie, coming home at half-past-ten, took her to task for what she had done.

"Moving those great heavy things!" he said. "Couldn't you wait an hour or two?"

"No, I wanted to get on."

"You might have hurt yourself, doing that."

"I didn't, however, as you see." Linn, slapping whitewash on to the wall, spoke to him over her shoulder. "What did the War Ag have to say? Are they turning Mrs Shaw out?"

"No, I've fixed it up," Charlie said. "They'll serve her with their cultivation orders but I shall do the work for her. The chap was quite agreeable and when it comes to seed and that they've got a deferred payment scheme. They'll loan me a tractor, as before, and I shall start ploughing as soon as I can."

Linn had stopped work and was looking at him. It was a while before she spoke.

"Was that Mrs Shaw's idea?"

"No, it was mine. I've had it in mind for quite a time."

"Why didn't you mention it?"

"There didn't seem any point until I knew what the chap had to say."

"What you really mean is that you wanted to get it all settled before finding out what I thought of it."

"Why, have you any objections, then?"

"It's late in the day to ask that now. You say you've already fixed it up. And if you can work both farms all right – "

"Oh, yes, there's no problem there. I shall have to have help, of course, but the War Ag will see to that. Why, with Slipfields and Stant put together, it's only ninety acres in all. I can surely manage that!"

Charlie went off, whistling a tune, and she heard him busy about the yard. She dipped her brush into her bucket and slapped the whitewash on to the wall. Yet another decision had been taken and she had been left out of it. Her anger and resentment grew.

At the end of the morning, when she had finished her white-washing, she went out to the yard and began dragging a butter-churn back into the dairy. Charlie saw and came running to help.

"I told you to leave that job to me!"

"I may as well get used to doing things for myself," she said, "seeing you're going to be so busy at Slipfields soon."

Charlie stood still, his hands on the churn, looking at her with a sharp frown.

"I shall never be so busy," he said, "that I can't do things for my own wife."

"Oh, a very pretty speech indeed!"

"Damn it all!" he exclaimed. "It was your idea in the first place that I should go and help Mrs Shaw."

"I didn't say you should run the whole farm for her!"

"She certainly can't do it herself. Not as the War Ag want her to ."

"What about that husband of hers? He's the one who should run the farm."

"He's not there, though, as you well know. She's got no one to turn to, only me. And he's not much of a mucher, anyway, from what I hear."

"You only hear Mrs Shaw's side of that."

"I'm talking about his running the farm. We know he was no good on that score. He always left the work to her."

Charlie lifted the butter churn, on its heavy oakwood frame, and carried it to its place in the dairy. Linn followed with her milking-pail and set them down on the bench.

"Are we quarrelling again?" he asked.

"*I'm* not quarrelling!" Linn exclaimed.

"Well, I'm surely not quarrelling by myself."

"The trouble with you is, you never think! What are people going to say when you're up at Slipfields so much of the time with a woman whose husband's away from home?"

"Why, that's just ridiculous! You know as well as I do – "

"What I know is beside the point! It won't stop people gossipping."

"You're surely not jealous?" Charlie said. He looked at her in some surprise. Jealousy, if that was the problem, was something he could understand. It might even draw them together again. His hands reached out to grasp her shoulders and he looked deeply into her face, trying to read her innermost thoughts and find his way to her innermost feelings. "You're surely not jealous?" he said again, and there was amusement in his voice. "Because if you are I can tell you this – "

"Oh, don't be so foolish!" she said. "For heaven's sake let's act our age!" She gave a quick, impatient shrug, shaking herself free from his grasp. "I'm a woman of forty-four and we've been married nearly ten years! I'm surely past being jealous by now!"

"That's all right, then," Charlie said. He turned away towards the door. "At least we've got that sorted out."

He went out to the yard and carried the separator in. Linn also went to and fro, carrying in her pails and crocks.

"The way I see it is this!" he said. "If we're too old to worry about being jealous, we're surely too old to worry about a bit of gossip!"

But the thought of it worried him all the same and he mentioned it again at dinner-time.

"If you were to go up and see her sometimes, as you've promised to do, it'd scotch any gossip before it begins."

Linn merely gave him a long, hard look.

* * * * *

The war was going badly for the Allies. Holland, Belgium, and Luxembourg had been invaded by the enemy and the British forces, driven back, had been evacuated from Dunkirk. Later in June came the fall of France. Immense German forces now occupied the West of Europe and only the Channel divided them from Great Britain.

"Seems we're on our own now," Charlie said, grimly, to Linn.

"Do you think they'll invade us?"

"God only knows! There are plenty of rumours flying about!"

But it was not only a question of rumours. He knew, by the orders issued to the Home Guard, that the threat of invasion was all too real. He was on duty two nights a week, patrolling across Flaunton Heath, watching for German paratroops, and his orders were to shoot any man who failed to stop and answer his challenge.

"How many Germans have you caught so far?" asked Billy Graves at the Hit and Miss. "Or are they all invisible?"

But although no paratroops fell from the sky, and people like Billy still made jokes about the invasion, the war was coming closer these days. England itself was under fire. Dover Harbour had been heavily raided; London and Birmingham had been bombed; so had Portsmouth and the Isle of Wight. Many people had been killed and many more had been made homeless. Women and children in their hundreds had been evacuated from the cities and from places along the coast. Kent was under shellfire from the German guns across the Channel and there was a photograph in the paper of a small girl, aged eleven, looking at the ruins of her home, where her mother and brother had been killed by a shell.

"And people in Scampton are grumbling because they've been told to plough up their cricket-pitch!" Charlie said.

It was a dry summer that year and he was glad of the open days. When he was not busy at Stant he was busy at Slipfields: cutting the rough tussocky grass; ploughing the yellow aftermath; harrowing and rolling the soil ready for sowing in the autumn. Smoke rose from the heaps of rubbish burning on the headlands and the smell of it was everywhere.

"One of those heaps burst into flames after dark last night," Helen said. "I had to go out and see to it."

"Damn, I never thought of that. I shall have to take more care." Charlie pointed towards the sky. "We shall have *them* down on us otherwise."

German bombers were sometimes heard passing overhead at night, going to raid towns in the midlands. Once a bomb had fallen on Baxtry, damaging a chapel there, and another had fallen in a field near Froham, killing three or four cows and a calf. So Charlie took more care after that, to see that his fires had burnt themselves out before he went home at the end of the day.

By the middle of August, he had ploughed thirty acres of ground at Slipfields, and the fields looked very brown and bare until the new growth of weeds sprang up to make them gently green again. Then, whenever he had the time, he went over and over them with the harrow, using the horses, Simon and Smutch.

"What a lot of trouble you take," Helen Shaw said to him.

"If a job's worth doing – " Charlie said.

* * * * *

In September he cut his own crop of oats at Stant and just as it was ready for carting, Robert came home on embarkation leave and was able to help in the harvest field. The boy looked fitter than ever before and he had a single stripe on his sleeve, which he had kept secret until now, so as to give his mother a surprise. Linn's joy at having him home was mixed with the fear she felt for him because he would soon be going abroad.

"Where are they sending you?" she asked.

"I shan't know till I get there. But even if I did know, I'm not allowed to tell anyone."

"Not even your mother? How silly you are!"

"I'll tell you this much – it's somewhere warm. Or that was the rumour back at camp."

He thought to satisfy her by telling her this. "It really is all I know!" But all through his fourteen days' leave, she would keep coming back to the subject, hoping to squeeze more out of him.

"Somewhere warm . . . Is it Italy? Or is it British Somaliland? What about Greece, is it warm there? I wish you'd tell me where it is."

She questioned him again and again until in the end he spoke sharply to her.

"Mother, can we leave it alone? You're spoiling my leave, going on like this."

He was out in the fields by day, helping Charlie to cart the oats. He was filled with astonishment at the changes he found on the little farm. He would stand sometimes and look over the fields and shake his head in disbelief. Slipfields, too, came in for his praise. He had seen its ploughed acres, neat and trim, when looking over the boundary hedge.

"Charlie must be driving himself, to have got through all this work," he said, as he walked with his mother about the fields.

"Oh, Charlie is like a dog with two tails. It suits him down to the ground, this war."

"Is anything wrong?" Robert asked.

"No, of course not. What should be wrong?"

"You sounded a bit sarcastic, like."

"Well, you know what Charlie is. You'd think, to hear him

talk sometimes, he was growing food for the whole nation."

"He's certainly doing his share, ent he?"

"Yes, and more!"

"What do you mean?"

"Oh, never mind!" She slipped her arm into his. "Let's talk about you for a change. I want to hear how you got that stripe."

"I've already told you."

"Well, tell me again."

"I really wanted to go down to Piggotts and have a word with Mr Madge."

"Oh, very well. Off you go. I suppose I shall see you *some* of the time."

* * * * *

Enemy aircraft were passing over more frequently now. Charlie and Robert sometimes went out and listened to them droning above. Air-raids had worsened on English cities and the bombing had become indiscriminate. Goering and his Luftwaffe were bent on breaking civilian morale as a first step in the conquest of Britain. Invasion was spoken of openly, even by the Prime Minister, and it was said that German troops were massed along the West of Europe ready to strike at a given signal. Mr Churchill, in a radio broadcast, had spoken of the cruel bombardment of London and had called upon the people of Britain to stand together and hold firm.

"Will the Germans come, d'you think?" Charlie asked Robert once, when they had been listening to the news. "And shall we be able to fight them back if they do?"

"I don't know," Robert said. "The fighting is all in the sky at the moment. The R.A.F. is doing it all. I suppose it all depends on that."

"I don't understand it," Linn said. "If the Germans are going to invade, why are they sending you abroad? Surely your place is here with us?"

"I'm leaving Charlie in charge of things here."

"I don't think it's any laughing matter."

"You can't have seen him in his tin hat!"

"What can the Home Guard do?" she said. "They're mostly old men and simpletons."

"And which am I?" Charlie asked. "Both, I suppose?"

"There are lots of things on the east coast to make it hot for the Germans if they do come," Robert said.

"Have you seen them?"

"Yes, in some parts."

"What sort of things?"

"I can't tell you that. But we're better prepared than we was last time."

"Last time?"

"In 1066!"

"Ah, nobody's tried it since then, have they? Except for the Spanish Armada, of course . . . "

"Yes, and just think what we done to *them!*"

On the last night of Robert's leave he and Charlie went down to the Hit and Miss for a last drink together. Linn was bitterly disappointed. She wanted Robert to stay at home.

"Why don't you come with us?" he asked.

"No, I don't care for pubs," she said.

"You used to work in a pub once."

"Not because I wanted to."

"All right," he said, "I'll stop at home."

But the moment Robert gave in to her, Linn's feelings went about turn. She did not like to think of herself as the sort of mother who ruled her son.

"You go with Charlie. Have a good time. I mustn't keep you to myself." She pressed ten shillings into his hand. "There you are. You treat yourself. You've earnt it, working so hard in the fields."

Early next morning she and Charlie went with him into Mingleton and saw him off on the train.

"You'll be sure and write to us, won't you? Even if it is from God knows where!"

"Yes, I'll write, when I've got time. But you mustn't worry overmuch if letters are slow in getting through."

"Worry? Of course not! How absurd!" She did her best to laugh at him. "The very idea!" she exclaimed.

"Look after yourself, young Rob," Charlie said.

He held Linn's arm as the train drew out.

The house seemed empty when they got back. Charlie went out to see to the stock and when he returned to the house, later, he found Linn upstairs in Robert's bedroom. She was standing by the chest-of-drawers, looking at the row of books which Robert as a boy, in his wheelchair, had read over and over again.

"I was thinking about when he hurt his back. Was he spared from being a cripple just to be killed in this horrible war?"

Charlie took her into his arms.

* * * * *

The next day, while Charlie was up at Slipfields, Linn had a visit from the vicar's wife, who came as the local billeting officer, finding homes for evacuees. She asked to be shown over the house and, seeing that there was a spare room with two single beds in it, she added the details to her list.

Charlie, when he got home from Slipfields, found Linn irritable and depressed.

"We've got to have evacuees. Mrs Roper has been here."

"I wondered when she'd get round to us."

"Strangers in Robert's room!" she said. The thought of it was hateful to her. "I've heard about these evacuees, coming from dreadful homes in the slums, dirty and smelly, with things in their hair."

"Surely they're not all like that?"

"We don't know *what* they'll be like! We've got to take them, lousy or not. We're not allowed to pick and choose."

"We must hope for the best, then, and keep some carbolic just in case!"

"It's all very well for you to laugh but I'm the one who'll have to look after them!"

"How many are coming, for pity's sake?"

"One or two, Mrs Roper says."

"Oh, well, that's not too bad. I thought from the way you were carrying on we were getting half a dozen at least."

"Yes," Linn said, in a tight voice, "I can see it's all a joke to you."

"Seeing we've got no choice in the matter, we may as well

knuckle down to it. There is a war on, after all, and we should try to remember that."

"Am I likely to forget when my son is away fighting in it?"

Charlie gave an exclamation. He was suddenly out of patience with her.

"And what is Robert fighting for? He's fighting to keep old England safe! The cities are far from safe just now. Hundreds and thousands of families are being bombed out of their homes. Just think what the war is like for *them* and think of those kids in the thick of it all!"

Linn was silent, avoiding his gaze. She turned away from him, awkwardly, shamed by the truth of what he said but still chafing against the fate that would bring strangers into her house. Charlie, watching her, understood. He was able to read her thoughts.

"We don't know we're born," he said, "compared with the people in the towns, and it seems to me the least we can do is to make the kids welcome when they come."

"Yes," Linn said. "Yes, I know." She drew out a chair and sat down on it. "We're lucky, I know, compared with some. It's just that I was rather upset . . . And Mrs Roper was so officious, poking into everything . . . "

"Oh, yes, I've heard about *her*! Did she ask to see into the coal-hole?" Charlie was laughing again now; trying to ease the atmosphere; giving Linn time to come round. "But I will say this about her," he said. "She's had the vicarage full of kids ever since the war began, so she's doing her share, we must allow that." He too pulled out a chair. He sat with his elbows on the table. "When are they coming, these kids of ours?"

"It could be quite soon, Mrs Roper says. They're pushing it through as fast they can because it's so bad down there just now."

"They're coming from London, then, I suppose?"

"Yes, that's right."

"I was in London once or twice, during the last war," he said. "But I shouldn't care to be there now . . . All those tall buildings shutting me in . . . Toppling down about my head . . . " He put out a hand and gripped Linn's arm. "Fancy having kids in the house! Us, at our time of life!" he said.

"That'll shake us up a bit, eh? That'll keep us on our toes?"

Linn gave a nod and tried to smile. She covered Charlie's hand with her own.

Chapter 13

The London sky at night-time was lit by the shifting criss-cross beams of the searchlights probing for German bombers. Sometimes a plane would be caught in a beam and the other beams would swivel to join it, making a glaring white patch where they crossed and chasing the plane across the sky. Then the big guns would go off and the noise of them, with the noise of the bombs, would fill the air, a double bombardment, shaking the houses again and again.

Philip was not afraid of the bombs. The air-raids at night were exciting to him. Being only nine years old he was too young, his mother said, to realize what the dangers were. But he had his fears, secretly, and what he feared most was being afraid. He hated to see his mother trembling, getting down on her hands and knees and crawling along the narrow hallway, into the cupboard under the stairs, as she did sometimes when the bombs fell close by. He wished she could be calm, as his father was.

"Philip, come away from that window and make sure the black-out is properly closed."

"Just a minute. I want to see."

There was no electric light. The power-station had been hit again.

"Philip's a bit of a fatalist, like me," his father said. But he drew the boy away from the window and made sure the curtains were closed. "Do as your mother tells you," he said.

"Yes, that's right, I'm a fatalist." Philip enjoyed collecting words. "If it's got my number on it — "

"Who have you heard saying that?"

"Dinny Quinn," Philip said.

"I might have guessed," his father said.

Mrs Quinn was their daily woman. Dinny, her son, aged seventeen, sometimes did jobs for Philip's father. He

211

painted the house and cleaned the car.

"Dinny's joining the Army soon."

"Thank God we've got a Navy, then!"

* * * * *

Philip's mother rarely went out, except to the shops in the High Street, but his father liked going out and on Sunday mornings in summertime he took Philip for a good long walk. They always went the same way: down through the subway at Noresley Green, along the quiet sunny streets, and through the big gateway into the park, with its drinking-fountain and band-stand and its snapdragons smelling in the sun. They would go as far as the Green Man, up on a hill overlooking the park, and would sit on a bench in the garden there. Philip had ginger-beer to drink and a big round arrowroot biscuit to eat and his father drank a glass of stout. Then they would walk home again.

"Who was that lady with the dog?"

"Oh, just a friend," his father said.

Sometimes his mother was ill with her nerves. She stayed in bed for days at a time and Dr Ainsworth came to see her. It was her time of life, he said. He prescribed a tonic and plenty of rest. Mrs Ash was forty-six.

Philip had to go and stay for a while with Evie Nicholls, his father's friend, who lived with her sister and little dog and had a canary in a cage. There were dark red carnations in the garden that took his breath away with their scent. He was allowed to take a bunch home, but his mother threw them out of the house.

"I never did like carnations," she said.

Philip took the petals off and put them into a glass jar. He poured water on to them and screwed on the lid, hoping that the scent would thus be preserved; but the petals only turned to slime and the smell of them when he opened the jar was an evil smell that made him feel sick. He threw the jar into the dustbin.

His mother got better gradually but she was not strong and sometimes she cried.

"Crying! Crying! What is it now?" his father said in a loud voice.

212

"Taking my child away from me! You had no right to do such a thing!"

"Somebody had to look after him."

"Yes, but not *her!*"

"Oh, for God's sake, not another scene! I can't stand much more of this!"

"Don't shout at my mother!" Philip said.

When his father had gone out, he went and stood at his mother's knee, putting his hands into her lap.

"I won't go to that place again. Not if you don't want me to."

"Oh, you can go if you like," she said. She was not crying now. "If your father asks you, you say yes. Then you can tell me all about it."

* * * * *

One night in June a bomb had fallen on Pitts Road School. The building had been badly damaged and the children had to stay at home till arrangements were made for them to go elsewhere. Philip didn't mind; he hated school; and now he was free to do as he pleased. There were always plenty of books to read.

Sometimes Jimmy Sweet came in and they played together in the garden. Jimmy Sweet was very fat and all the children in the district called him Fatty-Barrage-Balloon.

"Have you got a bible, Phil?"

"Of course we have," Philip said.

"Fetch it, then, and I'll show you something."

Fatty-Barrage-Balloon opened the bible at a page in the Old Testament and pointed to a passage there: "Hath he not sent me to the men which sit on the wall, that they may eat their own dung, and drink their own piss with you?"

Fatty gave a little snort, looking at Philip with screwed-up eyes. Philip slammed the bible shut.

"Your mother's calling you," he said.

At the back of Matlock Road stood the factory where his father was works manager. Sometimes Philip was allowed in to watch the men at work on the furnace, with its big iron door that rose on chains, and its little peep-hole at one side.

Behind the furnace was the stoke-hole and Philip stood watching Albert Verney shovelling in the shiny black coal. When Albert turned away, Philip threw the bible into the fire.

"What was that you threw in?"

"Only some rubbish, that's all."

The Old Testament was unclean. Philip would never read it again. But not everything in the bible was like that. Not the baby Jesus in his crib, with the ox and the ass standing by; not the boy in the temple, whose sayings Mary kept in her heart; not the bearded man with the gentle hands, blessing the loaves and the little fishes.

"Am I a Jew or a gentile?"

"What a question!" his mother said.

"Yes, but which?"

"Well, you're certainly not a Jew!"

"I'm a gentile, then?" Philip said.

* * * * *

The air-raids were becoming more frequent now. Hurlestone Park had a lot of factories, which made it a target for the German bombers, but it was the houses that were usually hit.

"You ought to go down to the shelter," Norman Ash said to his wife.

"With all those people? I can't!" she said.

But as the bombing grew worse she went, with rugs and cushions and folding-chairs, biscuits and cups and vacuum flasks. The shelter was under the factory: a large, deep basement, reinforced, which smelt of sandbags and creosote. All the people from the shops and houses in the block were allowed to use the air-raid shelter and they sat together on wooden forms or lay on cushions on the floor. There was a notice on the wall: "No cats or dogs or other pets. Please leave this shelter as you find it and take your bedding home with you. Signed, Norman Ash, works-manager."

"That's my father," Philip said.

"Tell me something I don't know!" retorted Fatty-Barrage-Balloon.

Sometimes, when the raids were bad, people came in from some distance away and Lilian Ash was indignant.

"That old Mrs Jones! She's got no right there. She comes all the way from Adelaide Road."

"I told her she could come," Philip said. Old Mrs Jones was a friend of his. Sometimes he went to tea with her. "She's got no shelter of her own."

"You had no business telling her that." And Lilian Ash spoke to her husband. "It's your job to see them and tell them," she said, "all these people who keep crowding in."

But Norman Ash was never there in the evening when the shelter filled. He was always at a Masonic lodge or fire-watching at Head Office.

"Fire-watching!" his wife exclaimed. "Do you expect me to believe that?"

"You can believe what you damned well like!"

He was always there in the morning, though, to carry Philip home to bed: up the stairs of the air-raid shelter, through the narrow factory yard, and across the garden into the house. Wrapped to the ears in a warm rug, Philip would stir in his father's arms and would feel the cold air upon his face; overhead the sky would be grey and in his ears would be the wail of the siren sounding the All Clear. His father would put him into his bed and would draw the bedclothes up to his chin.

"You've got another couple of hours before you need get up, lucky chap. Make the most of it while you can."

* * * * *

Old Mrs Jones had a large wooden packing-case in her kitchen and Philip, with his coloured crayons, had drawn make-believe knobs on the front, so that it looked like a wireless-set. He would sit inside the box and Mrs Jones would reach out and pretend to turn a knob, *click*.

"This is the B.B.C. Home Service. Here is the one o' clock news and this is Philip Ash reading it."

"Just a minute. I can't hear. I'll have to tune it up a bit."

She pretended to twiddle the knob and Philip spoke up in a big loud voice.

"Last night London suffered its heaviest raid of the war so far. Bombs fell on Pitts Road School and the Hurlestone Park power-station. Two hundred and sixteen enemy bombers were destroyed – "

"That's the stuff!" Mrs Jones exclaimed. "Give it to 'em, hot and strong!"

" – and the rest of the raiders were driven off."

"Serve 'em right, the rotten devils!"

"R.A.F. Wellingtons attacked Berlin and strategic enemy targets were put out of action. Three of our aircraft failed to return."

"Poor chaps. I hope they baled out."

"That is the end of the one o' clock news."

"You'd better come out now and have your tea."

Mrs Jones, although old, took an active part in the war effort. She collected shrapnel and tinfoil and was always knitting for the soldiers. She had even given her aluminium jelly-moulds to a boy-scout collecting at the door.

"They're needed to make Spitfires," she said, and whenever an English plane flew over, she would stand in her kitchen doorway and point to it with a grimy finger. "There go my jelly-moulds!" she would say. "Can you see them on his fuselage?"

September came, sunny and warm. England had been at war for a year. The raids on London grew worse than ever and sometimes in the mornings Philip's mother would take him out to see the damage that had been done in the night. Pemberley Road had been badly hit and five of its houses lay in ruins. One house had been sliced in half and a piano stood on a ledge, high up, with a vase of artificial flowers on it, untouched by the blast. Among the heaps of bricks and rubble a child's cot lay on its side with a golliwog hanging from its rail.

"Oh, the poor souls! How terrible! And only a stone's throw away from us!"

Lilian Ash went home feeling ill. She could not get it out of her mind, she said, and would never be able to sleep that night.

"Why do you go and look, then?" her husband asked impatiently.

216

"It's no good closing your eyes to these things."

As the air-raids grew worse, there was talk of a new evacuation scheme.

"Philip must go," his father said. "He should have gone at the very beginning but you wouldn't listen to what I said."

"Yes, he must go, I realize that, but I don't like the thought of sending him."

"Why not go with him? That would be best. I should feel happier in my mind if I knew you were both safe in the countryside."

"Yes, it would suit you, wouldn't it, to have me out of the way like that?"

Lilian Ash refused to go. A wife's place was with her husband, raids or no raids, she told her son. Philip would have to be sensible and not mind going alone.

"I'm not afraid of the bombs," he said. "I'd sooner stay at home with you."

"Your name's been put down," his mother said.

Philip called on Mrs Jones. He took his carton of shrapnel and his collection of milk-bottle tops. She would know what to do with them.

"I shan't be coming any more, I'm being evacuated," he said.

"Where to?"

"I don't know. It's a secret."

"I shall miss you," Mrs Jones said. "Who's going to read the news to me now?"

She gave him French toast for tea.

* * * * *

Outside the Evacuation Centre, motor-coaches lined the road, ready to take the children to Paddington Station. Philip stood waiting with his parents. His gas-mask, in its cardboard box, was slung by its string over his shoulder, and he had a label tied to his coat.

"I do think they ought to tell us where our children are going to."

"I don't suppose it'll be very far. Oxfordshire, that's what I heard." Philip's father was cheery and bright. "Oxford-

217

shire's not very far. We'll be able to drive down and see him at the weekend sometimes."

The children were getting into the coaches. Philip's mother hugged him tight and he felt her tears wet on his face.

"Don't! You're squashing my gas-mask!" he said.

"Cheerio, old chap," his father said. "We'll be down to see you when we know the address. — If we can get the petrol, that is."

"Write to us, Philip. You've got some stamps."

They stood on the pavement and waved to him. The coach drew away and left them behind. A light rain began to fall and he saw his father's umbrella go up.

When the coach reached Paddington Station, the air-raid warning began to sound, and the children were herded down into the underground. They stood packed together for over an hour, and a little girl next to Philip cried silently to herself, even though he held her hand. At last someone shouted "All Clear!" and the children were taken up again. Soon after that they were on the train.

Philip had no means of knowing what time it was. When other children in the compartment began to open their packed lunches, he decided to open his own; but he soon found he was not hungry and wrapped the sandwiches up again; the smell of hard-boiled egg and tomato made him feel sick. Later he gave the sandwiches to a girl who sat opposite, staring at him, and she gobbled them up in no time at all.

"Greedy thing!" somebody said, and she put out her tongue.

* * * * *

The train was travelling very slowly. Philip, who had a corner seat, looked out at the rain that was blurring the landscape. It seemed to him to be getting dark. He turned to the boy sitting beside him.

"Are we nearly there?" he asked.

"Nearly where?" the boy replied.

"Wherever it is we're going to."

"How should I know? Ask them out there!"

Outside in the corridor the two women in charge of the party patrolled up and down, regularly, looking into each compartment and quelling any squabbles that broke out.

"What about a sing-song? That should keep our spirits up! Let's start with 'Roll out the Barrel'!"

All along the slow-moving train, the children raised their voices in song, encouraged by the two attendants. They sang until their throats were sore; till all but the strongest had worn themselves out; but Philip, although he moved his lips, had no voice for singing songs, and his neighbour nudged him in the ribs.

"Why aren't you singing?"

"Never you mind!"

"You'll burst into tears in a minute, cock."

"Oh no I won't!" Philip said.

"Call this a train? It's more like a snail!" said the girl in the corner opposite. "Why don't they get a move on?"

"There's a war on, that's why," someone said. "I expect there's been a few bombs on the line."

"Anyone like a cigarette?"

"Get away! They're only sweets!"

"I wish I'd brought my tiddly-winks."

"I wish I was bleeding back at home!"

Blinds were drawn down over the windows and a dim bulb came on in the carriage roof.

"Anyone know what time it is?"

"Not me. I've pawned my watch."

"It's half-past seven," the attendant said.

"Cor! I thought it was midnight at least!"

"Miss, can you tell us where we're going?"

"You'll know soon enough. It won't be long now."

"*She* don't know any more than us."

"I hope the bloody driver knows!"

"Mind your language in there, you boys!"

* * * * *

The long, slow journey ended at last. The train drew in at a darkened platform. The children walked in file through

219

the streets, fumbling and jostling in the dark. Voices spoke and hands reached out, guiding them through a curtained doorway, and now they were in a brightly lit hall, where long trestle tables were spread with food and where women in white overalls were pouring tea from enormous teapots.

"Come along, children, there's plenty of room! Poor little mites, just look at them! They've been on that train for over eight hours! Come along, children, move down the hall! There's plenty of food for everyone!"

Philip drank a cup of tea, but he didn't want anything to eat. He held a buttered scone in his hand and pretended to take little bites from it. People stopped pressing food on him when they saw he had a scone in his hand. Later he left it on a ledge.

After the children had had their tea, they were lined up at one side of the hall, and a woman read their names from a list. Along the other side of the hall stood the rows of prospective foster-parents and their names, too, were called from a list. The organizers went to and fro, leading the children by the hand, and the foster-parents took charge of them. Philip was among the last to be called. His suitcase was brought and put at his feet.

"This is Philip. He's nine-and-a-half. Philip, you're going to stay on a farm, with Mr and Mrs Truscott here. Say hello and shake hands with them. You're a lucky boy. You'll like Stant Farm."

A man and woman looked at him. The man had merry twinkling blue eyes, deep-set under light-coloured brows, in a face as brown as mahogany, and his hand, squeezing Philip's, was rough and warm. The woman was rather beautiful but Philip knew it was rude to stare and glanced away from her with a frown. Her hand, when he took it, was smooth and cold.

"Well, Philip?" the man said. "Are you willing to take us on?"

Philip, not knowing how to answer, looked up at the lady organizer, who gave him a little pat on the back.

"Of course he is. He's a lucky boy. He's the only one allocated to you so far, but Philip won't mind that, I'm sure. He's used to it. He's an only child."

"Well, if it's all settled, then . . . " The man reached out for the suitcase. "What about saying goodbye to your friends?"

Philip glanced round the crowded hall.

"They're not my friends," he said with a shrug.

* * * * *

In the van, driving out to the farm, he sat between them, in the dark, his gas-mask balanced on his knees.

"The poor kid's nearly asleep," Charlie said. "He's just about done in with it all."

"Yes," Linn said, "he's had a long day."

"More than eight hours on the train, and only to travel a hundred odd miles! What a journey! No wonder he's tired."

"Bed straight away, I think, don't you?"

The motor-van rattled up the steep track. Philip was helped out, half asleep, and guided across the yard to the door. The cottage kitchen struck cold. There was a smell of old damp stone. Philip stood quite still in the darkness while Charlie, fumbling, struck a match and lit the oil-lamp on the table. A shiver shook him, whipping his flesh, and he stared at the rafters overhead. The kitchen ceiling seemed very low.

"Has the electricity gone?"

Charlie gave a little laugh.

"There's no electricity here," he said. "You're out in the country now, you know. It's all oil and candles with us, I'm afraid."

"Shall I light the fire?" Linn asked. "It hardly seems worth it at this time of night."

"Maybe Philip would like some warm milk?"

"No," Philip said. He shook his head.

"Something to eat, then? A biscuit, perhaps?"

"No, I'm not hungry," Philip said.

"Had a good feed at the Town Hall, eh?" Charlie stood looking down at him. "I know what you want! You want your bed!"

"Yes," Linn said, "I'll take him up."

She lit the candle and led the way. The staircase was steep

and very narrow. Shadows lunged at him from the walls and he cowered away from them, ducking his head. In the bedroom there were two beds. The ceiling sloped steeply down at one side, almost to the very floor, and the room was very small and dark, smelling of polish and old varnished wood.

Linn set the candle down on the chest-of-drawers and lifted his suitcase on to a chair. She unpacked his clothes and put them away, leaving his pyjamas on his bed. From a pocket in the lid of the suitcase she took his ration-book and identity-card. Philip stood watching her. He made no attempt to take off his clothes.

"D'you want any help in getting undressed?"

"No," he said, "I can do it myself."

"Is there anything you would like?"

"Well . . ." He glanced towards the bed. "Could I have a hot-water-bottle?"

"Do you really want one?" She looked at him uncertainly. "It means lighting the fire, you see."

"Oh. I see."

"You'll be all right. It's not really cold. There's plenty of blankets to keep you warm." She showed him how thick the bedclothes were. "I'll come back in a few minutes and tuck you up nice and snug," she said.

On her way out, she showed him the chamber-pot under the bed, but he glanced away disdainfully. She left him alone and went downstairs. Charlie was out on his rounds in the yard. She busied herself for a few minutes and then returned to Philip's bedroom. The boy lay on his back in bed, staring at Robert's old ice-skates, which hung from a hook in the rafter above.

"Whose are those?"

"They belong to my son. His name is Robert and this is his room. Those are his books on the chest there. He's away in the Army now, on active service, somewhere abroad."

"Fighting the Germans?"

"Yes, that's right."

She stood by the bed looking down at the boy. His face on the pillow was pale as wax and there were dark smudges under his eyes. She bent and kissed him on the cheek.

"Goodnight, Philip. Sleep well." She took up the candle and moved to the door. "Are you getting warmer now?"

Looking at her, he gave a nod. His shadowy eyes were half-closed with sleep. She went out, closing the door, and dimly he heard her going downstairs. He heard voices in the kitchen below and after that he heard nothing more.

* * * * *

"He seems a nice enough little kid. Comes from a decent home, anyway. We shan't have trouble with things in *his* head."

"No, he's as clean as a pin," Linn said.

"Seems more likely," Charlie said, "that *he'll* be looking down on us."

"What makes you say that?"

"No electric light for a start. Did you see his face when I lit the lamp? He could hardly believe his eyes."

"No doubt he'll soon get used to our ways."

"It's going to seem funny," Charlie said, "having a boy in the house again."

"Yes," Linn said, and was suddenly still, looking up at the mantelpiece where a snapshot of Robert stood in a frame. "I wonder where Robert is now," she said, "It's over three weeks since we heard from him . . . "

Charlie touched her arm.

"I reckon it's time we went to bed."

* * * * *

"You're not eating your bacon and egg."

"No, I'm not hungry," Philip said.

"You ought to eat it all the same."

"Can I have a piece of toast?"

"Yes, all right. You can make it yourself."

Charlie cut a piece of bread and Philip took it to the range. He stuck it on the prongs of the toasting-fork and held it close to the bars of the stove.

"What a waste of food," Linn said, looking at the boy's untouched plate.

"Here, I'll eat it," Charlie said. "Our young Philip doesn't know what's good."

Philip came back to his place at the table with his slice of bread toasted on one side.

"You've forgotten to do both sides," Charlie said.

"Oh, no, I didn't forget." Philip reached for the butter-dish. "This is French toast. It's better this way."

"Is it, by golly? I never knew that. I must try it some time." Charlie looked at Linn and smiled. Philip ate with neat little bites and licked the butter from his finger-tips.

"Where is this place?"

"It's called Stant Farm."

"Is it somewhere in Oxfordshire?"

"No, this is Worcestershire," Charlie said.

"Is it in England?"

"Yes, of course. Where did you think it was? Timbuctoo?" Charlie laughed and the boy looked away.

"Eat up your toast, young fella-me-lad, and I'll take you out to see the farm."

Philip got up and slung his gas-mask over his shoulder.

"You won't need that," Charlie said.

"We're supposed to carry them everywhere. It's compulsory, didn't you know?"

"Oh, all right."

Charlie took him to see the pigs. He scratched their backs with a little stick, then gave it to Philip to do the same.

"I suppose you've never seen pigs before?"

"Oh, yes, I have. Lots of times."

"What, in London?" Charlie said. "Do you they have pigs in Leicester Square?"

"No, but I've seen them all the same."

Charlie had a few jobs to do. He went into the barn for a bag of meal, leaving Philip in the yard. When he came out again he stared, giving a little startled laugh. The boy was wearing his gas-mask.

"You expecting an air-raid?"

The boy shook his head. His voice came muffled through the mask.

"I don't like the smell of the pigs," he said.

There was a joint of hot gammon for lunch. Philip stared

at the slice on his plate and wrinkled his nose at the beads of grease that oozed out into the gravy.

"What's wrong?" Charlie asked. "Don't you like the look of it?"

"No, it's all greasy," Philip said.

"I suppose you want a slice of French toast?"

"No, I don't want anything."

"You've got to eat *something*," Linn said. Worried, she took his plate away and put another in its place. She helped him to potatoes and beans and dropped knobs of butter into them. "There, now, how's that?"

Philip took up his knife and fork. He looked at Charlie, eating his ham, and watched as a strand of yellow fat was sucked up into his mouth. Then he looked down at his own plate, where the knobs of butter were slowly melting, coating the steaming-hot vegetables. He ate his potatoes and left the beans.

"I hope he's not always going to be like this about his food."

"The poor chap's feeling home-sick. He'll be all right when he's settled down."

Philip pretended not to hear. The pudding was brought. It was apple tart. He ate two helpings, with sugar and cream.

"He likes his afters, anyway."

When lunch was over, Philip asked for paper and envelopes. He wanted to write a letter home. He sat in the wide window-recess with the pad on his knees.

"This is a funny place where I am. It is a farm. They have not got a bathroom or proper lav, only a place out the back, it smells. I have to wash in the scullery. Their name is Mr and Mrs Truscott. She said I could call her auntie Linn. I hope you are well. How are the bombs? When you come will you bring my books, Arabian Nights and Robin Hood, all my books, there is nothing to read. They send their kind regards to you."

Charlie took him out for a walk, and he posted his letter in Ratter's Lane. Although it was Sunday afternoon, men were at work in the fields at Piggotts, getting the last of the harvest in, and Charlie, thinking to interest the boy, stood him up on a gate to watch.

"That's the barley they're working on. They're going all out to get it in. Everyone works on Sundays these days, now there's a war on, don't you know. See that field behind the house? They've got the tractors out there and they've made a start ploughing the stubbles . . . "

Philip was not listening. His ears had caught the sound of a train and his eyes were turned to watch its smoke as it puffed along the winding valley.

"Is it going to London?"

"No, it's going to Chantersfield. This is only a loop-line. The London trains don't come this way."

Charlie lifted him down from the gate and they began to walk back to Stant. Overhead an aeroplane droned and they craned their necks to look at it.

"It's only one of ours," Philip said.

His upturned face was empty and bleak. Charlie felt cut off from him. The boy had come from another world.

"Come on, Philip, I've got an idea." He reached out and grasped the boy's small hand. "I'm taking you up to Slip-fields," he said. "I want you to meet a friend of mine."

Chapter 14

The village school at Scampton, which normally held eighty pupils, now held a hundred and twelve because of the influx of evacuees. There were not enough desks for everyone and some of the children sat on forms. Philip, on the end of a form, was constantly being edged off, so he went and sat on the floor by himself and read "The Adventures of Tom Sawyer." Nobody seemed to mind what he did.

"I never went to school at home."

"You must have done," the headmistress said.

"No, I didn't. My school was bombed."

Out in the playground he read his book. A village girl came and slammed it shut, jamming his fingers between the pages.

"Why don't you cockneys go back home?"

"Leave me alone or I'll hit you," he said.

Sometimes, after school, Philip loitered along the river with three other evacuees from Flag Marsh Farm. They poked among the rushes and reeds and threw pebbles at the ducks. Once they went down to the railway line and placed pennies on the rail, so that a train would run over them. Philip, when he got home to Stant, showed his smooth flat penny to Linn.

"You mustn't go down to the railway line. It's against the law and it's dangerous." She looked at him with an anxious frown. "I want you to promise you won't go again."

"Oh, all right," he said with a shrug.

* * * * *

He no longer carried his gas-mask about with him everywhere. Nobody else did, not even at school. The district had never had a raid.

"You people here," he said to Linn, "you don't really know there's a war on."

"I ought to know well enough, since my son is away fighting in it."

"You never get any air-raids, though."

"A couple of bombs fell at Froham," she said, "not so very long ago."

"A couple of bombs! I heard about *them*!" Philip gave a derisive snort. "One of them fell in a field!" he said.

He leant against the dairy bench, watching her as she weighed the butter and patted the half-pounds into shape.

"We had our windows blown in at home. There was broken glass all over the place and lumps of plaster came down on my bed. But you should see the streets all around. Some of the houses are just piles of bricks with people buried underneath. Sometimes people are blown to bits!"

"Yes, it's terrible," Linn said. Often she was at a loss to know how to answer this boy, who only seemed to come to life when talking about these terrible things. "You should be glad you're out of it."

"I'm not afraid of the bombs myself. I'm a fatalist, like my dad."

"Are you indeed?"

"Yes. I am."

He turned and wandered about the dairy, peering into the pans of milk. He bent over one and blew on it and the cream became wrinkled in little waves.

"Where's uncle Charlie got to?" he asked. "Up at Slip-fields, I suppose?"

"Don't blow on that milk, if you please," Linn said. "It isn't hygienic. I've told you before."

* * * * *

When uncle Charlie was at home, he always found things for Philip to do, such as helping to fill the oil-lamps.

"You hold the tundish steady for me and I'll pour in the oil."

"Why do you call it a tundish? We always call it a funnel at home."

Lots of words were different at Stant. When there came a drizzle of rain Charlie called it a "duck's frost" and when he was hungry he said he was "clemmed." Once he called across the yard, "Come and see this moggy here," and Philip expected to see a cat. But the "moggy" turned out to be a calf.

"You're queer, the way you talk," Philip said, and sometimes he mimicked Charlie's speech. " 'Paasture'!" he said. "Whatever's that? I don't know what you're talking about!"

"It wouldn't be *you* that talks queer, I suppose?" Charlie said with a little smile.

One of Philip's little tasks was to look for bits of broken china lying about the garden and fields. These he hammered out on a stone until they became reduced to grit. The grit was then thrown down for the hens and they came running to peck it up.

"Why do you give them grit to eat?"

"It helps them digest their other food and it means their eggs'll have good shells."

"Why does it?"

"Why d'you think?"

"I don't believe it does at all."

"Seems you're a disbelieving Jew."

"Oh no I'm not!"

"What are you, then?"

"I'm a gentile," Philip said.

Some of the chickens were laying away. Charlie set him to find their nests, and he crept along the hedgerows, peering into the undergrowth. Once he found eleven eggs and carried them home in his cap.

"Good boy! You've got a keen eye!" Charlie gave him threepence to spend. "Get yourself some sweets," he said.

Philip was good at finding the eggs. He often earned a few coppers like this. But Linn was inclined to disapprove.

"His parents won't thank us for spoiling him."

Philip was saving to buy a kite. He had seen one in the village shop. It was blue and yellow and cost three-and-six. Once, on a Friday evening, when Linn had her cashbox on the table, he looked inside.

"Gosh, what a lot of money!" he said.

"Fingers out, if you please," Linn said.

He watched as she took some money out and pushed it across the table to Charlie.

"What does she give you money for?"

"That's my wages," Charlie said. "That's what I get for running the farm." He put the money into his wallet. "Your auntie Linn is my boss, you see. The farm is hers, every rod, pole and perch, and that's why I have to keep in with her." Charlie screwed up his face in a wink. "I have to watch my p's and q's, otherwise I might get the sack."

Linn closed her cashbox and turned the key.

"I do wish you wouldn't talk like that. What is the boy to think of us?"

"What that boy thinks," Charlie said, "would probably fill a ha'penny book."

* * * * *

Charlie had his hands full, running the two farms together, and doing guard duty two nights a week, and sometimes when Linn came down in the morning she would find him asleep in a chair by the hearth.

"Why didn't you come to bed?"

"It hardly seemed worth it, just for an hour."

Immediately after breakfast, he would be off to Slipfields again.

"I wonder you bother to come home at all."

She often made such remarks these days. Charlie had come to expect them. Once, when he had been on guard duty, he showed her a tear in his tunic sleeve, where he had caught it on a fence. "Could you mend it for me?" he asked, and Linn, in an off-hand way replied: "Why don't you take it to Mrs Shaw?" He hung the tunic up on a peg and went out without a word. Later he mended the tear himself.

At Slipfields he was drilling wheat, as directed by the War Ag. They had sent him a tractor twenty years old and he churred and clanked about the field, with Helen Shaw behind the drill, watching over the seed in the box.

"They must have got this one out of the museum!" he said, shouting above the noise. "It's the Adam and Eve of all tractors. I bet they can hear us in Mingleton!"

"Never mind! It's doing the work!"

"How's the seed?"

"It's getting low."

Charlie, on reaching the headland, drew up beside the standing cart, in which were stacked the sacks of seed. When he stopped and put on the brake he did it clumsily, with a jerk, and Helen was thrown across the drill, hitting her face on the open lid. Charlie switched off and jumped to the ground. He went to her, all concern, and saw blood starting out from two cuts, one on her forehead and one on her lip. Her knuckles, too, had been cut and grazed. He took hold of her hands and turned them over, wincing to see the torn, wrinkled skin and the blood squeezing out in glistening red beads.

"We'd better go in and I'll clean you up."

"No, it's all right, it's nothing," she said. She looked at her hands, where they lay in his; then, gently, she drew them away and plunged them into her apron-pockets, searching for her handkerchief. "There's so much junk in these pockets of mine!" She glanced at him and gave a laugh. "Where is that wretched handkerchief?"

She found it at last — just a piece of old rag — and dabbed at the cuts on her mouth and forehead, catching a little trickle of blood just before it reached her eye.

"Here, let me do it," Charlie said.

"No, I can manage, don't fuss," she said. Again she gave a little laugh and showed him the blood on her handkerchief. "All in the course of duty," she said. "I have nothing to offer but blood sweat and tears!"

"It was my clumsiness, jerking like that. I got in a tangle with my gears."

"You're tired, that's why." She met his gaze. "On guard all night and working all day. You ought to go home and get some sleep."

"Now who's fussing?" Charlie said.

"Yes, well, shall we get on?"

"You sure you're all right?"

"Right as rain."

Soon the seed-box had been refilled and they were able to

resume work, churring noisily up and down, followed by a few foraging rooks. The day was damp, with a faint gleam of sun, and a white mist hung about the woods.

* * * * *

Philip, crouching under the hedge, watched the tractor as it crawled to and fro, and smelt the paraffin fumes on the air. Now and then he heard Charlie's voice, calling out to Mrs Shaw, and heard her laugh as she answered him. But he could not hear what they were saying. They were too far away for that.

He was moving along the hedge, peering through the tangled thicket, when suddenly a pheasant flew up and went drumming away towards the woods, uttering its harsh kok-kok-kok! Startled, Philip turned and ran, putting his hands over his ears; he hated the noise the pheasants made; it went through his head and made it hurt. He ran away from it, down to Stant.

"Where have you been?" Linn asked.

"Oh, just playing," Philip said.

"Not on the railway line, I hope?"

"No, I went up to Slipfields," he said.

Linn took two plates of sausage and mash from the oven and put them on the table. She and the boy sat down to eat. They never waited for Charlie now, for she never knew when he would be in.

"What did you go to Slipfields for?"

"No particular reason."

"Did you see your uncle there?"

"Yes, but I didn't speak to him."

"Why ever not?"

"He was busy, that's why."

Linn reached for the teapot and poured out the tea. She put the boy's cup in front of him.

"What was your uncle doing?" she asked.

"He was driving the tractor," Philip said.

"Did you see Mrs Shaw?"

"Yes, she was riding behind the drill."

Philip, with his knife and fork, was playing with his

mashed potato, smoothing it over again and again until it looked like an igloo, he thought. Now and then he glanced at Linn: quick little glances, darting at her, out of the corners of his eyes; and there was something in his face – some slyness in the way he smiled – that suddenly filled her with irritation.

"I do wish you wouldn't play with your food! Why can't you eat it properly?"

"There's no need to take it out on *me*," the boy muttered, half to himself, "just because you don't like *her*."

"What did you say?"

"Nothing," he said.

"If you were talking about Mrs Shaw, I've never even spoken to her."

"You don't like her all the same."

"Get on with your dinner," Linn said.

* * * * *

By the time he had bought his kite, the weather had changed and it was wet.

"You can't fly a kite in the rain," Charlie said.

"Oh yes I can!" Philip said.

But the kite when wet soon slumped to the ground and its coloured panels were smothered in mud. Philip washed it under the pump and took it indoors to dry by the fire. He then went out to play in the barn, where Charlie had rigged up a swing for him.

The kite as it dried fell against the stove and bits of burning wood and cloth dropped to the hearth and burnt holes in the mat. Linn, who was upstairs making the beds, smelt the burning and hurried down. She stamped out the smouldering bits on the mat and, snatching up what was left of the kite, thrust it into the open stove. At that moment Philip returned. He saw and gave a great howl of rage. "Rotten cow! You've burnt my kite!"

"Don't you dare speak to me like that, after what you've done!" Linn exclaimed. "Such a stupid, dangerous thing! You might have set the house on fire!"

"I wish I had!" Philip cried. "I wish this house had been

233

burnt to the ground!"

He turned and rushed headlong out again and stayed away until it was dark. By then Charlie was in. He spoke to the boy with severity.

"I hear you've been calling your auntie names."

"What did *she* do? *She* burnt my kite!"

"You burnt that kite yourself, my lad, by putting it too close to the stove." Charlie was standing on the hearth. He pointed to the black-edged holes in the mat. "Just look at the damage you did down here and think how bad it might have been if your auntie Linn hadn't found it in time."

Philip, avoiding Linn's gaze, came and looked at the holes in the mat. He touched one with the toe of his boot and its charred edge crumbled into dust.

"Well?" Charlie said, still severe. "What've you got to say for yourself?"

"I'll pay for a new one if you like."

"And where will you get the money from?"

"I can write home and ask for it."

"Now you're being silly," Linn said. "No one expects you to buy a new mat."

"All your auntie expects," Charlie said, "is that you should say you're sorry to her."

Philip shifted inside his clothes. His glance flitted quickly up to Linn's face and then down at the mat again.

"Sorry," he muttered, and folded his lips.

"I should think so too!" Charlie said. "If only you'd listened to what I said about flying that kite in the rain, none of this would have happened, you know." He reached out and ruffled Philip's hair. "But there you are. It's over now. You've said you're sorry and that's that."

"Come along, Philip," Linn said. "Your tea has been waiting this half hour or more."

Later that evening, when the boy was in bed, Charlie talked to Linn about him.

"The trouble is, he's too much alone. He doesn't seem to make friends at school and we *are* a bit cut off up here. If we had another evacuee – "

"One's quite enough, thank you! I've got enough to do as it is."

234

Linn was writing a letter to Robert and Charlie was doing his War Ag returns. They sat at the table with the lamp between them.

"I think it's all wrong that we should have an evacuee foisted on us when we're so busy with the farm."

"It's only the same for everyone."

"What about your friend Mrs Shaw? She hasn't got evacuees. Why is that, d'you suppose?"

"I don't know," Charlie said. "Mrs Roper called on her but nothing ever came of it. I suppose it's because she's all alone." He turned over a form and frowned at it. "It seems rather a pity to me. A kid would be company for her up there, and she'd make a good foster-mother, I think."

"From what you've said about Mrs Shaw, she can't even look after herself, let alone a child as well."

"I may have said that. I don't say it now. She copes pretty well, considering."

"Yes, with your help."

Charlie sat still, watching her. He tried to read her closed face.

"I know you don't like my going there but surely with things the way they are – "

"Since when has it mattered what I like? Not for a long time past, I think."

"Oh, for heaven's sake!" he said.

"I suppose you'll say it's no business of mine if you work yourself to a standstill?"

"The autumn work is all done now. Life will be easier till the spring." Again he watched her as she wrote and, knowing it was a letter to Robert, he said: "Did you tell him Daisy had dropped two calves? It's part of her war effort, you tell him that. Daisy was always a favourite of his. He'll be glad to know she's doing her bit."

"I've already told him," Linn said.

* * * * *

She wrote to Robert every week, filling page after page with news of the farm, but she had not heard from him for over two months and it worried her, a constant pain, eating away

235

at her heart and her mind.

"I don't even know if he's alive!" she would say whenever she posted a letter. "Anything might have happened to him!"

Then, one day in early December, three letters arrived at once: only the briefest notes, it was true, barely covering one page each; but to Linn they were Robert's presence itself; she saw him in the room with her and heard his voice in the few pencilled words.

"Things are beginning to hum now and it's nice to be doing something worthwhile," he wrote in the last of the three letters. "I can't say much but you will be getting news soon and it will be worth hearing I hope. When you hear it, think of me!" And, in a postscript, Robert wrote: "Remember that billy-goat we had? Remember what Charlie called him that time? Well, *he'd feel at home where I am now.*" These last words were underlined.

"Billy-goat? What does he mean?" Linn said.

Charlie read the postscript again.

"I called that old goat Moses once." He looked at her with his slow-spreading smile. "I reckon our Rob's in Egypt," he said. "This is his way of letting us know."

Before long there was news coming through of the British offensive in North Africa. Charlie got his atlas out and showed her Egypt on the map. He put a little pencilled cross at Sidi Barrani, on the coast.

"That's where it's humming and that's where he is! 'Doing something worthwhile', he says, and he never spoke a truer word! They're giving the Eyeties what-for out there and it seems they'll soon have them on the run!"

Then another letter came, even briefer than the others.

"Everything's fine. I'm fit as a flea. But time is going on wheels now and I'm as busy as an eight-day-clock so don't worry if you don't hear from me for a while. Best wishes from the billy-goat. Happy Christmas! Toodleoo!"

Linn was torn between pride in her son and fear at the dangers she imagined for him.

"Happy Christmas!" she said, with a catch in her voice. "What sort of Christmas will he have, poor boy?"

Philip, coming into the kitchen, saw the letter in her hand.

"Was there any post for me?"

"No, not today," Charlie said. "You had a letter only last week."

"Yes, but I've written home since then."

"Well, give them time," Charlie said.

Outside in the chicken-ground, afterwards, Philip helped to collect the eggs.

"Why was auntie Linn crying?"

"Was she crying?"

"You know she was."

"Well, she'd heard from our Rob, you see. He's away in the war and it worries her."

"It's not only that."

"What is it, then?"

"It's her time of life," Philip said.

* * * * *

He had written to his mother asking if he could spend Christmas at home.

"You have not been to see me yet. Why don't you come? I don't like being stuck in this place. I want to come home and have Christmas with you. Send my fare and I'll come on the train."

But his mother, when she answered his letter, told him he must stay where he was.

"We are still getting air-raids. You are safer where you are. It is very kind of Mr and Mrs Truscott to have you, so be a good boy and don't play them up. I will soon be sending you a parcel for Christmas."

Philip put the letter into the stove and Linn, who had watched him reading it, saw the emptiness in his face as he poked it down among the coals.

"Perhaps after Christmas, in the new year, your mother might come and stay," she said. "You must write and say we're inviting her."

"No. She won't come. I know she won't. She wouldn't want to leave my dad."

The boy, having watched his letter burn, dropped the poker into the hearth. He came to the table where Linn was

237

making pastry.

"She wouldn't like it here, anyway."

"Oh? Why not?"

"Well," he said, and gave a shrug. "No proper lav. No bathroom and that. She wouldn't like it. She'd have forty fits." He went to the window and peered out, wiping away the steam from the glass. "My mother's not used to that kind of thing. She couldn't stand it for five minutes."

"In that case you're right and she'd better not come." Linn took a piece of dough from her bowl and began kneading it vigorously, pushing at it with floury knuckles. She glanced now and then towards the boy.

"Is that what you tell them when you write home? About all the things that are wrong with the place?"

Philip was looking out at the rain, pretending not to hear what she said. Suddenly he turned away, muttering something under his breath, and she watched him climbing the stairs to his room. His sullenness taxed her patience at times. She could never get near him, try as she would, and often his cold, sharp, critical gaze made her want to box his ears. Charlie could talk to him easily enough but her own efforts at friendliness only seemed to rouse his contempt.

Philip, in the bedroom above, stared at the books on the chest-of-drawers. They had no interest for him whatever. Their titles made him curl his lip and inside, as he already knew, their contents were dull and dry-as-dust. "Elementary Physics." "Meteorology for Beginners." "Lives of the Great Astronomers." He took out this last, which was old and well-thumbed, and turned the pages listlessly.

He carried the book to the window-recess and reached for his box of coloured crayons. On a blank half-page at the end of a chapter he drew a purple barrage-balloon and all round the margin he drew falling bombs. There were very few pictures in the book and these poor few were black-and-white. He coloured the stars in a diagram of the Great Bear and gave Tycho Brahé a blue moustache. A printed caption caught his eye. "Tycho Brahé, with Johannes Kepler, was one of the great astronomers of his time and contributed much to our understanding of planetary motion."

"So what! Who cares?" Philip said with a sneer.

* * * * *

Just before Christmas the weather turned cold and there was some snow. Charlie took a horse and cart and went up to the woods at the top of the farm. Philip went with him and helped to collect the dead boughs that lay about everywhere on the ground. Charlie sawed them into logs and Philip threw them into the cart. They then drove across to Slipfields and Mrs Shaw met them in the yard.

"I've brought you the logs I promised you."

"Yes. So I see. You're very kind." She reached up and helped the boy to the ground. "*And* you've brought Philip to see me."

While Charlie unloaded the logs, tipping them out on to the cobbles, she and Philip ran to and fro, picking them up as they tumbled out, running with them to the door of the shed, and hurling them in as far as they could. Laughing and breathless, they raced each other, stumbling over the wet rolling logs, picking up one or two at a time, sometimes snatching at the same log and running with it to the shed door. Charlie leapt down and joined in the game and the logs went hurtling faster and faster, thump, thump, thump, until they were all safely stowed in the shed.

"Phew! Am I puffed!" Philip said. He pressed one hand against his side. "Cripes!" he exclaimed. "Haven't I got a stitch!"

The boy was crimson to the ears and his cap was tilted over one eye. He looked up at Helen's bright laughing face and saw that her nose was smudged with dirt.

"Hoo! Look at you! You're all dirty!" he said.

"Where?" she asked.

"On your nose!" he said.

"There, is that better?" She rubbed her nose.

"No, you've only made it worse!" Philip shrilled with laughter again. "Oh, I've got such a stitch!" he said.

Helen removed his cap from his head, smoothed the hair from his hot forehead, and replaced the cap tidily.

"Come indoors, both of you, and I'll give you a hot

drink," she said.

Philip and Charlie followed her in. She gave them cocoa in big brown mugs and opened a tin of ginger biscuits. Philip took one and dipped it into his hot cocoa, holding it there until it was soft. Charlie sat smoking a cigarette, watching Helen across the room.

"Well, it'll soon be Christmas, eh?"

"Yes, another three days, that's all."

"I've been wondering," Charlie said, "whether you'd come and spend it with us?"

"No, I don't think so." She shook her head. "I don't think that would do at all."

"I hate to think of you up here, all alone in this lonely place."

"I'm used to it. I don't really mind."

"Yes, but at Christmas!" Charlie said. "What are you going to do with yourself?"

"I've got my wireless-set," she said, "and I'll have a good fire, thanks to you."

"You'll need it if the forecast's right. They say we're in for a hard spell."

"Don't worry about me. I'm all right."

"Well, I can't make you come, I know." He drank his cocoa and put down his mug. "Philip and I had better get on. Poor old Smutch will be feeling the cold."

Helen went with them to the door. Philip bounded across the yard and climbed up into the cart. He sat on the seat and took the reins.

"I saw your wife one day last week," Helen said in a quiet voice. "We met on the bus going into town."

"Did she speak to you?" Charlie asked.

"No, just nodded, that's all," Helen said. She looked at him: a straight, steady look. "I don't think she likes your coming here."

"Why, that's nonsense!" Charlie said. "It was her idea in the first place that I should come and give you a hand."

"I think she's changed her mind since then. I think, perhaps, you should keep away."

"If I kept away it would still be wrong! There's no way of pleasing her nowadays!" The words burst out of him, bit-

240

terly, and he looked away, feeling ashamed. "Take no notice of me," he said.

"I'm right, then, in thinking she doesn't approve?"

"Oh, it's not you, it's everything! Whatever I do, it's never right! That's nothing new. It goes back years. Long before you ever came."

"Is it really as bad as that?"

"Sometimes it is," Charlie said. "Sometimes I feel – Oh I don't know – " He stood staring across the yard, watching Philip in the cart. "I suppose I'm being unfair in a way. It's her son, you see, he's away in the war, and she worries about him all the time . . . Then there's our young Philip there . . . He rubs her up the wrong way sometimes . . . "

"Charlie, I want you to look at me."

He turned towards her, his face well-schooled.

"Well, what is it? I'm looking!" he said.

"I want you to look me straight in the eye and tell me I'm not the cause of it all."

"I'll tell you this much – "

"What?" she asked.

"You've still got a dirty face!" he said.

He walked away and climbed into the cart. She went and opened the gate for him. He raised his hand in a little salute, looking down at her as he passed, and Philip doffed his cap to her.

"Thanks for the cocoa, Mrs Shaw!"

* * * * *

After breakfast on Christmas Eve, Charlie and Philip walked into town. The motor-van had broken down and Charlie wanted to buy some spares. While he was at Sutton's garage, Philip went shopping by himself. He bought a yellow duster for Linn, a packet of razor blades for Charlie, and a handkerchief for Mrs Shaw. He bought some paper-chains for himself and three little pine-cones painted gold.

They walked back across the fields but as they approached Scampton village Charlie turned off at the railway sidings and, after a glance up and down the road, lifted Philip over the fence and nimbly vaulted after him.

241

"We'll take a short cut along the line."

"Won't we get into trouble?"

"Not if nobody sees us, we shan't."

"Auntie Linn told me off for coming down to the railway line."

"Yes, well, and she's quite right." Charlie took a look at his watch. "But there's no train due till twelve o' clock. That gives us half an hour or more, and we only need ten minutes, that's all."

He shouldered the sack containing his spares, and together they scrambled down the steep bark, on to the narrow railway track. It was quite warm between the two banks and only a few patches of snow lay in the shadows of the trees.

"Supposing a train was to come along?"

"It won't," Charlie said. "There isn't one due."

"Yes, but supposing?" Philip said.

"Well, what if it did?" Charlie said. "You'd hear it a mile off, wouldn't you?" And then, as they walked along, he said: "There's nothing to be afraid of, you know. You're perfectly safe if you walk at the side."

"Oh, *I'm* not afraid!" Philip said.

And to show how unafraid he was, he walked between the glistening rails, enjoying the thud of his boots on the sleepers and stretching his legs to make them reach. After a while he came to a stop and stood looking up and down the line.

"Which way is it to London?" he asked.

"I told you before," Charlie said. "The London trains don't come this way. This is only a loop-line."

Philip frowned. He did not understand.

"We'd have to go into Mingleton to get the London train," Charlie said. "Don't you remember, when you arrived, you came to the station in Mingleton?"

"London is *that* way, then," Philip said. He stood looking back the way they had come, to where the narrow single-line track curved away into the distance. "How far is it, along the track?"

"It's about a hundred and fifteen miles." Charlie studied the boy's wistful face. "Not thinking of walking it, are you?"

"No, it's too far," Philip said.

"Come along, then," Charlie said.

When they were close to Scampton Halt they had to walk on the side of the bank, taking cover among the trees, so as not to be seen by the man in the office. They went crouched low, like Red Indians, stealthily making their way past the Halt and then dropping down to the line again.

In many places along the track the granite chips that formed its ballast were littered with fragments of broken shell, some yellow and some brown, some patterned with swirling black stripes. Philip kept stopping to look at them. He saw they were snailshells, broken in bits.

"Why are there so many snailshells here?"

"Because of the thrushes," Charlie said. "They bring the snails to the railway line and smash them on the granite chips. They eat the snails and the shells are left."

"What about when the trains come along?"

"If they've got any sense, they fly out of the way."

But about a hundred yards further on, they came upon a dead thrush, lying just inside the rail. Charlie turned it over with the toe of his boot.

"There's one that left it too late," he said.

Philip stooped and picked it up. It was hard to believe the thrush was dead, so warm was its body between his hands, so bright were the feathers on its breast. But dead it was; there was no doubt of that; its head lolled on its limp broken neck and its eyes were just two blobs of blood.

"Poor little bird," Philip said, and held it close against his face, touching its feathers with his lips and feeling its death inside himself, secretly, in his heart, where it hurt. "Poor little bird," he said again, and stroked its pretty speckled breast, tenderly, with the backs of his fingers.

He hated the thought of the dead thrush lying on the railway line, where another train might crush its body, so he took it to the foot of the bank and laid it in the long grass, underneath a hawthorn bush, and covered it with handfuls of leaves.

"Come along, Philip," Charlie said. "We'll be late for dinner if we don't watch out."

Soon, in another half mile or so, he was leading the way up the steep bank, over the fence by the railway bridge, and out into Ratter's Lane. They were almost at the farm when the twelve o' clock goods train, running on time, passed along the valley below. Charlie turned and looked back at it.

"There you are! What did I say? You can hear them a mile off, can't you?" he said.

They stood and watched the train's progress, marked by the travelling coil of smoke, and Philip thought of the bright speckled thrush who had left it too late to fly away and now lay dead in the grass of the bank, buried under a mound of leaves.

Chapter 15

Soon after Christmas there was news of terrible fire-bomb raids on the City of London and the docks.

"I hope Philip's parents are all right," Charlie said. "I don't think they're anywhere near the docks but they get their share of the raids just the same."

It was a great relief to him when, early in the new year, Philip had a letter from his mother.

"How are things at home?" he asked.

"They've got burst pipes," Philip said. "They had to have the plumber in."

"Sounds as though the weather there is just as bad as it is with us."

"Yes, it's bitter, my mother says. The windows have been blown in again and she says the wind is howling through."

"They're still getting raids, then, at Hurlestone Park?"

"Yes, of course," Philip said.

His mother, in her Christmas parcel, had sent him a brown balaclava helmet, a new pair of gloves, and a thick woollen scarf, and now that the weather had turned severe, Philip wore them all the time.

"She must've known we were in for a hard winter," Charlie said, "sending you those warm things to wear."

"She still hasn't sent my books, though."

"Books won't keep you warm," Linn said.

"Tell me something I don't know!"

"Now, then!" said Charlie, frowning at him. "You mustn't be rude to your auntie Linn." And a little later he said to the boy: "What about Robert's books upstairs? Have you thought of reading them?"

"No, they're boring," Philip said.

"It'll be a good thing," Linn said, "when this young man returns to school."

"*If* he can get there," Charlie said. "The way things are going we shall soon be cut off."

* * * * *

Often in the morning, when Charlie went out to feed the stock, he had to dig his way through the snow, which had drifted over the farmyard walls and piled itself up, eight feet high, against the doors of the barn and sheds. The pig-sties were buried to their roofs and so were the hen-coops in the field. Wherever he went about the farm, he had to carry a spade with him, to dig a pathway through the snow and to break the ice on the drinking-troughs.

For some days the farm was cut off. No baker's van could come up the track and Linn had to bake her own bread. Charlie took the horses out, pulling a snow-plough made of rough boards, and cleared a passage as best he could, all the way to Ratter's Lane. The Council snow-plough had cleared the roads and they were now roughly passable, at least for those who travelled on foot. Linn began watching for the postman again: she had not heard from Robert for over a month; but the postman never came to the farm.

"I don't think he's trying hard enough. He can't be bothered because of the snow. Surely there must be a letter by now?"

"I'll go down to Scampton and see," Charlie said.

But when he had struggled down to the village, there were no letters waiting at the Post Office, and he returned empty-handed.

"Try not to worry yourself too much. You know what happened last time. You waited and waited, weeks on end, and then three letters came at once."

"How can I help worrying when Robert is fighting," Linn said, "somewhere out there in North Africa?"

The news from the desert had been very good. The British had taken Bardia, in Egypt, and were pressing on into Libya.

"We seem to be doing well out there. We're pushing the Eyeties back all the time."

"It still doesn't mean that Robert's all right."

"If anything had happened to him, you would've heard immediately. No news is good news. It must mean he's safe."

"Safe?" she exclaimed bitterly. "Robert won't be really safe until it's all over and he's back at home! And who knows when that'll be? The last war went on for four long years. How long will this one go on, d'you think?"

"We won in the end, though, didn't we?"

"Only when thousands of men had been killed! Thousands of lives just thrown away!"

Charlie made no answer to this. He knew he could never comfort her.

* * * * *

Snow fell again for two or three days. Then it stopped and there were hard frosts. On washday, when Linn hung her clothes out to dry, they stiffened immediately on the line, and she had to bring them in again, to dry them as best she could indoors. They hung from strings across the kitchen and dripped all morning, wetting the floor. The whole house smelt of wet clothes; steam rose and clouded the windows; moisture dripped from every wall. Whenever someone opened the door, thick smoke gushed from the chimney, and the clothes became covered in smuts.

"*Must* you keep coming in and out?" Linn demanded, rounding on Philip, and to Charlie she said angrily: "I told you that chimney needed a clean but you're always too busy elsewhere to do what needs doing in your own home!"

"Come on, Philip," Charlie said, "this is no place for you and me."

"Grumpy old thing!" Philip said. He pummelled his way through the wet dripping clothes.

Sitting on a box in the woodshed, he watched Charlie splitting logs.

"Auntie Linn doesn't like me. I can tell by the way she looks at me."

"Nonsense! Of course she does! She gets a bit fussed about things, that's all."

"I don't care, anyway. I didn't ask to come to this place."

Philip had picked up a bunch of straws and was twisting them round and round in his hands until they made a tight-twisted ring. "How long do you think the war will last?"

"I don't know. You've got me there. We should all like to know the answer to that."

"If the war ended tomorrow, I should go home, shouldn't I?"

"Yes, you'd go back to your mum and dad."

Charlie's axe came down on a log and the two halves, cleanly split, toppled from the chopping-block to the floor. He kicked them aside, on to the heap, and stood for a moment, axe in hand, looking at the boy's wistful face.

"We shouldn't see you for dust, should we, once the war was over?" he said. "You'd be off like a shot on the London train and that'd be the end of you."

"I might come and see you sometimes."

"Well, now, I wonder!" Charlie said. He gave a little teasing laugh and touched the boy's balaclava'd head. "I don't think you'll give us a single thought, once you're back in your own home. Why should you indeed? No reason at all! Like you said a moment ago – you never asked to come to this place."

He set a log on the chopping-block, split it with one stroke of his axe, and paused again.

"As soon as the weather gets better, young Phil, I'll take you up to Flaunton Heath and show you the Observation Post, where I shelter when I'm on sentry-go."

"Why not today?"

"I'm too busy today."

"Are you going to see Mrs Shaw?"

"I don't know. I might, if there's time."

Philip slid from his perch on the box and threw his twisted straws aside. He came and stood close to the chopping-block, watching Charlie splitting the logs.

"I suppose Mrs Shaw is your fancy piece?"

"No," Charlie said, "indeed she is not!"

"What is she, then?"

"Just a neighbour, that's all."

Charlie stopped and picked up a log and set it on the

chopping-block. His axe lay resting in his hands.

"You shouldn't say things like that," he said.

"Why not? Where's the harm?"

"I reckon you know that well enough. You were just trying to stir me up."

"What if I was?"

"You shouldn't, that's all."

Charlie began to swing his axe, lifting it high above his head. The blade was descending, straight as a die, when Philip's hand fluttered out below and flipped the log from its place on the block. Charlie saw it and stiffened himself. His heart leapt into his mouth and a terrible heat turned his bones to wax. The axe came down – he could never have stopped it – and the blade bit deeply into the block. Philip, seeing the look on his face, gave a high-pitched crowing laugh and spun in a circle, hugging himself. Charlie stared at him, feeling sick, appalled by the danger the boy had run. His whole body prickled as though on fire.

"That was a damned stupid thing to do!" he said in a voice tight with control. "If I'd hit your hand with this axe of mine – "

"You didn't though, did you? I was too quick!"

"If you ever play that trick again, I'll give you a hiding you won't forget, and that's not a joke, so don't you smile!"

Charlie put up a shaking hand and wiped the sweat from his upper lip. He still saw, in his mind's eye, the boy's small hand crushed to pulp, under the axe on the chopping-block. The thought of it suddenly blinded him and he was filled with a black rage.

"Go on, get out, you little sod! I can't trust you. You'd better get out!"

"No, I'm not going to!" Philip cried.

"Didn't you hear what I said to you?"

"Yes, I heard! You swore at me!"

"Playing a damn-fool trick like that! I've half a mind to tan your hide!"

Charlie's anger was still like fire. He stared at the boy and the boy stared back, sullen, tight-lipped, defying him. Then, from the house, they heard Linn's voice, calling them in to their midday meal. A flicker crossed the boy's face and

249

he looked at Charlie warily.

"It's dinner-time. She's calling us."

"Who's *she*? The cat's mother?"

"Auntie Linn, then," Philip said.

"Yes, all right, you'd better go in."

As the boy sidled past him, however, Charlie reached out and grabbed his arm.

"No more tricks in future, mind? Promise me that before you go in?"

"Stop it, you're hurting me!" Philip said.

"I want that promise," Charlie said.

"All right, I promise. Cross my heart."

"See that you keep it," Charlie said.

He let go of the boy's arm and sent him on his way with a smack on his rump.

* * * * *

There came a few days when the weather relaxed. The wind went right round to the west and there was a sudden surprising thaw. The ice in the yard grew treacherous and Charlie worked hard to clear it away, but as soon as he had cleared the flags, snow slid from the roofs of the sheds and the yard was just as bad as before.

Out in the fields the snow still lay: shrinking a little and flattening itself; even melting here and there; but, for the most part, still lying thick, smooth and wet and glaring white. "It's waiting for more," Charlie said, and on the fifth morning, sure enough, the wind went round to the north again and heavy snow-clouds darkened the sky. "We're in for it now and no mistake!" He could feel the snow in his stomach and bones.

Linn looked out of the kitchen window and saw the postman coming up the track. She went out to meet him in the yard but the only letter he had brought was a bill for pig and poultry food.

"Isn't there anything else?" she asked.

"Sorry, Mrs Truscott, that's all there is."

She watched him trudging away again. It was now more than six weeks since she had last heard from Robert. Her anxiety for him increased every day. This was Saturday and there would be no more deliveries at Stant until Monday morning. Shivering, she went indoors, where Philip was putting on his gumboots.

"Any post for me?" he asked.

"No, nothing," Linn said.

"I wish they'd send my books," he said. "There's nothing to do in this old place."

"Why don't you go and play outside?"

"That's what I *am* doing, can't you see?"

* * * * *

Charlie was in the lean-to shed, filling a can with paraffin from the tank on the bench. When it was full he turned off the tap, removed the tundish from the can, and screwed on its cap.

Out in the yard, close by the door, Philip was lying in wait for him, a wet slushy snowball in his hands. It exploded fully in Charlie's face. Spluttering, he set down the can, wiped the worst of the snow from his neck, and made a lunge towards the boy. Philip turned and ran for the house and Charlie lumbered after him, stooping to gather snow as he went.

"I'll get you for that, my boy!" he said.

Linn was at the kitchen-table, washing up the dinner-things, when Philip burst in, shrieking with laughter, and Charlie ran in after him. The door swung open against the wall, a chair was sent toppling against the dresser, and the crockery rattled on its shelves.

"What on earth – !" Linn exclaimed. "Mind what you're doing, both of you!"

The draught was making the chimney smoke and she hurried across to shut the door. Charlie, with his snowball in his hand, cornered Philip at the foot of the stairs and caught him by his jacket collar.

"Now, then, my lad, you're for it!" he said. "A taste of your own medicine!"

"No, that's not fair!" Philip howled. "Not down my neck, you rotten pig!"

"Will you say you're sorry, then?"

"No, I won't! I'd sooner die!"

"All right, you've asked for it! Here it comes!"

The snowball was touching Philip's cheek and moisture was trickling down his neck. Squirming, he struck at Charlie's hand and the snowball fell to the kitchen floor, plopping and bursting on the tiles. Crowing with triumph, he kicked at it, spreading the snow about still more and sending it spurting everywhere. Charlie caught hold of him by the arms, swung him giddily round and round, and suddenly hoisted him up in the air till his head was almost touching the rafters.

"Now, then, I've got you, haven't I? What've you got to say for yourself?"

"I shall say *something* if you don't watch out!"

"What'll you say?"

"Sod, hell and damn!"

"Is that what they teach you to say at home?"

"Mind your own business! Put me down!"

"Ask me nicely and maybe I will."

"Stop it! You're tickling! Put me down!" Philip's voice rose to a shriek. His face was as red as a turkeycock's. Charlie's hands were under his armpits, holding him in such a way that his arms were helpless, flailing the air, and even his feet, although he kicked out, could not quite reach Charlie's stomach. "Stop it, I tell you! You'll give me a stitch!"

"Oh, for heaven's sake!" Linn said. "You'll send the wretched boy into fits."

"He's got to say he's sorry first."

"Devil! Devil! I shan't. so there!"

Philip, red in the face, looked down, and Charlie, laughing, looked up at him. His fingers moved under Philip's armpits, tickling him and making him squirm, and suddenly Philip, pursing his lips, leant forward in Charlie's arms and spat directly into his face.

"Ach! You dirty little grub!" Sobered, Charlie let the boy down. He groped for his handkerchief and wiped his face. "Where did you learn that dirty trick?"

Linn, with an exclamation of disgust, darted forward and

gripped the boy's arm. Angrily, she gave him a shake.

"Aren't you ashamed of yourself?" she said. "Spitting in people's faces like that! I don't know what we're to do with you. You're a hateful, dirty, horrid little boy!"

Philip was now as white as white. His face was contorted, his lips compressed. Writhing, he pulled away from her, punching her stomach with both his fists. Linn reached out with the flat of her hand and caught him a clumsy smack on the head. He rushed from her and stamped up the stairs. The bedroom door opened and closed and they heard the creak of the floorboards above.

"Such behaviour!" Linn said. "He wants a good spanking, that's what he wants!"

"It's all my own fault," Charlie said. "The boy's highly strung and I got him worked up. You could see he was sorry afterwards."

"*I* couldn't see any such thing! There was no sign of shame in his face at all!"

"Maybe I'd better go up to him."

"Maybe you'd better leave him alone!"

Linn got a cloth from the scullery and began wiping the mess from the floor. Charlie stood watching her.

"I was just going out," he said. "I thought of taking the boy with me."

"No need to ask where you're going, I suppose?"

"Mrs Shaw is almost out of oil. I'm taking her up a two-gallon can." He went to the door for his jacket and cap. "There's a lot more snow on the way," he said, "and she'll have run out in a day or two."

"What about us?" Linn said. "We'll need it, too, if we're snowed up again."

"We've got plenty in the tank."

"It won't last long if you give it away."

"Two gallons of paraffin! You surely don't grudge a neighbour that?"

"I hope she pays for it, that's all. *I* have to pay for it, don't forget."

Linn, having hung up the floor-cloth to dry, returned to her bowl of washing-up, and Charlie looked at her cold, clenched face. Sometimes, she seemed a stranger to him and he wondered if all marriages ended like this, with discontentment on either side. He and Linn still loved each other; their lives were close-linked in so many ways; but how long could love last when carping disapproval on one side and baffled withdrawal on the other hardened into a daily habit, shutting out trust and sympathy?

He took some money out of his pocket and planked it down on the table.

"There you are, it's paid for," he said.

He crossed the room and called up the stairs.

"Philip, are you coming down? I'm going up to Slipfields. You can come with me if you like."

There was no answer from above and Charlie, after listening a while, shrugged and left the house by himself. He collected the can of oil from the yard and set out across the fields. The north wind was now blowing hard and the dark clouds, piling up in the sky, bulged with the burden of snow to come. He turned up his collar and bent his head.

* * * * *

Philip, at the bedroom window, saw Charlie crossing the yard and watched him trudging up the field, by the pathway already worn in the snow. The boy wanted to follow him. "Yes! I'm coming! Wait for me!" – The words went hallooing in his mind. But when he reached the bedroom door, something caught him and held him back. He kept seeing Charlie's look of disgust in that moment when he had spat in his face, and the thought of it made him turn away. When he looked through the window again, Charlie had already gone from sight.

The light was poor in the little bedroom. Philip took a pillow from his bed and laid it on the window-sill. He hoisted himself up and sat on it, with his box of wax crayons in his lap, and one of the books from the chest-of-drawers. He opened the book at the very beginning where, on the fly-leaf, in a neat, tidy hand, was written the name, Robert Mercybright. He crossed out the name with a red crayon and began writing a letter home. "Dear Mum and Dad and Mrs Quinn . . . "

The room was cold. He was shivering. He hunched himself up, inside his jacket, and pulled the sleeves of his jersey down until they half-covered his hands. His fingers, grasping the crayon, were numb. He breathed on them to make them warm.

Downstairs in the kitchen Linn finished her washing-up and put the china away on the dresser. When every piece was in its place, she began clearing the kitchen table, taking the bowl out to the scullery and emptying the water into the sink. She returned and wiped the table clean and hung the tea-towels up to dry. The clock on the mantelpiece said half-past one. Philip had been in his room half an hour and that, she felt, was quite long enough to have taught him a lesson he deserved. He would catch a chill if he stayed there too long. She knew she would have to go up to him and help him out of his fit of the sulks.

Philip, hearing her step on the stairs, scrambled from his seat on the window-sill and closed the book he had been writing in. In his haste he dropped it and the coloured crayons spilt from their box and went rolling about over the floor. He kicked the book under the bed, but it slithered across the polished boards and out again at the other side, fluttering open on the mat that covered the floor between the beds.

Before he could reach it, Linn had come in. She saw the book and picked it up and her face, as she turned over the pages, became darkly flushed. The fly-leaves were covered with scribblings and the margins of every printed page were defaced with childish crudities. "Sez you, Clever Dick!" "Who's Copernicus when he's at home?" "Newton stinks and so do you!" "Dung and pisswater! Hah! Hah! Hah!"

"How *dare* you do that to my son's books?"

She moved quickly to the chest-of-drawers and began to look through the rest of the books. There were about a dozen in all and every one had been defaced. The scribblings and drawings glared from the pages, leaping at her and hurting her, filling her with unspeakable rage. That Robert's books, which he had so loved, should be defiled in this careless way with dirty, ugly, meaningless words! Trembling, she looked through every one, and Philip stood watching her, pale and sharp-eyed. When at last she turned to him she was filled with loathing and disgust. She could never forgive him for what he had done. He would always be hateful to her now.

"How *dare* you ruin Robert's books? Oh, yes, you can cringe, you horrible boy! You deserve to be whipped for what you've done!"

"Don't you touch me!" Philip shrilled.

"I shan't touch you, never fear! But I shall certainly write to your parents and tell them about your behaviour today. Spitting in Charlie's face like that! Scribbling filth in Robert's books! I just don't understand you at all. After we've taken you into our home and done all we could to look after you – "

"I didn't ask to come to your house!"

"We didn't ask to have you, either, but we've done our best, Charlie and me, to make you feel welcome just the same, letting you sleep in my son's room – "

"Rotten old room!" Philip cried. "Rotten old dirty stinking farm! Everything here is horrible and I've written home to tell them so!"

Linn took a step towards the boy, but he darted past her, ducking his head. His foot caught in the edge of the mat and he stumbled forward, awkwardly, knocking his knee on the iron bedstead. Rubbing himself, he glared at her and edged his way towards the door.

"What do I care about your son?" he said, with an ugly curl of his lip. "I hope he never comes back from the war! I hope he's dead and blown to bits!"

"I think you'd better get out," Linn said, in a voice she could only barely control. "Go on, get out! Get out of my sight!"

"I'm going, don't worry!" Philip cried. "And I'm never, never coming back!"

He ran from the room and clattered downstairs and she heard him go slamming out of the house. Then she heard his step in the yard and when she looked out of the window she saw him vanishing into the barn. She turned to the books on the chest-of-drawers, gathered them up into her arms, and carried them out across the landing, into her own bedroom.

* * * * *

Philip stood in the middle of the barn and stared at a rope that hung from the rafters. Earlier, a cow and her two calves had been housed for a while in the barn, and a few strands of hay, which had been the cow's feed, still remained in the rope's noose. Philip reached up and pulled it out, strewing it over the stone-flagged floor. He went and fetched a wooden box, clambered on to it, breathlessly, and placed the noose about his neck.

The rope was old and very hard, chafing against his tender skin. He raised his hands to tighten the noose but the knot was too stiff and refused to budge. It hurt his fingertips, making them sore, and he held them for a moment against his lips, sucking them until they were soothed. Looking down at his booted feet, he inched his way to the edge of the box. The rope's noose was very wide; much too wide to encircle his neck; and although its lower edge was under his chin, the knot was high above his head. Cautiously he put up his hands and tried again to tighten it.

Suddenly the wooden box, placed insecurely on the flagstones, tilted away from under his feet and he clattered, sprawling, to the floor. The rope, as it slid from under his chin, jerked it upwards painfully, its roughness scraping his lip and his nose and bringing the hot quick tears to his eyes. Heart pounding, he scrambled up, and the rope with its noose swung to and fro, two or three feet above his head. He stood for a while, watching it, giving a little whimpering cry, then went and peered through a slit in the wall.

The house was visible from the barn. Its door was obliquely opposite. He climbed on to a pile of sacks and settled himself to watch and wait. The sky was darkly overcast and a few flakes of snow were fluttering down, absently, with no will of their own, but tossing about this way and that as though reluctant to reach the ground. Through the narrow slit in the wall the wind came blowing, stinging his eyes, and up in the great high roof above he heard its whining song in the beams and the way it whispered and shuffled and crept as it played among the loose, shifting tiles.

* * * * *

After a time the house door opened and he saw his auntie Linn come out. She picked her way across the slush, went into the dairy, and closed the door. Philip waited a few minutes and then crept from his place in the barn. He crossed the yard and went into the house.

The warmth of the kitchen surged about him, bringing goose-pimples up on his skin and making him shiver like a dog. He took his overcoat from the door and put it on. He buttoned it up, right to the throat, and put on the warm balaclava and scarf that his mother had sent him for Christmas. He found his warm woollen gloves and stuffed them into his coat-pockets.

After glancing through the window to see that the dairy door was still closed, he went across to the kitchen cupboard and took out auntie Linn's cashbox. It was locked, as it always was, but Philip knew where to find the key. He took two pound notes and some loose change and, delving under his overcoat, thrust the money into his trousers pocket. Carefully he relocked the cashbox, put it back into the cupboard, and hung the key in its hiding-place. Quietly, with trembling hands, he closed and locked the cupboard door.

Outside in the yard the wind struck cold and as he passed the end of the house a flurry of snow came whirling at him. But he was snug in his helmet and scarf, with his thick-napped coat buttoned up to the neck, and the wind and snow were nothing to him. He crossed the yard, treading quietly, and climbed over the five-barred gate. Once on the track he felt free to run. His rubber boots kicked up the slush and the wind behind him helped him along, making him feel he could run forever.

He met nobody, all the way; not even in Ratter's Lane; so that when he climbed the fence by the bridge and slid down the bank to the railway line, there was no one to see him and turn him back. He was alone in a white silent world, under a sky dark with clouds full of snow, and the daring of it warmed him inside.

At either side of the railway track the snow was piled up two feet high, so Philip walked between the rails, where trains had flattened out the snow until it was only a few inches thick, dirty, discoloured, and spotted with oil, barely covering the wooden sleepers. There had been no drifts on this stretch of line because it was sheltered from the wind, but here and there, during the thaw, the snow, which had drifted as high as a man up on top of the northern bank, had slid down the slope on to the track. The sheer weight of the piled-up snow brought it tumbling down in a rush, like a miniature avalanche, and where there were no bushes to stop it, it fell in heaps on the line itself.

Philip, walking along the track, witnessed one of these falls of snow, only twenty yards ahead. He heard it rumbling up on the bank and stood quite still, nervous, alert, while it rippled and billowed its way down the slope and came to rest with a dull-sounding crump, spreading right across the rails. It wasn't enough to block the line. Philip had seen, as he walked along, where similar mounds had been flattened out, dirtied and blackened, by the trains. But now, as he went on his way again, he kept a sharp eye on the steep north bank and listened for the rumble of toppling snow. It must be a terrible thing, he thought, to be buried under an avalanche.

There was scarcely any wind along the line. The high embankment shut it out and its whining song was only heard in the telegraph wires strung from their posts. Overhead, high in the sky, the fluttering snow was thickening, and soon it began to fall more quickly, big wet flakes that flopped in his face and gathered, glistening, on his brows.

Now and then, as he tramped along, he thrust his hand into his pocket and felt the money hidden there, snug and warm against his thigh. When he got to Mingleton he would buy a ticket and get on a train and if anybody questioned him he would say that his mother had been taken ill and that his father had sent him a telegram telling him to come home at once. Charlie had said it was two miles along the line to Mingleton but two miles was nothing, Philip thought, and there was no hurry, anyway. He liked the quietness of the line, and the snow coming down on him, wetting his face. It was a bold, adventurous thing to be walking along all alone like this, with nobody knowing where he was. Sometimes he glanced over his shoulder, through the rapidly falling snow, watching in case a train should come; but he knew that he was perfectly safe because, as Charlie had said that time, even if a train did come, you could hear it a mile off, couldn't you?

Somewhere along the bank, just here, was the place where he had buried the thrush, but he couldn't tell where it was, exactly, for now it was buried under the snow. The thought of the thrush, killed on the line, gave him a strange feeling inside: of pain and pleasure twisted together; melting, hot, like tears in his heart. When he thought of Charlie, however, he was filled with unbearable guilt and shame, because Charlie had been a friend to him and he had spat in Charlie's face. It was the devil that had made him do that; it was something he hated and wanted to kill; something he couldn't talk about for no one would ever understand.

Trudging on along the line, he felt he was leaving the sin behind, hidden and buried, like the dead thrush, in a secret place that couldn't be found. The snow fell, cold in his face, and he bowed his head to it, hunching himself, feeling it soaking his woollen helmet, which sagged cold and wet on the back of his neck. It seemed a long way to Mingleton. He had not even reached Scampton Halt yet. He lengthened his stride and hurried on.

* * * * *

Linn, having finished her chores in the dairy, went to the barn and looked inside.

"Philip?" she called in a loud voice. "It's high time you came indoors. You'll catch your death of cold out here." She opened the door wider still, to let more light into the barn, but the boy was nowhere to be seen. "Philip, are you hiding?" she called.

She crossed the yard and went indoors. The fire had burnt low in the stove so she raked the ashes and put on more wood. She then went to the foot of the stairs.

"Philip, are you there?" she called.

The house was as silent as the grave. She climbed the stairs to the boy's room and, finding it empty, descended again. When she hung up her jacket and beret, she noticed that Philip's coat was gone; he must have come in while she was out and followed Charlie up to Slipfields; but at least he was wrapped up warm, she thought, for his balaclava helmet and scarf had also gone from their peg on the door.

Snow was falling steadily, piling up on the window-panes. The kitchen was dark and she lit the lamp. While she was replacing the glass, there came a loud knock at the door and when she went to open it, the postman stood there, wrapped in his cape. He put a letter into her hand. It had come by the second delivery.

"I could see it was from your Robert," he said, "so I brought it out to you straight away."

Linn was almost overcome. She had never expected such a thing.

"Won't you come in for a cup of tea?"

"No, I'd sooner get back, thanks. I don't much like the look of this snow." Waving to her, he turned away. "I hope it's good news from your boy," he said.

Linn, at the table, close to the lamp, put on her spectacles and read her letter. It seemed to her that the writing was strange but soon, as she read, she understood why.

"I'm writing this with my left hand and making a mess of it too," Robert wrote. "I am in hospital (cannot say where) with a broken right arm and two fractured ribs. Believe it or not I fell down some steps! (I'm expecting to get a medal for that!) One of my ribs punctured my lung so I shall be out of action for a while and it looks as though they'll be sending me home for a spot of leave. I hope you're proud of your soldier son! Expect me soon, in plaster, Rob."

Linn put her face in her hands and wept. The news was too incredible. Robert, her son, was coming home. She thought of him in a hospital ward, hundreds and hundreds of miles away, in pain, perhaps, and more ill than he said. But what were a few poor broken bones so long as he was still alive and was coming back to England again? Even the punctured lung, she thought, was nothing if he was coming home to be nursed. He would be safe, at least for a while, and perhaps by the time he was fully recovered, the war might be over and victory won, at least in the desert, anyway.

She read his letter again and again. It made her laugh and cry at the same time. How long would it be before he came? The letter had no date on it. It could have been written weeks ago. He might already be on his way, travelling homewards, even now. She pictured him stepping off the train, stiff in his plaster, sheepish, amused, looking at her with his deep dark gaze. "I hope you're proud of your soldier son!"

She was still laughing and crying when she heard Charlie out in the porch, stamping the snow from his boots on the mat. When he walked in she stood looking at him and he knew at once that she had had news.

"Robert?"

"Yes! He's coming home!"

"I can't believe it – "

"Yes, but it's true!"

"Have you had a telegram?"

"No, a letter – "

"Here, let me see!"

"He's broken his arm and two ribs," she said, watching as Charlie read the letter. "The poor boy's in plaster. He fell down some steps. One of the ribs has punctured his lung – "

"Laws! That sounds pretty bad!" Charlie said.

"Yes. Poor boy. It's terrible!"

But her eyes, her smile, her tone of voice, all belied the words she spoke, and Charlie saw that to her it was not terrible at all – it was the answer to her prayers.

"Will he get over that all right?"

"Yes, of course. We shall see that he does!"

"I wonder when he'll get to us."

"Oh, I wish I knew!" she said. "The silly boy hasn't put a date. It could be tomorrow. It could be today! His letter might have taken weeks so it could be any time at all!"

"I can't believe it!" Charlie said. "To think of our Rob coming home to us! I can hardly believe it's true!"

"No more can't I! But it is! It is!"

Linn's face was radiant. She laughed through her tears. It was years since Charlie had seen her like this. She was the Linn of the old days, looking at him with joyous eyes, letting him share her happiness; letting him come close to her, in thought, in feeling, in sympathy. She put out her hands and he clasped them tight. They looked at each other, exchanging new warmth, drawn together in hopefulness by this astounding piece of news, that Robert was coming home to them.

"Oh, Charlie, I do wish he'd come!" Linn could scarcely contain herself. "I wish he'd come walking in at that door, now, this minute, and no delay!"

"He won't come like that, without warning, you know. He'd be sure to send us a telegram first."

"Yes, of course, how stupid of me!" Laughing, she drew away her hands, putting them up to her warmly flushed face. "I shall have to be patient, shan't I? But at least I can get things ready for him – "

"It's rare old weather he's coming home to. It's snowing again, did you see? We're in for a blizzard by the look of it."

"Robert won't mind the snow!" she said. "He'll be glad to see it, after all that sand!"

But the snow brought Philip into her mind and she looked at Charlie with a frown.

"Hasn't the boy been with you?" she asked.

"No, he was still upstairs when I went."

"Oh, yes, but he's been out since then. I thought he must have gone after you."

The thought of Philip darkened her mind, because Robert was coming home on leave and would see what the boy had done to his books. It was the one dark blot on the day, spoiling it and bringing distress. She began talking to Charlie about it, telling him everything that had happened, and how she had sent the boy out of the house.

"I was so angry about the books! Such a mess he's made of them! Robert's books, that he loved so much, all scribbled over with rubbishy words and with silly drawings everywhere! They're all quite ruined, every one."

"What did you say to him?" Charlie asked.

"Oh, I don't know!" She spread her hands. "You can imagine what I said." She paused for a moment, looking at him. "You must admit he's a difficult boy. Spitting in your face like that, after you've been so good to him! And then the things he said to me!"

"What things?"

"He said he hoped Robert was dead. He said he hoped he'd been blown to bits."

"I don't wonder you sent him out."

"He said he hated this house and the farm and everything here was horrible."

"Yes, well," Charlie said. "He didn't mean it, I don't suppose. You know what kids are. They say these things."

"Yes, I know. I tell myself that. And what with his being away from home . . . I know we must make allowances." Linn, with a sigh, turned away. She put Robert's letter into its envelope and stood it on the mantelpiece. "Anyway, I sent him out. He went into the barn – I saw from upstairs – but I don't think he's there now, unless he's hiding somewhere."

"I'd better go and look for him."

"Yes, make him come in and be sensible. Tell him we're having an early tea. He can make himself some toast at the fire. He always likes that. It's his favourite thing."

Charlie went out into the snow and Linn, bending over the range, drew the kettle on to the hob. Her feelings had undergone a change – Robert's letter had done that – and now when her thoughts dwelt on Philip, the enormity of what he had done no longer took first place in her mind. He was only a child, after all, and the farm was a lonely place to him. Perhaps, as Charlie had once suggested, they should ask for another evacuee; if Philip had company of his own age he might not be so difficult; she would have to give the matter some thought.

As she busied herself, laying the tea, she glanced repeatedly out of the window. Charlie was going all round the yard, looking into every shed, and distantly she heard his voice as he called the boy's name again and again. The snow was falling more swiftly now, filling the sky and darkening it, and Philip, it seemed, was not to be found. Where could he be? she asked herself; and in her heart, for the first time, she felt a stab of anxiety.

* * * * *

The mid-afternoon passenger train from Chantersfield to Kitchinghampton was running over an hour late. It had been held up at Chantersfield because the fireman had failed to arrive and much precious time had been lost while a man had been found to take his place.

Now, having stopped at Baxtry and Froham, it was on the last lap of its journey and would run non-stop to Kitchinghampton. Here was the chance to make up lost time, and, the line being clear and the signals at go, the driver was letting his engine rip. The fireman had the stoke-hole open and was shovelling on more coal. Snow fell and melted on his back and sizzled against the boiler-breast. He slammed the door shut and stood erect, flinging his shovel into the bunker and wiping his hand across his face. The driver, with his hand on the regulator, watched the pointer on the speed-gauge as it crept steadily up the dial.

"I reckon we'll give them a treat today!" He meant the passengers on the train. "Show them what we can do, eh?" he said, and had to shout to make himself heard. "We'll be in Kitchinghampton by half-past-three so they won't have much to grumble about."

The needle crept up and up on the dial until it read eighty-five miles-per-hour. The driver looked out at the thick flying snow.

"Bloody weather!" he exclaimed. "Looks as though it's setting in." Withdrawing again, he wiped his face. "The forecast was right for once in a way. We're in for a blizzard and no mistake!"

The fireman pounded his chest and coughed. He spat out a mouthful of coal-dust and phlegm.

"Did you feel a bump?" he said.

The driver pulled on the regulator, easing it out, fractionally. His eye was on the pressure-gauge.

"A fall of snow on the line, I should think. There'll be plenty of *them* along this stretch."

"Whereabouts are we, do you know?"

"Just coming up to Scampton Halt."

"I don't know this stretch of line, it's new to me," the fireman said.

"You haven't missed much!" the driver said.

The train went rattling through the Halt and Fred Mitchell, in his office, stood at his desk and watched it go past.

"They're fairly burning it up today, by God!" he said to himself with a little grunt. "Seems their hands've slipped with the coal!"

Dimly, because of the muffling snow, he heard the blast of the train's whistle as it ran into Glib Hill Tunnel.